COLLARED

By Stephen E. Scott

Prologue.

Natalie pulled the taxi door shut and sank back into the seat after confirming her address. She did not want to talk.

Her mind was full of the enjoyment she had just left, after deciding she needed to have a clear head, tempting as it was to have another glass of wine but she needed to leave and to be able to think straight.

The Bangladeshi music did not grab her attention and her thoughts of tonight within a quarter of a mile slipped back to her childhood. She unconsciously squeezed either side of her tummy with her hands that had crossed and folded across her lap. The feeling gave her a little reassurance. She opened her eyes and stared blankly out through her reflection in the rear window, her face contorting with those memories. The tiled or polished wood floors of the corridors and dormitories, the tiled or painted walls, haunted her with the hollowness their utility created as she fled along them, searching each night for a new place to hide. For most of the time, these memories remained unthought.

Many of her friends from those days were still friends, not that she met them as often as she would like. Some she had lost contact with and wondered how things would be when the opportunity to meet up came.

Natalie like most people throughout their lives, had to face the lows that come with living. In her life however, the lows for her, had been lower than most people would ever experience or perceive and would put their own tribulations into a perspective that would make them in many cases, appear insignificant.

Few people would be strong enough to live with those childhood memories and to overcome them, to live a normal life but Natalie is one of those few.

Most people would find it difficult if not impossible, to forgive or forget the experiences that Natalie endured and would welcome the chance to get revenge. Few people get that chance.

Most people are not actually strong enough even if they get that chance, to carry out all the things they have talked or thought about for years after, to take that revenge if the opportunity comes along.

Natalie is one of the few.

Dedication

To Samantha, my beautiful daughter, who helped me develop my original idea into the fundamentals of this story, while we were enjoying ourselves on holiday in Turkey and for suggestions for the cover. I hope you like how Collared has turned out. Thank you for taking an interest. Love you....Dad x

Special Thanks

Firstly to Michael Dearden who adapted the photo for the front cover, in the same way as he did for my first book, New Pews for Sunday.......Brilliant....and for the cover of the paperback...Thank you again Mike.

Secondly, to Chris and Heidi for giving me a picture of their home and guest house, "Penrose" in Lostwithiel for the cover.

Thirdly, to Shan who spent significant time reading through the book before publication.

1) TAXI

Natalie felt the motion of the taxi as it turned right off the road, into the crescent shaped drive of her house and then the converse turn as the taxi driver followed the left hand bend as he approached the front door, the same bend that would take him out of the other gateway and back onto the secluded, rural B road in Oxfordshire.

She opened her eyes from dozing after the birthday party she had been to only four miles down the road, the affect of five glasses of wine and a night's chat and frivolity having its calming influence after a long week in work on the tax office help line. Josephine, Joe for short had liked The Best of Dean Martin CD Natalie had given her. Natalie was happy to be home. This house despite an imposing, opulent appearance when constructed in the mid Victorian era from stone, cropped into large brick style blocks, with doorways and windows surrounded by Sandstone inlays, had always been a happy house.

She opened the rear right hand door of the black Mondeo and put her right leg out so that her brown flat healed loafer pressed down on the Cotswold gravel path that lead her up to the newly replaced, single grey granite step in front of her solid wooden front door. The taxi driver had stopped exactly where she had asked him.

He turned to look back at Natalie, partly to make sure she was not going to bolt and run inside as she already had one leg out of the door. "That's £9.50."

Natalie gave him a note and waited for the change with an expectant look on her face. The taxi driver stared back, the whites of his eyes emphasised by his dark skin as he waited for her to blink and convey submission. Her expression didn't change.

"I haven't got any change luv, sorry. It's only 50p. I'll give it to you if I pick you up again."

"It's not 50p, it's £10.50. I gave you a £20 note."

The taxi driver instantly became more confrontational in his tone. "Naa you don't. I know what you give me so don't come with me. I give you change of twenty and you get ten back so I lose out. No way. Are you getting out or what? I need to get on."

Natalie's expression still remained for the most unaltered, her eyes unblinking, her stare intensifying at hearing his attitude, his English heavy with Indian influence.

"I know exactly what I gave you so I would like my change." Natalie always separated each type of note into separate denominations within the compartments of her purse. She repeated herself, this time a little slower and more purposeful. "I want my change please." Her eyes remained fixed in his direction.

"Are you getting out or do I drag you out? I got no change, I told you this again."

"You're from Lahore aren't you? There or Calcutta."

"I live here! My home no concern to you. Now get out of car."

Natalie took a final deep sniff as if to convey her disgust at his attitude, smelling through his body odour infused with curry perspiration and cardamon chewing breath, his cheap pungent citrous smelling aftershave. She stood with her back next to the car as she faced the front door and listened to it move off, running her fingers gently along the right side of the body, confirming what she had felt just before she got in, when she stumbled off the curb and caught herself from falling. She had put her hands against the door and rear side panel; where there was a deep large dent followed by a crease in the metal from an accident.

The sound of the car's exhaust had a slight blow and growl in it and she heard the squealing of its brakes and hollow bottoming sound of a worn suspension as it hit the driveway lip back onto the road.

She felt used and angry as she walked slowly along the path, feeling the jaggedness of the stones pressing
through the leather soles of her shoes.

"How easily people lose their integrity," she thought, "for so little and for what!"

She took a few slow deep breaths and gave out a few long sighs as she cleared her head and filled her nose with the smell of the Honeysuckle that surrounded the front doorway, dissipating the taxi drivers presence from her sense, the slight curdling sick feeling from him, his taxi and attitude being replaced by a calm and satisfied feeling from being back at home. She thought of Joe's hug when she had opened her present and that meant more to her at this moment than the taxi driver.

The large double fronted Victorian house stood looking at her. The light from the moon found reflections in both of the large double windows that formed the front of the two bay windows, top and bottom of the house, like four pairs of eyes looking at her as she pondered along the path after the taxi had driven away.

It emanated total darkness from inside. Natalie never left a light on, despite the repeated suggestions and warnings of her friends to do so, in order to make it look like someone was in. They were always concerned for her. The curtains were drawn to all windows at the front of the house that looked out towards the roadway and always remained drawn, no matter what time of day. Her neighbours had become used to it since she moved in eight years ago, after inheriting the house from a long lost relative, her long dead mother's cousin Margaret. She still had a few fond memories of Margaret from when she and her mother went to visit; up until she was about seven.

She enjoyed the games of hide and seek in the large, flat, private garden. The rhododendrons and hydrangeas proving perfect cover for an excited little girl hiding from two grizzly bears prowling the grounds of her castle. The back of the house did look a little like a castle as directly opposite to the upstairs front bay windows, were two walled roofs which you could sit on by coming out onto them from the patio doors of the two rear bedroom which were above the kitchen on the left side and what was referred to as the garden room on the right side of the house. Natalie decided to use the right hand rear bedroom, the slightly smaller of the rear rooms as her bedroom. It had an en suite, which also had a door leading onto the landing, close to the first floor stairway that lead to the loft bedrooms and storage rooms built into the attic space.

Her friends concerns for her safety often brought the same type of response. "Who would want to do anything like that to me? she would say. "I'm fat and ugly."
At five foot ten inches and size twelve, her friends might agree she could trim down a little but she was far from ugly.

She had beautiful, naturally curly black hair which tussled over her shoulders to mid way down her back. Her face had high cheek bones but their affect on her attractiveness to some, was lessened but the fullness of her face, something she knew would return if she could trim back down to her preferred size ten. Her dark, almost black brown eyes had a sadness across them but backed with an intensity of concentration that riveted you to stare back at her when you were looking at her. Despite her being slightly overweight, her body curved and pointed in all the right places and her legs often brought compliments, especially from the bar men and waiters, even waitresses at The Pheasant and Feathers, her local which she had just left and where they too, looked after her.

She took in her final appreciation of the late night, warm July air and put her right hand onto the door, leaning her weight against it, feeling the edge of the lock against the side of her fingers and slipped the key in with her left hand. One final, purposeful deep breath accompanied her few anxious thoughts and Natalie felt back in control.

The hinge on the front door needed some oil but it was useful as the "eecking" noise it made could always act as a good warning to a thirty one year old woman living on her own.

The door thudded shut reassuring behind her, the echo reverberating throughout the wide empty hallway. The noise of her keys clattered and jarred in her ears as she accidentally dropped them into the usual copper dish on the hall table. She ran her left hand along the wall as she walked to the stairs. She stopped at the open door to the lounge and questioned if she had left it open as it now was. The large round brass handle felt cool. Natalie continued to the stairs, passing the closed door into the dining room on her left, her length of pace almost measured to perfection as her toes grazed gently against the bottom step.

She turned her head to listen at the silence of her now familiar home. She took in a deep slow breath, almost analysing the spectrum of smells. She could smell the furniture polish she had used yesterday on that solitary hall table, the highly polished teak slippery to touch.

There was a smell of the flowers from inside the lounge which had escaped through that open door and there was another scent, something familiar. She smiled to herself as she stomped tiredly up the bare, stained wooden stairs.

2) PRESENCE

The bedroom door had a similar reassurance from the solidness of its manufacture despite being over a hundred years old, as she lent against it to push it shut. It needed to be trimmed slightly as it was always sticking in the frame.

Her red scolloped summer dress was laid over the blue bedside chair and her matching red bra and knickers she dropped into the laundry basket just behind the en suite door. After opening the bedroom window for some fresh air, Natalie eased herself into the coolness of the sheets and put her hand out for her book and then stopped, her arm still outstretched.

She lay still, listening to the sounds of the house. Every house had its own sound she felt and now in the silence, she was feeling her home around her and there was a strangeness to its life.

Natalie's hand came back to the bed and she lay with her arms by her side, her head just raised off the pillow, her ears scanning each individual creak and sigh, each movement of air that brought sound.

She picked up her black dressing gown from the bottom of the bed in the same movement as getting up and walking to the bedroom door. The door jolted open as she tugged on the brass handle and she stood motionless in the doorway, her head turning slowly from side to side so as not to make any extra noise of her neck moving against the fabric of her gown, as she listened.

The landing light switch was halfway along the landing at the top of the stairs, some thirty feet away from her bedroom. She never used this at night anyway, there just didn't seem any point.

The silence continued as her ears and mind coordinated like radar, analysing the house for deviant signals. Her concentration and stillness detected the same familiar scent within the mix of odours around the house.

"Is anyone there?" She said it not expecting an answer. Who in their right mind would answer, "it's only me," if there was anything sinister. She smiled a little uneasy this time to herself, at the thought of some horror picture, where the would be victim seriously expects a stalker or intruder to answer the question.

Nathalie closed the door again, shoving it with her hip and walked back to the bed. The room felt warm and she lay on top of the sheet just in her dressing gown, still listening.

It must have been about thirty minutes before she dropped off to sleep, her hearing segregating every single reverberation her ears sensed but she felt her scrutiny answered.

It was about an hour before the man dressed in black from head to toe moved within the en suite, having gone through the landing doorway into the bathroom when Natalie went to her bedroom door, to listen along the landing. He had come prepared with a tiny can of oil which he put onto the hinges of the en suite door, leaving it for five to six minutes before moving the door, to look through the crack on the hinge side of the door, at Natalie lying on the bed.

He listened to her breathing which had turned slow and deep, a sign of sleep, something he had been used to. The temptation to go into the bedroom and stand over her, goaded him; his mind fighting with this compulsion, comparing it to the logic of remaining secreted as an apparition, a suggestion of a presence without identity, within the shadows and rooms of her home as he enjoyed his invisibility.

His compulsion became over ruled by his need to use a bathroom, the excitement of unknown surveillance creating the need to urinate. Each step he took along the landing was slow and purposeful, testing for creeks in the floorboards, avoiding putting his full weight on an area which could transmit his presence.

The downstairs toilet provided welcome relief. He found a large bowl and filled it slowly at the kitchen sink, pouring it carefully down the toilet pan to dissipated the urine so Natalie would not discover it the next day.

He opened the fridge, putting his finger on the pressure plunger switch which turned on the light and eventually started the warning bleeper, telling you the fridge door was open; using the light from his mobile to look inside for something to eat. The ham rolls he made tasted fabulous after which he was careful to wipe up all the evidence.

His walk upstairs was again slow, each downward step previously memorised so that on accent, he would not trigger an unwanted creak or groan from the old stairway, sometimes missing out a step which he knew would send out an alert in the silence. He looked in again at Natalie sleeping, by creeping up to the en suite door and looking through the gap on the hinge side and then crept upstairs to one of the attic rooms at the front of the house for some sleep. His thoughts were of tomorrow.

3) SATURDAY

Saturday morning brought the luxury of a lay in. Natalie opened her eyes at 10 am and smiled to herself as her first thought of last night and bedtime passed through her neurones.

Once awake, she found it difficult to go back to sleep. She had always been like that since about the age of eight, just after her mother died of an unexpected brain haemorrhage at thirty two. It was, if once awake, there was a subconscious need to be in control, so that the same thing wouldn't happen to her. Sleeping with lots of other people around her as well, also meant that she had been woken up by the sounds of those already up in the morning routine so the opportunity to go back to sleep never happened. Being woken in the middle of the night also meant she found it difficult to turn over and go back to sleep and that had often meant lying there upset, thinking or anticipating, very frequently draining her of refreshed energy for the next day.

This night after her return to bed, she had slept soundly and felt fully refreshed. For once she thought, "a Saturday morning and it was sunny." British summers were so unpredictable and inconsistent, not long and dry as Margaret had told her they were like,
"when I was a girl." Her second thought was of the lady who left her this house.

The back of the house was south facing and the sun came in through the windows all day, making the rooms very bright and warm. She walked to the en suite to use the toilet and to take a shower, leaving the dividing door from her bedroom open. Natalie didn't check the other en suite door leading onto the landing, why would she? It was impossible for anyone to see into her private bathroom from any other angle; through front or side bedroom windows. The back garden was completely private and the bathroom window had heavy frosted glass. She felt safe.

As she sat on the toilet she heard the slightest of creaks from the floorboards and the hint of a smile formed.

Her intruder pressed his right eye up to the crack in the landing door as he stood motionless, watching. He watched her wipe herself still wearing her dressing gown and then go to the sink to wash her hands. His eyes focused on her reflection in the mirror above the sink, on partly exposed breasts as her gown hung open. Natalie felt her hair and ran her fingers back through it, pulling it back into a pony tail and assessed if she should wash it. Her breasts rose inside the dressing gown which flapped shut across her chest, hiding her reflected torso from him.

His face twitched with early frustration but he was used to waiting.

As she turned towards the shower, Natalie held the gown shut with her right hand so that it didn't get in her way as she turned on the shower taps. She stood, leaning against the glass shower cubical feeling the water getting to the set temperature the gauge was set for.

He adjusted his position so that his eye had an altered field of view, to take in the shower cubical. He took a deeper breath and held it to gain control of his breathing, letting the air out slowly through pursed, dry lips.

Natalie took off the robe and placed it to the right of the shower door. She loved the feel of the warm water pounding initially on her head as it pumped out of the raindrop shower above her and then the sensation of it cascading down and around her body. The thing she enjoyed most was the solitude of her showering, the fact that she could lather herself as much and as frequently as she wanted and that she didn't have to pass the soap or shower gel to the next girl waiting her turn.

When she took over this house, she had the bath moved and the bathroom done out with modern Italian ceramic tiles with vines of yellow and highly polished chrome fittings. The shower was a large oblong, with a wooden floor at one end as the drying area, giving her plenty of room and her own self contained world where everything was to hand.

The steam inside the cubical become a fog and combining with the opaque blue shower glass, made her body become difficult to distinguish.

The man waited on the landing, straining to see her through the crack in the door. As he watched and his mind fantasised about what he couldn't see, he moved slowly to the open side of the door, pulling it further open, very slowly and carefully, just in case its hinges made a noise. The door moved silently and freely. He held it steady with both hands, with just half his face had Natalie seen him, peering around the door, his right cheek pressing against the door's edge, which also brushed against his close cropped, full head of grey hair.

He moved his head slightly to get the feel of his hair and head being rubbed, like a cat brushing itself up against some-one's legs looking for an affectionate response. The door's edge reminded him of the dormitory and the shelf inside the cupboard next to the showers, which his head used to press against, as he twisted inside to look through the tiny hole he had drilled in between the tiles and into that storage cupboard, which he used to look at the girls and then boys showering.

Natalie was enjoying every second. She moved her head forward so that the water ran down the back of her neck, down her swan back and over and around her small and rounded firm buttocks which she pressed against the glass, causing the water to bubble and cascade around her hips to find a less restricted route across the top of her bottom and into her groin before running down her legs.

She stood motionless, listening to the hiss of the water coming out of the shower head, the lower rumble of the shower pump in the background of her hearing. Her mind followed the relentless stream of water as it enveloped her.

The intruder moved to his left unconsciously as he watched her saturation, causing an untested part of the floor to creak. He stood rigid, his eyes wide with uneasy surprise, watching to see if Natalie had heard his misfortune.

He watched her head turn slowly towards the open door and he shifted back behind the door, looking in through the crack again, checking on whether he should move off down the long landing and into one of the front bedrooms.

Natalie just seemed to be standing now with the left side of her face pressed against the shower glass. She could see the change in lighting coming in from the landing, through the partly open door but she had not seen his movements, he had been too quick but she had heard a creak, albeit a quiet one.

Her voyeur pressed his back against the wall and continued with his leaching, watching her seemingly continued unawareness of his presence as she lathered herself three times more, pressing various parts of her body slowly and sensually against the glass as she enjoyed the slippery, pressured sensation against her bottom and breasts. Even he thought it was a strange way to shower but it still excited him.

Natalie stayed inside the cubical, drying herself and then walked back into her brightly decorated, multicoloured bedroom, her dressing gown wrapped tightly around her. She hesitated at the foot of the bed and turned the vivid almost neon blue duvet back to make the bed, tucking the end under the matching pillow. He watched her through the two doors, walking around the bed, her feet skating across the white long pile carpet as she walked, he thought towards the rich, red curtains with large sunflowers. Instead of hearing the curtains being pulled open, he heard the bright green fitted wardrobe door in the front alcove being opened and the sound of clothes hangers being slide from one side to the other as she selected what to wear.

Her brief absence from his gaze compelled him to move, his brain questioning the logic of possible discovery with his impatience to see what she was doing. He stepped over the part of the landing floor which had almost given him away, not to repeat the incident, pushing the door deliberately right back to the wall so he could make an unhindered exit if needs be.

Each step he took was slow and measured, placing each foot down on the bright yellow bathroom carpet, heel first and then transferring his weight to his toes as he prowled closer to the bedroom door which he pushed half shut so he could hide behind, in order to continue his scrutiny. He felt in control, his successful stealth increasing his deluded bravery. The effort of hiding behind this door had been in vain as he couldn't get the angle between the door and the frame to see Natalie in front of this one wardrobe. Impatiently, he half put his face against the other edge of the door as he had done earlier and looked around into the bedroom.

The early morning sun lit up the red curtains, making them and the sunflowers vibrant. Natalie's bedroom was a complete non co ordination of a colour scheme, something which had escaped him when he had been in it the night before as he familiarised himself with her house. He had not turned any lights on as he explored. The darkness of the house had hidden this mish mosh after he had broken in through the kitchen door, having climbed over the locked wrought iron side gate to the left of the house.

Natalie stopped moving the hangers and stood one hand leaning on the rail, her left hand feeling the material of the yellow sun dress she appeared to be selecting. She stood motionless and then took in a slow, deep breath, like she was sniffing the air around her or the fragrance of the laundered, waiting clothing.

Thirty to forty seconds passed without her moving. He started to rub himself and then stopped before he lost control as he stared, transfixed by the accentuation of her bottom and lower back, her position of leaning into the wardrobe, exaggerating her sensual lines. It was too soon for that he thought.

She turned directly towards him unexpectedly, a sudden transformation from inanimate to fluid motion, taking the dress and hanger she was holding off the rail, holding it in front of her face and body as she turned, a welcome barrier to his immediate exposure.

He stepped back behind the bathroom door, that moment of survival, gratefully received by her undetected stalker. He pressed himself again to the wall, looking as best he could in that moment of surprise, at her approaching the bathroom with her yellow dress still held out in front of her face. The space behind the door didn't give his portly 5' 8" frame much seclusion but he eased it silently, as open as he could, so that it provided the maximum amount of shielding as possible.

This premature unenvisaged confrontation had not been in his planning. As he stood rigid initially holding his breath, his mind racing as to what he would do should she discover him behind the door, he admonished himself for being so foolhardy so soon and now risk possible discovery. Her skating foot steps grew louder as she approached the bathroom door, her left leg drawing friction from the bed duvet as it rubbed against it and he heard this, knowing her entry was only seconds away.

His right hand gripped the small pen knife in his right pocket, used more for opening beer bottles than anything else but its three inch blade could still eliminate her. He speculated, her turning and seeing him behind the door, his punch to her face to disorientated her and then his plunging the blade into her throat. He had never done anything like that. How many times would he have to do it to kill her. There was still so much terror to create that an early killing was certainly not how he wanted things to be.

The pen knife needed to be brought out of his pocket but that would cause the door to close to allow him the space to do so. It would make a significant "click" on opening and that would give him away should Natalie hear it. The decision was made, he would see if he was discovered and then punch her in the face and follow that up with whatever came next.

He braced himself ready to lash out should she find him behind the door. His body went tense. The wall pressed hard on the back of his head as he tried to immerse himself into the tilling.

Natalie walked into the bathroom singing Volare, one of her favourite Dean Martin songs off the CD she had bought Joe. The difference in the carpet texture changed her way of walking. She loved the feel of the long pile of the white bedroom carpet pushing against and in between her toes and then by comparison the more cropped pile of the yellow bathroom carpet.

As she swished in, waltzing as she sang, the hem of her dress caught the end of her tooth brush which was protruding off the edge of the sink, knocking it into the basin. Its movement was enough to catch her attention which made her turn towards the sink, her long damp hair now facing her predator.

Natalie's reaction turned her back to facing towards the bedroom and she hung the hanger over the top of the en suite door on her third attempt, each simple action causing him to anticipate his need to attack. She turned and picked the tooth brush up and then cleaned her teeth. As she lifted the hanger off the door, she pulled it away from the wall and walked back into her bedroom, its closing exposing him but Natalie was ahead of the door's edge and his presence remained unseen.

Now with her unintentional assistance, he looked through the gap in the now three quarter closed door at her putting on matching yellow bra and knickers. As he watched her hold and feel the underclothes close up to her face, he wondered at the rational of smelling your own clean underwear before wearing it. His thoughts instantly changed to the degeneracy of smelling them after Natalie had taken them off.

The sound of the hair dryer was a welcome relief, allowing him to breathe normally as he watched her bend over and fan along her hairs length. Natalie left the hair dryer on the bed and paced to the bedroom door, yanking it open.

The door bell rang. "Coming!" she shouted, as she glided her hand along the banister rail and followed its right hand turn down the stairs to the hallway.

He followed her along the landing to look down at the front door and who was calling at 11 am on a Saturday morning.

"Are you ready for our tea and crumpets?" Her neighbour Jane asked.

"As always Jane. You spoil me lovely," answered Natalie, reaching out and taking hold of Jane's extended right arm.

Jane squeezed Natalie's hand with her left hand, giving her a warm, affectionate smile at the same time. Jane was two inches taller and had been a tall girl and lady for her generation. Her hair which she dyed regularly, as she didn't want to be part of the blue rinse mob as she referred to them, was a light brown, virtually the same colour as her own had been before it turned white almost overnight when her husband Michael had passed away twenty four years ago. She had in the main, a serious face from her days as a police woman and her need to portray authority. Her sternness dissipated on greeting Natalie for their Saturday morning get togethers and her blue eyes smiled warmly behind her silver rimmed oblong glasses. Her forehead had faint frown lines, far less than anyone would have expected from such a serious face but the laugh lines around her eyes were far more prominent.

It had been Jane who called on her, when Natalie had been found and inherited the house and it was Jane who instigated the search for Natalie when Margaret died and the house remained empty for two years after Margaret's death, ten years ago.

Jane had remembered Margaret's cousin and her daughter coming to the house on occasions, not frequently but often enough to be remembered and to obviously be, relations Margaret cared about.

The solicitor Margaret used was known to Jane, Margaret had made sure of that. Natalie was her only surviving relative and she made Jane promise that she would do her best, along with this solicitor to find Natalie.

At five years old, Natalie had not remembered Jane all these years later, until Jane had reminded her that on one of the visits, she had to arrest the two grizzly bears trying to eat the princess and had put Margaret and her mum into handcuffs, for being naughty grizzly bears. Natalie's memory had strained to recall the event and she felt a bit embarrassed by not remembering it as well as Jane but her mind had suffered a lot over the years since her mother's death. She did however remember the "Bear Police Lady", even if she couldn't remember Jane as Jane. That had meant a lot to Jane, sixteen years later when Natalie eventually moved in at twenty one and this rekindled memories of when Natalie had been a little girl and Jane had been a thirty seven year old police woman.

"One second Jane." Natalie turned back towards the stairs and took another long, slow breath in, her eyelids shut as she concentrated. That smell was still there.

She shut the door as she turned to walk arm in arm down the gravel path to Jane's house for their Saturday ritual. Jane didn't go out much socially and didn't really want to after her husband had died. Now sixty three one of her joys in her later life was now having Natalie as a neighbour and a friend and someone she could look after when need be.

The intruder walked into the front bedroom and watched through the gap in the curtains as they walked through the gate and out of sight to Jane's house.

He lifted both his arms and smelt his armpits. He could do with a shower and a change of shirt as the perspiration from his excitement was now becoming a detectable odour.

He walked into the en suite and picked up the towel Natalie had used to dry herself, giving it a long sniff with his face buried in the fabric. There was the smell of vanilla shower gel and Natalie.

His shower was quick and efficient, drying himself with the same towel, putting it back on the linen basket to the left of the sink, where Natalie had draped it.

After dressing and then taking his shirt upstairs to the attic room where he had slept that night, he opened his small hold all bag and took out a clean identical black shirt from the seven inside the bag, putting his used shirt in a clear polythene bag to ensure its segregation.

"Time for something to eat I think. What have you got in your fridge Natalie?" He said to himself as he walked down to the kitchen.

4) CLOSE SHAVE

After making himself a cup of tea, he emptied the electric kettle and refilled it with cold water to make sure it felt cold to touch should Natalie come into the kitchen when she came home.

The two honey roasted ham rolls he made with English mustard was enough for him with the tea.

He wiped up the crumbs and shook them out into the sink from the dish cloth he had used to wipe around the work surfaces. His watch showed 11.50. There would be about another 20 to 25 minutes before Natalie returned, judging by the routine he had watched over the last three weeks of following her around, noting down times and destinations, movements and habits.

He went to look at the wooden back door and the small glass panel he had replaced after smashing it with his elbow. The putty had dried, holding the glass he had measured a week ago when planning his entry, firm within the old frame. The broken glass was in the brown recycling bin and he had been careful to wrap the broken pieces in a plastic bag, still with the cris crosses of masking tape around them, which had stopped it from shattering into too many pieces.

The dining room had an archway leading in from the kitchen which was fitted with two half arched slatted wooden doors painted blue on the dining room side and black on the kitchen side to match the black granite worktops. When open, the through room measured forty two feet long. There was little sign of use. The oblong silver framed glass table had a film of dust across it, in which he thoughtlessly ran his left index finger, looking then at the gathering on the end of his blue protective glove. He did the same on the black waist high wooden sideboard which was against the opposite wall to the hall and stood between the two pieces of furniture, looking around the room. The black high back, modernist chairs also had dust on them.

Looking around there were no ornaments just long, clear, uncluttered surfaces. The room and table would have easily sat ten people with plenty of space to move around. His eyes were drawn to the light grey carpet which looked as if it hadn't been walked on much. The area under the table showed no signs of scuffing from people's shoes while having dinner. Even the two sea scape pictures didn't lift the feeling of emptiness this room conveyed.

At the far end of the table was a small pile of The Event, the area's local paper. There were five copies of the same addition from the third of June with Natalie's picture on the front page, holding her winning flower arrangement. He stared at her face with a big beaming smile and visualised how she looked when she was a child, picturing her development through her teenage years to her twenties, to her picture now.

Like most local papers it had the usual adds for local tradesmen which he glossed over as he thumbed through to the back page. He returned to staring at her photo and those missing years and started reading the write up that accompanied it, even though he had memorised it, having read it over and over again in the retirement home.

The annual summer fair brought out a better crowd than usual, thanks to an unexpected dry and sunny day. The organisers are pleased to say that this year with a greater attendance, the stall owners and committee all felt it worth while, with £1000 being raised through entrance fees, to be donated to the children's ward of

St. Bridget's Hospice.

The hospice was proposed as the recipient by one of the committee members, Miss Natalie Thomas, herself a winner of The Best Unexpected Flower Display, in which contestants were asked to create an unconventional flower display which they felt best reflected their life.

Natalie's display combined large brightly coloured blooms with herbs and spices, giving it a uniqueness of scent which won the judges unanimous vote.

What makes her display all the more astonishing is that Natalie is........

"Thanks ever so much as always Jane. I loved those croissants as well. You'll be getting me fat, well fatter."

The front door burst open as Jane turned the key and exerted unnecessary force in trying to help Natalie back into her home.

He looked at his watch 12.20. "Shit" he thought. He had lost concentration on his timings and had become too involved with studying her, the paper, her dining room and speculating.

The hall door to the front of the dining room leading into the hall and front door was open. The sounds of their entry steps were clear on the wooden floored hallway as they both came in to exchange their hugs and goodbyes.

The two arched doors to the rear were still open so he could sidle back into the kitchen if he needed. The lounge to dining room door in the front right hand corner was shut and he had forgotten to try it this morning after putting some oil on the hinges last night before Natalie had come home. It hadn't squeaked last night when he first oiled but it had before and he didn't want to try now, not with two people in the house.

"I'll tell you what Jane, let me get that pack of cards for you now, save you coming back around. I don't need them. I'm pretty sure they are in the living room. Do me a favour take the cake into the kitchen and put it in the fridge for me."

Jane walked down the hall and paused at the open dining room door. She was about to close the door but decided to change her route and go through the dining room to the kitchen having seen the two arched doors open. She closed the hall door behind her as she walked into the dining room. It gave a slight groan.

The intruder moved away from the other side of the arched doors and towards the main kitchen hall door ready to move back into the hallway and away from Jane. Jane opened the fridge and put the cream apple turnover she had bought Natalie onto the second shelf.

"The cake is on the left of the second shelf down," she shouted, her head pointing to the open kitchen door. The intruder was now standing by the dining room door at the foot of the stairs. If he walked up the wooden stained stairs he would surely make too much noise. His hand gripped the round brass handle ready to dive inside should Jane or Natalie sound as if they were coming back into the hallway.

"I can't find these cards in the living room Jane, they must be in the side board in the dining room," Natalie called in response to the instructions about the apple turnover.

"Sorry Natalie what was that?" Jane was walking to the kitchen hall door as she called back, her hearing not as good as Natalie's which she had witnessed on previous occasions and which boarded on the extraordinary.

There was a sudden tightness to his chest as the possibility of being discovered prematurely and not on his terms, started to make him perspire. As Natalie repeated herself to Jane, he could hear her walking towards the hall door to make herself more audible to Jane's hearing. The dining room door gave a quick, sharp, short creek as he pushed it open and jumped inside out of view, just as Natalie arrived in the living room doorway into the hall.

Jane had walked up from the kitchen and was now standing midway along the rear part of the hallway with the stairs on her right, the dining room door having been closed by the intruder.

Natalie walked to the dining room door. "I think they are in here," she said again as she put her left hand onto the door nob.

"Hi Natalie, I've a small parcel you need to sign for here."

Natalie turned back towards the front door where Alan, The Postman was standing in his red shorts, black trainers and red Post Office T shirt, his short black hair just visible under the side of his red baseball cap. She walked towards him rubbing her hands to get rid of the moisture.

From the kitchen she could hear the bleeping of the fridge door. "I think the fridge door is still open Jane from the cream cake on the left of the second shelf down." She laughed as she said it, conveying that she had heard Jane's information of earlier.

She walked to Alan while Jane walked back into the kitchen. In the dining room the intruder stood with his back against the door, listening to either side of the room simultaneously. Jane was now back in the kitchen walking towards the bleeping fridge which was in view from where he stood at the door.

He heard Natalie go back into the front living room and assumed she was putting her parcel down. "I'll just find a pen," she called to Alan. "I usually keep them in the top draw of the side board."

The dividing door into the dining room was on the opposite

side of the room to the hall door and gave a loud "eekk" as Natalie opened it, to look for a pen. He was now kneeling down behind the high back black chairs that were positioned four along each side and one at each end of the table, hoping his black shirt would be enough camouflage to keep his presence unnoticed. He mentally breathed a sigh of relief for not opening that dividing door into the lounge earlier as it would have made a noticeable noise.

"I don't need a pen Natalie, you sign this screen," Alan's call from the front door stopped her entering the dining room.

She turned and followed the line of the low backed three seater, green leather settee that formed one side of the square shaped U, the three settees made around a green granite coffee table; all of which focused on the fire place which formed the fourth side. Her hand skipped from the one settee to the next which ran parallel to the fire place wall and when her hand ran out of settee, she turned diagonally to go back out through the door to Alan.

"Thanks Natalie," said Alan, "have a nice day. Do you mind if I stay here a sec, just to sort some of these things out."

"No, not at all. I'll leave the door open if you need the hall floor." Alan stepped inside and put his bag down and started his quick sort out.

The intruder was trapped with all three exits having someone present. "Jane I think the cards are here in the dining room." Natalie followed the settees again and went back into the dining room.

Jane came in from the kitchen and joined Natalie as she foraged around in the bottom draw of the side board, which was on the other side of the table to where he was kneeling. He kept low and silent, hardly daring to breathe, keeping his head bowed, not even looking at them as they searched for the playing cards, just in case they turned around and spotted his face through the gaps in the seat backs.

Jane stood up guiding Natalie at the same time, the playing cards in her hands.

"Thanks Natalie, I'll see myself out. Are you sure you don't want these back?"

"No I'll never use them."

Jane walked out with Natalie between her and the intruder, Natalie's body acting as an additional shield, closing the dividing door after she left Natalie in the dining room.

"See you Natalie," called Alan, as he picked up his bag and closed the brown wooden front door, as Jane came out and they walked down the path to the tarmac drive together. Natalie turned towards the kitchen, still with her back to his position, her left hand skimming the top of the side board. She stopped as she felt the change in surface where he had rubbed earlier and removed the thin film of dust. She spread her arms wide like a bird flying and caught hold of the arched doors pulling them closed behind her, turning at the last second to face into the room before the doors clicked together on the ball catch.

She paused and thought to herself, "I will have that apple turnover before the pastry goes hard and another cup of tea."

Her sandals clicked across the white tiled floor as she crossed to her kettle to the left of the sink and put her left hand out to grab the handle. It wasn't there. The handle was on the right hand side where he had put it.

5) PREPARATION

The fifteen minutes of listening to Natalie make a cup of tea and eat the apple turnover seemed hours as he stood silent, even for a predatory prowler like him. He moved to stand behind the left hand side arched door, should she come back into the dining room.

Natalie washed up the cup and folded the cake box, putting it into the stainless steel kitchen bin. She walked over to the arched doors and put her hands on the handles and paused.

He looked at the shadow created by her body which obscured the light coming through the slats where she was standing in the kitchen. Both of the other doors were still closed from earlier as he had not wanted to risk any noise by opening them. The earlier fifteen minutes for tea and turnover seemed by comparison to this twenty seconds or so a click of the fingers. What was she going to do? Her shadow moved from side to side. What was she thinking about? Was she coming in or what? He stood with his back to the wall in case she flung the doors open, with his head and body twisted as much as he dare, for a quick response, transfixed to the shadow coming through the slats.

The light reappeared and he listened to her sandals walk to the kitchen door and then along the hallway towards the stairs and the dining room hall door. The chairs on the other side of the table offered the same camouflage as he crouched down behind them, just in case she came in from the hall.

He knew to stay in the dining room as she would be back down again to go out shopping. She would be out for about ninty minutes.

For the second time, he watched her walk down the path and to where a friend was waiting in a red Range Rover Evoque. The path lined up to the left hand front passenger door and she jumped in. Natalie turned her head back over her left shoulder in the direction of the living room bay windows as the Evoque slowly pulled away.

"What in hell's name was that? You idiot!" His mind admonished his earlier actions as his size ten soft soled shoes thudded up the stairs. His previously slow concentrated steps in the close presence of Natalie, now relaxed and angry, almost striding up the staircase and then along the beige carpeted left hand side of the landing back to Natalie's bedroom.

Her bedroom door was sticking. Good. He tried it four or five times and looked along the frame and the edge of the door for the signs of contact. He knew what he was going to do with this door.

His feet pumped across both sides of the two landing walkways as he weaved front to rear of the house and back again, three times each side, testing to see if any other floorboards creaked with his exaggerated weight. The board he had stood on earlier by the en suite was the only board that made a noise and he glared at it to embed it in his memory.

The landing doorway to the second floor attic rooms was open but he deferred considering going up there at this stage. As he circuited the long double sided landing, he occasionally leant against the polished mahogany coloured wooden bannister and stood up on his toes to exert downward pressure, all with the aim of finding any more squeaking boards. The landing passed his tests.

At the front of the house, at the far end of the sixty foot first floor walkway, away from Natalie's room, was a double glassed, brown upvc, sash cord, top and bottom opening window. The council rules on replacement windows being in keeping with the area, style of house etc were irrelevant to him.

The heavy, deep red curtains matching all the other front windows, both top and bottom to the front of her house, all of which hung from pelmet to floor, regardless of window size, were new, just four weeks old; not that he was aware of that, nor did he appreciate their ageless condition.

He pulled one of the landing window's curtain edges back to look out and check no one was around. The retaining catch moved freely as did the top opening section when he lowered it and put it back into its closed position.

The doorways leading into the two front bedrooms were opposite each other, just beyond where the top of the split stairway became the first floor on either side of the house. He went into both and now with the light just about permeating in from outside, he noticed they were identically decorated.

"Guest bedrooms!" He thought.

Both beds had white lace trimmed linen and pillows, daffodil yellow carpets, a pine bedside table but no light and matching double door wardrobes in the front alcove on the outer wall of the house and except the red curtains, everything was covered with clear polythene sheeting. In the rear, outer wall corner of each room were the original oak doors leading into the now adjoining bathrooms, which again matched with single stand up bath in white, placed in the centre of the room and away from the outer wall and window, with green padded window seat; so that you could walk fully around it. Both were fitted with the same chrome fittings as in Natalie's en suite. The toilet and sink were on the opposite wall to the door in from the front bedrooms, with the sink closest to the bath. In the gap between the toilet and the landing wall was a doorway into the third and fourth bedrooms at the rear of the house. There was also a third door adjacent to these rear doors, leading onto the landing, about half way towards the rear of the house, closer to Natalie's bedroom and her en suite on one side and the doorway to the second floor stairs on the other.

The doorway into the rear right hand bedroom from the bathroom squeaked a little until the oil he put on the hinges worked its way in, lubricating silence. He checked the bathroom door onto the landing, remembering he had forgotten to check the bathroom landing door opposite. "Sorted!"

He stood, puzzled as to why this third bedroom was decorated identically to the front two and again covered in polythene.

His observation of Natalie's movements had only covered the last three weeks and no one apart from Jane, Natalie and the man in the red Evoque had come to her house. That was a good thing from his point of view.

It just struck him odd, now that he had daylight and time to take in the decor, why there was no variation in these bedrooms and why on close inspection, everything looked new and why the polythene?

The doors to the fourth bedroom on the rear left of the house were locked both on the landing and from the Jack and Jill bathroom, between it and the front bedroom. His shoulder confirmed their security and then he leant back against the landing door looking down the stairs to the hallway below to get his breath.

He wandered back into the left hand rear bedroom, musing to himself. "Even the mirrors are the same!" Talking to his reflection within the silver oval, leaf designed frame.

His watch showed forty minutes had passed, there was plenty of time before her return.

There was no dust on his blue gloved right index finger as he rubbed it around the bottom of the mirror's frame. The same glove skidded around his chin as he assessed his stubble growth. It was now nearly two days since he shaved. He hated beards and moustaches, it wasn't clean to him, he would have to shave before Natalie came back, he should have done it when she was in Jane's earlier. Why didn't he?

His eyes looked tired. There were puffy bags under them and his eye lids hung heavy on their sides. He turned his head to present either side of his face to the mirror, a second assessment of his beard and his skin which looked weathered and cracked, the sort of skin you see on an old sea captain after years of exposure to the elements, drenched in salt filled waves crashing over the bows of his fishing trawler, catching cod in The North Sea.

There was nothing about his past sixty eight years that had exposed him to weather wearing conditions that could account for this facial ageing. His stare was unfading. His self assessment critical, scathing. Nothing but his behaviour, his debauchery could be pointed at for his cragginess, his furrows and lines that had infiltrated his skin from the age of twenty three after he had finished his training and when he felt compelled to misbehave, when placed in the close proximity of children and vulnerable teenagers.

There was remorse after each incident in those early days but as the frequency, opportunities and his authority increased, the remorse past quicker and quicker, the need to indulge again returning at an ever increasing rate. This face, this degradation, his perception of himself, was the epitome of Dorian Gray's painting in the attic. Each crack and cranny he put down to God's retribution on his appearance. The belief that the eyes were the windows to the soul, showed his soul as a blank, lifeless effigy. There was no glint or spark of excitement, no flicker of humanity, just a constant expression of indifference which looked at everyone he met, until he put on his display of interest.

Over years of subterfuge, he had learnt to act and people were seduced by his wit and consideration, consideration which drew his victims close through their trust in his compassion and purveyed concern. There had been rumours, tell tales, accusations, even a short, half hearted police investigation going back years and he had always been exonerated from any wrong doing, his victims often defending him with the hope of future leniency. There was none.

He placed both hands on the wall, either side of the mirror and stared threateningly at himself, looking deeper and deeper at the features of the face looking back. This was not him. He should not look like this. He had always been particular about his appearance, to be smart, presentable but his life had not been his to live but to serve and those he served suffered.

The lower buttons on his black shirt were stretched, his stomach now filling the capacity of the fabric where as years ago, his chest and shoulders had been more likely to stretch the seams. He pushed his body away from the wall and stood back from the mirror so that he could see more of himself. At five foot eight, his change of shape made him look shorter than he was. His stomach didn't overhang his black leather belt like those beer swilling football yobs he hated but it had distended in a way that had not been intended or encouraged and he reviled himself. The fingers of his right hand curled and clenched into a fist as his anger with himself increased. His right arm swung back as he closed on himself in the mirror, his stomach and torso disappearing out of sight as his face filled the reflection. His left hand slapped flat against the green emulsion painted wall to the side of the mirror and his right fist quivered with aggression as it threatened to smash the harrowed face looking back at him.

"No!" He turned away, walking back out onto the landing through the bathroom door.

The stairs up to the second floor echoed even with less heavy footsteps, as he plodded up to review the layout with more detail than tiredness and Natalie's presence allowed last night.

The first door on the left at the top of the stairs was locked and was directly above the fourth locked bedroom below. It was an odd design he thought. The one staircase from the rear of the house leading up to a squared off U shaped walk way with doors leading into the rooms off it.

Again with more time to think and visually measure, the second floor landing appeared to more or less follow the first floor double landing. This was a big house, bigger than it looked from outside. It certainly looked wide being double fronted but the depth of it was deceiving and the number of rooms inside were more than he had imagined.

The front left hand room where he had slept had a single bed in it, just the mattress, no bedding but he had used his back rain coat as a blanket but even that had been too warm and he had thrown it off during the night.

These roof rooms were really warm. "The design of this house must have been years ahead of its time, with rooms in the roof," his thoughts distracted from Natalie, as he wandered between each of the other accessible rooms.

There was little in each of these rooms. Three had single beds, all unmade. The rear right hand bedroom was the largest and all that it contained were four enormous, old fashioned wooden wardrobes standing back to back in the centre of the room. He circumnavigated them slowly, opening one of each of their double doors one by one. Inside there were just old dresses and ladies coats that dated back years, probably Margaret's covering her life, judging by some of their styles and condition. They didn't hold his attention as he flicked the occasional hanger to move a garment that had hung lifeless for years. The wardrobes were by no means full.

Each room had connecting doors and he oiled each hinge so that he could move silently between each when the time came.

Now with all the hinge oiling done, he started to think of the coming evening. If her habits of the last three weeks were constant, Natalie would be home this evening on her own and he looked forward to his perverse idea of party games.

38

6) DAVID

Natalie's arrival home this time was expected. He sat patiently on the bottom step of the stairs to the attic room eating a Mars Bar he had taken out of his hold all. As they walked to and from the car with shopping bags, Natalie crunching up and down the gravel path, he listened to David her friend, talking about going out for a curry that evening.

"Don't go out for a curry," he thought, "DON'T." His calmness quickly left him as he heard David bring this variation into his plans. He listened, his teeth grinding as his annoyance towards this infiltrator grew.

"It's a nice idea." Natalie's voice trailed off in volume as she walked into the kitchen, her words no longer carrying to where he was sitting.

"Is she going to go for this curry?" He got to his feet and started pacing around the rear area of the landing just outside the en suite door. As the two of them walked to and from the kitchen, he would stop and listen again to their conversation. There was not much of it, so perhaps that was a good sign, that Natalie was not really interested but he couldn't be sure.

"Cup of tea David before you go?"

He could see the top of David's head through the bannister spindles and his pause, as he looked at his watch.

"Yes, go on then."

He moved, his fingers rigid with agitation, his hands in front of him as if he were holding a massive beach ball. The longer

David stayed the longer he would have for Natalie to say she would go for a curry, if she had't already. His preoccupation with this get together again distracted him and he stood on the creaking floor board outside of the en suite. He glowered at his foot and the floor in disbelief and froze, motionless.

"Have you got someone staying with you Natalie?" David called into the kitchen as he looked up the stairs to the sound of the floorboard.

"No why?"

"I thought I heard something upstairs."

Her intruder watched the top of David's dark brown hair rise up the stairs as he started to walk up to the first floor to investigate. He turned, cursing himself mentally for his second moment of careless. He took two stairs at a time up to the second floor, pushing his weight down through his legs to make his assent as quick and as quiet as possible.

David was about thirty five and taller than himself, not by much but enough to make a difference when combined with a thirty year difference in age. The last thing he wanted was a confrontation with him.

"It's nothing David, don't worry. It's an old house. It creaks and squeaks all the time." Natalie had come out of the kitchen as soon as she heard David start to go upstairs.

"I'll just have a quick look to be sure. You need an alarm in here Nat."

Natalie raised her voice and injected unexpected sternness into it, as if she was telling off a naughty boy. "David leave it. You're wasting your time. It's just an old house. Come and have your tea." He looked down onto the top of her head as she stood facing towards the front door.

"Okay!" He turned around and walked back down the half

flight of staircase he had just climbed, his solid healed, brown slip on shoes, cracking down on the wood with his slow, reluctant steps.

The sound of his steps brought a sigh of relief to the disturbed predator as he lent back against the wall of the first unlocked bedroom along that second floor landing, his ears focused like sonic radar at David's location and direction. He decided to stay in that room and sat down in an old red armchair that he hadn't noticed earlier, which was partly covered by a sheet that had been thrown on it, showing only the bottom part of its front legs.

Despite its obvious age, it felt comfortable. As he pulled the sheet off the right arm, its exposure revealed the years of wear, the heavy red dralon material worn thin and some of the wooden frame showing through. It still felt comfortable enough for his purposes. Looking at the open door to the landing prompted him to get up to push it three quarters shut, enough for secrecy but open enough for warning, should David decide to try and take a second look. His pen knife blade glinted from the sun coming in through the velux roof window before he slipped it into the worn arm, between the frayed material and the partly exposed frame, its handle standing like a tiny obelisk for quick extraction.

7) REFLECTION

The relative silence of the second floor and his need to remain hidden brought on drowsiness and he dosed off to sleep, part listening, part day dreaming the recollections of the care home he once ran.

Unknowingly, he sat smiling to himself as his memories started to gain momentum. His mind became mixed with the layout of Natalie's house and his recollections of the terror he had been able to inflict on the children, friend by day, Bogeyman by night.

Those too young to understand became too frightened almost to go to sleep, especially if they had misbehaved in anyway during the day and had received any sort of correction from any member of staff. He was made aware of any misdemeanour and every child and the Bogeyman was always mentioned. Eventually every child knew they would receive a visit from the Bogeyman for being naughty. Their overall behaviour was often commented on and his caring, humour filled authority was often praised by unsuspecting visiting clergymen, who witnessed his brotherly approach with the children.

The other staff as they changed over the thirty six years he remained in charge, may have suspected something but his devotion to be the one to stay on night duty, night after night, allowing them welcome free time, apart from when he took holidays, eliminated any real conclusion to his doings.

The dormitories were hardly welcoming, being white tiled from floor to ceiling, echoey, hollow rooms, easy to clean, twelve unfortunate orphans or troubled children in each, four dormitories in total. He remembered his first, hesitant perversion. The silence of the sleeping children made the sound of his heeled shoes as he tried to walk down between the beds, like small thunder claps, causing him to cringe with awkwardness as he tried to put each consecutive step down, gentler than the last, each "click" quieter, his first sordid secret almost exposed before its conception.

The picture of his own progress that night made him smile now, a memory not forgotten but not thought of until the sound of David's shoes; his head oscillating from side to side, looking at those young seven to nine year old faces above the bed clothes, like a silent Daleks trying to glide silently past each bed, selecting its victim. That first child, a boy who had punched another boy, nothing vicious but it had been seen and stopped before it could escalate.

He remembered removing his shoes to walk back out. Those shoes were never worn again at night.

David's footsteps had brought back that memory as his mind ironically compared it with his first transgression. After that he wore moccasin slippers which allowed him to move like a ghost as even soft soled shoes like he was wearing now, squeaked on contact with the tiled floors.

The arm chair seduced his brain into reliving his disgrace as success. The more he transgressed the better he became at leaving the children penitent for their behaviour, his calculating, manipulative suggestions convincing them generally that they had deserved the Bogeyman's retribution. The Bogeyman's face he created. A simple black ski mask that covered his face, except the eyes which were cut out. He had embellished the mask with a sad mouth and droopy, sad eyes and eyelids with white paint which often conveyed vulnerability and hesitancy to his young victims, who on seeing the mask were somehow drawn to the sadness of the beast that was threatening them, a sadness which he told them, had been cre-ated by their behaviour, for which they would have to make amends, in order to be forgiven.

He always left each child with a few, slow, soft, pressured strokes across the back of their heads after removing the blue surgical glove from his right hand, as he settled them to go back to sleep, turning their heads away from the way he was going to walk out of the dormitory and the whispered words in their ears, in a made up growl voice to disguise his own, "you've made The Bogeyman very happy. Be good."

Tonight, he couldn't quite decide if he was was going to need that mask.

8) FURTIVE

The front door slamming brought his senses back to the here and now. The pen knife quivered as he stood up, prompting its retrieval and insertion into his trouser pocket as he listened for Natalie's whereabouts, now that David, he assumed had left. There was the faint sound of a car starting but he couldn't be a hundred percent sure as he was too far up and embedded in the house for the sound to reach him clearly.

There was no sound from below. Had Natalie left and gone with David for that curry? The silence infused with his imagination. There was still no hint of noise from below. His ears strained to pick up any sound waves that floated around the house carrying signs of Natalie but after 10 minutes of on edge expectation, there was still only silence.

Where was she? He needed to know to be in control. If she had come up stairs when he had been dozing, he could walk straight into her and that would spoil the fun. Each footstep he took down the second floor staircase was even slower and more deliberate than his earlier movements around the house. The single bannister on his left side gave additional support to take his weight as it transferred and was spread between his legs, his feet, his descending body and the uncarpeted stairs, until he stopped on the second from bottom step, listening.

His breath smelt in his cupped hand which covered his nose and mouth to subdue the noise of his breathing. The halitosis had been an unexpected bonus for his alter ego as The Bogeyman, as not cleaning his teeth and leaving off the mints he sucked most of the time during the days, gave an even more sinister and credible entity to his chosen victim as it passed through his mask, while he beguiled and damaged them with his deception.

The mints and toothpaste divorced any immediate connection between him and the night time demon that possessed the multiple bedrooms and left his stench of breath. When children spoke up, were found crying, ran away and were recovered and questioned, The Bogeyman's breath was nearly always mentioned.

Now, his eyes tried to bend their sight around the corner of the stairs through its doorway, onto the beige first floor landing, to see if there was any sign of Natalie. There was no sight or sound that indicated she was still in the house. The next few steps allowed him to see through the bannister which formed the square O shape of the stairway, where it split to go to the left and right hand side of this elongated rectangle of a double sided landing. There was still no sound coming up from downstairs. A few more tentative steps towards the front of the house took him away from the locked fourth bedroom door and closer to the top of the staircase. Again he glanced a look over to see if Natalie was down in the hallway, keeping as far back as he could, his back rubbing against the landing wall.

The door to that previously locked fourth bedroom, flung open with Natalie spiralling out of the doorway, her back turning to face him as her long black hair whipped around with her momentum, flicking strands across his face. She locked the door, paused for a second or so and walked down to the rear of the landing towards her bedroom, her back still towards him.

Startled, his body rigid with tension at the shock of her nearly bumping into him, he took two careful steps and crouched down by the side of the bannister, again with the hope that should she turn around, the dark brown, mahogany uprights would blend in with his black attire enough so that on a quick glance, he would go unnoticed. Natalie did not turn around but hipped her sticking bedroom door shut, leaving him crouching on his hands and knees.

The sound of her shower emanated from the far end of the landing, through the en suite landing door and to where he was still crouching. He took very thoughtful controlled steps down the stairs and into the kitchen, using her second shower of that day to boil a kettle and make himself a cup of coffee, cooling the kettle as before with cold water.

The time was now 5.30 and he still didn't know if Natalie was showering to go out for a curry with David and Co or if she was preparing for her usual Saturday night in, the TV on and a book, which appeared to be her relaxation for a Saturday night from his previous three weeks observations.

He walked from the kitchen, through the odd sort of adjoining "space" which he couldn't define but that sort of "lost bit" within Natalie's house where there was a bit off the right side of the kitchen, with cupboard storage in it but no appliances, no dishwasher or washing machine which were in the kitchen but just a "gap" in continuity from the kitchen to her beautiful garden room.

The grey rattan, weather proof three piece suite, two double settees and a chair with bright yellow cushions with blue peacock feather design for the seat and back rests stood out, "bang" straight in your face; against the pink painted walls that formed the archway effect of this conservatory, this garden room, which was about twenty five feet long, approximately the same length as the kitchen on the opposite side of her house.

After initially sitting on one of the double settees, he changed and sat in the chair, which again with the two settees, formed a squared off U shaped layout, around a matching rattan coffee table. The left side of the garden room had a centre patio door, opening and facing the kitchen, downstairs toilet and back door protrusion directly opposite. Sitting in the chair with his back to the entrance into the garden room from the kitchen, after two or three minutes started to un nerve him. She could, or David could, if he came in, approach him from behind.

A little unsettled, these subsequent thoughts encouraged him to move to the right hand settee, from which he could look at the kitchen opposite, through its windows which were on either side, so that he could look into the kitchen itself and beyond to the pathway on the far side, the one he had used to get to the unsighted kitchen door, through which he had gained entry last night. This seating position also meant he could see anyone coming into the garden room, through its entry door as soon as possible.

Happy now with his musical chair selection, he sat into the squidgy cushions and enjoyed his coffee. From where he sat he could hear Natalie's shower directly above him. With the vision of her from that morning in his mind he gave himself a quick indulgent squeeze as he visualised her lathering herself and pressing her buttocks against the shower cubical's glass walls.

The coffee's caffeine did not kick in as he was expecting. The heat from the garden room, his sleep deprivation and age, all caught him unawares and he fell into an unguarded, deep sleep for twenty minutes, with the sound of Natalie's shower from above, droning in his ears.

He woke with a start, his eyes looking naturally straight across from his seating position into the length of the kitchen in which Natalie was preparing something or other. Whatever it was didn't matter. There was the possibility that should she look across, she might see him sprawled on of her rattan settees, an old man dozing.

There was little to hide behind, only the back of the settee on which he had fallen asleep. The walls of the garden room were relatively low in order to give it, its maximum affect for the capture of the sunlight and its warmth. It had been purposely designed long before add on conservatories had been thought of, by the original owners; to have as much light in that room and as much of a view of the garden as possible. There were three narrower windows on the end, with five wider and matching, virtual floor to ceiling windows along each side, the centre windows one either side, now replaced with opening patio doors and all in council approved brown upvc. On this late afternoon, on an very sunny July day, it had lulled a perverse, psychopathic, paedophile into an untroubled sleep.

His breathing instantly became shallow and rapid, as a result of this unplanned agitation. He sat still, his puffy bagged eyes glancing around him. Apart from the other matching settee directly opposite, there was nothing to hide behind, except for kneeling down and hiding face first into the seating cushions of the settee opposite or getting up and hiding behind the back of the settee he had fallen asleep on. There was a small CD player on the floor behind him, no TV, no book case, nothing other than these two settees, a chair and a coffee table that could offer him the minimum of cover.

His gaze did not divert from Natalie. Her every move was stared at without her knowledge to see if there was the slightest recognition off his presence. There was none. As soon as she turned her back on him, he slithered around the side and back of the settee like a magnetic snake, unable to break free of his contact with the rattan. The coffee cup remained on the table.

From behind the settee, he looked at her still doing whatever she was doing but now again he felt safe and in control. He knew where she was, what she was doing, more or less but she knew nothing about him. Then he saw his coffee cup.

He had felt momentarily settled, as he peeked out from behind the settee like a child playing hide and seek and looked at her, in her pyjamas or her onesie or what ever the stupid description was, for the all in one jump suit or leisure suit that people had been introduced to through imaginative marketing. He could see that it was a Tigger onesie or pyjamas and his mind was sent back to one particular girl that had been brought to the care home at the age of eight by social services, with a full set of Pooh Bear character clothing and pyjamas after the unexpected death of her relatively young mother.

There was no father to be found. From birth certificate records, it would have appeared that the father and mother never married and although the name of her father, James Morris appeared on the birth certificate; her mother Mary Mills had never changed her name and there was no record of a marriage. Against "occupation" on that girl's certificate was seaman for her father and civil servant for her mother.

Had that child been lucky enough to have found relatives, she would not have been subjected to an orphan life for six years and the depravity of someone appointed to look after her welfare. She had become one of his favourites very quickly and he had visited her more than most.

At fourteen, she had eventually been found a family prepared to offer her a foster home, a family caring enough to go the extra mile for her particular needs. Initially, he had missed her as she had developed early at eleven but he soon found unfortunate replacements.

He stared at the floor as his memory of that girl, as she had been then, relived in his mind and then looked back at Natalie and waited for her to go and settle in the large front lounge on the left side of the house for her Saturday evening. His coffee cup drew his attention again.

9) TEASING

Natalie deadlocked the front door and walked into the front left hand lounge. Unlike the living room which had a doorway leading into the dining room, there was a second doorway at the far end of this long lounge coming back into the hallway, just beyond the stairs. Between that door and the doorway into the kitchen was another downstairs shower room and toilet.

His watched showed 7 o'clock. The TV was on but not very loud, as the sound barely made it out through the still open door and up to the first floor landing, where he had crept after washing his coffee cup once Natalie had left the kitchen. As he waited, the plainness of the landing stuck him. The beige carpet had registered but now these beige walls were so bland by comparison to the other three bedrooms which were all painted with the same green emulsion and Natalie's room which had blue walls.

As he leant nonchalantly against the doorway of the stairs to the second floor, listening to Natalie walking to and from the kitchen, first with her tray of spaghetti carbonara, then with the New Zealand, Villa Maria Sauvignon Blanc he had seen in the fridge after her shopping, now in the wine cooler in her left hand, a large bulbous glass in her right and book under her right elbow; his eyes noted the two identical low storage ottomans, directly opposite each other on either side of the landing. Both were painted white with plain, bright yellow padded lids which looked comfortable enough to sit on. Apart from these two large, oblong storage boxes, there was no change in colour around the landing, no pictures, no ornaments, just beige, the bannister and wooden bedroom doors.

Pushing himself away from the door frame with his shoulder, he made one step towards the ottoman on his side of the landing and stopped as Natalie came back out of the lounge one final time to go to the kitchen.

The doorway provided further support for the next twenty minutes as he leant against it, listening.

There was no one outside of the front of the house to see him look out from behind the curtains of the front window of the landing. The right hand side bedroom door glided open with the push of his foot, ready to be his escape route as he draped the curtain over the top of his head while he undid the latch. Gripping the top opener, he slammed the window down to the window sill, the thudding vibration transmitting its contact back up into his fingers, its movement silent until the crash sounded along the landing and down to the hall and Natalie's lounge.

Looking over the top of the bannister, down towards the hall, he could just about see the top of Natalie as she rushed out of the lounge and stop by the front door. He knew what she was thinking. "What was that? Where had that noise come from?"

He tried to sense her, static, concentrating, her mind trying to analyse what had just happen. Twenty seconds passed. The living room door on the other side of the hall, swooshed as she pushed it firmly so that it would open fully. The sound of her bare feet, from being laid out along the seven seater white, L shaped leather settee, padded on the hall's wooden floor. Her footsteps went silent as she walked onto the living room's blue carpet. The bannister creaked from his weight, as he leant further over the front end section to look down into the hall and for Natalie. He froze as the creak ended not to create a second giveaway.

The dining room door handle rattled, warning him Natalie would be coming back into the hallway having walked through the two rooms. She emerged slowly, her right hand running along the face of the door, across the frame and onto the hall wall.

He felt excited as he studied the perturbed look on her face. She was breathing quickly, like she had just finished running. The bannister groaned again as he pushed it, coaxing the wood to attract her attention and he stood back against the window that he wanted her to find.

The sound of her coming slowly up the stairs changed as the balls and soles of her feet started to make little squirting noises, as her cautious progress became more sweaty. It was a warm night. He felt it as well and a bead of perspiration ran down the side of his left temple which was wiped away with his blue surgical glove.

The back of Natalie's head glided back into his view as she came higher up the stairs. From her movement, it was obvious she was ascending the stairs in the same way as he had earlier when moving up to the second floor after David heard the floorboard. The upper part of her body was firm, just her right arm extended to guide her hand along the bannister rail. The impression of a semi automated marionette, coming out of a large nineteenth century German city centre clock, chasing her husband or a thief came to mind. Natalie directed her strength through her legs, pushing her body weight upwards and forward in an effort to be inanimate and quiet as possible, while she investigated that unexplained sound.

He felt superior already within his game. Three elongated side steps from the bannister took him to the right hand bedroom doorway. His legs and body were drawn inside as he backed into the room, like he was being sucked inside the room by a vacuum cleaner, his neck and head riveted towards Natalie, the appearance of an overweight, out of condition, black pointer dog waiting for his master's instructions.

Natalie hesitated at the divide in the stairs, uncertain whether to go left or right, turning to face the front of the house in her quandary. The black pointer dog retreated his face to behind the door frame, his eyes still able to watch her, in her cotton Tigger patterned pyjama top and shorts. The red curtain flapped open from a gentle gust of wind, enough to lift and move it slightly in a wave through the fabric, like the bottom of a matador's cape, teasing the bull with small ruffles. Natalie's hair moved as the gust moved along the landing. She raised her left hand to feel the air still passing her.

Her head dropped as the thought of "how?" was conveyed through her body. He moved back into the room proportionately to Natalie walking towards the landing window, keeping her in view the whole time, her hand still outstretched in front of her, feeling the air movement against her skin.

The breeze caught her perfume and body smell as she pulled open the curtains, wafting their combination around the landing, through into the darkened bedroom and into his nostrils. This was an early treat and he smelt every molecule until the scent passed beyond his sense's capability.

Natalie stood with her hand out through the open window, waving in the air where her fingers should have been touching the glass.

"What?" was all she said, as he watched her became visibly that little bit flustered by her confusion, as her hands felt around the fallen window panel for something, a gripping point with which she could close the window back up. It dropped slightly, her hands missing the grip as she lifted the window to its closed position. Her tormentor smiled to himself as he watched her reactions and the difficulty she seemed to have as she fiddled and fussed with the locking catch, trying to decide which way it would turn to lock shut.

"Awoe" after breaking a nail, she closed the curtains and stood with her hands on her hips, her back fully turned against him. He scanned her from hair tip to heal, his baggy eyes squinting as his thoughts twisted his face. The curve of her buttocks just appearing below the bottom of her Tigger stripped yellow and black pyjama shorts, catching his focus and his lust.

She jumped at he sound of a slamming bedroom door . "Jesus Christ!"

Natalie turned quickly, apparently in fright and looked back at the front window, her mind providing the logical explanation, which she surprising voiced to herself. "Ah the wind must have caught the door."

She shook her head disbelievingly and then stood silent, seemingly assessing the landing for another probable cause.

He waited for her, watching through the gap in the adjoining bathroom door where he now stood, having quickly moved through the bedroom. He relished the aftermath of her reaction as well as the shriek she had made when he slammed the bedroom door.

Her hand rested on the brass door knob, hesitant to open the door into the bedroom. His excitement mounted as he could hear her hand fiddling with the brass. The bathroom door onto the landing opened silently for him, the oil having successfully lubricated the hinges and he stood almost side ways on in the threshold peeking down the landing towards Natalie.

"Was she going to open the door and go into the bedroom?"

He was ready to move back to Natalie's bedroom if she did. Her hesitancy passed and she opened the bedroom door, the latch springing loudly back as she let the knob free from her grip. He saw her body move through the doorway and then tried to hear her walking through towards the bathroom door he had closed behind him into the Jack and Jill bathroom.

That adjoining door opened suddenly, making him jump back quickly onto the landing. Natalie's movements had been so quiet through that front right hand bedroom, that he had not heard her, despite his ears straining to pick up any noise. The bathroom to landing door in which he had just stood came to his aid again, providing a natural shield to his discovery, forming a wooden barrier between the two of them. His soft soled black shoes pressed heavily into the landing carpet as he turned and like a slow motion Gazelle, strode towards Natalie's room with lengthy, controlled, quiet, springing steps.

His hand was already outstretched to push open her door when he realised she had pulled it tight. The moisture from his face and lips spread onto the surface of the wood as his face and head brushed against the surface of the door. She still had not come out of the bathroom onto the landing and he looked at that bathroom door with defiance as he rushed to go into her en suite through the landing doorway. The floor board creaked again as he inadvertently stepped on it a third time since the start of his internal stalking. He held his breath with anxiousness, willing not to be given away by his clumsiness, his face starting to turn red, when at his age from this exertion, he needed more oxygen than less going to his lungs.

Natalie came out of the bathroom doorway and pushed her feet into the pile of the carpet, hesitating as she again assessed the landing and then continued to move slowly towards her bedroom.

Her feet swished and caressed the carpet as she lifted them off the pile and glided them alternately from side to side across its surface, like a mine sweeper searching for mines.

She stood still after three or four steps, facing her bedroom door and then turned and went back downstairs into the lounge, leaving its door nearly fully open.

His mouth opened with a grateful "paahh", taking in a deep, deep breath, followed by more quick breaths as he bent over with his hands on the sink in Natalie's private bathroom.

Even in the dimness, her en suite mirror was no kinder to him than the bedroom mirror had been earlier that day, only now his craggy, bag eyed face was bright red.

His normal pasty face, sun lacking complexion eased back while he looked at the redness dissipate in the mirror, as his lungs recovered from holding his breath.

There was a glimpse of realisation as he looked at his face and then directly at his own body, putting his hands onto the roundness of his stomach. His age had caught up with him and here, now, he was stalking a young, fit woman by comparison; not small, sleepy, frightened children.

This was the first time he had ever broken into any house and stalked anyone and it was bringing a new excitement and danger. His reflection became his confidant as he stared at himself and his thoughts questioned this reality.

Eventually there would be confrontation which was the whole purpose of being there but first he must weaken her through fear so that he had the advantage, an advantage that was so much easier when he had prowled those night time silent, children filled dormitories.

The cold water on his face and the black towel removed the traces of sweat, the chill injecting additional invigoration to his thinking. He wiped the inside of his collar where the water had run down his neck and then rubbed his eyes with the towel, its movement on his droopy eyelids, feeling like he was scratching his eyeballs beneath. The towel remained scrunched in his right hand, partly obscuring the lower part of his face and he stared at his own eyes.

Was there any excuse for how he was and how he had been? Since being retired, virtually all opportunity had disappeared just leaving empty compulsion and frustration. His eyes still looked lifeless even when thinking and reflecting as he was doing. His humanity and decency had long gone. Any godly, spiritual ethic a thing long ago in his past. He needed to un-nerve Natalie more, to create more unbalance in any calm logic she may have now, as a grown woman.

The expectation of creating more "bumps in the night", ..."ghostly"........ unexplained events, like the window, like the wardrobe door she would find later, now galvanised a glimmer of spark in those dead eyes in the mirror. When you become as depraved as he had sunk in life, normality was your coffin and hell your excitement.

The black towel dropped to the floor as he leant forward to put his face right up to the mirror, to look at every aspect of his now full face in close up, the intricate detail of his worldly, existing portrait. The scram, long since healed to the right of his right eye, now a line within his age, a deep, determined de-fence from a child one night, a feisty, strong, black haired girl. There were two small indentations to the right of his chin, the same girl a couple of months later, just before she left, a well struck blow to his face with the heal of her shoe, the only thing she could reach from her bed as he leaned over her, his stinking breath escaping the confines of his demented, sad lipped mask. The smile of recollection was stomach churn-ing had anyone bar himself seen his image in that mirror. His lips distorted in an almost satanic, "Elvis" smile, a lip curl de-void of music and pop and filled with the grotesqueness of a demon; psychotic with power, his earlier torments this night, now encouragement for further terror.

In her bedroom were the built in wardrobes, the green painted doors of the one in the front alcove and the pink painted doors of the larger wardrobe built into the second deep recess, on the other side, to the right of her double bed.

He ran his hand along the top of the duvet and then slipped it underneath the cover and squeezed and rubbed the mattress where Natalie's bottom and hips would lie, bringing it back out and sniffling it slowly and deeply, imagining his hand just rubbed around her buttocks and thighs.

The clothes on the left side within the pink wardrobe were arranged in ascending order according to length, shortest on the left, becoming longer to the right. The two bifold doors, each reached about three feet into the bedroom when fully open, their ends protruding well beyond the bedside table with the alarm clock. The dressing gown Natalie had placed at the bottom of the bed, he rearranged to the pillow end of the bed.

The bathroom mirror drew his attention again as he walked through her en suite to go back out onto the landing, stopping to look at himself again, his image now looked calmer, not red faced but with a steeliness of expression that conveyed a surety, a determination. He had left the first, tentative level of fright and now with distorted confidence walked towards the middle of the landing and the top of the staircase, looking down into the hall.

The sound from the TV seemed quieter than before. "Had Natalie turned the volume down so she could hear things better?" The question repeated in his mind as he took the first three of the left hand divide in the staircase down towards the lounge. His shoes for the first time didn't seem to want to co operate with his desire for silent footsteps. Each stair caused them to give out a small "Shuuuuush" and "eeck" as his weight first pressed down on his decent, transferring to the other foot on the next wood stained step.

He stopped, standing still totally, his head the only thing with the slightest of movement, looking between the lounge door and the stairs below his feet. The lounge floor he could see was polished and he assessed that these shoes would make the same warning sounds to Natalie when he finally went in, to stand behind her while she read. These same sort of shoes latter in life, like his slippers, had served him well when walking those dormitories but in the relative quiet of this house, when his victim was still awake and an adult, they were not fully allied to his plan.

His left arm flexed, helping to push him backwards as he reversed up the three steps back onto the landing. Natalie came out of the lounge carrying her empty dish. He went static. Luckily, her head was bowed so she didn't look up towards the landing. As she went into the kitchen, he returned to her bedroom to consider what to do with his shoes.

"Was he being too careful?" He thought to himself. "The first aim having broken in successfully was to create fear and unnerve her. The first window had been the start but he need to do more so that when he did reveal himself, Natalie would collapse in a gibbering heap, leaving him stronger to do anything he wanted, her own fear having defeated her."

He mulled these thoughts through, trying to establish a course of action. The shoes were a minor issue which he hadn't noticed before but he didn't want them to spoil things. In one of her draws he found some black socks which proved to be a struggle to get over his shoes. He sat panting on the bed after managing to get them on. Leisurely, he lay to one side his elbow on the pillow and thought to himself until he unintentionally dozed off.

The decent into the hall this time was silent and it had virtually gone dark outside. Ignoring the lounge for the moment, he walked into the kitchen and out to the garden room to the CD player. There were four CD's lying next to it. The Best of Dean Martin, the same one as Natalie bought Joe after an evening two weeks ago where they shared three bottles of wine and the CD had been the one they left playing four times without changing, as it was "so good". The other two were by two different groups he had never heard of and the final one, "Movie Themes".

He squinted a quick glance down the listings and his selection was made. The Dean Martin CD was still in the player. He swapped the disks, putting Dean carefully back into its case. Turning the volume right down he set up his chosen track to be the next to play. The red arrow told him when it had reached maximum volume 30. The remote had batteries in it and he made sure it decreased the volume as he pointed it at the player. He stood by the entrance arch, ready to leave to go to back to the kitchen and through to the dining room and then living room if he needed to escape to another part of the house should Natalie start searching the ground floor.

"Dah, dah, da, DAAHHH" the theme from 633 Squadron exploded through the speakers. He threw the remote over the top of the first settee with its back directly facing him onto the yellow and blue peacock feather decorated seats and moved quickly into the kitchen to watch for Natalie.

In the lounge, the sound of the brass band of The Royal Welsh Guards swooped in and crushed the sound of the softly playing TV.

Natalie flinched at the sudden noise as she looked up, putting the book she was reading down next to her as she got up and left the lounge to investigate, following the sound from the CD player.

In his anticipation of Natalie, he forgot his own plan and found himself standing next to the door at the back of the kitchen into the rear toilet and storage area. It was too late to go back across the kitchen to the dining room. She might see him and he still wasn't ready for that yet, not on her terms. He ground his hands together in anger with himself.

Natalie in these thirty or so seconds, had come in from the hall and gone through to the garden room. The intruder craned his neck to see her through the kitchen window, across the red paved patio area with its large wooden round table and six chairs, which lay between him and the garden room opposite. To him, her confusion was obvious and that drew a snigger of laughter as he gloated in his second success. He pressed himself back against the wall, in the hope of making himself less noticeable. Despite his excitement, his hands continued to rub around themselves.

Natalie held her head with both hands, cupping her cheeks as she stood looking down at the CD player, not even bothering to turn it off or down in the first minute of her walking into the garden room. She picked up the CD cases and appeared to investigate them but she now stood with her back towards him, so he couldn't see her face. This frustrated him, he squeezed his hands together ever harder as his tension increased. She eventually turned the CD off just as Laura's Theme from Dr Zivargo started and put the cases back down against the CD player.

As he watched her leave, listening for her going back through the other side of the kitchen to the lounge, he leant back against the toilet door, his tension ebbing as he relived the last couple of minutes, his recollections divertIng his concentration. He looked at the repair he'd made to the back door glassing and it made him feel smug again.

Natalie opened the tall American style fridge door at the far end of the uncluttered granite work tops that ran from the side of the fridge towards the door into the utility room where he was standing. He froze rigid again, his swallow stopping half way through, his Adam's apple stuck, afraid to move.

If she closed the door and looked his way, there was nothing between him and her. "Had she noticed if the utility room door was open or shut?" The question though logical was a panic reaction.

His thoughts thrashed around. If he moved, would her eye catch it. He felt himself beginning to go red as he held his breath again. He concluded if he didn't move and she saw him, she saw him.......if he did move and she saw him, then the same, she saw him but if he managed to close the door and she didn't see him, then he had won this moment.

He watched her swaying in and out of the fridge as she selected something more to eat. Moving microscopically to the other side of the utility room, he slowly and gently pushed the door shut and stood behind waiting. He could hear the click of a knife on the granite.

Natalie shut the right hand fridge door which had partly acted like a shield and walked back to the hall, shutting the kitchen door behind her as she went back into the lounge with a couple of slices of Stilton cheese, peanuts and apple, to go with her wine. His surgically gloved left index finger held the warning plunger in and he then cut himself a chunk of Stilton on the granite surface which bordered the dividing wall into the dining room, deliberately leaving crumbs where as Natalie had previously wiped hers up from the granite on the opposite side of the fridge.

"For the moment," he thought, "a short break." The utility room became his bar for ten minutes as he ate the cheese and peanuts and downed it with a 33 cl bottle of Stella Artois, leaving about a quarter of the beer in the bottle. The cap clipped back on, enough for his purposes and he went back in the kitchen and opened the fridge door, this time without holding in the warning plunger.

The small bottle shattered everywhere even though he

dropped it directly onto the floor in front of the fridge door. Before he slipped through the arched doorway into the dining room he ushered some of the larger fragments together so that the bulk of the broken bottle tried to gave the impression it had fallen off the shelf, where four had been lined in the right hand door.

The fridge started to send out warning bleeps as he broke off the bottom part of the bunch of green grapes and retreated into the dining room shutting the arched door behind him, eating a grape one by one as he opened the door into the living room, ready for his exploration into the lounge when Natalie returned to the kitchen. The muffled sound of her feet padded past the dining room's hall door as she moved towards the kitchen and her tormentor walked in the opposite direction, separated by the dividing wall.

She stopped at the kitchen door, the open fridge door emitting a halo of light across from the other side of the L shaped kitchen. The pungent smell of the beer hit her nose and Natalie remained where she stood, staring at the light and towards the beer and the broken glass on the floor. She put two and two together.

"How on earth could that have happened? I'm sure I closed the fridge door. Natalie, you're loosing it! Too much wine girl." She said it out aloud, in a tone that sounded like she was scolding herself off for being so careless. Natalie returned to the lounge to get her slippers and collected the dust pan and brush from the utility room, methodically sweeping the floor from the far side of the kitchen towards the glowing fridge, the buzzer still bleeping at her. After disposing of the larger pieces of glass into the kitchen bin, she felt the floor cautiously through the floor cloth for more shards on the white tiles as she moped up the beer. Natalie finished and closed the fridge door which put the kitchen into darkness as she had not bothered to turn the light on. He thought that odd.

She put her right hand onto the granite to use as a guide and touched the cheese crumbs he had left. "Cheese?" She exclaimed aloud, rubbing her fingers and then smelling the Stilton now smeared onto her finger tips and the palm of her hand. She stopped and thought.

Her stalker smiled to himself from the doorway of the dining room into the living room, although a little disappointed inwardly for such a controlled reaction from her. He had expected a little more agitation. Still, there was more to come and he moved quietly from the living room across the hallway into the lounge and stood behind the door waiting for Natalie to return to her book and wine.

10) CLOSER

His eyes adjusted to the light or the lack of it. The red curtains still closed, prohibited any real moonlight shining onto the front windows from permeating through and into this large, oblong lounge. Not even the white L shaped leather settee or its two matching, two seaters added any whiteness within the overall gloom of this room.

As he looked around, he could see four matching tall floor lamps with thin stainless steel shaft and bamboo style, square paper shades, two against the dividing hall wall and two directly opposite against the outer wall of the lounge. None of them were on. The 50 inch flat screen TV stood in the opposite corner to the front door of the lounge he now stood behind, its light dappling around the furniture and furnishings of the room. Underneath yet another square formed by the leather settees was a huge Turkish rug, predominantly red from what he had seen last night before she came home but with symmetrical patterns where he could see, with deep royal blues, yellows, pinks and greys. It protruded beyond the backs of all the seating, like a clifftop roadway, where he could walk without going onto the original polished wood block flooring from when the house was built.

There was one high sided, teak side board with crystal cut glasses inside the glassed, three shelf double sided display, all of which had been Margaret's favourites. This stood between the two floor lamps by the dividing wall to the hall. From the ceiling hung two old circular chandeliers, with five legs coming off their central stems, tiered with droplet crystals which became smaller in size the further away they were from the centre.

This room had no lack of available lighting should Natalie switch some lights on but he was happy hiding in the shadows. Even the light from the TV could catch him but he intended to be behind her, so his presence would go unnoticed.

The small part of her buttocks poking from underneath the bottom of her shorts stayed in his stare, as Natalie came back into the room and walked to the large L shaped sofa. She really did have fantastic legs, beautifully formed calf muscles and shapely long thighs but then they had always been like that. He felt himself start to stiffen while he stood behind the open door, intoxicating himself with his bravery and daring at now being in the same room. The picture on the TV sent jumping, changing, erratic flashes of colour and light around the shadowy room, which would have been in complete darkness if it had not been on. The smell of spaghetti bolognese still lingered but he could smell her as she walked within two feet of where he stood behind the door and he took lustful, deep, slow breaths to take in her scent. She stopped by the first settee and stood with her feet apart, a perfect display of her bottom and thighs, moving after a few seconds until the back of the settee obscured them from his gaze. She bent over, almost unnaturally to pick up her glass of wine off the pink marble coffee table with a slow enticing bend, stretching her shorts, the curves of her buttocks distinct, drawing the excitement out of him. She stood up straight with the glass in her hand and took a sip, putting it back down with the same provocativeness. He moved the pen knife in his right pocket to one side so that he could reach himself better.

Natalie sat down and picked up her book and he waited, staring at the back of her head and black hair.

The first small, slowly paced footstep, moved him eight inches closer to her. The second step the same, the third, the fourth and his heart shook in his chest with the effort of pumping his blood around his body, the adrenaline like the accelerator in a car, pushing his engine to go faster. He stopped with an unrushed glide behind her, his bodily movement the opposite to his racing bodily functions. The feeling of his heart beating in his chest made him think that it must be so loud that she would hear it. He looked down on Natalie's head pondering the sense of his approach to the possibility of her sensing him. Would his own heart give him away? The smell of her now was stronger, her skin, her perfume, her hair.

The fingers of her left hand ran across the face of the page, tracing the words of the story she was reading. The dappling light from the TV made the room flicker with hints of life, of shrouded colour, his own face, fixed with concentration and recollections. He leaned over Natalie's head even more, inquisitive to see the book that kept her engrossed, his eyes unable to see any words.

Natalie shifted in her seat. He pulled back his head, the slightest of touches from her hair against the end of his nose, the mere touch, forcing the smell of her hair into his nostrils as he took his next, measured breath, slowly and pedantically, his brain counting the seconds of inhalation, comparing them to the capacity of oxygen he needed to fill his lungs; the fewer, the deeper the breaths, the more silent he could be, like a black panther hunting his pray, crouching in the undergrowth. Here, the undergrowth was Natalie's own home. Its layout now more familiar to him, now that he had laid down his patterns, his runs.

Natalie lent forward and took another, larger drink of wine, the sound of it, as she purposely sloshed it around the inside of her mouth, her tongue swimming through the chill, tasting the gooseberry flavours of New Zealand; making him want to kiss her, to take the wine from her mouth and savour it and her lips again.

She sat back against the back rest and he returned to hovering above her head, her movement causing her strapped Tigger top to slip downwards and pull to the left, revealing the side and curve of her right breast and a slanted exposure of her cleavage. Natalie did not adjust her top, why would she? She was alone. He looked at her legs curled up on the settee, her right calf plumped up from lying on top of her left leg underneath, its shape and curve transfixing him, as his eyes roamed greedily over her body. Natalie's left hand still traced the story on the page but he had now lost interest in what she was reading.

His excitement was now pumped. The steps he took to move away from her were as slow and as short as those when he had approached but now backwards and out through the hall door. As he moved down the hall to the kitchen and the toilet in the utility room, his hearing remained directed back towards Natalie and any sound that conveyed his detection. All he heard was the sound of the TV become fainter as he walked through the house away from the lounge.

After relieving himself in the utility room toilet, the perverted prowler walked through the dining room and sat in the blackened living room on the green leather settee facing the curtained front window, listening to the TV from across the hall.

When he looked at his watch, 11pm. Natalie would be going to bed soon.

11) SOLITUDE

For a half hour while he sat silent, reflecting his visit into the lounge, listening and waiting for Natalie to go to bed, his thoughts were dragged back to thinking of his new home, the retirement home, approximately two miles away.

Was this going to be his existence, one surrounded by all men, ageing like himself, put out to pasture; pondering the meaning of life now that the majority of their lives had passed. He like they had no close family, just brothers or sisters if they were still alive and he didn't have either.

The black socks he had fought with earlier were well and truly moulded to the shape of his black desert boots as his contemplations found his eyes unconsciously looking at his feet.

His one surgical glove had a small hole in the thumb on his right hand, which he had caught in the zip of his trousers earlier. "There are spares in my hold all," he thought pensively "but I don't think I'll want them on later." His thoughts about touching Natalie's body directly without this five fingered condom came and went as his angry, speculative misgivings about his forthcoming care home years forced him to ring his gloved hands and fingers together, their integration ripping open the torn thumb even more.

Six of the men who were in the home before him had come from around the country and now two months after joining them, he was already sick of listening to their stories, their lives, their comparisons with each other, their accents. The other two he had worked with and he was well used to them.

The picture of F. James Connelly, a very tall, now bulbous,

rotund man with wild grey beard and thick unkept matching hair, who had spent most of his life in the North of Scotland and who spoke with an indecipherable Scottish accent having been born, raised and worked there all his life; planted itself as the quintessential image of these six other boarders. Now, for some unfathomable reason, he had been brought to a retirement home in Oxfordshire, to share his twilight days bemusing, confusing eight other relics and three staff members, with regalia, anecdotes, thoughts on life and spiritualism as death drew closer, where the only decipherable word anyone could understand was, they all assumed, within his repeated gabling was "haggis."

For the first time in over twenty four hours, his mind moved away from calculation, assessment and intrepid anticipation, by the thought of this man. He appreciated the comedy within the situation. "Even God has a sense of humour," he thought to himself but that thought was short lived as the overwhelming frustration of trying to understand what on earth he was trying to say, every time he opened his mouth returned within an instant and now, pummelled any patience out of him.

The thing was, it wasn't just him. There was a frigging Welsh bloke from North Wales, that sang "Onward Christian Soldiers" in Welsh or "My Hen had a bad eye" or whatever the Welsh National Anthem was, at the drop of a hat, confirming to his mind, that every Welsh man thought they were Tom Jones. After eight weeks, apart from everyone referring to him as Father Taff, he still couldn't remember his name, Geriant, Gerwen. Glyndwr or something beginning with G or double G, something idiosyncratic to a language with words that didn't use vowels. When he spoke, he had a breathy, guttural tone to his voice and spoke so softly and quickly, that he wanted to give him a bloody good punch in the mouth, to annunciate whatever English he was trying to speak, in order to get rid of that Welsh North Walean twang. He was almost as indecipherable as bloody F. James Connelly.

As his silent contemplation became more aware to his thinking, he could feel the anger of his unacknowledged schizophrenic behaviour, rise within his blood. His hands stopped rotating and twinning and became clenched in an aggressive, controlled ball, vibrating almost as the exertion of distain and speculative perceptions, flowed from his brain and manifested themselves within the form of two combatting fists fighting for supremacy.

Agitated acutely by his situation, he pushed himself into the back of the settee, the cool of the leather acting like a damper for his mounting loathing towards his fellow relics, as it pressed against the back of his neck. His hands now gripped both knees as he tried to refocus on Natalie.

The sound of the TV had amalgamated with his pondering. It was the sudden silence and the sound of the lounge door clicking shut that brought his attention fully back to the present. Natalie's footsteps to go upstairs were very quiet with her slippers on but he moved to the hall doorway and listened to the shuffle of her feet on the steps. As she walked to her bedroom, he glanced up at her on the landing, while the shadows hid his form, as he emerged from the living room. Her bedroom door squawked as it shut tightly into its frame.

"Christ! What on earth! How the bloody hell?" Natalie's vocal surprise was loud and clear enough to be heard downstairs.

From below on the stairs, he heard her walk into to open wardrobe door as she went to the bed. The clatter was significant. Natalie had not seen the door, not expected it to be in her way between the bedroom door and the bed and had walked straight into it. The bifold door bouncing away on her initial impact, springing back to hit her head a second time, her hands reacting in surprise as she first walked into the door but without any effectiveness to stop the door when it bounced back.

He smiled, wickedly, grotesquely, his face distorting, the same Elvis curl in his lip he had deliberately developed after someone had told him in his early twenties that he had the look of Elvis about him. At that time he had black hair and far longer side burns than now, having gone grey but that comment had twisted his self perception into him thinking he was something he wasn't, giving him a misguided stardom. By day, he would often slip into an Elvis caricature, engaging with the children with a line from one of his songs, in a voice that sounded like Elvis to his ears but not to anyone else, even though they all got to know who he was pretending to be.

To the younger children he was funny but once past thirteen, his uncoordinated leg shaking, hip swivelling gyrations, impressions that were exactly like the scenes in the films in his minds eye; were as nerve jarring, squirmingly embarrassing, as if he had been one of those unfortunate children's drunken, talentless father giving an unwanted exhibition in a wedding. For those older ones, if they had made him feel awkward and a little self conscious by their sniggers and lack of cheers and participation, they were remembered for later that day.

The sound of Natalie's confusion and accident gave him another feeling of accomplishment, displayed right across his face, as his cragginess scrunched, to give his features the appearance of an old dried out shammy leather cloth.

The bedroom door opened with its customary noise, Natalie standing, rubbing her head and arm.

From his position on the stairs, hidden by the darkness, almost leaning up along the steps above where he stood, he could just about see Natalie's upper body silhouette, its language clearly assessing her home for some sort of answer. He remained still, enjoying his undetected presence. Natalie turned and pushed the door tight again, the wood grinding as she did so.

12) ESCALATION

His watch showed 11.15. He waited until 11.45 to carry on going up the stairs, there was no rush. His accomplishments so far, made him happy. Each one of his steps brought back memories of those tiled dormitory floors, his shoes which used to make a soft, hissing noise and hint of a squeak as the soles pressed down with his weight. He felt he had perfected the intimidation of those soft soled shoes, replacing on occasions the slippers from his earlier years.

With each step now, he made the comparison of the here and now, to those clinical corridors, with this carpeted landing in complete darkness, nothing other than beige walls to give the impression of illumination. Without any light from anywhere, not even moonlight coming in through the heavy, thick red curtains; there was just different degrees of black, shadows and darkness.

The thought that he was invisible, having virtually laid himself out along the stairs, a black clothed spectre blending into the darkness excited him. Appearing from within darker shadows and disappearing back within them at will, a ghost like entity in control of Natalie, dictating her emotions, her reactions and movements thrilled him. These thoughts, this imagination brought goose bumps out along his arms and the back of his neck as he walked carefully into her en suite, avoiding the squeaking floorboard outside of its doorway.

Natalie had fallen into a deep sleep, the sound of her breathing familiar to someone listening for unconsciousness. The dressing gown he had put at the top of her bed was now obviously heaped in its usual place at the bottom of the bed, rather than lain ready for use the next morning, a sign of frustration from Natalie throwing it there.

He lifted it off the bed and respectfully placed it on the low, bow legged chair that was to the left of the window, opposite the green wardrobes, a remnant from when Margaret had owned the house and this chair, which had been Natalie's princess' throne.

He gently pulled the silk belt out of the belt hooks, holding the silk of the dressing gown so that it didn't ruck up and hinder the belt from pulling through each loop. It was almost loving.

He walked calmly into the en suite, glancing at Natalie lying on top of the bed, the shape of her legs catching his eye again, even within the darkness of her bedroom. He jammed one end of the belt under the door and arranged the end so that it would bunch up and catch on the door, stopping it from pulling through.

The other end he coiled around the water pipes running up behind the basin pedestal.

Leaving the en suite, he pushed open the bedroom door adjacent to Natalie's sticking door and walked down to the front landing window.

With the crash of the upper windows slamming down onto the window sill, he bounded silently back with elongated strides like Monty Pythons Minister of Silly Walks to Natalie's door and held the door knob. Within seconds it moved within his grip.

"Aaahhh this bloody door! Why won't you open? You bloody thing. Why won't the knob move?"

Natalie was half shouting at the door exasperated, half questioning why although it was stiff, why it wouldn't open.

"Aahh!" The impact of her hitting the door, transmitted through the wood and the door knob he was holding.

He heard her leave her bedroom.

"Aaaahhhhh God!" The sound of Natalie sprawling across her en suite floor, tripping bare foot over the silk belt was as clear to him as if he had been standing in the bathroom watching. He imagined her arms and hands grasping out for support as she fell but the door from her bedroom and the sink were all behind her and the shower cubical too far away from her momentum of fall to be of any help.

He envisaged her lying in a heap, holding herself, another injury or hurt adding to another moment of confusion and questioning, as he stepped into the spare bedroom and stood back within its blackest shadows looking out of the partially open door, waiting for Natalie to gather herself and to come out of her bathroom. After a few minutes, she walked out onto the landing, her body hidden of detail and definition, just a semi crouching, walking, slightly limping effigy within the darkness, brushing herself off and adjusting herself as she was just about to walk passed the door of the spare bedroom.

She stopped, a statue, the shape of her legs, an vague outline within the emptiness of light. Her head turned towards him slowly, the shape of her hair changing like a halo of black shadow. Natalie pulled the bedroom door shut with a loud, determined yank. The sound of her footsteps thudded along the landing to the front window, the breeze giving away it was open again. As she lifted the window shut and secured the latch far easier this second time, he pressed his ear to the bedroom door and listened for her footsteps and mumblings, not quite catching everything she said to herself as she walked back to her bedroom.

"Don't say .....latch...on, another fu........thing to pay for."

The stalker tutted quietly to himself, shacking his head. The one thing he kept on about to those kids was bad language. "There was no need for it," he would tell them. "Anyone could swear but with so many other words to use, only a clown, some nerk swears because they haven't got the intelligence to do anything else. Bad language was the pits, " he used to say. His ears continued to strain, only catching part of what she was saying to herself.

"Aahh, this ..odding door. Fu........open." Natalie thrust her hip into the door to open it, like a footballer fouling an opposition player about to run around him, the wood squealing again as the edge jumped away from the frame. Natalie didn't bother to close it tight this time, leaving it ajar.

Silence resumed. I thought you would know better than that Natalie," he thought to himself as he heard her and he waited for her to go back off to sleep.

13) CONTACT

The latch of the bedroom door he had been standing behind, opened silently and he moved like a phantom across the landing to her door, which gave the slightest of creaks as he pushed it fractionally more open, to look at Natalie lying on the bed rather than in it. That made things even easier.

The door groaned again as he rocked it back and forth, deliberately trying to stir Natalie with its sound infiltrating her hearing. She started to stir, moving her legs along the length of the duvet, the quietest of rustling sound as it shifted with her movement.

He moved the door again. This time she opened her eyes in that kind of sleep where you see but your mind will forget the instant you close them and she raised her body up onto her left elbow. Her head turned towards the creaking door, he stepped back out of the doorway, out of view. Natalie flopped back down onto the bed, the duvet emitting a louder "ppooohhh" sound as her body sank back into its softness.

She was instantly asleep but he waited another ten minutes, just standing in the doorway looking at the silhouette of her exposed, long, legs. He took his surgical gloves off and scrunched them into his left trouser pocket, taking out the much used mask.

There was the merest of movement from her as he sat on the edge of her bed, the mattress moulding to his weight, the slope of it almost encouraging Natalie to roll towards him and his waiting hands.

Even in the darkness, his eyes tried to take in every inch of her over and over again, like a photocopier trying to remember every feature, every aspect, blemish, freckle, every sinew and muscle, so that he would have a lasting image of this moment. He felt elated, his fingers tingled, his goose bumps were back and they felt like a wave of pulsing electricity on his body, causing him to twitch and shake as the impulses moved through his skin.

Her hair smelt as he remembered from the lounge a few hours earlier but this time, there was the luxury of Natalie being asleep and he nuzzled his nose into their black strands, taking in long, purposeful breaths of her scent. His hand hovered above her left thigh, close enough to sense the warmth of her leg, the exchange of body heat between his finger tips and the top layer of her skin, the sensation of feeling but without exerting any pressure on her. He guided his hand along the contours of her legs, down across her calves and back up to their divide in her shorts.

His brain stored every second of memory it could in these anticipating moments so that he would be able to remember every moment of this silent analysis.

Natalie's left leg flexed as he put his hand gently onto her warm flesh, mentally absorbing the sensations of touch, the smoothness of her legs, his fingertips pressing virtually unfelt through the lightness of his touch, kneading the relaxed muscle of her thigh.

His excitement had stretched his trousers and this containment added to his sexual awareness. He caressed and rubbed her leg for about a minute and his touch was so intentionally light that she remained asleep.

Natalie's head was turned away from him. He put his face next to her left cheek and lingered, his lips close enough to kiss her through the open zip mouth he had woven into the mask, as one of his preferred modifications from years ago. He didn't give into the temptation but he moved them just above her skin in the same way his hand had hovered moments earlier over her legs. There were faint traces of the wine she had drank, its smell on her breath as she lay sleeping innocently, her breathing still in deep sleep; slow, long breaths. His lips were wet as he passed his face over hers, smelling her skin. They inadvertently touched her face as he drawled over her complexion, her naturalness. They were so wet, they slipped across her face, like a dogs tongue when it licks your hand. Even their contact didn't wake her. He wiped his lips with the back of his hand to stopped his saliva dripping down onto her face.

Natalie did not use make up, she couldn't but he didn't know that though he had a suspicion, as he had never seen her remove it. He hadn't seen any around her bedroom or anywhere else but now this close and with time to think, time to focus on the woman lying below him, it dawned on him that she didn't use it. In this light, almost complete darkness but this close, Natalie was beautiful, perfect, his senses of touch and smell seemed heightened within the minutes he had sat next to her in the darkness, seeing her, sensing her, other than just with his eyes.

He continued to stare, his eyes fixed on hers, almost willing her to open them so they would be looking straight back into his. His thoughts drifted to how blind people coped and how their other four senses it was said developed to compensate for the loss of their sight. He looked around in this black filled room and thought this is what blind must be, black, no light, no shape or form, no definition or clarity, just black. In those moments of sitting above her, with his eyes straining to see anything around the room or even Natalie on the bed with any distinction, he felt thankful that he had his eyesight throughout his life and that it had served him well, within the perversity of his caring. His eyes dropped, almost in a silent pray of thanks and compassion for those who were less fortunate to be without sight.

Natalie stirred, the back of her head turning flat against the pillow, her face directed towards his, his lips and nose less than an inch from her own.

"Nat. Natty." He whispered gently, softly, moving his mouth close to her left ear, speaking in his practiced voice, just loud enough to wake her but not anyone else sleeping close by or even in the same bed. "Natty, Natty, wake up, wake up Natty, I've got something to show you. Natty wake up darling, The Bogeyman is here."

He moved his head even closer so that his skin sensed hers, the exchange of warmth between their two faces now tangible by proximity, even without making contact, the mask the only thin barrier between them, except for where his naked cheeks were exposed through the cut outs he had made in order to rub his skin against those he preyed on. Another later modification.

"Natty!"

Natalie's eyes opened but she had no focus. In the darkness, she could immediately hear him, his breathing. She could smell him, his halitosis pungent this close, instantly turning her stomach, reigniting traumatic memories; his odour draping itself across her tongue as she took in that first conscious breath, his face so close to hers that she could taste his presence.

She screamed, her legs recoiling up to her chest, returning Natalie to a near embryonic cocoon, her hands ramming down into the mattress either side of her body, lifting her body away from the duvet, her thighs exploding with power springing her away from him, pushing her so that her bottom now sat on her pillow. She screamed a second time but his left hand had followed her retreat and clammed over her mouth stifling its crescendo, pushing her head back so that it almost touched the wall behind the low level wrought iron style weaving headboard, the metal edge pushing against Natalie's neck, apposing his pressure.

"Ssssshhhuuuuuuuuussshh. Who is going to hear you?" He moved himself up the bed, pushing himself forward with the aid of his right hand, sitting close up to her coiled up body, her knees instinctively brought up tight against her chest, her both hands now grabbing his left arm as he held his hand over her mouth.

His voice was smooth, un flustered by her reaction. He spoke with a calmness and exactness, practiced initially forty odd years ago in front of a mirror and developed over years of offending, its tone ambiguously threatening and calming, his prey subdued by its misguidance that if they behaved, they would remain on the safer side of calm and on his good side.

His words were spoken with a feeling of admonishment, of disappointment; his breath vapourising each syllable into Natalie's face.

"It's been a long time Nat. Do you know I never thought I would see you again. You left without saying goodbye, do you remember? I do. You left that month I was away and I never thought I would see you again. My little, lovely Natalie." He paused,.......and then pushed his face forwards towards hers and took an emphasised sniff to smell her, "you're not so small now." His left hand went around her pulled back legs and he slide his fingers along her right thigh, downwards towards her bottom. She squirmed and shook to avoid its contact, giving out an "eeeeeekkkkky" growl from the back of her throat. His left hand diverted and went down onto the duvet and he leaned on it.

Natalie remembered that month seventeen years ago for a

number of reasons. It was a month of safety, where her sleep was not disturbed with an awakening, a hand rubbing along her legs, The Bogeyman mask she knew so well, being above her face, his stink making her feel sick, her fumbled, bumpy journey to the toilets to vomit after he had left, the rise and aches of bruises from knocking into other children's beds and the doorway as she tried to quickly but discretely leave the dormitory.

She remembered it for the excitement and anticipation of being fostered by Mike and Rhianne Morgan, two people she lived with until she was found as Margaret's only living relative and her inheritance of this house and the £250,000 Margaret had saved from the insurance payout following the death of her husband and her frugalness.

Mike and Rhianne had taken an instant likening to Natalie, partly because of her politeness on their first meeting, partly because Natalie looked like she could have been Rhianne"s natural daughter with similar high cheek bone features, brown eyes and black hair and same body shape, her legs being longer than her body and partly because of Natalie's disadvantage and they felt she deserved a chance for normality.

As registered foster parents and having adopted Jonathan and Helen when they had been babies, Natalie's transposition from care home to being loved, all happened the month he was away, "on a break" while under police and council investigation.

Natalie remembered a police man and woman coming to talk to her, two weeks after she went to live with Mike and Rhianne. It had been the police woman who talked to Natalie the most about what was happening. She remembered her voice sounded familiar but she couldn't place it but that police lady had been so gentle and caring in the way that she spoke to Natalie, that she had never ever forgotten those first four weeks of her new life. She had not been able to describe The Bogeyman only that he, it, wore some sort of mask with a sad face from what she could remember but she had told the police lady that he stank when he spoke and that his voice didn't sound like anyone she knew.

That voice now with some signs of age was breathing its stench over her again, infiltrating her nose, sliding down into her lungs.

"Natalie, ...my little Natty."

Natalie sat staring blindly towards his face, unable to distinguish any real features even as close as he was, the darkness cloaking his distinction; her other four senses pin pointing him exactly.

He leant forward again, her thick, long black hair an untidy, disheveled bouffant from laying on the pillow, strands touching his face, the enticement of a tickle against his skin.

Natalie knew he was The Bogeyman from the care home. She had never seen his face, even though on one occasion when she was older and had started to fight back as her strength increased, she had partly pulled off his mask and gouged the right side of his face.

Her shaking, seemed to him involuntary, he could feel it radiating through the mattress like ripples across water hitting the bank. This was one thing he loved, the confusion, their own fright within their minds freezing their thinking as to "what to do", giving him power to command obedience.

Natalie's voice squeaked with staccato fear. "How ....did....... did you ......find me? Why me again, not me.... again."

"I'm so glad you asked!" There was glee in his voice, just for a second and then he returned to his controlled flow of speaking.

"Your flower display, that's what brought me to you. As soon as I saw your picture, I knew it was you. You've grown into a very beautiful woman and I'm glad to have found you again. You were always one of my favourites and now we can enjoy some more time together, so much more ....grown up time.... shall we say, where you don't have to go back to sleep."

Natalie moved herself up the pillow towards the head board, further away from him, the dissipation of intensity from his breath, momentary relief for her.

The sad mouthed mask moved closer again, the stench becoming more concentrated in front of Natalie's face. She screwed her nose in an attempt to close her nostrils to the smell and it manifested itself to her, as an image of Pepe Le Pew, the cartoon skunk and the drawing of his smell coming from his tail. His breath was a lasting memory from her childhood and one which she knew she would have to get through tonight. Natalie checked that the gold painted key she had put around her neck when she had come to bed was still there, hanging on a gold chain, a facade of jewellery. She felt for it, the significance unnoticed by this skunk.

The movement of her left hand was almost totally hidden within the darkness of the room.

"Uuhhh"

The effort of lifting the battery operated alarm clock, off the bedside cabinet and smashing it into the right side of his head and the start of her defiance, drew every single molecule of concentration from her remaining senses, to ensure that she struck him accurately and hard. As he fell across the bed, almost across her recoiled knees, Natalie was up on her heels and jumped over the lower part of his body on the bed, his legs instantly weakened by the impact, the pieces splintering and showering down onto his lap.

Despite his age, he recovered quickly, shaking off the impact within seconds, the adrenaline from sitting on her bed pumping, making him more athletic, younger than he was.

Natalie's left shoulder bumped into the door frame, kinking her body sideways and through the opening. "Stay away from me, stay away from me." Her bedroom door had screeched almost as loud as her voice as she slammed it shut on her way out onto the landing, her voice conveying the uncoordinated fear, a mind filled with the terror that he played off. She screamed as she ran into the oblivion of the darkness of the shadowed landing, her left hand running along the wall for guidance. Her fingers touched the frame of the door to the first spare bedroom. The door thudded against the wall as she rammed her hand against the wood, the impact catapulting the door on its oiled hinges to life. There were no locks on any of these bedroom doors but she closed this one behind her so that she could hear the click of the latch into the receiver.

"Come on Natalie, that's no way to be, not after all this time." His voice, still controlled, slow, purposeful, direct; preceded him walking out of Natalie's bedroom. "That was not a nice way to greet me!"

As she stood inside the spare bedroom, her back leaning against the door, listening; she heard his words coming through the still closed door of her bedroom. The tell tale squawk of the door opening and rubbing against the frame, told Natalie exact where he was, as he came through her bedroom door onto the landing.

"Natalie!" He shouted her name, a mixture of anger, frustration and excitement as he walked out onto the landing. Instinctively, he put his hand up for the light switch and then remembered it was half way along the landing at the top of the stairs, where they joined the landing. "The light in Natalie's bedroom," he thought to himself, "that will give some light on the landing."

Turning back into her bedroom he menacingly and slowly pushed the light switch down into the on position, expecting the light to give him the luxury of seeing the landing and where she might have disappeared. The switch clicked but the yellow, green and blue, Art Deco shaded light in the centre of Natalie's bedroom did not turn on. He flicked the switch three or four times but remained standing in darkness. He looked back into the room towards the light hanging down from the centre of the room and questioned himself as to if he had turned it on to the prequel of these circumstances; he could not remember.

Natalie moved quickly through the bedroom and waited at the door of the adjoining bathroom, moving as far away from him as she could. The sound of her hand thumping on the door as she felt for the handle gave her location away. This time his footsteps were quicker across the landing, he wanted Natalie to know where he was, how close, it heightened his excitement. He wanted each footstep to increase her fear and her derangement.

His fist thudded on the bedroom door, transmitting aggression through its sound on the wood. The door sprung open, hitting the stop spring on the skirting board, shaking and vibrating from the impact as it bounced back towards closing again; helped by his left foot giving the base of the door a hefty shove as he turned the brass knob to open the door, adding to the affect of his pursuit.

He moved from one shadow to the next, his body merging with the blackness of the bedroom he had just entered. His voice was full of menace, a mono syllabic tone lifeless of compassion, rehearsed, refined to intimidate. Natalie knew exactly where he was standing before he spoke.

"Natty, come on Natty. I used to enjoy our get togethers. Come on Natty let's play. I'll be the father."

Natalie turned and opened the door into the bathroom, the light within the bedroom didn't change. Closing it quickly and quietly behind her, she moved across to the opposite door leading into the other spare bedroom and opened and closed it with an over loud slam.

He smiled to himself. From experience he could imagine her flailing around in the dark, bumping into things, her mind detached from her limbs. He pictured Natalie, her face now older with that same panic stricken expression. His mind drew the picture of the adjoining bathroom, the bath in the centre of the room, her frantic analysis, should she, could she hide in the bath or behind it, would HE find her there, would she be trapped, what was there to hit him with. His imagination build up the story on the other side of this door that he had his hand on ready to open. Hesitation, expectation heightened his exhilaration. The chase he loved it. A tiger hunting down an antilope.

This door he opened very, very, slowly, his black clad body morphing from one room to the next. The excitement produced an uncontrollable, unconscious smile, his lips stretched as wide as his mouth would move into that expression; the result like a bedevilled hyena, psychotic from the first taste of blood, its prey desperate to get away.

His eyes had become used to the lack of light and he looked around in what he considered was a totally dark room. The white ceramics of the bathroom suite did provide a blurred outline, his hand draped on the top of the bath as he followed the circumference of the fitting, his focus straining to look into the bath and then around the back of it, his imagination misleading him to thinking he would find Natalie cowering behind or within the bath. He stopped, his brain staring into the expected image he had created seconds earlier.

"It was the other bathroom door! Clever girl Natalie. No not girl, you're not a girl anymore are you but a woman. I've never done this with a woman, this is going to be fun."

His thoughts were almost vocal, his lips moving underneath his mask without sound as he worked out what was happening. Natalie had been able to open and close that first bathroom door without him knowing and it was the other door into the second spare bedroom he had heard her slam.

Natalie stood in the open doorway of the second spare bedroom, ready either to go out on the landing or back into the room, if he were to go through the bathroom door onto the landing, she held her head to one side listening.

His confidence was growing with each passing second and he felt himself with his right hand, his hardness a sign to him of his manliness and superiority. The opening of the bathroom door was conducted like a ritual as he tried to project his hearing through the unopened wood and into the bedroom beyond where Natalie was standing. The door knob turned silently, his grip firm and he held his breath so that there was no sound from anywhere. When the door had opened enough into the second bedroom, he glided around it as if magnetised, his movements almost a dance and the door his partner. Despite his efforts, Natalie heard the door brush against the carpet and she stepped out onto the landing, closing the door behind her in synchronicity with his entry. The light switch by the door also failed to turn any light on and he wondered if there was a power cut in the area. The lack of light was not helping. For his age his eyesight was good, only needing glasses for reading but here, going from room to room with no light coming in from outside and thick red curtains drawn, each room was as dark as the last and the next. Paradoxically, he let out his held breath with a long, slow blow through pursed lips to be as discrete and as invisible as possible now he was in this second bedroom and then, immediately after taking in his next breath, exposed his presence by calling, "Natalie, come to Father, Natalie, come to me. Let me see how you've grown."

Natalie could hear his taunts through the closed door as she guided herself across the landing, past the front landing window, where she paused.

She turned to start to move down the right side of the double landing, back towards her room and the stairway to the second floor, taking long exaggerated footsteps. Half way along, he came out onto the landing, immediately trying to focus on Natalie, now half way along the other side of the landing.

He spoke in a comic, mummified voice, his arms extended for five to six steps and lumbered, impersonating the mummy he remembered from the Hammer House of Horror films he used to watch as a child and teenager.

"Naaaaaataaaaalieeeeeeee, Naaaaaaaataaaaaaaalieeee."

He walked towards the front of the house in order to get to the other side of the landing, ignoring the chance to use the stairs to cross over in case he misjudged them in the darkness. Her stalker did not want to injure himself. He passed the front landing window and thought how dull he had been at not opening the curtains in the rooms he had just come through, his thoughts so single minded on Natalie that he had made life difficult for himself. Still obsessed, he passed the landing window without pulling back the curtains to give some sort of light to the landing.

His impression brought back the horror down those corridors. She knew exactly what he was doing by the way he called her name. Her footsteps became quicker and shorter, her feet landing harder. She broke into a frantic run, her body twisting away from him, her head rotated still in his direction, her right hand still on the bannister. Natalie swivelled her hips past the ottoman storage box, the subtleness of her agility unseen to him as his eyes strained to distinguish where she was along the still dark landing.

"You bastard, stay away from me." Natalie shrieked, her fear enriched his elation, his immersion within her survival instinct, making him smile more and more, a child with its favourite toy, an excitement difficult to contain. He could just about see a silhouette flailing about on the far side of the landing, a moving impression of fear.

Natalie grabbed the handle of the locked bedroom door adjacent to the stairs to the second floor.

"Jesus Christ! Why won't you open?" Her voice was screeching as she shouted at the door.

He loved it, the feel of fright in her voice, the panic and confusion. The sound of the door knob rattling across the landing and Natalie fighting with it, making him tingle.

Natalie turned away from the locked door, the sound of her pulling on the door knob jangling in both of their ears. To him its sound was reassuring. He imagined Natalie's mind must now be in turmoil. She was frantic, in cohesive, fleeing anywhere she could, to get away from him. This pursuit electrified him, this present embellished by his memories of his past; this young woman regressed to her childhood and here he was now, descending on her.

To Natalie, the sound was exposing her position, her vulnerability and she knew it. She gave it one final rattle and then turned, her brain thinking about the next move, her next step, her hands reaching out for the door frame leading to the stairs.

"You bloody bastard!" She shouted down the blackened landing. Her thoughts followed her words. She knew he hated bad language. Children's names came to mind, where as a result of a swear word, a wrong word, the wrong way to answer, The Bogeyman had visited them the same night.

She had discovered his alter ego. The Bogeyman despite his mask, reeked of a stench that had imprinted itself indelibly on her mind. His mask had hidden his face but not his identity.

Natalie thought of her hospital visits and now within this eclipse darkness, where nothing had form or was distinguishable, where shadow merged with shadow; she remembered the Irish doctor's voice talking to her, the pen light shining across her pupils, its light neither blinding nor illuminating, just a change in shade, in colour. The room where they examined her was full of bright, bold colours. His voice had been soft, lyrical, virtually loving as he sat with her and talked to her about her future, her traumas and tried to coax her into telling him what had gone on.

She remembered the discussion her mind had with her conscience; to tell this doctor what was happening in the night or to keep it to herself, because if she did divulge the truth, she would end up the worst for it. Her brain engulfed her mind with memories, how the doctor took her hand and placed it on his face.

"I want you to feel this, I want you to feel everything and I want you to tell me what you feel."

The doctor had softly placed Natalie's left hand on his face. In these seconds of decision, she recalled those repeated visits. The memories of touching his face, the smoothness of his skin, his glasses which she often dislodged off his nose, came back virtually as basic instructions to her now, on the landing.

His voice, thick with a southern Irish accent, which had made her feel comfortable and warm, flowed now with her recall, with unexpected affection within her present predicament; his explanation, his encouragement, to expect the best outcome in the future, her future. He had tried to be upbeat to a young teenager, to be positive at a time when most people of Natalie's age, found normal life a struggle as their hormones kicked in.

"This may not be a permanent condition Natalie, I want you to understand this. Our tests have showed there is nothing wrong with your eyes and that this condition, you not being able to see at the moment, is not because of any damage we can find to your eyes themselves, which is great news. Sometimes, there are things which affect us............
.......something which has affected you, which we can't really explain....do you understand? Is there anything that you want or would like to tell me, anything that is bothering you. Are any of the other children bullying to you?. Tell me Natalie. Is there anything I can help you with?"

She remembered him taking her hand with his but this was different when he took hold of it, of her. She had no problem with touching his face, to learn, his explanation of her other senses compensating was unbelievable, confusing. How could they possibly do that, compensate for her eyesight. How could they know they would? In those milliseconds of memory going back sixteen years ago, Natalie saw herself after a second or so, pulling her hand shyly away from the warmth of his grip; her mind illogically fearful that he might try and take advantage, despite a female nurse always being in the same room. She felt guilty again at that reaction then, a reaction which had been almost involuntary, her body withdrawing from the touch of a man. She wished she had said sorry to that doctor.

Her thoughts saw her own face, her expression as if she had been the doctor looking at her. She watched the two single tears that had flowed down both of her cheeks during that consultation, the knowledge inside her head that this masked effigy, this sad faced night visitor would never be found out and that should she say anything, she would not be believed. She didn't say anything.

Sixteen years later, her black apparition was thirty five feet away along the landing, walking nonchalantly towards her, confident in his superiority. Natalie could hear his footsteps along the carpet, his shoes still with a black sock over each one. The doctor had been right. Her other senses had developed and compensated as best they could for her impaired vision.

"Natty, come to me. Father Elvis wants me to talk with you about your behaviour." His words crept along the landing before him, their sound filled with history, with intimidation. She could hear him closer, the slow, soft imprinting sound of his footsteps pressing into the carpet, catching up with the sound of his voice in her ears, the faint smell of his infected tongue carried to her by his expiration of breath. She knew exactly where he was, just about to walk past the storage ottoman.

Natalie stayed still, her ears and nose mapping his movement towards her like radar. There was the faint thud of his left knee against the ottoman, the sound of his black trousers brushing against the cane weave of its sides. She heard his body bend with the faint "uh" from the back of his throat as he leaned down to rub his knee, the sound of his trousers rubbing against his skin as his hand rubbed his knee.

His menace was so focused on her that he had forgotten about the ottoman being any sort of obstruction on the landing.

His next calling of her name was embellished with his annoyance at walking into the ottoman. "Natalie, come here and let me look at you."

Natalie turned and stormed up the stairs to the second floor, running her right hand along the hand rail for guidance, counting the steps as she ran. Her left hand lifted the chain and gold key from around her neck, the chain getting caught in her hair. She gave it a yank to free it from her longest strands.

She stood in front of the first room with its locked door and ran on the spot. She shouted down, her voice with a manic terror in it. As she heard the sound of her own words, she knew the affect they would have on him. Natalie turned the key in the lock as she shouted down, the sound of her voice and heavy footsteps drowning out the sound of her unlocking the door.

"Stay away from me you bloody bastard. Get out of my bloody house. Get out. Leave me alone. You've done enough to me."

Natalie hurriedly put the chain back over her head, her feet still pumping steps out on the worn carpeted floor, the lack of pile giving each step a hollowness with the old wooden floorboards underneath.

She turned away from the now unlocked door and moved along the landing with long, quiet steps not to give her position away; her finger tips just touching along the walls until she felt the frames of the doorways, pushing open the next door on the left and then the one on the right, so that they would swing right back into the room. Natalie pounded out her next couple of steps, transmitting her progress along the second floor corridor and quietly opened the furthest door to the third spare room on the right hand side of the house.

The sound of his footsteps as he climbed the stairs told Natalie he was enjoying the chase. They were not slow and laboured but steady, firm, repetitive stomps on the stairs case. He used the sound of his pursuit as another weapon of fear knowing his victim would be listening for him coming, wondering how close he was, hoping their hiding place would be safe.

Her pursuer stood at the top of the stairs and instinctively reached for the light switch on the left hand wall. The click reminded him that none of the lights were working. The moving shadows of the doors attracted his attention and he walked past the first door Natalie had unlocked. He didn't bother trying it, he knew it was locked and he walked along the thread bare carpet. Natalie was right, she knew him, he was enjoying himself. As he reached the first door on the left which was still coming to rest from being thrown open, he put his left hand on the edge to stop it and walked into the room. He could feel his heart pumping partly from the effort of walking up the stairs, partly from holding his breath earlier and from the exhilaration of stalking Natalie.

The darkness held him still, a murky outline within the door frame, his eyes straining to look around and distinguish anything other than different shades of blackness. His silence and the silence of the room convinced him Natalie was not there and he turned, undeterred to walk along the landing, deliberately emphasising each step with heavy weight to convey his approach.

Natalie had stepped into the bedroom and waited to see if he opened the first right hand door she had pushed or if he walked along the corridor to the door she now stood by, listening from just inside the room. She knew he would be struggling in the darkness.

He lowered his voice, talking from the back of his throat, a deliberate tactic to scare his targets, his phrasing of his taunt, emphasising Natty, Elvis, Bogeyman and naughty children with a quiver, a psychotic imbalance to normality.

"Natty, Father Elvis has told me about you and he has called The Bogeyman. We don't like naughty children and you have been naughty. You know what naughty children have to do don't you."

His quiet, controlled footsteps sounded slightly louder with each step he made towards her. She could feel his approach through her bare feet, the old floorboards conducting his weight along their lengths. She knew he had passed the first door and was now halfway along the landing.

Natalie moved through the room, passing him on the other side of the wall, she could sense him. His intimidation no longer frightened her, words that before had terrorised her as he searched for her on the occasions she managed to get away from her bed, her voice frozen with fright. She felt the wooden chest of draws against the dividing wall to the landing and moved around them. The floor creaked and she went rigid as her foot pressed down on the floor. She wondered if he had heard it. Her next step was even more careful, her toes brushed again the old green carpet, its colour faded, indistinguishable within the gloom.

The dividing door closed quietly behind her. Natalie was careful to hold the door knob and turn the latch into the receiver, she did not want him to hear that she had moved into the next room, ready to go back out onto the landing and into the room she had unlocked.

"Natalie, come and make The Bogeyman happy." She scowled, her face angry at hearing these words again as he pushed open the far door to walk into the room she had first hidden in. She heard him bump into the chest of draws and she knew he was halfway down the room towards the dividing door. She moved stealthily backwards through the door onto the landing and repeated the same closing procedure with the latch moving into the receiver.

She opened the previously locked door and closed it behind her. Putting her left hand onto the wall, she walked around the edge of the room and stood with her back against the wall facing the door and waited, listening.

The dividing door of the other bedroom slammed shut as he

flung it closed for its frightening affect and walked through the room and back out onto the landing and stood by the previously locked door. Natalie knew he was there.

She could hear the excitement, his eagerness, the devilment in his voice through the old, gnarled wooden door, as if he were still talking to a child playing a happy game of hide and seek. "Ooh Natalie. You are getting better at this. I like this. You are getting me more and more excited. Come out, come out where ever you are. Is she in the bath? No. Is she behind the bath? No. Ohh my goodness where can she be?"

The memory of trying to hide under the curve of one of the old stand alone Victorian baths came to mind, the modern replicas she now had in those inter connecting bathrooms, an inverse homage to her childhood hiding places. She could picture him edging his way around it to try and surprise her, the thought in his mind that she would be hiding in the same way as she had a long time ago. Natalie smiled to herself, a confident, reassured smile.

He turned to look at the door which was locked and put his hand on the door knob. She heard the metal of the latch touch as the door moved within its closed position, his hands causing it to move three to four millimetres, enough for it to rattle. His mind caught up. "This door was locked" and he turned away to walk down the landing again, ignoring all the rooms he had been in. The corridor turned left at the end and she could hear his pronounced footsteps getting quieter as he plodded purposefully down the rest of the landing.

Natalie listened hard. She could hear the other doors opening along the second floor landing, the faintest of sounds clearer to her than most other people with all their senses, the sound of him walking around the rooms, banging into furniture, of moving things to see if she was hiding behind them.

After ten minutes of searching he stood back at the top of the stairs just outside of the unlocked room Natalie had stayed in.

His excitement had turned into frustration at not being able to find her. He was not used to losing at hide and seek but he was not used to playing it with adults. She heard the agitation in his calling of her name. "Natalie, you and I need to get together now. You know you have got to make The Bogeyman happy before he leaves you. All naughty children have to do that. You know that don't you!"

He took his first step down the stairs and stopped. Rolling his lips as he thought over all the rooms he had been in, he turned to look back at the door at the top of the stairs.

His mind tried to look for faults in anything he had just done. "She wasn't in any of these rooms, I know that. She didn't pass me, so she is not in one of the bedrooms or downstairs. This room is locked. I know that since breaking in and she definitely came up here and she can't get out because the front door is deadlocked and the windows are all locked."

This time he hesitated as he put his hand onto the door knob, staring at the door, disbelieving that it would be anything but still secure. He twisted the knob very slowly, listening for the latch to fully retract. The door knob grated as he turned it. When the knob was fully turned he paused again, expecting the door to resist any effort to open as he pushed it with the side of his right arm and shoulder. The door flipped open, catching him off balance causing him to stumble into the room.

Natalie had listened to the door, holding her breath as she pressed herself against the opposite wall. As he lurched in, she gave out a little frightened squeak through the top of her nose. It was enough for him to hear her. She knelt down.

"Aahh you clever little girl! You're in here. Where are you? Where is my all time favourite girl. Come to your father."

The door clicked shut behind him and Natalie knew he was in the room, his eyes straining to distinguish anything with the lack of light. She stay crouched on the floor, like a sprinter ready to start a race, her bare legs tucked down behind her arms, her long black hair hanging in front of her shoulders, obscuring what little colour there was on her strappy top and the lightness of her skin. If he had been able to see her, she would have looked like some wild animal waiting to pounce on its prey. Natalie gave out a second high pitched squeal.

He walked towards her, the sound of her fear now that he was in the same room, the stalking over, making his heart pound to the point he felt sure Natalie would hear it and add to her terror. His erection was solid, fuelled by this game of cat and mouse. The empty room made his voice sound hollow, like the first echo coming back to you after calling out in a cave or a canyon, words removed of life, just the sound travelling through the air.

"I can't wait to play over favourite game, do you remember?"

14) CAPTURE

He tried to get his hand under his penis and scrotum to give himself relief. His head felt as full with blood as his genitals, causing him to feel outside of himself as his brain tried to gain control of his thinking again over the deluge of feelings his groin and his legs were sending. The room felt like it was whirling and he was caught up in a tornado, a tumbling, twisting, uncoordinated lather of limbs, body and sensations. Natalie's voice, her laughter penetrated his bubble as he struggled to establish control. This had happened in an instant. All the planning, the preparation around the house, his unseen presence watching her, his control, gone.

As he reeled in pain, he thought he heard the door close and the sound of the lock being turned but he couldn't be sure. His own unexpected screams and cries of pain were filling his ears, swamping other sounds around him. He thought he had heard Natalie run past him in the dark. As his reactions subsided, in these fifty or so seconds of derangement he was sure he heard the sound of Natalie's heavy, quick footsteps as she ran down the stairs to the first floor bedrooms.

He swallowed, mixed in between cries and groans, the nausea passing, a sub conscious attempted to stop himself from being sick. The darkness of the room had turned against him, no longer his ally. It cloaked his awareness. In those disorientated moments he had become unable to distinguish which way was up or down, his mind rotating in the blackness of that room, his own weightless universe contained within four walls.

The wood of the floor joist he now straddled felt rough, even spiky against his now ungloved hands and fingers as he tried to feel between his legs, to hold his throbbing penis and testicles. The wood was rough but solid when the house was built and had flaked with shards splintering away from the body of the beam over the hundred years or so since being laid in place. The shards pricked and dug into his finger tips as he tried to cup himself to give himself relief. The edge of the beam dug into his thighs and bottom as he squirmed around adding significantly to the pain his groin had felt when his feet had gone through the floor.

Time had become distorted. These few mind twisting seconds where his senses had burst into unexpected responses, his hearing detecting the "sshhhiiiish" of the carpet strips covering the holes in the floor as his feet pushed them into open air, his feet and body following, his decent short and abrupt, less than a second, the wooden joist slamming into his privates, his teeth jarring as his head whipped back, the taste and smell of vomit forced up through his trachea into his nose and mouth, kicked up out of his insides by this immobile wooden battering ram.

Each thoughtful deep slow breath was intended to ease the numb, bruising throbbing pain. His initial cries and screams were replaced with throaty, chesty groans and pitiful nasal whimpers, the sort a whingeing dog gives its owner when whining for food or a walk. His hands pushed down on the floor around him as a survival instinct to get himself out of this hole. The other un disturbed strips of frayed, threadbare carpet gave way to the weight of his hands and arms pushing against any lack of substance as his writhing effort to recover, forced them to fall into the bedroom below.

The sound of a bedroom door opening below him drifted up between the open cris cross of joists, touching the extremities of his hearing. His mind had not narrowed it down to the other locked bedroom door, directly under this one. As his legs dangled and jiggled about, giving the impression of an old toy, a monkey on a stick; he could feel something fumbling for his legs.

The lack of floor didn't give him any help at all. As he fell forwards, backwards, sideways grasping around to find something firm to push against apart from the joist he was stuck on, his legs and ankles were being groped. His imagination gave him an image of demons dragging lost souls down into the depths of hell by their arms and legs.

He found it harder to move his right leg, it was being held and pulled on. Mixed with the hard chafing and edge of the wooden beam, he felt the warmth of his own blood oozing out of the scagged splinter impaled cuts his legs had suffered in that second of unexpected decent. This increased the feeling of pain his throat was experiencing from his groin. The pressure from the steel handcuff clamped around his right ankle. The rachet noise of it being forced shut clicked into his hearing, his awareness of what was happening still had not caught up. His left leg was yanked down, catching his testicles on the joist, reintroducing another wave of pain, producing another level of wincing, a stomach initiating, guttural "uuuurrrr", taking any defensive evasion from capture away, his left leg momentarily weak, hanging and jangling, lifeless.

The partner cuff dug into his shin as it was clamped tight, its edge sharp and hard against his skin, his left trouser leg unable to provide any protection from the steel as it had ridden up his leg. He still wriggled and squirmed, trying to ease himself off the beam and back up into the room but his position hardly moved. He leant forward putting both hands onto the beam in front, his distended stomach parting in the middle as the wood divided his portly shape either side of it.

His forehead got closer and closer to the beam until it eventually pressed against it, his feet the pendulum to his body. As he leaned forward, his manacled ankles came up behind him until his heels and the handcuff steel jarred against the underside of the joist, his painful, slow movements like that of the nodding duck ornaments of the 1960's, where it would get closer to the glass of water with each swing until it's beak immersed itself, paused and would then restart the increasing osculation cycle again until its beak found the water again, a perpetual motion for as long as there was water in the glass to give it life.

His water ran out quickly. The joist had delivered the killer blow from the start and he had not been able to recover.

Natalie listened to the grunts of effort above her, the sounds of discomfort and pain as his attempts caused the beam to groan with the movement of his groin and belly, the wood supporting his weight, two arms and legs hanging as he straddled it. The silence of his defeat followed. His arms hung down into the void of the bedroom below, his wrists about six inches lower than the ceiling. The temporary exhaustion of his body, its stillness bringing increasing relief, brought back his ability to think, the realisation after only ninety seconds since he started to walk across the floor to where Natalie had exposed her position with those frightened mouse like little squeaks and the thin strips of aged carpet folding and being pushed through the floor where the floor boards had been removed: that it was he who was now the prisoner.

The touch of Natalie's right hand on his left leg filtered through his panting, its movement along the left side of his body and then the inquisitiveness of her fingers as she felt along from his shoulder and down to his wrist. As the cold of her second set of handcuffs chilled his left wrist he jerked upwards, a reaction followed by the thought that he should have worked out what was happening. He lifted his right hand away instinctively and brought it back up above the floor frame and onto the beam supporting him.

"Give me your other hand, now!"

His eyes widened as he heard the defiance and strength in Natalie's voice and it altered his thoughts to ones which told him that if he complied he would make his situation worse.

His voice had lost its intimidation, its sarcasm, its confidence. It was now full of concern for his self preservation. He could see himself just hanging there. "What are you going to do?"

"Give me your other hand now." There was no patience or compassion in her voice, just the tone of a cold jailer giving an order.

"No! No way Natalie, no." She heard the desperation in his voice and she smiled.

His mind had rejoined him totally and he heard her step down the four rungs of the ladder and walk to somewhere in the bedroom below. Her movements were shielded both by the darkness and the joist, a solid barrier to any line of sight to many parts of the room. There was a metallic sound......of something and he tried to think what. He heard her footsteps back to the ladder and the aluminium "churr" as the blue moccasin slippers she had put on, scuffed back up the four rungs.

"Aaahh.... what the.......what are you doing?" He screamed out as a different sort of pain ran from the back of his left calf muscle and shattered his recovery, a hot, burning intense concentration of Stanley knife blade stabbing into his leg. His both hands tried to grab for his limb and he felt the imbalance of his body twist, his movement changing his position resting along the length of the beam to where its edges and solidity reminded him of its unfriendliness. The blood that had seeped into his trousers squelched slightly against the beam, as his groin and thighs jumped on the three by six support, the acuteness of its position pressing hard into the soft areas of his body.

Natalie's voice was condescending. "Sorry! I haven't got a pen knife. Do you still have the same one with the black handle? Now, give me your hand or the same thing is going to happen again.........and possibly again. You know you have been naughty." Her last words were his own.

"Natalie, my beautiful Nat....." His word were cut short as the second impact of the blade penetrated his trousers and skin, its sharpness like a blow lamp, burning along his legs and pounding into his head.

"Aaahhhhhh......Jesus Christ, ...holy shit girl." His body involuntarily repeated the same reaction as with the first stabbing.

Natalie was calm, indifferent and the level of sarcasm was increasing in her voice.

"Now now, we don't like bad language do we, it's not nice." Again his own words from years ago started to increase his awareness of the predicament he was now in.

Her instruction was unemotional. "Give me your hand please."

He lowered his right hand down below the beam where it hung alongside his already cuffed left wrist. He felt her feel for his arm and down to his hand, as his stomach and chest retook their uncomfortable position of lying along the wood. The cuff clamped his second wrist and he looked like a piece of black beef threaded along a gigantic barbecue skewer, his hands and feet below at either end, his body above.

"Natalie!" He turned his voice into a pitiful whine hoping to appeal to her.

The bedroom door closed and he heard the lock turn. The sound of her footsteps back up to his room made him lift his head with expectation. Perhaps his last contrived call had softened her.

The bedroom door lock turned with the key she had around her neck, both rooms now returned to their locked state. Natalie turned the handle to check and the door rattled in the frame. He heard her walk back downstairs and then silence.

15) RECOLLECTION

Natalie turned the electric back on at the consumer unit in the utility room and made herself a cup of tea. As the kettle boiled she held her hands out in front of her and felt the shake in them. The black leather stool felt momentarily cold as her bare legs slipped back into the seat, her open back underneath her short top against the leather padding, adding a second quick refreshing chill to her skin.

In between sips of tea, she leant forward from the stool, her hands leaning against the edge of the granite work tops as she regained her composure. In the background she could hear him calling her name, the sound of his stench embellished voice, a muffled, pleading call through the wooden door and down two flights of stairs. Its sound made her smile again and her thoughts of her forthcoming plan made her smile until it turned into a spasmodic giggle, a nose snorting tiny giggle that slipped after ten satisfying seconds down to her throat and turned into a tongue clucking, head nodding laugh and into a deluge of unrestricted shoulder shaking hysteria. Natalie slipped off the stool as her laughter gained control of her body, her scheming, her awareness and control, her relief vibrating down along her arms, her breast shaking as her body rocked, her legs giving way, robbed of any strength as she collapsed onto the floor of the kitchen into an quivering embryo, the sound of her cackling reaching up through the two floors, hitting his ears with the devilment it contained.

She rolled over onto her front, the cold of the tiles cutting through the warmth of her skin, giving her an indication of which way around she was on the floor. His predicament was as perfect as she had planned but even better than she had hoped for.

Lying on the wooden beam, her uncontained happiness entered his ears as delirium and his already painful skewering along the joist made him think the worst was not yet over.

Natalie turned over onto her back and felt the cool of the tiles. As she lay there, her laughter eventually subsiding, her breathing slowed and returned to its normal rate. In the darkness, she stared at the ceiling, seeing nothing, her mind floating off into a night time daydream, her memory bringing back her planning over the last three months. The sound of his voice punctuating the silence evaporated from her consciousness and Natalie drifted into semi slumber, her thoughts starting with a visit a couple of months ago to Jane next door.

"So, tell me about this new job and why you want to have a job Jane, you've been retired for years." Natalie could see herself asking Jane as she held her cup of Saturday coffee.

"It's a bit of something to do. It's a bit boring doing very little or nothing each week except for seeing you every Saturday and the other odd occasions. It's only part time, three mornings and possibly two afternoons but nothing on the weekend, well not for me."

"And where is it?"

"It's a new retirement home, only a small one for ten people, well ten men actually, in Chestnut Drive, so it's cooking some breakfasts and mid morning tea that sort of thing and lunch and if they need it, some help for evening dinner, perhaps some laundry. It will get me out of the house just for a couple of hours. I went there on Tuesday for an interview, well not really an interview if I'm honest as I've known the new warden for years. I used to work with her in a way years ago and she also goes to our church, so it was more of, well just a chat. She ran me last Monday and I went Tuesday. It's not really a job either, it's more a volunteer thing really, but still, I'll see how it goes. If I don't like it or it's too much I'll stop."

Natalie remembered the conversation. She had gone over and over it after she had left Jane's that day, the surprise that there was to be a new retirement home for "them" so close to where she was now living, seventy miles away from where she had lived with her mum before she died and the children's care home she had ended up in, which had not been that far away from her mum's house. Now, although only seventy miles between locations, it seemed unbelievable to her that here was a chance that he may be one of those that came to stay in this new retirement home Jane was talking about.

She moved her hands across the tiles, enjoying the cold ceramics, her thoughts re enacting her feelings from months ago. She felt determined to trace him, to try and ensure that if he were still alive, by how old he would now be, that he would somehow be offered a place. Natalie remembered walking into Jane's dining room as she thought about this possibility and how she could go about things. She knew straight away that she would have to get herself noticed, possibly even going in with Jane to this care home to be seen by the men who had been offered accommodation but then how would she know if he were one of them. "His breath" she thought. "I would know his smell anywhere. He's poured himself over me enough for me to know how he smells."

Her fists clenched on the floor as her anger rose again at re-thinking these thoughts from that Saturday morning.

"Natalie, just be careful lovely where you put your coffee. I've gots lots of papers on the dining table. These croissants will be ready soon."

Her recollection was so vivid. She mouthed her answer now lying on her kitchen floor as if she were calling back to Jane as she had done that morning, her mind transported back through time. "I will Jane. What are all the papers for?"

Natalie caught herself doing it and laughed at herself, bring her consciousness more to the surface. Her eyes opened and she moved her arms slowly across the floor around her body, like a mine sweeper, spreading her fingers across the tiles, using each millimetre to take in their coolness and lift her from her relaxed slumber and bring her fully back to awareness and focused.

Jane's answer unexpectedly excited her.

"They are the pictures of the men I'll be looking after when I start so that I know who is who. I think it will be nicer for them if I know who they are already, so that I don't have to ask who they are, don't you?"

Despite not being able to see clearly, Natalie's blank gaze towards the kitchen ceiling turned from a vacant, innocent look, intensifying as she continued to recall what she found laid out on Jane's dining table. Her expression flowed from anger to contempt, her thoughts fuelled by disgust at the memory of "him", her eyes narrowing with determination, her mind bring him back into focus in the room above; mixing in with her discovery.

Natalie's minds eye watched her put the coffee cup down on a window sill in the dining room and then run her hands lightly over the paperwork, feeling various piles and configurations, her dexterity careful not to disturb their order. She had expected to find a large wall chart with ten photos on or ten glossy photos in a pile but as her fingers explored, she came across lever arch files and clip files of varying sizes, laid out even to her in a methodical order for Jane's convenience. There seemed to be a disproportionate amount of paperwork, for such a small, part time job.

Her left hand grazed against an open cardboard storage box and she diverted her fingers to feeling up its side. Her touch went passed the top edge and onto the filling that lay stacked higher within the box. Her fingers felt its end and Natalie ran her hand across the top of the pile, the slipperiness of the glossy photo, distinctive from the rest of the paper.

She saw herself with the photo held close to her nose, her left index finger trying to trace around the outline of the face, across his eyes, his jaw.

She remembered Jane's voice gentle and full of concern as she brought the croissants in on two Royal Crown Derby plates." Natalie are you alright darling? What are you trying to do? Are you able to see anything in that photo?"

"Who is it? Is this one of them?" Natalie looked towards Jane, her face with an eagerness across it.

"Yes. He's nearly always sucking mints and nearly always grumpy with the others. His name is Byron but for some reason he likes to go by Elvis. Well actually, I know the reason. He used to be in charge of a children's care home until he retired and he used to think he looked a bit like Elvis Presley when he was a young man and used that as a joke with the kids, you know, get them to sing and all that sort of thing."

Natalie's heart had jumped on hearing Jane talk about this Byron? It had to be the same person. Jane's few sentences summed him up. It couldn't be anyone else.

She remembered those frequent occasions when he tried to ingratiate himself to the children, breaking into his impression of Elvis Presley, swivelling his hips, encouraging the kids to do the same, often resulting in the young ones jumping and squirming excitedly as they joined in the musical mayhem he created. She remembered she shuddered with revulsion at that memory, knowing when she had grown older, she unravelled his alter ego.

It was that Saturday morning that started her thinking.

16) REALISATION

An hour had passed and the joist did not become any more comfortable as he tried to adjust himself along its length given his handcuffed restraint. Calling Natalie's name had become tiring and after about thirty minutes he started to think that it might start to annoy her. His time alone in blackened seclusion started to raise his concerns. His immediate pains from falling through the floor had dissipated to a tolerable level and he started to think about getting free.

The steel of the handcuffs dug into the outsides of his wrists as he pulled them away from each other in a vain, frantic effort to break the chain. With each tug and yank against his bondage, he felt his head temperature rise with his effort, the perspiration building from small droplets forming on his forehead to multiple face hugging streams of fear, emerging and attempting to run down his cheeks, before being sucked into the fabric of the mask. His ankles stubbed against the underside of the beam as his feet jerked up as a counter balance. He held the underside of the joist as he threw his feet upwards behind him, hoping the chain would give way but it just caught against the timber, sending the wood's resistance up along his legs and through his body, his groin and abdomen sensing bruising discomfort as his legs swung ineffectively to break his restraints. His anger exerted him more, until he resembled a thrashing kebab, still live and aware of its fate, trying to unthread itself from a skewer about to be laid across a barbecue grill.

His hair wilted against his scalp and the back of his neck, his sweat immersing his entire head and face, the effort of trying to defeat his unyielding shackles raising his temper, his temperature escalating rapidly, the mask retaining every jewel of heat behind the aged, sad mouth, that had softened and deceived the innocence of every young child he had visited.

What strength he had was soon drawn from him, his age and weight far from helpful in trying to achieve a super human escape and he lay still along the beam trying to steady his breathing. His black shirt and trousers aggravated his body by their touch, encapsulating his limbs which oozed from every pore. His shirt was wet with damping body fluids which ran around his skin. As he lay still, he could feel the trickle of perspiration running down and around his thighs and groin, down his calves to become absorbed by his socks.

The air around him gave him no relief, the temperature of this attic room was significantly higher than the ground floor or bedrooms he had been excited to prowl earlier. His mask had lost its friendship. It was now a spiteful companion, as if teasing him by putting a hand across his nose and mouth to restrict his breathing. He felt claustrophobic as he wished for the feel of cool air on his face and its freshness for his lungs but his thin woollen ski mask was designed to keep the biting chill of mountain snow and ice from cutting into the skin and now it withheld any relief and swamped his face as if someone was pushing a pillow down onto him. He tried to get the bottom of the mask to ride up his face by pulling his chin back along the beam. It moved slightly but the abrasion of the wood started catching in the fabric, cutting into his skin as the lower part of his face jaggedly moved back towards his tubby body.

The bottom of the mask moved up momentarily as he tried to use his motion along the beam to ease it off but the neck section below his chin was too long and it simply ruffled up and then rolled back under his chin.

As each effort and moment of thought passed, he realised his situation was worsening. He was no longer in control and unless he could intimidate Natalie into releasing at least one pair of handcuffs, he could see no way of over coming the strength of the joist.

His arms pressed sharply against the wood as he tried to reach around its girth, to get his fingers up to his face and under the now saggy hem of his old cowl but his arms were too short and the beam too large. As he twisted himself around the beam he felt his balance slip which ever way he tried to stretch around to release the mask. He grabbed the beam for the security of being able to lay along it before tipping to the side. The vision of himself suspended upside down hanging from these cuffs, like a missionary capture by cannibal pygmies carrying him to the boiling pot on a fire, did not bring the usual post card humour with it. He didn't know how long Natalie intended to leave him here and he preferred to be prostrate along the beam rather than hanging, knowing his suspended weight would drag the life out of him.

As these thoughts went through his mind, he knew he had to remain calm, that there would be a chance sometime to escape; after all, Natalie was blind, what could she possibly do. His mind caught his thought and reworked his conceited conclusion. "Look what she had done already! Look where you are at the moment," he thought to himself.

He gasped and panted for oxygen, his mask poaching his head and face. He felt like a pot holler crushed against an immovable stone face, trying to get his nose above water to take a breath. As he panted deeply, the perspiration within his sodden ski mask seemed to get drawn from its material and up his nose in droplets, the sensation of fluid causing him to jerk with a reaction he envisaged would be that of a drowning person. He had never cut holes out for his nostrils as he had always been calm and surreal, a tormentor and apparition that had haunted the halls and more so, the minds of naive children. Now his own sweat, its smell and saltiness threatened his ability to breathe as his mask reached saturation point.

17) CONFRONTATION

Through his heavy breathing, his ears eventually picked up the sound of the door being unlocked. He tried to turn around, to look towards the doorway but he couldn't pivot enough to do so. The sound of the door locking again followed and in the still, space like darkness of that room, he lay rigid and listened.

"Natalie, are you there? Are you there my lovely girl?" He turned his head, trying to listen for any noise which would indicate her presence in the room with him. The sound of his own puffing and panting the only sound he could hear.

His voice started to sound uneasy. There was a shudder within it, he was asking the question but at the same time he was frightened at hearing any answer.

"Natalie, lovely girl, are you there? Natalie."

Natalie stood silent behind him, the affect of his breath through his struggle had corrupted the air in the room, his body odour added a different tone within the overall degenerated perfume that he had fermented within the hour or so of his struggling. The room reeked, the stale air carrying curdling wafts that made Natalie's stomach turn over, her developed sense of smell enhancing its pungency.

His voice went up an octave as it cracked in its higher pitch, his uneasiness evident to Natalie. She smiled to herself with an malicious sneer at hearing him, the inference of pleading in his voice. Her mind jumped to what she would be doing and she couldn't contain an unexpected quick outburst of laughter.

"Natalie!" He jumped, his head turning towards her laughter. "Natalie, come on lovely girl, please take these cuffs off, I can't move."

She said nothing.

His voice had more earnestness as he tried to avoid appearing to plead for her help, conscious not to show weakness. "Natalie, come on now, this has gone far enough. This is not you."

He tried to compose himself and sound accommodating, unthreatening as he repeated and softly called out the variations of her name. "Natalie, Nat, Natalie ...."

Her silence remained for fifteen minutes, not the sound of her breathing, not the slightest movement to make the faintest of sounds from her clothes moving over her skin.

"Natalie!" His voice eventually raised and she heard the start of his desperation as she stood motionless behind him. She knew he would start to think if he was now in the room alone, if somehow she had left so quietly that he hadn't heard her leave. The silence and dark would make him wonder if she was still there, if she was coming back, in the same way she used to go to sleep wondering if The Bogeyman would come to visit her in the middle of the night. Natalie used to go over in her mind if there had been anything she had done that day that would be reported which would make The Bogeyman turn up on the edge of her bed.

His shoulders and body slumped forward onto the beam with a muffled cascade of weight while she maintained her total silence; just standing, thinking, her expectations rising. She felt the fight beginning to ebb from him as she listened to his breathing eventually slow down to its normal rate, his effort to get air earlier drowning out any stray sound that may have come from her as she hovered behind him.

Her voice when she eventually spoke was calm, controlled, sarcastic and menacing. "I think you have been a naughty boy. The Bogeyman knows what to do to people who are naughty. You've been naughty haven't you, very naughty."

He jumped again. The silence had swayed his belief into thinking she had left the room.

The scuffing of some of the removed floorboards being pushed across the floor made him try to repeat his earlier attempts at looking around. His bondage and stomach didn't want to help.

"What are you doing, Natalie what are you doing?" His voice now transmitted more concern and this appealed to Natalie as she listened, still in silence. She felt for the alignment of the boards across the open gaps of the joists and struggled as they clunked and jarred into place on his right hand side.

He could hear the effort in her breathing as she moved the boards from where they had been laid them after removing ten of them from the floor weeks earlier and then again....... silence.

He tried to see what might be happening around him. "Natalie!" ....silence.

His ears strained to hear the slightest of sounds, he listened for any creaks in the wood that betrayed her presence, her breathing........silence.

The eventual sound of her slowly, feeling footsteps along the board, her weight stealthily transferred, the board conveying her movement by the side of him, made him shiver with an unnerving chill. His hands tried to reach out to get hold of something of her, his desperation at being shackled rising as he felt less dominant. The underside of the joist bit against his left arm as it pulled around to allow his right hand leeway to grasp out for Natalie. Straining fingers caught empty warm air as he tried several times to catch hold of anything.

Natalie could hear his efforts as she stood motionless beyond his reach, listening to his efforts.

Her voice came slowly, gently out of the darkness, her words soft and calm, almost loving but the underlying tone infused with derision, dispelling any affection. "Are you alright?.....are you ok? Look at me my darling. Look at me. The Bogeyman is here and we have to make sure he's pleased with you before he can leave and you can go back to sleep." Her last command, the words he used to use, brought an intense sense of relish within Natalie at being able to replay his torments.

"Nata........"

"Shuuusshhhhh." Natalie cut his attempted protest short.

"I said.....look at me.......look up at me."

Natalie heard the joist creak as he twisted on it in order to look towards her voice. There was still so little light available to illuminate anything, that her form was still just that of a dark shadow, her legs and arms the only thing lighter than shades of black. He felt her right hand placed on his head, her thumb pressing down into his forehead. Natalie used this as a guide. His right hand could still not reach any part of her as he moved it slowly this time to try and find contact with some part of her.

"Look at me." She felt his head rise as he followed her instruction.

"Ttzzzzzzzzzzzzzz." The pepper spray she was holding in her left hand found his pupils behind the ski mask, instantly burning his eyes, creating streams of tears.

"Aaaahhhh! What are you doing you mad bitch?, Aaahh, good god, Aaahh, Aaahh. His voice, his screams instantly confirmed she had been accurate in following her right arm and hand.

Natalie's voice was filled with sarcasm. "Now now. You know The Bogeyman HATES bad language. There are so many other words you could use.....aren't there!"

Her hand grasped the top of the ski mask tightly. He could feel his hair being pulled as it got caught up within her grip as he reeled against the affects of the pepper spray. Natalie yanked it off his swirling head with one angry, vengeful pull. He felt the burning sensation of a good number of his hair follicles being taken with the mask, torn out by their roots.

"Aaahh, for pity sake."

Natalie's mock sarcasm and astonishment tickled her amusement. As he puffed his cheeks and gritted his teeth to try and gain control of his pain, the tears cascading down his face, he could hear the laughter in her voice. "Well! ....who have we here.? Is it The Bogeyman? Why no...it's ....it's Father Byron. Well, who would have guessed? Can you still do Elvis?"

18) TURNING POINT

Natalie deliberately slammed the bedroom door to ensure he heard her departure. She paused and then rattled the key in the lock repeatedly to emphasise the door being locked and his isolation.

Father Byron's eyes were bloodshot red, watering incessantly, blurring his vision, burning, pulsing. As he writhed around, trying to reach his eyes with his hands to give him some relief from the pepper spray, the sound of the door shuddering in its frame as Natalie left put his agony into a separated state, shocked by her thunder like exit. The subsequent moment of silence in the darkness of his room, that brief ten seconds of muted suspension stopped his brain from experiencing the fiery turmoil as he listened to the silence and realised his solitude was now at Natalie's command. The start of Natalie's deliberately delayed key rattling drew his attention and when the last rattle dissipated in his hearing and silence enveloped him again, his squirming resumed as if a switch had turned back on his sense of touch, the feeling of a erupting volcano permeating through his tears and behind his eyeballs like meandering lava, burning through to his optic nerves.

Father Byron pulled on his handcuffs, the chain straining against the beam, the effort of his tension on the wood trying to combat his returned pain. His brain managed one coherent thought, he was Natalie's prisoner and his writhing continued.

19) INTERLUDE

The pinging of the fridge door turned Natalie back to push it shut. The ham sandwich tasted delicious. She threw the packaging in the bin and returned to the stool by the kettle. In the quiet of the kitchen she could hear the sounds of Father Byron filtering down through the house. She sniggered to herself.

The eight inch wooden spoon she felt for and took out of the utensil jar by the side of the gas hob, became her imaginary microphone.

"It's now or never, come hold me tight, kiss me my darling, be mine tonight…………" Natalie's left leg quivered as she sang through the Elvis song in the centre of her kitchen, recalling Father Byron's impersonation of "The King". She moved her body in a less than rhythmic way, mimicking his awkwardness at not being able to move as smoothly as Elvis when he sang to the children. She started laughing to herself at her caricature of him, the memory of his black hair as it had been back then, kept long in the front with strands hanging down across his forehead for as close a look to Elvis' hair style as he could get.

Natalie started to play with her own hair, pulling strands down in front of her face, Elvis style. Her laughter developed into a long, deep belly laugh and then morphed into a hysterical cackle. She gripped the edge of the worktop by the kettle as she bend over, her laughter shaking her whole body, drawing the strength out of her legs. It lasted for two uncontrolled minutes, as she relished her situation and his, strapped across the joist. Natalie wiped the tears away from her eyes with some kitchen roll as her laughter started to subside.

She looked upwards through the ceiling towards the attic room, visualising.

20) SUSPENDED

His watch showed 1:45. The switch which illuminated the display, gave an audible click as he released it, something he had never noticed in the fifteen years of owning it but then, he had never been so quiet before. It was just over one and a quarter hours since he sat on her bed. The light flicked on again with a click as he double checked the time. Father Byron could not believe it was so short a period. His own discomfort seemed like hours, a complete mismatch of reality to imagination.

He resigned himself to waiting, persuaded by his recent efforts to free himself in some way, that he was not going to be able to break the handcuffs or the wooden beam. Calling for Natalie was also a waste of effort. His thoughts hoped for Natalie's retained childhood goodness, that she had not totally turned into a homicidal killer who regularly strung up her victims.

The picture he had seen of her in the local paper seemed to be projected onto his mind like a bill board lit up in the darkness. Wherever he directed his head given his restraints, that image wouldn't leave him, her smiling, matured face instantly recognisable to him as one of his favourite girls. He had loved her spirit, her positiveness, her overall level of happiness, despite being in care following the early death of her mother. Natalie hadn't been a rude child but she did ask questions and stuck up for others which was one of the reasons why The Bogeyman chose to visit her so frequently. There had been a strength about her, something which appealed to him and something which he had to break to be in control. It had been a challenge, a contest he as an adult knew he would always win, eventually.

His thoughts now were more hesitant, more fleeting, unsure now what to expect. That determination within her as a child had clearly stayed and now as an adult, she was a real threat and he could not see how to overcome her conviction.

As he lay along the beam he suddenly thought about his watch. The light cast the faintest of illumination into the bedroom below but even twisting his wrist to try and direct what little light it gave out failed to show what was below. There were a few edges of things which he couldn't identify but some seemed to be metallic and there was some sort of reflection off things where the window should have been. He listened to the click of the light switch on the rim of his watch and again he lay there in total darkness ....wondering.

The bedroom door lock almost echoed as Natalie opened it with focused determination.

He looked down into the abyss of darkness and was just about able to make out a blurred, fuzzy shape, devoid of any definition or substances as his eyes tried to disseminate Natalie from the surroundings.

Natalie could smell him, her hearing pin pointing his position, the sound of the creaking joist, his trousers brushing against the timber, the handcuff chains jangling between his heels.

"Natalie, you lovely girl, I knew you wouldn't ......aaahhhh."

The Stanley knife blade sliced through his trousers into the back of his right calf muscle. His legs jerked upwards. Natalie waited until she heard his movement only seconds later as his legs lowered after their initial involuntary reaction and repeated the stab a second time, aiming six inches lower towards his ankle.

His legs jerked away a second time.

"Aaahhh, dear God girl. Why are you doing this? I never did anything like this to you."

Natalie looked up in her darkened seclusion, her eyes staring with defiance, her voice conveying her expression. "Worse !"

The blade bayoneted his leg a third time, parting the muscle with its inch long point like a vindictive surgical incision. As the scolding sensation passed he could feel the warmth of his blood oozing onto his skin and running down the back of his dangling legs, these new wounds reminding him of the two earlier ones in his left leg.

Natalie slammed the door, its vibration filled with her anger and he felt it, the sound amplified by the silence in and around the house, injected now with almost twenty years of pent up aggression.

The key turned slowly in the door lock. Natalie was really beginning to enjoy herself. She knew he would be thinking about what she would be doing next and she wanted to play the same mind games that she had to endure. Those nights of lying in bed, frightened to go to sleep, frightened to stay awake.

His reaction as she walked into the room confirmed her intentions. There was more fear in his voice now after stabbing his second leg. His anticipation made him struggle again against the handcuffs, the futility of his efforts, again oblivious to his mind. He had to get himself free. What was she going to do? The handcuffs started to draw blood from out of his bruised wrists.

Natalie controlled her anger and excitement. Her voice came softly out of the darkness "Don't struggle, don't hurt yourself trying to get away. You can't. I am with you now. We are together, let's enjoy each other."

He recognised his own words and pulled harder against his shackles.

"What are you going to do? Leave me alone. Get away from me."

"Exactly in the same way as you did with me."

The crash of the four foot square board behind him increased his anxiety. Natalie felt for its edges and the joists it lay across to make sure it wouldn't tip into the gaps between the framework of the floor when she stood on it. The old board groaned as it took her weight. She held her left hand out in front of her to buffer his back from bumping into her. The pressure of her grip on his right shoulder surprisingly stopped him from thrashing around.

"Stay away from me. Stay away from me. Stay away from me." His voice increased in pitch as it turned into pleading.

Natalie grabbed his forehead with her right hand and pulled his head back. He started screaming. "Get away from me. Jesus Christ, get away from me."

Natalie's sarcasm was filled with hate. "Language Father or you'll meet Stanley again. Now hold still. You'll see it will be better for you if you do." He remembered what he often used to do after saying those last same few words. His body went stiff as the memories of his earlier life twisted in his mind. The fear of receiving the same attention as he had perpetrated crawled slowly through every ember, like a fungus devouring his self assured sanctity. The impending perceived abuse corrupted his thinking, his recollections now had more than a hint of fear attached and superimposed his memories on his future.

The front of his neck was taut with Natalie pulling his head back as far as possible. He felt the uneasy pressure in the back of his neck as his scalp was forced towards the top of his spine.

"Don't struggle, don't move." Natalie's voice was firm and direct, indifferent whether he did or didn't.

He felt her fingers move down to just above his eyelids and then her hard nails felt for the coverings of his eyes. His head twitched to evade her slow clawing towards his eyes.

"I said don't move. If you do, I'll slice your eyeballs."

His already static body went stiffer than the joist he was straddling on hearing Natalie. Her calmness and intimidation were a paradox. He felt certain if he moved Natalie would carry out her threat, yet if he didn't move he would put himself into an even weaker position and her dominance would be even greater.

She kept the palm of her right hand firmly on his forehead and meaningfully and purposely pushed his head further back. Byron felt his heart palpitated. He closed his eyes, fearing Natalie would spray more pepper spray into them.

Her voice was low and stern "Open your eyes...now!....now!"

"What are you going to do?"

"This"

"AAAAAHHHHHHH, Aaahhhhhhhh, Aaahh, AAAAAAHHHHHH."

Natalie stood back as his head jerked violently from side to side as he tried to alleviate yet another deluge of scorching pain in his eyes. His body followed his head, shuddering through its portliness, his over weight stomach giggling behind his clothing as it pressed against the top of the beam, enveloping some of the sides of the wood when he laid full length along his support in an effort to get his hands up to his eyes. The floor creaked from his movements, hard, quick, reacting involuntarily in a cacophony of heavy effort, the sound of his legs thrashing underneath the joist, the harsh metallic jangling of the handcuff chains pulling between his ankles cutting into his skin, the same from his handcuffed wrists, the chain resisting his movements when his torso's reaction tried to jerk erect, dragging him back downwards onto the beam.

Natalie could see his reactions through the sounds she was hearing. The old wood groaned repeatedly and told her he was writhing, his groin and coccyx transmitting his restrained body weight through the beam as his predicament hindered free flowing movement. She visualised him as an old infirm arthritic rider sitting in the saddle of a horse, trying to shift his position but instead of smoothly sliding around in the saddle as he looked around the countryside, he was stiff and restricted, his leaning forward to backwards, an erratic fight against his manacles and seat, his age and weight adding cumbersome hindrance to his mobility and she laughed.

His shrieks of pain pounded into her ears and she relished each wave of agony as she took them greedily into her mind. Each cry, each expulsion of misery, his panting, screaming, bellowing, the vocal indication of his own unvisualised impending degradation, was beginning to satisfy her infinite lust for revenge. She felt her body tingle with the volume of his contortions, his voice failing to form words only sounds of infliction. Her heart pumped, the adrenaline surging, mixing with the joy of her superiority.

Natalie waited for his contortions to subside and then felt along his right arm down to his wrist and held his hands still, inserting the key into the handcuffs.

"Bring your hands up above the beam, do it now, you have one chance."

Despite his discomfort and probably his weakened but still

superior strength, he obeyed Natalie and brought his hands above the joist, letting her re cuff him. He was still screaming out withered cries of pain as the pepper spray continued to burn his eyes.

Natalie pushed him forward, sending him to lying full length along the beam. The sound of the wind being forced out of his lungs as he wallowed along the joist, told her he was where she wanted him.

"Lift your legs, get your feet up to here." She struck the beam with her hand so he knew what she wanted him to do.

Father Byron puffed heavily with the exertion required of him to get his feet up to the underside of the beam. Natalie helped support his legs by holding onto his right ankle and tried to unlocked the cuffs while holding his feet below the wooden beam. She failed to do it as he couldn't hold himself in position. His feet swung downwards. He winced and groaned again as the edge of the beam pressed into his genitals.

Natalie felt the dampness of his socks around his ankles slip out of her fingers. Her impatience was obvious. "Dear God, if you don't get your bloody feet up here, I'll cut them off."

Natalie took a deep breath, her composure regained quickly.

"Big effort now Elvis. Lift your feet above the beam." She looked towards him, his struggling movements slow and laboured, just a change in his overall shape like floating, perambulating wax in a 1960's table lamp. Byron tried to swing his feet backwards and up above the wooden floor support, squealing as his already bruised privates pressed hard and awkwardly against the beam. Natalie instantly tired of his fat grunting and groaning as she listened to him trying to pendulum his legs backwards enough so that his feet and ankles rose above the wooden support.

"Get your feet up where I've told you, you fat bastard or I'll gauge your eyes out. Do it now."

Her voice, her attitude sounded to him like Lucifer was talking to him. It was devoid of any warmth, any human tenderness. It sounded factorial, threatening, controlled, almost psychotic.

He groaned with the effort of lifting his ankles again up to the underside of his supporting wooden saddle and felt Natalie unlock the cuffs. She listened to his long, slow, relieved sigh and she could feel his misguided expectation at being released, his misinterpretation of her unlocking the ankle cuffs.

"Thank you Natalie. I knew were a good girl."

She put her left hand onto his right shin and helped his leg come above the joist and helped place his toes onto the beam. Her touch reassured him that this was all coming to an end. "Now the other foot." His left foot joined his right on the beam.

"Are you alright?" He heard an unexpected warmth in her voice and he slumped, drained of resistance along the length of the beam, his feet resting on the top edge behind his body. It was over..............

..................There was a long silence as his relief filtered through his hot sweaty body.

Father Byron raised his head, his ears perked like a pointer dog as he heard the click of the handcuffs on his ankles but unaware he had been re shackled, his mind trying to decipher the source of the sound.

"Na........what on earth?" He felt her foot push into his right hip and then space.

The old double bed mattress billowed out unseen dust in the

darkness of the locked room below as he landed in a tumble of confusion, shackled arms and legs, his right hand thumping onto the wooden floor beyond the mattress, a soft island on a sea of solid oak floor; the mattress not capable of fully disguising its hardness, the solidity transmitting directly into his body, through his rib cage and along his limbs.

"Uuuhhh." The wind in his lungs was knocked out of him despite his cushioned landing. He lay there stunned, the total darkness within this void of substance, confusing his comprehension of position. He heard a snigger and the latch of a lock closing the door above him.

A torrent of despair flooded his perceptions and he realised Natalie had not relented, nor submitted. His unfathomed decent from the room above sent him into unconsciousness.

21) COCOON

Father Byron came around slowly, his eyes seeing nothing but blackness, a shapeless, empty, boxed universe. He rolled over onto his right side and appreciated the luxury of the old lumpy mattress. His body regressed into its fetal shape and he lay still for a time, thinking and wondering what had happened and what was going to happen next.

He had lost track of time and even speculated that he had fallen asleep. He looked at his watch....nothing. The fall when he landed with his right hand missing the mattress must have smashed the watch on his wrist when it hit the floor.

His legs felt a little shaky, especially when he stood on the mattress while it undulated beneath his feet.

He held his hands out in front of him as he tried to walk around the room, in an attempt to establish what was shrouded in the blackness that surrounded him.

"Holy shit. What in God's name?" He recoiled from where he thought the window should have been in his mind's eye, his fingers burning as hot stabbing points of aggression, repelled his attempt to find out what was in front of him and a possible way out. He rubbed his hands and fingers together and felt the slippery, warm and somehow sticky conglomeration that turned out to be his own blood seeping through tiny slices and holes in his hands and fingers from the razor blades, drawing pins and tacks which cut through his skin like tissue paper.

His mind could not immediately work out what was happening. No window. No light from anywhere. He turned repeatedly, losing any perception of which direction he was facing and stumbled on something which rolled under his left foot. "What on earth?" As he fell forward, his hands felt like they had ignited as these defences venomously dissipated his unintentional lunge. His arms stiffened to save himself and pushed his body away, his head writhing with numbness as the feelings of agony injected another dose of fire through his skin.

"You bloody bitch, what are you doing?" He screamed his abuse, still not processing what was happening; what he was experiencing. "Aaahhh." His already bleeding legs from the Stanley knife cuts, felt more dagger like penetrations through his trousers into the skin of his shins and the quadriceps of his thighs. He jerked around, trying to rub away the scalding, needle like traumas to his legs. There was a sharp, shooting pain to his right ankle as it twisted on something which in that second of contact felt round, the movement perpetuating along the length of his right leg and turning his right hip, pulling the fibres in his groin. He gripped himself between his legs as his tendons felt like they were going to snap, his legs buckling, felling him into a bundle of tumbling disorientation. His arms, face, back, his legs attacked by menacing steel and metal edges, drawing more and more blood out through small insignificant singular insertions into his skin which when combined, drew the flow of strength out of him.

The metallic clatter of objects being knocked by his body, bumping against other things jarred in his ears, the sound loosing its innocence and now initiating fear, his heart jumping with anxiety, his chest feeling tight, stopping him from taking deep, calming breaths. His mouth snatched at air, his lungs panicking for more oxygen. His head felt clouded, thoughts obscured in mist, fingertips trying to grip the worn wooden boarded floor as he crawled in a bewildered circle.

His body and mind combined into a conglomerate of diffusion, an ambiguity between the lightless reality he was lost in and the fear of further injuries with the belief there was hope, a belief that was quickly ebbing.

The room lit up like the centre of the sun; blinding white light flooding towards the middle of the floor where he lay, nursing as best he could, the tiny wounds perforating his arms, hands and legs where tiny streams of blood leaked from his skin.

His hands went protectively in front of his eyes, trying to shield the intensity of the glare which within seconds of il-lumination, was hurting his pupils, forcing him to squint, his forehead deeply furrowing with the effort of trying to focus on anything around him through narrowed eyelids. The heat from the 500 watt floodlights started to build up around him very quickly. As he turned in every direction, twisting like a decapitated worm on the oak floor, each light stared directly at him, defying him to look back at them, their intensity cre-ating eye burning, pupil dancing lights blocking his vision no matter where he looked.

Natalie listened at the door. She could visualising his writh-ing from the sound of his arms and legs flapping and kicking against the floor, the sound of clatter, his podgy body exhaling his breath in loud, effort filled exertion resonating through the floor. Natalie could hear him through the hollowness, the wooden floor acting like sounding boards.

She leant against the wall and thought about the electrician who had asked why she wanted so many bright, hot lights in this unused room. She could tell from the tone in his voice that he had not really believed she had wanted it for growing orchids.

"These are the wrong type of lights. You need heat lamps not flood lights. They will give out far more heat than these lights."

"No, I am happy with these, just secure them to the floor and the walls like I've asked, in a kind of square all around the room so that they are all facing inwards," had been her reply.

The electrician had been concerned she was making the wrong decision and tried a second time to advise her.

"These will be so costly to run, eighteen 500 watts flood lights."

She could hear his voice now foremost in her mind as she enjoyed the sound of Father Byron in the background. "These are exactly what I want. I want them at different heights and screw the light or the stand that it's on to the floor so they can't move or fall over, or the higher ones to the walls." Her lips smiled without intention as she remembered her last comment that ended that conversation.

Natalie turned the light switches off and the darkness to Father Byron's eyes was even blacker than any darkness he had been in before. He rubbed his eyes, pushing the knuckles of his index fingers deep into their sockets, giving relief to his aching eyeballs that had fought against the onslaught of light. He flopped back down with his eyes shut. Within the darkness behind his eyelids, he saw the illusion of coloured speckles dancing in front of his pupils. As he lay there, momentarily relieved, he could not decide if his eyes were following these flashing speckles or they moved in synchronisation with his eyeballs. Prostrate, he stared towards an unseen ceiling.

The lights burst on again with an explosion of silence, boring their brilliance through to the back of his retinas. Whichever way he turned, there was a blinding white glare obscuring any definition, disguising whatever there may have been there with him, within the four walls of this discarded room, now used for his torture.

Natalie flicked the switch to off and waited twenty seconds and then turned them on again, the same disorientation hitting Father Byron a second time. She happily switched the lights on and off for different length of times, over the next twenty minutes. Byron's exasperation and increasing tiredness could be heard within his exclamations and reactions to the lights being turned on, his moans of pain clearly filling with increasing anger as each blackout teased him with the thought he might be able to do something about the lights but his hands and arms were stabbed by sharp, defending prongs and points puncturing his flesh on every attempt, causing him to recoil and curse Natalie.

"You bloody bitch of a woman. What have you become? You were never like this. Natalie stop this. This is enough. THIS IS ENOUGH" His aggression rose as he shouted around the room, not knowing where Natalie would be. He rubbed his hands and arms to try and alleviate the burning sensations and stood, unmoving in the centre of the room, almost spiked into static submission.

"Natalie, please this is enough......... Please." He sank back down onto his knees and his determination ebbed out of him with a long sigh of anguish.

Natalie turned the second switch on which operated the timing mechanism she had the electrician install, linking it to the light switch and absorbed his frustration with such childlike relish. She giggled as she listened to his rekindled rantings through the door. The volume of his voice faded gradually as she walked down the stairs to the first floor and into her bedroom to sleep for what was the rest of the night. Natalie closed the door, pushing it into the frame with her hip. She snuggled down in her bed, closed her eyes joyfully, enjoyed the feel of the duvet and thought she was not in a rush to get up tomorrow; it was Sunday.

22) CAVE

Father Byron reached out to feel for the old mattress he had fallen on when Natalie kicked him off the joist. His fingertips jerked back away from the wooden floorboards as he felt for it. The tiny holes made from whatever had defended the lights earlier, the razor blades that had sliced almost unseen slits through his skin, the barbed wire that the suppliers had brought to Natalie's house, thinking it was for the top of the rear wall of her garden; all made their effectiveness known. In his confused bewilderment he had not realised he had received so many injuries, until now. His hands and fingers felt like they were on fire as the pressure from trying to crawl back to the centre of the room, tortured the nerves exposed by the cuts in his skin.

The old bed felt comforting as he crawled onto it and slumped onto the bumpy, uneven softness. His body curled up instinctively, his knees tucked up against his chest. He listened to the relief, the expulsion of his own breath, the only sound he could hear and it felt inexplicably reassuring. His lungs eventually emptied and for a moment of blackened isolation there was total silence.

He rolled onto his back. There was nothing. No reflection, no glint, not the faintest glimmer of light from anywhere in his colourless universe. He stared around the room, concentrating on seeing anything and nothing filtered an image into his eyes. This was cave darkness, just as he remembered when he went to Dan yr Orgof caves in Wales years ago, when they turned the lights off and he couldn't see his own finger touching the end of his nose. He tried it. Seeing he couldn't see his own finger unnerved him even more. The mattress undulated underneath him as he knelt up and shifted himself around in a clockwise direction vainly hoping he had been mistaken in missing any sign of light. He hadn't.

The bed bellowed out its response to his heavy body crashing back along its length as he let himself collapse. His mind entered into pondering and quickly escalated into agitation, his thoughts half thought, half explored were swamped by more thoughts tumbling over the ones in front which were forced to leave his mind. He put his hand onto the top of his left pectoral which felt tight, a sharp ache cut through the sub layers of his skin, scoring into him from inside his body. He took a slow breath and concentrated on being in control of his body, willing it to behave normally. The blade of anxiety cut into him no matter how slow he took each breath. Beneath the scorching feeling that burnt into his muscle, he could feel his heart beating, fluttering irregularly. He moved his right hand down from the top of his chest and armpit to his heart and pressed his palm against his shirt. It felt damp with his perspiration but through the cotton, the irregularity made him fearful.

His memory of walking those corridors, his control, the nemesis he had become, that elation of misguided authority over the children he cared for now, in these last ninety minutes came back to haunt him, creating a feeling of guilt from the fear he now felt; for the first time in forty years. In the darkness he sensed unforgiving retribution hanging over him. He had totally lost all control over Natalie and he knew it. His age had now become his disadvantage in the same way that the children's ages had been theirs when he was younger and fitter.

The mattress despite its lumps and wear drew him to curling back up and slipping off to sleep. As he became drowsy and his body relaxed into the contours of the old bed he said a short prey for God to look after him and for his safety. As sleep took his consciousness he listened for God's answer. Silence.

The timers switched all the halogen bulbs on again in a wall of blinding white light, passing through his closed eyelids, startling him awake again. He was just as blind with all the light around him as he was when surrounded by complete darkness. He vainly looked around, kneeling up on his bed but the brightness glaring at him from every direction pounded his eyes into submission. There was nothing he could distinguish, no shape, no glint of metal, no edge, just 9000 watts of relentless intimidation.

Father Byron dropped his head onto the mattress, his forearms either side of his ears, his hands clasped around the back of his head in an attempt to block out the light. The lights continued to burst on and off throughout the rest of the night with total irregularity, their intensity waking him when he slipped into unconsciousness, the immediate darkness like the inside of a coffin.

23) MORNING

Natalie opened her eyes, her mind instantly turning to her captive. She lay still for a few moments, her thoughts reviewing the events so far. The warmth of the bed begged her to stay as she absorbed the feeling of the warm duvet against her skin. Natalie sat up after a few minutes of indulgence. The sunlight illuminating the red curtains must have been very intense as their colour seemed stronger to her this morning. She looked towards the window and stared, transfixed by the difference of colours her eyes could see. Natalie moved her head to increase the change of angle with which her eyes looked at her surroundings and the colours of her bedroom looked more distinctive. She looked towards the window as she walked to her en suite. Her mind felt unnervingly bemused at the change of colour that usually surrounded her each morning. Despite the strangeness of this morning, her shower was leisurely, she had no need to rush. He wasn't going to go anywhere.

24) LEASH

After toast and coffee, Natalie walked slowly from her kitchen up the two flights of stairs. Her eyes were expressionless. They neither moved one way or the other, just stared blankly before her as she walked, almost trance like, her hands feeling the walls and surroundings on her ascent to the second floor, stopping for a while outside his locked door.

Natalie's voice was sarcastic. "Father Byron. Sorry! ......Mr Bogeyman....are you there?" Natalie laughed to herself. Her mind heard herself as if she was someone else, sniggering, giggling, outside of her self inclusive bubble. She pressed her forehead against the door, listening through the wood. His wheezing, laboured breathing seeped back through the grain. She could tell from the slowness of his breathing that at this moment he had fallen back into sleep. Natalie didn't look at the timer, she wasn't bothered how long he had been granted rest bite or when the timer would turn on the lights again, blinding him; the most important thing was he had had to endure nine or so hours of eyeball blinding, hot lights boring down on him, depriving him of sleep, tormenting his body and its tiredness.

Her fingers played across the override light switch as she thought about the forthcoming day. It was 10.15 on Sunday morning, but there wasn't going to be any Sunday roast for Elvis. The click of the switch was also the switch to Natalie's smile. Her lips beamed with excitement as she heard him react to the blaze of blinding halogen destroying every shade of darkness within his unconventional prison.

"Is this you, Natalie is this you? God, sweet Jesus girl. This has got to stop. Natalie this has got to stop. This is insane." His voice sounded withered, its control, its menace drained out of him by a virtually sleepless night tormented by instant transitions from light to darkness playing with his mind, his physical recovery to regain strength removed by the tortured night.

Natalie brushed the walls with her hands for guidance as she went up to the second floor and the room she had lured him into. She pushed the door open so that it would creek above his head. She felt tingly with anticipation.

There was escalating uneasiness in his voice as he tried to clarify any shape, anything that Natalie was doing in the dark. "What are you doing, Natalie, what are you doing? Where are you? What's happening?"

Natalie could hear him stumbling on and around the mattress, the sound of his rubber soled shoes, now sock less and exposed, squeaking on the floorboards, intermixed with silence and then muted puffs of air and the vibrating rumble of a compressed spring, as he stomped clumsily over the mattress, swirling in a state of anguish, fright rushing through his body.

Natalie unhooked a binding clip on a chain and let it slip through her fingers and through a gap between the joists, listening to the rattle of the metal as it lowered closer to the floor. The tinkling of its chain stopped and the tension and weight went slack as it started to coil up on the floor below. Her left hand clasped the chain so that no more length would run through to below. She pulled some of its length back until there was weight again in her guiding left hand and knew that the end was now hanging in mid air.

Her voice was direct and firm. "I want you to grab the end of this." She rattled the chain.

"What.......where....what are you talking about? I can't see a thing. Turn a light on so I can at least see what you want me to do."

Her voice became even more stern. "Listen.....it's not far from you. Grab it."

"I don't know where it is, what you are talking about."

"Grab it. The chain. Listen." She jangled it. "Listen and grab it."

Natalie rotated her left wrist and the chain started to swing in an ever increasing and rising circle as it swished slowly around the room below. She felt and heard the end hit Father Byron in a clatter of steel as the weight of the chain jumped and jarred to find its momentum and equilibrium.

Father Byron's voice had not lost any of its anxiousness. It sounded disturbed. "What on earth was that? What are you doing?"

Her voice hinted a subdued reminiscence, resentment within every word.

"Get hold of the end. I won't tell you again. If you don't I will leave you in here. No food. No toilet. Nothing. No light........ just like me. You choose."

Father Byron's voice reflected a reciprocal resentment, a tone layered with trepidation as to how Natalie might react to his answer. "What! .....What do you want me to do?" He reached out to try and catch the swirling chain as it bounced against his upper body. His right hands gripped it after a few attempts. Natalie felt the tension.

"Hold onto it........." She felt the recoil in the chain as Byron pulled his end. "Put the end around your neck."

"What? What end! I can't see anything. What end?"

"Feel for it like I have to. It's not hard." Her voice remained calm but direct, emotionless but the tone disturbingly intimidating. Her response entered his ears and made its way to his brain. That nano second of delay swept another chilling realisation into his awareness that he was in a situation way beyond his control. He had unwittingly instilled merciless revenge, an uncaring emotionless state into his favourite victim, borne out of his own depravity.

He hesitated again, uneasy at getting an answer to his question. "I've got it. What now?"

"Put it around your neck, NO WHERE ELSE OR I'LL KNOW. Her voice came down from above him like an ethereal command. He felt himself shudder with fear. Her dominance had now totally usurped his history. His mind jumped back to prowling those corridors and his helplessness now, started to dredge some buried guilt from deep within the remnant of any decency he used to have; fuelled by his own self pity for now being Natalie's prey.

He fumbled with the end clasp and eventually heard it clip onto the chain he had obediently wound reluctantly around his neck. Natalie heard the metallic clink as it formed a steel collar around his throat. She smiled again to herself and then gave the chain a vicious yank. Natalie could tell from the surprised strangulated noise that came from the back of his throat that he had obeyed her instructions. Her fingers curled around the ringlets of steel and tightly gripped the chain that draped down into the room below her.

His voice spluttered and rasped from deep within his throat as the chain pulled against his flesh and stretched his neck violently, catching his Adam's Apple; his head jumping towards the open ceiling above, the darkness within the room where Natalie stood, blending with the darkness which surrounded him. Nothing was evident, nothing distinct, not even the hint of any glint from the chain, just the sound of its jingling, irritatingly piercing his ears.

Father Byron took hold of the chain with his right hand and tried to pull it away from his skin, like he was stretching an elastic band. The chain remained as tight around his neck. He wondered to himself if he had been too easily compliant in obeying Natalie. His thoughts quickly reviewed the last five minutes looking for the point where he could have, should have said no and regained control. The was no opportunity as far as his analysis could see. His mind jumped back, scrolling through the events of the night before, looking for the same moment where he could have regained dominance. Whether it was fatigue or uncomfortableness but he couldn't be bothered to logically scrutinise each thought and drifted back into the moment and his resignation to his current predicament.

He vainly hoped that his plea would miraculously appeal to Natalie's inherent goodness. He tried to sound friendly and concerned.

"Natalie, come on darling girl! This has gone too far now. Think of the consequences."

The chain yanked his neck again, his brain instantly thinking back to how his voice may have sounded to Natalie. Had he come over as patronising, condescending, threatening. He didn't have time to reach a conclusion. Natalie pulled on the chain again, the steel strangling against his Adam's Apple. He coughed as he grabbed at his throat, his voice gargling out his reaction.

Natalie's voice threatened injury. Its tone solid, unwavering, monosyllabic. "These are the consequences. Seventeen years of consequences waiting for you and what you did. Now it's my turn but I have not got the luxury of time."

His anxiousness rose making him pull on the chain again. He

heard the steel links like a ricochet of sound travel along the length of his leash and envisaged it becoming taught in Natalie's hands. He wondered why there was no audible reaction from Natalie against his forceful retaliation. Even in his tired and weakened state, even allowing for his age, surely he was still stronger than Natalie; surely she would have been pulled at the other end of the chain. There must be some sound of her reaction but nothing. In the silent seconds that followed, he pondered. The darkness hid the well oiled pulleys that were fixed to the ceiling trusses in the room above which added to Natalie's strength and control, increasing the ferocity of each tug, ten fold.

"I'm going to lower down a blindfold so that you can go to the bathroom. I don't want any accidents. You stink enough already. Don't try anything or I'll yank you back here and certainly don't try to take the chain off from around your neck; I'll know that as well and it will be the worse for you. Remember, I can hear and feel everything so go to the bathroom and nothing else. I'll know exactly where you are." Natalie's voice remained identical in tone as moments earlier, her instructions equally disturbing.

Despite the warning, Father Byron's mind jumped naturally to thinking about getting free once out of the room, instinctively putting his hand back onto the chain around his neck.

Natalie heard the links touch together, the slightest of jangles, their touch and the change in tension transmitting along the chain to Natalie's fingers. She pulled her end of the chain, his throat responding with truncated, strangled gasps.

"I told you I would know. Do you want to test me." Natalie exerted her authority with another pull on the chain, the heavy plastic, wide grooved pulley wheels adding venom to her biceps.

His throat strained again. "Okay, okay." His voice crocked out his defeat, his compliance.

Natalie smiled to herself, hearing his submissiveness.

"Here is a blindfold. Feel for it as I lower it down to you. Byron started to wave his arms around his head like a demented helicopter with broken rota blades, whirling hopelessly in the dark.

"Come on before I change my mind." Natalie knew this would add pressure to his situation. She could hear the jangling of the chain as it transmitted his franticness in trying to located the dangling blindfold.

Her voice snapped again with intimidation. "Come on. Hurry up."

"I'm trying Jesus Christ help me......I'm trying."

Natalie relished the imbalance in his voice. His feebleness stoked her excitement.

She felt his hand brush against the dangling string with the blindfold tied to it.

His voice sounded full of relief, of jubilation, a sense of almost wanting to impress Natalie that he had successfully got hold of the it. "I've got it, I've got it."

Her voice sent him his orders. "Put the blindfold on and stand still. I'll let you out and go to the first bathroom on the right. Nowhere else or I'll know and don't touch the collar. Natalie felt the string pull as he drew down more slack so that he could remove and then secure the heavy black elasticated blindfold around his head and then felt stillness.

"Don't move....at all. If I hear the chain jangle I won't let you out."

"Which way is the door? Natalie! I can't see anything. Which way is the door?"

"Shut up and stand still. I will tell you when you can speak."

Natalie secured the end of the chain onto a hook on the wall, making sure it was tight. She heard his throat respond.

She went down and opened the door of the room he was in. "Don't move." Natalie switched the lights on again as she went back upstairs, this time for her benefit.

"I'm going to direct you out? Do exactly what I tell you or I will drag you back by your throat. Take two paces forward."

The brilliance of the illumination below lit the room as if Natalie was looking into a glowing fluorescent pond with only one fat black fish sculling beneath the surface. She could see his blurred body, a shadow refracted within the waves of light. Natalie now knew which way he was facing.

"Turn to the right and walk three steps slowly and stop." Natalie could see his effigy moving towards the doorway.

In his new blindness, he started to stress out. The lights heated him from all directions. Now standing, they felt even more intense than when he had been lying on the mattress. Natalie could see his bodily darkened shadow moving around as if being buffeted by large breaking waves.

"I said stand still....stand still, why are you dicking about? I'm going to count to ten and by ten you should be by the door. If you're not then that's the end of it. No toilet for you." Her words resonated in his memory and she knew it. This time he felt the pressure, the panic of having to the count of ten to get something done, to comply with the order but this time it was not her that had to decide whether to come out of hiding and face The Bogeyman.

Natalie started counting, slow, firm, deliberate, impartial numbers, conveying a cold indifference to Father Byron, evoking threat and punishment with very number in her countdown.

"One.............turn left,........ two steps...........................Two."

She could hear the build up of his franticness, the sound of his shoes shuffling and scuffling on the bare boards, his stumble and then the mattress puffing as he bumbled across it.

"Turn left, take four steps.".................three.

She heard him turn, the sound of his shoes, his clothes moving over his skin, touching his body. Natalie called down mischievously over the sound of his squeals of pain as his searching hand and fingers were pricked and cut with renewed burning sensations as he felt vainly for the bedroom door but found the sharpened points of barbed wire and modified razor blades that had so carefully and skilfully arranged around three quarters of the room to protect the floodlights and prohibit his approach to the boarded up window. Only the doorway remained more or less unhindered without any of the obstructions and defences and the lights on this side of the room nearest to the doorway had been mounted at virtually ceiling height, looking down into the room.

Natalie thought back to when she and Jane hauled up the two reels of barbed wire and how she dressed herself up in an old thick quilt padded black coat, two pairs of jeans, the first layer, one of her own pairs; the second top layer, one enormous pair she bought from the Oxfam shop for her "fat friend" who was not very well. She smiled again to herself as she remembered how the lady serving her and who could see she was blind said "I think dear, that this particular pair are far too big for you. Perhaps I could help you to find a smaller pair," until Natalie gave her the concocted explanation of buying them for her friend.

She saw Jane and herself methodically and cautiously unrolling these reels and slowly working from the left side of the room to the right side, testing each protruding point for sharpness and filing them, to make them more aggressive so that when struck with speed rather than caution, they would draw blood. Natalie remembered how finicky it had been to cable tie the sixty razor blades to the barbed wire and how satisfied she had felt when she tighten the last one. The triangular four pointed tacks, like those used by the police in stingers they would throw across the road to puncture tyres of runaway cars, had proved to be very frustrating when trying to insert them into the gaps within the wound barbed wire. In the end, she had left most of those to Jane. The drawing pins dropped in front of the barbed wire had been an after thought but every point, every edge worked to contain and torment her captive.

Natalie grinned to herself as she imagined what she must have looked like in those two pairs of blue jeans and black quilted coat, heavy walking boots, with a steel food colander on her head like a German helmet and a steel food sieve over her face, both tied around and to each other with some of her old tights. She remembered Jane's uncontrollable hysteria as she collapsed on the floor laughing at her battle dress. It was easily fifteen minutes before Jane could start building the defences and they laughter together every time Jane relapsed as she laughed at Natalie's appearance. Natalie's make shift head protection had been useful as the wire had sprung and jumped at taking a few bites at her during her preparations. The image of herself and her efforts brought out sniggers which infiltrated her voice as she admonished Father Byron.

"Now now, there are plenty of words we can use without using swear words. You know what happens then."

"Don't use my own words back at me you bitch."

Father Byron's erratic frustration came tumbling out of his mouth without thought.

Natalie heard the eventual patting of the palms of his hands on the wall which was not fronted by barbed wire or razor blades, which he didn't appreciate were either side of the wooden door. He was so close to the opening.

"This is not fair.....where is the bloody door?"

"Naughty man, naughty man swearing like that. What would God say if he were here now?"

Natalie's face was smiling from ear to ear as she taunted him from her memories and she started singing Elvis' "Wooden Heart", with her own modifications .....''can't you see I love you, please don't break my neck in two, that's not hard to do cos I don't have a wooden heart." Byron could see the scene from G.I. Blues and he took hold of the chain in case Natalie yanked it again. She burst into laughter, just about getting the next two numbers out.

"Four.......turn left four steps.....five." As punishment for answering back she sped up the count, knowing the increase of pressure by the shortening of time would escalate his level of panic. It worked.

He whined his anxiety out like a belligerent child, not able to get their own way. She knew his mind was starting to convect into turmoil and she was loving it. Natalie could see his thoughts racing. He had to find the door, to get to the toilet, to stop the chance of him dirtying himself. He didn't know how long this was going to last. His mind was going back to a child like state, where everything was black or white. It was there or it wasn't. The concept of time to a child had no essence, no definition. A minute could be a minute or an hour. One was just a shorter wait than the other and when you are frightened, a second could seem longer than a day.

Natalie wanted these ten seconds to disappear in Byron's concept of time and to become an eternity. She wanted his heart to pump and for him to hear it, as if it wasn't his own, with him willing it to be quiet so she wouldn't sense it through the silence, within his darkness.

Byron's frantic efforts continued. Natalie could feel the tension on the chain increase and then subside as he moved with an increasing frenzy of desperation without coherent thought in trying to find the door, his only thought to get this toilet privilege before it was snatched away from him. "Jesus Christ, aahhh, what the hell?" Blades and points sliced and punctured his fingers and hands.

"Six......seven....eight." The pressure to find the door increased with each number and Natalie's enjoyment started to leave her control. She started to laugh and immediately thought it would aggravate and intimidate Byron even more without any calculated intention on her part this time. The hollowness of this artificial cavern, the open floor and the exposed ceiling trusses in the room where Natalie stood in which she had David secure the pulley mechanism for the "piano that she was going to store", in this unused second story attic room; seemed to convey a crypt like burial chamber. She deliberately stopped her laughing and held her breath and in that split second of her silence took in Byron's emotions.

The simple task of trying to find the door blindfolded was not a mammoth task but Natalie had complicated it with revenge. Byron tired, hungry and frightened, his mind fighting with itself to think straight, had lost the logic of searching systematically or listening to Natalie's instructions, both totally escaped him. He, now in desperation, virtually flung himself from one wall to another, impaling his hands over and over again. The wire spikes dug through his trousers into his legs. His guess at the door's location would be lucky if his stretched, taught, anxious fingers found the old varnished oak door.

Natalie could feel his disorientation, his blind thrashing below, his black silhouette spiralling. She followed the black crossing around the room, her hearing able to pin point his movements, the sound of his shoes on the floorboards, the slapping of his hands on the old papered walls where they reached over or through the gaps in the barbed fencing. She paused for a fraction of a second in order to heighten the tension, his stress. Would he find the door before she counted ten? The pause made her think that she should make sure he found the door, she didn't want any damage or mess on her carpets or furnishings later.

"Nine......it's behind you....COME ON........can't you even find the door............."

Father Byron's shoes squealed slightly indicating his turn in the opposite direction. Natalie hoped her scorn would get the result she wanted. The sound of his clothes, his breathing, the movement of his body through the room across the floor conveyed he was moving in the right direction. She heard his hands slap onto the door.

"Ten"

"I've found it, Natalie, I've found the door." Father Byron sounded out of breath and triumphant.

Natalie's voice was slow, deliberate and menacing. "You were too late. I counted ten." She tingled with excitement as she listened to herself and his following pleas.

"No Natalie please, I've found it, please let me use the toilet, please."

"I've told you, you were too slow.............soooooooo."

Byron's voice had become flooded with desperation. "Natalie...please, PLEASE......look, I've found the door. Listen, it's open, look, listen girl."

Natalie fumed at his condescension within his pleading. That one word. She spat back her retort. "I'm not your girl. You were too..."

Father Byron's brain was frantic. His only thoughts, to persuade Natalie that he had succeeded in finding the door before she had finished counting to ten and to let him use the toilet. "PLEASE, please Natalie.

Natalie was tingling. The euphoria of her control ran through every nerve in her body. She was deliberately teasing him with failure, knowingly escalating his fear of confinement. Her own experience of being trapped now gave her the edge, each pause in her voice, each transmission of sound from every movement she made, she knew would scream through his brain as he tried to analyse what she was doing, where she was moving, what would come next.

Her face smiled with ecstasy as she spoke down to him in a slow, threatening voice, her lips almost conveying her excitement as she tried to remain in control of herself and not slip into hysterical laughter.

"This is the one and only time I will give you a second chance. If you are not quick enough or you disobey me.......that's it." She put her right hand over her mouth to aid her self control and to stifle the smile that almost changed the tone of her voice.

The chain pulled through her hands, bobbling erratically over her fingers as Father Byron took up the little slack there was as he frantically made his way through the doorway onto the landing. His voice immediately came back at Natalie, filled with aggravation.

"I can't see a thing. Can I take this blindfold off. Natalie, where is the light switch?"

"No don't touch it. I'll tell you if you can."

Her voice mocked back her answer adding to his frustration. "You tell me. You spent enough time looking around my house thinking you were clever, that I didn't know you were here. Your stench was everywhere."

Her mind placed her memory of his body odour and breath into her nostrils and throat as she spoke, almost as if she had sprayed a vapouriser of pungent, repugnant perfume onto her neck; his combination of B.O. and halitosis competing like lower and higher key notes of fragrances so carefully concocted by perfume manufacturers when creating irresistible and lasting aromas.

The thought of his smell turned her stomach. She could tell it was him even as a child, while hiding from The Bogeyman in a cupboard or behind a bath. Natalie swallowed to clear the gagging feeling in her throat. Her head jerked to one side as if to disperse his smell.

Her mocking instructions continued. "You know where your right side is don't you. Turn that way. It's the next door on your right and you don't need lights. We don't need lights. You're in my world now. Hurry up before I pull you back in."

Natalie yanked on the chain and she heard its tension reach Byron's neck. "Aarchh."

"Hurry up." Natalie voice rose in volume. The chain pulled slowly through her fingers again as Byron walked tentatively down the landing feeling his way to find the bathroom door. The house was really dark, no light coming in from anywhere outside. His right hand touched a light switch and flared at the nerve endings in all the cuts in his hands. "Thank God!" he thought to himself.

Its click didn't alter things and his head dropped slightly with despair as the darkness persisted to shroud everything into indistinguishable black. He touch the blindfold. Somehow Natalie knew. "Don't touch the blindfold. I'll rip your neck off. No more warnings."

He paused and rubbed both his eyes. Natalie could hear him closing the bathroom door as much as he could and the sound of the chain rubbing and jarring between the door and the frame.

She waited, glad that he was relieving himself and that there would be less risk of him dirtying the carpets or furniture later.

25) OBEDIENCE

Natalie felt the change and movement along the chain. Father Byron's voice followed, reaching Natalie like a second wave indicating his movement back onto the landing.

His voice conveyed his exhaustion. "Natalie! Please Natalie can we stop this now. I'm so tired by all of this now. You've had your revenge surely by now. Let's stop all this now before things really go too far."

Natalie's reaction swept away any glimmer of absolution. The steel noose tore at his throat as she pulled violently down on the chain, the pulley configuration increasing her strength. Father Byron gagged as his Adam's Apple was caught again within the impetus of the recoil. He grasped at his neck as the force of Natalie's anger pulled him off balance, prostrating him along the floor.

His voice rasped, unable to find its normal tone and pitch. "You bloody evil bitch...aaacchh......stop...stop."

"Get up you fat bastard or I'll drag you along the floor and choke the guts out of you."

Natalie pulled again, forcing Father Byron to scramble along the landing, trying to keep up with the retraction back towards his bedroom prison. The chain had no flexibility, just solid, interlocking, unforgiving links jarring and clinking against each other. The old mattress billowed out more dust as he collapsed back onto it, relieved to feel the chain go slack and slumped almost exhausted by his efforts to reluctantly get back to his crypt.

Natalie again tied off the chain so that Byron couldn't move and then went down to lock the door.

His knees hurt as he manoeuvred himself from off his stomach onto both of his joints. The sound of his efforts registered with Natalie. She knew he was getting tired, very tired and this is what she needed.

"I've locked the door." Natalie said with a secretly relieved smile.

Natalie pulled on the chain to bring Byron back into her world. "Unclip the chain from your neck, take the blindfold off and wind it around the chain."

Natalie released the tension of this steel leash so he could unclip it more easily. The chain dropped away from his neck and Natalie pulled up the excess and put it to one side on her way out, locking the door behind her. She walked casually down to the first floor and turned the timing switches back on.

"Aaahh .....God not again." She heard the dismay in his voice, the ebbing of his spirit. Another couple of hours and he would be ready. "Be careful! Don't burn yourself."

26) PURSUIT

For the next three hours the lights blazed and extinguished erratically creating delirium in Byron's mind, ebbing his strength even more, burning and blinding his vision for a second time when he tried to open his eyes, lulling him into the expectation of relief when they went out and destroying his recuperation when they came back on. In the blinding or blackened silence, through the numbness of isolation, of sanity deprivation, Father Byron writhed and twisted on the old mattress, his mind jumping between his past and his thoughts as to now and why he deserved to be trapped in this room and Natalie. The relentlessness of his exposure, his tiredness, his prickling, sore little stab cuts and slices on his hands, arms and legs, all added to his lack of logical thinking. Closing his eyes against the lights and lying back on the mattress to sleep, just relax or just wait, escaped his thinking. His brain repeatedly focused on his condition, his situation. It could not break free from the confines of this unused bedroom. It strayed into his history but found no reason. All he could conclude, no matter how many thoughts blasted around his head, was that this was unfair. This should not be happening to him.

"Are you awake?. Natalie's voice was authoritative. "Are ..... You.... Awake?

Father Byron looked up to the hole in the ceiling from where her voice bellowed down. It sounded like a railway station announcement, still devoid of any emotion, a statement of fact, a call to act, to be aware.

"Get up...now...............look up here."

Natalie heard the mattress puff and squeak as he stood up and tried to balance himself while it moved under his feet. He looked up obediently, innocently, not thinking as to why.

"I'm here!" Natalie could tell by his voice that his head was looking upwards from the slight strain his extended neck was putting on his vocal chords.

"Sssssssssssssssssssss." The two cans of pepper spray covered his head in vapour, engulfing his eyes with their blinding concoctions. Father Byron instantly shied backwards away from their combined cloud, the tiredness in his body re surging with unplanned effort to move him to safety but his movements were uncontrolled. He wheeled mindlessly around his confines, his eyes scolding, pulsing in their sockets. The barbed wire drew more blood as he spiralled from one coil to another around the room, in a deranged pirouette of pain. His eyelids were shut like vault doors, sealing his pupils with a glaze of capsaicin. Byron pushed his knuckles hard into his sockets in a reactionary attempt to alleviate the spray's burning attack on his orientation. He coughed involuntarily which bent him over while he was spinning around incomprehensibly, injuring himself with almost every turn or movement on the metal that guarded the floodlights and any possible attempt to reach the boarded up window. As he spun, twirling around at half his height, his efforts to stand steady on his feet evaded him, stumbling down onto his knees, his head and face spiked against the sharpened ends of the barbs and tacks, the drawing pins burning vengeful holes into his hands and knees. Byron's efforts to breathe seemed to fight against his will to do so, causing his respiration to hiss and gasp from the pepper spray infected air. The skin of his eyelids stretched and squelched with the force he exerted to try and stop the heat generated by the chemical mix. Byron consciously tried to open his eyes, fighting against the nerve reaction to clamp his eyelids shut in an effort to alleviate the inferno that he felt was melting his eyeballs. Nothing helped. The tears gushed from underneath his closed eyelids, streaming down his cheeks, spraying off like rain drops as his head jerked and swirled in his disorientation.

"Aaahhhhh, aaaahhhhhh, ahhhhhhhhh,"

Nothing by searing agony engorged his body, igniting in his eyes balls and transmitted to his brain, which then distributed the sensations to every nerve in a cacophony of writhing.

"I can't see! I can't see!"

Despite the lights blazing within the room, Father Byron could not focus on anything, not even the brilliance around him. Nothing had any form or substance. Where the light would if less intense, have shown him his surroundings, the pepper spray and the halogens combined to create an aurora of distorted illumination, which blended and merged everything around him. Before there was just a wall of white light, now following Natalie's attack, light seemed to have pain, substance, which danced in front of his eyes.

Natalie skipped down the stairs to his first floor room and stood outside the door, listening to his screams and the scuffing and groaning of the barbed wire as it repelled his flailing body.

The door creaked as she pushed it slowly open, hoping that its sound would filter into his ears and add to her intimidation. It did. As the door bumped against the wall, Father Byron's cries paused. Natalie could not see his head cock to one side like a puzzled spaniel but she knew the creaking hinges had been heard. Byron's pause was momentary, a fraction of a second until taking his next breath and his screaming resumed. As he crushed his knuckles into his eyelids, his careering around the room slowed. Natalie could pin point where he was, one foot on the mattress, one on the floor. She held her hands out,

166

searching to make contact with some part of his body. His right elbow brushed eventually against her left fingertips.

"Father Byron let me help.....sshhuuussshhhhhh....it's going to be fine."

"Whaaaaaat?" There was hesitance, disbelief in his voice, his movement paused. She followed his voice three foot into the room.

Natalie took out the two cans of pepper spray from her back pockets and covered him again with two simultaneous jets.

"Aaahhhhhhhhhhhhhhhhhhhhhh, Jesus god, aaahhh, aahhh."

Natalie stepped back to the right of the door, her back against the wall to avoid his erratic, podgy body bumbling around in front of her in agony. She laughed for a couple of seconds and then gained control of herself.

Her voice conveyed new tones, controlled distain. "RUN............ Run Elvis. I'm going to inject acid in your eyes........run, like I had to.................RUN."

His continual screams and cries told Natalie exactly where his face was. She stepped forward, using it to increase the momentum of her left handed slap across the right side of his face. Its impact knocked him sideways, his right foot stepping back onto the mattress which twanged and squeaked as his legs and feet tried to keep his balance.

Natalie stood back again and shouted. "Run....how many more times!"

Father Byron's addled brain took in her order and started to move him towards the door, his body disconnected from mindful co ordination. Within the brightness of the lights she watched the impression of his stumbling, twisting, leg buckling lurch towards the wall, his right hand hesitating and tentative as it reached out to feel his way out of the door but hardly leaving his right eye as he continued to try to dissipate the blaze that was trying to burn out his corneas. He bounced against the wall, his right shoulder jerking towards his chin, another pain integrating in the mix already transmitting through his nervous system.

"Turn to your left ....run you fat bas....."

Her voice stopped abruptly as she heard the effort of his laboured backhand swipe as it swung towards her. She stood back as he lost balance and listened to his hand pass her face, feeling the waft of air and then his body falling against the wall. She leant in towards the blackened impression of his body judging where his head would be and slapped him hard across the left side of his face for a second time.

"Aahh you bloody bitch." His voice conveyed his tiredness, surprise and increased Natalie's confidence.

Natalie sounded demented. "Ruuuuuuunnnnnn,"

This time Father Byron fell through the doorway onto the landing, still rubbing his eyes as he squirmed around his stomach on the floor. Natalie stood over him and sprayed him again. Byron's screams increased even louder as his body jerked and gyrated.

"It's going to be acid next time." Her voice was now attuned into his hearing despite his writhing. Byron grabbed out at the floor and tore at the carpet, his fingernails dragging him away from Natalie still screaming, the pepper induced salty tears streaming down his cheeks, his eyes blood red, the white around his corneas burnt to bleeding point by the repeated dowsing.

Natalie listened to his body drag along the carpet and she let him crawl along the landing. The door to the bathroom he had used earlier opened silently but Natalie knew exactly where he was. She walked along the landing and flicked the light switch on. The two crystal chandeliers burst on now Natalie had turned the lighting circuit on within the electrical consumer unit. She blinked.

"Wow." She thought to herself. What is that?" This time it was Natalie who rubbed her eyes and stared along the landing. "What?" For a few moments she paused, a digression from her pursuit of Byron, this time her own mind confused. Within the light she had turned on, Natalie looked along her own landing, its colours clearer than normal, slightly more distinct. She rubbed her eyes a second time. When she opened them again, her lack of vision felt normal. Natalie wondered to herself in that split second of confusion, if she had seen what she had thought she had seen.....

"Aaaaaahh, aaaahhh." Father Byron's perpetual screaming brought her diverted attention back to him. She closed her eyes and focused........that second of concentration brought back the image of those corridors that she hid in and she knew Father Byron would soon know feelings and have thoughts that he had never experienced before and she relished her expectation.

Byron felt drained. His mind was telling him to stop screaming, to stop giving his position away to Natalie. He had to get away. He had to hide. Even with the landing light on she would not see him. Byron could not decide how best and in what order to use his hands, whether to rub his still burning eyes, the heat and sensations excruciating, his vision when his eyes flicked open for a second between rubbing them, completely blurred. He tried to gain control but the pepper spray had won that battle, usurping his attempts to focus through tortured eyelids which he mentally strained to open.

The chill of the enamel Victorian style bath brought cooling relief to the right side of his face. It became an obstacle in front of him as he dragged himself by his elbows into the bathroom. He tried to press his eyes against the side of the bath for more relief but his face and the bath were incompatible shapes.

"I know you are in the bathroom. Don't turn on any taps." Natalie did not want him to wash his eyes. She started signing the Elvis song she had heard him sing so often. She sang it menacingly, with staccato venom in every word. "It's.. now.. or.. never, come ...hold.. me.. tight. Kiss... me ..my ...darling, be ...mine... tonight. Tomorrow... will... be ...too... late. It's now... or... never, my... love.. won't ..wait."

Unknowingly he started to mime the words to the song he had loved singing but Natalie's echo was coming back to haunt him. His consciousness clicked onto the fact he was almost singing along. He pushed himself reluctantly away from the cool bath towards the adjoining bedroom door. His elbows slipped on the white tiled floor, so his humongous effort to crawl away was worthless, he hardly moved. The edge of the bath numbed his right wrist as it slapped along the top edge. His arms flailed around in an effort to find something that could give him support to get up onto his feet.

The bathroom door slammed shut and Natalie stood over him, her eyes staring ahead of her, not looking at his crumpled body on the floor. The door closing froze his body. His nerves quivered throughout, shaking him as if he were shivering from the cold. Instinctively, he looked up at the sound of the door, the sound of it slamming shut in the frame accelerating his heart rate. The bathroom was black, the landing light just hinting below the door.

"Sssssssssssssss." The pepper spray swamped him again. "Ahh-hhh......aaahhhhh...Dear God was that acid?" His mind was racing. "She said she would use acid the next time." That thought exploded, his level of fear thrashing it around inside his head like the ball bearing being fired around a pin ball machine, its momentum dying quickly off as he realised it could not have been acid. There was a fleeting moment of thought that he would not recover from dose after dose of this pepper spray, if she kept using it. There was no reasoning with her. He knew with each escalation of things that he was in serious, serious trouble. The possibility of permanent blindness came to mind. An article he had read years ago about the ethics of its use, when the police first introduced pepper spray to their arsenal came to mind. These thoughts were quickly lost. His renewed screams echoed off the tiled walls and floor. Even through the amplified sound of his own voice reverberating around the bathroom, he heard the click of the pull cord turning the spot lights on in the ceiling.

Natalie's eyes winced away from the glare and then stared ahead of herself again. Father Byron's black clothed body stood again out against the white surroundings. His shape was still condensed on the floor, squirming, screaming, struggling to lift his tubby frame back unto his feet.

"It's now or never, come hold me tight." Natalie started to sing Elvis' song again. Father Byron shivered involuntarily as he finally managed to push himself up to standing again. His hands were saturated from wiping the tears that gushed uncontrollably down his face. Natalie could see the contrast in colour and shape as he feverishly and repeatedly rubbed his eyes with his fingers, his knuckles, the palm of his hands as he tried to introduce some relief into his eye sockets.

"It's time for the acid." Her words taunted him, adding more screams, more volume. Father Byron's heart jumped into his mouth with an immense wave of nausea flooding his senses, his brain instantly processing the threat. His right hand was shaking as he reached out to find the door leading to the adjoining bedroom. He knew he had to get away from Natalie. The hinges he had oiled two days before glided effortlessly in silence. The bedroom carpet brushing against the bottom of the door was still audible between the now slightly hoarse and ebbing cries and told Natalie exactly what he was doing.

Byron's head was befuddled. The nausea made him want to bend over and find the toilet pan to be sick but his balance had gone. He felt like he was on a rolling ship. His legs, his body, his arms were uncoordinated as every part of him seemed to be fighting against each other and his mind swam in a muddle of impulses and reactions. His right hand went back to his eyes and back again to gripping the door frame. He pulled himself through to the bedroom, his left hand reaching out to find the light switch. It froze on making contact, his brain questioning whether it was better on or leave the room in darkness; what would make it easier for Natalie? What would be best for him. Light would help him see but added other layer of discomfort on his eyes in those brief moments he could actually open his eyelids. The nerve in his left index finger made the decision for him as its twitch pressed the switch down.

His eyes blinked and remained without focus. The shape of the bed was a blurred lump of furniture. He lent over and put his right hand on it, feeling the softness of the quilts beneath the polythene but it made him want to jump onto it and sleep but his eyes could not clarify any detail.

"Why can't I see a bed?" The question came without him thinking, his unconsciousness teasing him. It was almost humorous to him when he realised he had thought it, if he had not been so frightened. He squeezed the quilt, encouraging it to become distinct, to show him its design but nothing changed.

"I can't stay here. I need to hide. I need to get out. Where did I put the front door keys?" His thoughts started to regain cohesion within his confusion. He felt his way to the door at the far end of the room and within those sixteen feet of travel, instantly felt he was beginning to get away, a misguided concept just from experiencing twenty to thirty seconds of relief from

Natalie's pursuit.

The bedroom door leading back onto the landing opened as silently as the first leading into the room. Natalie could distinguish within the overall noise of his floundering, his efforts to be quiet and to escape from her somewhere within her house, the sounds of the far door opening across the carpet. She leant against the wall of the shared bath room he had just left and listened.

Father Byron twisted out onto the landing, his feet stepping out what could have been some sort of an advanced reverse turn if he had been waltzing; still with the fleshy part of his thumbs where they formed the palms of his hands pushing into his eye sockets. There was no relief. The capsicum was scolding his eyeballs, the repeated vaporisation had impregnated his tears, coated his skin, the fumes feeding the fire.

Natalie's head poked out from behind the bathroom door frame and she stared expressionless down the length of the landing to where she knew he was standing. Father Byron could not see her. He tried to look around as to which way he should go but his eyes could see nothing just blurs of colour distorted by the wash of tears flooding across his pupils. He remembered being a child and having drops put into his eyes at the eye clinic after his parents became concerned that he was short sighted. His sight was blurred then and he hadn't liked it. It had made him feel claustrophobic, like he was beneath the surface, struggling to get the water out of his eyes so that he could see clearly. He had hated going to the swimming pool or being in the sea for that reason. His mother had tried to reassure him that he had not gone blind but at five years old, he remembered his panic and now, sixty odd years later, in this brief interlude from pursuit, that sensation returned. Standing on the landing, not able to see any defining lines or specific shapes brought the memory of that clinic back.

His footsteps where heavy and awkward as he continued to stumble around the landing. The bannister gave him the extra strength his legs were lacking and he followed it across its width from where he had come out of the bedroom, at the front of the house. In his turbulence, the thought of opening the red curtains covering the window he had opened and slammed to torment Natalie, didn't enter his thinking. All that mattered was to get away and hide, to regain some sort of control of himself, to stop his eyes from burning.

The bannister led him to the opposite front bedroom. The door burst open, banging into the wall as his hand and his following weight, timbered through the doorway onto the floor like a fallen tree. His body fell hard, the unexpectedness of the door flying open caught him completely unprepared. The carpet scrapped hard down his right side of forehead and face as his still handcuffed hands and arms failed to dampen his fall, giving him angry carpet burns as his head ploughed along the floor. The impact jerked his head, his awareness struggling to hold his mind open. He lay there for forty seconds feeling his head swelling and the pressure building up inside his skull. The headache was almost instant. Another wave of nausea swept over him.

His brain fought with the deluge of impulses, not able to analyse which was hurting the most. Natalie heard his groans and sighs as he rolled onto his back.

The floor started to feel like a friend, his fingertips massaging the carpet and he relaxed into the fibres with a momentary feeling of safety. The carpet smelt new, the scent of which confirmed what he had seen when he had been prowling around the house, though its smell had eluded him at that time. He breathed in deeply, strangely appreciating its odour while his eyes were shut as tight as possible as he tried to cope with and subdue Natalie's last attack.

Father Byron started to stare up at the ceiling, still with tears welling up in his eyes, nestling like tiny pools in the recesses of his eye sockets. He lay still, feeling those salty pools cooling against his skin, against his eyelids. The nearest of the two 1930's crystal chandeliers that hung at either end of the landing cast shadows around the bedroom but within the restricted light that crept into the room, the distinction of Natalie's brightly coloured decoration and furnishings were muted. As he turned his head to his left to face the door onto the landing, those puddles of tears cascaded down his cheek, around his nostrils and across his lips, their saltiness now exposed to his taste. They were almost refreshing as his tongue felt their entry into his mouth.

He rubbed his head. His temples and forehead were pounding and his sight could still not distinguish anything around him. Despite his relentless tearing from the capsicum derivative, Byron started to wonder where he was in the house. His thoughts fought slowly through the conglomeration of pains, his concentration held back as if trying to stride through waist high water; to place this room and how he had got into it and from what direction. The crushing, spinning feeling in his head felt worse as he pushed his mind to think clearly.

The carpet felt soft against his cheeks as he turned his head from side to side, its smell intensifying as his nose came closer to it. He only did it once and stopped as the feeling of wanting to be sick swept from his stomach into his throat, the feeling accompanied by the smell of vomit destroying any fragrance from the new carpet. He put his hand over his mouth and forced himself up hurriedly onto his knees in case he had to run for the bathroom. It was instinctive. The feeling passed quickly and as quickly as it did, Byron started to think "where was the bathroom? Where would he have run if he had been sick?" He now felt totally confused. His legs felt heavy as he lurched towards the door and the light switch. The wall forced out the air in his chest as he fell against it by the switch. The light didn't come on when he pressed the switch down. He tried three times but the bedroom light remained off. Natalie heard the thud of the back of his head against the wall in his despair to the fact that she had taken the light bulb out of the pendent fitting. It made her smile again.

"The next time it's acid." Her voice was infused with glee as it drifted purposefully across the landing, into the bedroom and Byron stopped the instant her words reached him.

"Dear God, I've got to get out, I've got to get out." His thoughts reacted again to her words which chilled him. The corridors of the care home came to mind unwittingly. He twisted his body along the wall towards the other bedroom door, his head remaining in contact with the wall as he rotated three hundred and sixty degrees, once, twice, three times until his head came into contact with the door frame at the rear of the room. The light from the landing chandelier struggled to maintain any intensity to the far end of the room where he was standing. He felt for the bathroom door handle and paused.

"Why am I running? She's blind! She can't see me! She can only hear me! Am I better off hiding and being quiet?" The door handle slowly turned back to allow the latch return into the receiver as he hesitated, his thoughts gathering momentum. The immediacy of the pain from the pepper spray had passed, he was no longer screaming, his mind had focused on getting away and he suddenly realised that despite the fact his eyes were still streaming with tears, he was not screaming.

He listened to his own thoughts, trying to work out the best thing to do. "Could I be quiet enough? I think I've got control........I'm not screaming.......I'm quiet. No she's still got to be really close. I need to get somewhere where she won't find me but where am I now? When I came out of that room........oh god, I can't remember, where am I?" His heart was pounding again as his thoughts worked him up into a panic. The identically decorated bedroom hid its identity in the half light and his eyes cloaked the rest. The frame of the doorway pressed against his cheek as he slumped momentarily to recover, its edge digging into his skin, unknowingly helping him to regain a fraction of his concentration.

27) CAT AND MOUSE

The CD player from the lounge threw the song upstairs, so that the level of volume just reached into the bedrooms, clear enough to be heard if you stopped making any other noise and concentrated on listening.

This time it was Elvis singing but with Natalie's voice accompanying the CD, slipping in her own modified words. Natalie had gone down stairs while he had worked his way through the bedroom and put on the CD of Elvis' Greatest Hits she had bought three weeks ago. She shivered just from listening to this song. Byron's eyes were wide with fright, his flesh started to prickle, he knew now what was to come next.

"You ain't nothing but a hound dog, hiding all the time. You ain't nothing but a hound dog, hiding all the time. Well you ain't never caught a Rabi and you ain't no friend of mine."

Natalie's voice could be heard above the music and Father Byron knew the significance of the word changes.

He pushed himself away from the doorway he was leaning against which lead back onto the landing and found the doorway leading into the adjoining bathroom. This time he was more careful as he turned the door knob and pushed against the door. The door didn't move. He turned and pushed again, it did not give way. The wood gave a groan as it resisted his efforts.

"Oh God help me here.....help me to get away." His silent, mouthed plea for help had risen to a heightened level of prayer on hearing Elvis' voice and that song. He pushed again at the door and it failed to move. He wanted to be as quiet as he could but his agitation and efforts seemed futile. The door creaked and groaned indiscreetly as it resisted being opened.

The sound of Natalie's stomped footsteps coming back up the wooden stairs reached his ears over the sound of the music. Even his shoulder failed to move the door. He looked around, his mind now in a frenzy. He repeatedly tried to force the door open by pushing all his weight against it but the door stayed secure. Byron became aware of the noise he was making as he tried to force it open.

"What's wrong with this bloody door? Please open. I bloody oiled you a few days ago. You bloody bastard.....OPEN." His mind was twisted in anger and fragility, plated like inter-woven emotions. His nerves were on end, burning through his body more fiercely than the excruciating heat that had almost devoured his eyes. He tried again to push against the wood, now more conscious of doing it silently but it resisted over and over again. The tears welled up and ran down his cheeks but his time they were generated by his own terror. He felt his right hand shaking as he held the door handle, the vibration rippling from his fingers up his arm to his shoulder and then reverberating across his chest and into his other limbs. The shaking throughout his body made him aware of how fright-ened he really was. Even tightening his grip on the handle in his frustration to get the door to open, did not stop his body from shaking.

The perspiration running down his face mixed in with the tears from his eyes. The palms of his hands were saturated from wiping his eyes and dribbling saliva from around his lips. His fingers slipped again on the round brass door handle as he tried to turn it while he pushed against it to open. It still resisted.

"You bloody, bastard door." He shouted uncontrollably, mo-mentarily forgetting that his voice would expose his position to Natalie if she didn't know already. His body crumpled slightly, pulling away from the door as he clung to the brass knob. The door started to open towards him.

The floor jarred his body as he let himself collapse in a heap as he looked towards the now partly opened door. His hands squelched as his rubbed them together, the fluids from his head lubricating his palms. For a minute or so he remained still, trying to work things out. Both his eyes still hurt and were useless to him. They would not focus, they could not distinguish, they couldn't do anything to really help him.

Byron sat on the floor and for the first time in those unnatural, fleeting seconds of assessment, wondered if he was really, permanently blind. His next thought after this, his momentary contemplation; was he now like Natalie?

Elvis' voice tickled his ears as it floated up from the ground floor. Its distraction within his inertia closed his thinking off to the fact he was sitting on the floor. His shoulders and legs twitched momentarily in an unconscious homage to The King's gyrations as he instantly became caught up with the words of the song, which dragged back vivid recollections of his nightly activities in the care home.

Those long corridors, devoid of personality, character, of individual distinction, briefly became his refuge and filled his head with memories and images. In seconds, with Elvis' voice in his head, he was walking along those uniform white, clinical tiled passages. The red oblong boarder tile that broke up the blandness, five feet up the wall, strobed passed his eyes like the long white lines in the centre of the road disappearing under the bonnet of a moving car. His mind displayed that movement and now during this unexpected recall, the fear he knew he had generated with each step, with each tile as it moved passed his eyes while he walked purposely slowly, stalking after his prey, now transmitted itself into his own heart as he strained to look around the gloomy bathroom with murky, injured eyes. He knew he was the prey and no longer the predator. Byron felt the fear and horror he had wanted to create within his victims during his pursuits then, now as his own feelings. He could not control his emotions now as he had done then, despite knowing his own history.

He wrapped his arms around his chest to try and stop his body from shaking, his fright exaggerated by his own memories of prowling those child tormented corridors. His right sleeve felt wet against his cheek as he again, tried to wipe some clarity into his eyes.

Natalie stamped on each oak stair as she walked up from the ground floor, the sound of her feet growing in volume as she got closer to the the first floor. That sound disappeared and Byron knew she was on the carpeted landing. She stood motionless, listening. He willed his body to stop shaking, the noise of his own quivering forming a barrier to any sound her feet may make on the carpet. Natalie slowly and carefully took her first few steps silently on the deep pile beige carpet, stopped and smiled to herself.

His fingertips dug deep into the fibres of the bedroom carpet and he started to drag himself towards the now disturbed door leading into the adjoining bathroom. The door pulled open into the room and he crawled past it onto the cold tiled floor, pulling the door virtually shut with his foot. The bathroom felt cold and the light from the landing which had struggled along the length of the bedroom, now just squeezed through the partly open bathroom door, casting a dim sheet of light along the white tiled wall next to where he was lying. He looked at the bath in the gloom, his own shadow just visible, cast from the reflection off the tiles onto its white enamel, the meagre illumination silhouetting the bath like a great white shark rising out of the surface of the water on the attack and about to swallow him whole.

Within these sanitary confines, the tiles seemed to echo back his whimpering, with a hollowness that made him finally realise he was actually crying. Father Byron lay strewn across the floor and felt even more vulnerable, more alone and now, the sudden reality of his crying, made him even more aware of the fear rippling through him. He heard in his ears, his own heart pounding from its effort within his body, bouncing back through his chest from its contact against the floor. With his eyes unable to distinguish anything with any accuracy, he forced his ears to try and compensate as he strained to find the sound of Natalie's presence. Those cold, familiar corridors which he had controlled, remained in his consciousness and the similarity of his lying, virtually hiding in this tiled bathroom, merged with his memories as he clasped his hands over his mouth in an effort to stop his sobbing. Byron rolled onto his back, his head bumping against the floor as he tried to gain control until he pushed himself against the bath, sitting up with his back against it, his knees curled up to his chest. He sat still for what could have only been thirty seconds and then heard three deliberately emphasised steps from the landing.

The threat of Natalie opening the door and having acid sprayed in his eyes made him scurry around the other side of the bath on all fours to make himself more inaccessible. His movements were draining his already sapped strength. He waited, the back of his head against the cool enamel, his hands again cupped over his lips, his fingers covering the length of his nose, to muffle all breathing sound.

The edge of the bath became his support. It moved slightly as Byron used it to to get up onto his feet, his weight bearing down unnaturally on one edge. His heart jumped as it twitched, a perverse feeling of guilt swept over him at the misplaced thought that he had somehow dislodged it from its secured positioning in the centre of the room.

The rim guided him around its circumference and as he followed it, in now virtual darkness, the only light through the cracks of the two doors. He tried to measure and gauge if any aspect of the bath would hide him from Natalie. His two hands tried to crush the bath's rim into submission as if the more anger, the more force he could exert through his frustrated grip would make the bath concede to becoming a good hiding place. He held on to the cold, curved edge and the bath told him, he was too big to use it as a hiding place, either in it or behind it.

His memory had suggested hiding in the bath with a towel covering him, a make shift cloak of invisibility but no amount of memories or imagination would help him hide now from Natalie.

Having got himself up onto his feet, Byron felt around for the pull cord to turn the lights on. He stumbled and significantly more by luck, got his left arm caught up in the cord by the door leading into the next bedroom. He tugged at it, the lights instantly blinding him with their intensity and the brilliant reflection off the white tiles. Still his clarity was bent and distorted though pupils unable to focus; the immediate impact bludgeoning Father Byron with an unexpected venom of electric brilliance. Misguidedly, he had thought turning the light on would help him to find out where he was in Natalie's home. The complete opposite was true. He didn't know whether he was on the right or left side of the house, facing the front or back of this large, impressive suburban home; he had become lost in the constructed maze of similarity, the attack on his eyes now fully disorientating him as to which bathroom or where it was in the house. He only knew that if he left it and went back onto the landing, he wouldn't know the front from the rear of the house and being caught by Natalie and the acid while he still couldn't focus, was the one thing he had to avoid.

The enjoyment of his prowling footsteps, squeaking on the tiled floor in his hay day, seemed a long way off as he thought about those occasions now, while he wrestled with his confusion and his own attempts to escape. He felt terrorised as he struggled to listen for any sound of Natalie. Byron leant against the wall, his brain regurgitating those nightly walks. He saw her hiding, quivering with fright but tonight his own fear had surpassed hers in his reasoning. He had not wanted to do anything permanent to her as as child but Natalie was threatening to use acid to burn out his eyes and there would be no arbitration with her revenge driven threats.

Age and inactivity over years of physical slovenliness had erased any nimbleness or athleticism and trying to move stealthily around the bathroom, given his tiredness and injuries was beyond his flexibility. Each movement dragged out unwanted groaning effort from the back of his throat. His sounds were filled with desperation, fright, cramped muscle pain from crawling, grovelling around the floor on his hands and knees, trying to be illusive in his attempts to disappear from Natalie's senses.

His mind sought for refuge in his perception of his superiority but he couldn't regain control of his emotions. Squirming, straining he pushed himself out of the bathroom into the rear right hand bedroom. This time he opened the door easily, remembering it opened outwards from the bathroom. His left hand slapped against the wall, searching for the light switch. It felt like déjà vue as the pendant light flashed on, the blur of colours not telling him anything different from the previous bedroom. Nothing was different. He questioned himself. Had he gone back into the bedroom he just thought he left. His mind was spinning. The merging of the bed, the wardrobes, everything within the room had lost any distinction and the room from the shapes and tones within his blurred vision, looked like the one he had just crawled out of.

Father Byron's frustration fuelled his fear, he couldn't think straight and he needed to. He needed clarity, his head craved it. His mind went from the past to the present and back again. When his thoughts were of the past he lost the awareness of the present and what he was doing and that was dangerous, as he could give himself away. The sound of his own voice and the final ebbs of his crying reached his ears again, bringing him back to the bedroom. His lips quivered as he started mouthing his thoughts out to himself.

He crouched back down into the smallest bundle his bloated body could reduce to, a beaten reaction to his isolation and entrapment. He held himself, not that he was cold but for self comfort. Byron nestled himself between the dark chest of draws and the wardrobe, his head leaning against the firmness of the wood, its solidity providing a temporary feeling of safety. His eyes glanced furtively around and saw nothing clearly as he slumped exhausted to one side. He sat still for about a minute feeling it was a lot longer. His head made a rumbling noise which confused him until he realised he was unknowingly rolling it against the side of the wardrobe. He stopped and adjusted himself, clasping his arms around his folded up legs, holding his knees as close to his chest as his stomach would allow. Byron started rocking gently, his own movement unconsciously comforting.

Within this artificial solitude, his thoughts jumped back nearly sixty odd years to when he was five and he used to cocoon himself in the corner of garden shed, hiding behind the deck chairs propped against the back wall. His mother had a spontaneous temper, subsiding as quickly as it erupted and she rarely bothered to seek him out down the shed if she couldn't find him in the house to slap. That space behind the deck chairs became his hollow refuge until she calmed down. Between these two pieces of Natalie's furniture, Byron returned to his child like self and he continued to rock slowly, as he remembered himself as a little boy. A few new tears welled up in his eyes and his body shivered as the pictures of his childhood and his mother rolled through his mind.

His memories were interrupted as he heard Natalie's voice as she joined in at the start of Elvis' next song. He could hear the threat, the irony, her excitement with the lyrics.

"Well bless my soul, what's wrong with that? I never thought this would happen to me....I got stung....YEAH....I got stung... YEAH."

"Oh God, I can't believe this! This is not right. I would never have thought Natalie would have turned out like this. She's............she's so malicious.....she wasn't like this! What on earth would have made her like this? Dear God! She's......she's evil...yes...she's not malicious, she's evil. She's not going to listen to anything I say! How on earth can I get away from her?.........I need to get out.......I need to get out!"

The restart of this thinking process between the furniture, despite the pulsing, burning feeling still in his eyes caused his heart to accelerate again. Unwittingly, his attempt to gain calm and control, to think clearly, had made him more aware of his predicament and his heart rate responded.

He looked around the bedroom again, wishing for focused vision, his concentration diverting from his thoughts momentarily to his eyes in the hope that he would be seeing things around him more clearly. The furrows in his forehead hurt as his skin creased with him squinting to try and distinguish definite outlines and objects. The red bedspread on the bottom quarter of the bed, covering the white linen sheets, the light blue, flower patterned wallpaper, the bright yellow carpet appeared to his eyes as a conglomeration of mess, the tears bending the light refraction through his corneas like raindrops distorting the view through a pane of glass; obscuring the true form and substance of what he was trying to look at.

Byron rubbed his eyes and head furiously in another effort to clear his vision and relieve his pain. He willed his eyeballs to push forward out of their sockets, to focus and tell him where he was, what was around him. His eyes refused to cooperate.

His anguish boiled over. His anger transforming into hatred. Byron gritted his molars while his lips thinned in a distorted effort to spitting out his mouthed, silent thoughts.

"Dear God!........I need to get out of this bloody house. Where am I? ...,WHERE AM I? God forgive me, I need to kill this bloody bitch if I can't get out." Thoughts turned to adrenalin which forced his legs to push him back onto his feet and through the far door back onto the landing.

Natalie stood singing manically on the opposite side and at the far end of the landing to the front of the house and stared towards her stumbling, frantic target. She gyrated "Elvis style" knowing she would be just a blur, illuminated with the dappling and irregularity of light created by the Portuguese crystal, a dancing, highlighted spectre to his blood red eyes. She was loving every second of her rendition. Her face glared defiance that he dare interrupt.

Natalie stopped her unseen performance half way through the song and leant on the bannister looking at his bumbling, twisting, swirling attempts to find cohesion, to get some sense of where he was and where he was going to hide next. Although the single chandelier had brilliant illumination, the far end of the first floor would have benefited from the second chandelier being switched on, to light the rear half of the landing. Natalie herself, now had a puzzled look on her face as she watched his body, arms and legs fling around like a demented puppet. There was an unusual clarity about him and she enjoyed his erratic flailing.

Father Byron's left hand found the wooden bannister and it slid along the polished, oak surface, directing him across the rear width of the house away from Natalie's side of the landing, his right hand still squelching the tears out of alternative eye sockets. The landing had an illuminated haze at the far end away from him. There was the slightest hint of her body shape within the electric glow but at nearly sixty feet away, Natalie's body outline was a mere dark crack within the glints and patterns thrown by the crystals that livened up her end of the first floor.

All of it was lost on Father Byron. Nothing he could do would give a quick fix cure to his vision. He disappeared into the second doorway. His right hand felt along the wall, having missed Natalie's sticking bedroom door and he found himself in Natalie's tiled en suite. There was nothing he could recognise within the unlit bathroom. It felt cooler than the last bathroom and that instant change of temperature felt like someone had put a cold cooling flannel on the back of his neck. It gave Byron his first real moment of all over body relief in almost two days. He pressed his back against the tiled wall and its chill refreshed him through his shirt, icing the sweat that was dripping all over his body and that had soaked his clothing, more than the initial chill of wandering into her en suite. He breathed in the cooler air and it inflated his lungs. This unexpected relief invigorated his rejuvenation.

"Where ever you are, come in here and I will smash your skull. You won't beat me....you .....you ......girl." He said it with the derision that reduced a girl, a woman to an object, his target.

Natalie stood still at her end of the landing and even over that length of distance, she heard his careless, vicious words, spoken out aloud. "Oh really!" She thought to herself, her mindset viciously derisory. "Like I'm scared of you now........ooohhhoooohh." Her mouth turned into a wide, grimacing smile. Her eyes flashed in his direction, following the path his words had come from. She knew exactly where he was and she knew what she was going to do next, having heard his voice come from her en suite.

The fingertips of her left hand glided nonchalantly along the top of the bannister as she imitated an ice skater, her body rhythmic as she flowed within the words to Suspicious Minds which had started playing and now filled the landing, adding her own vocals.

"You're caught in a trap. You can't move on, because I hate you too much baby...... yeah."

Father Byron paused over the sink as he was just about to wash his face and eyes with cold water, knowingly defying Natalie's previous orders. His throat almost growled on hearing one of his favourite songs and one he used to sing to the children as Father Byron, getting them to do Elvis' performance moves.

He knew he used to sing it very quietly as he sought out Natalie's hiding places but only ever sung this song when he stalked her. She couldn't listen to these songs for years and had forced herself to do so when she reached her early twenties, knowing.......hoping, she would have the chance to use them for her own ends.

Byron's hands hovered in mid air, disturbed from his intention to bathe his eyes, the immanency of Natalie appearing next to him as he used to do to her, now putting pressure on him to decide if he should continue to wash his face or to move on, not to get caught and not to have her spraying acid in his face. His throated squeaked as he strained to make a decision. It was only a few bars of that song but his anxiety flared up like a firework rocket shooting into the sky and exploding, dragging his heart with it, creating a pain within his chest as its pumping accelerated even more. His head rapidly looked from side to side seeking guidance or instruction from the space that surrounded him. He had always used the start of that song when he found Natalie, to physiologically enforce on her that she would never get away and now he knew its meaning here.

He splashed the quickest swill of water into his eyes and automatically turned the tap off, wiping the water away from his face with his sleeve as he moved back to the same door leading out onto the landing, feeling his way along the wall with his left hand. Above the music he could hear the sharp "ting" of what he first thought was a symbol. He listened, trying to remember if he had heard that instrument in this song before. Byron hovered by the bathroom door listening to Natalie, wondering if he should go out onto the landing.

Natalie repeated her own words still singing along to Suspicious Minds as it moved towards the ending where Elvis would sing the same lines over and over again while he gyrated the song to a close.

"I've got the acid here, you can't walk out, because I hate you so much baby..I've got the acid here, you can't walk out, because I hate you so much baby....."

Natalie could see Elvis on stage and so could Father Byron but now with Natalie's alterations, it suddenly dawned on him, she must be striking a bottle of acid in her hands with something or other to make the high pitched tinging noise.

"Lord Jesus, please let her see sense. She's going to do it. Oh dear God help me here. Please help me when I need it."

His prayer was as rushed as his wash. The imminent urgency of his capture and his future burst from his forehead and face as his terror pumped fresh beads of sweat, amalgamating with the water droplets still on his face; the tension in his body making him feel rigid, the sinews in his arms and hands throbbing from gripping the door frame.

Natalie ambled along the landing, turning the front chandelier off as she walked passed the light switches opposite the stop of the stairs where they joined the first floor. Having heard the taps running from her en suite, she started to think that if he regained more clarity with his vision, he would struggle to see clearly if it remained as dark as possible.

The reduction in light and the return to gloom prompted him to move out of the en suite. Natalie heard him across the far end of the landing, his marionette like awkward, semi lurching, semi wobbling attempts to put one foot in front of the other, in an attempt to find his next hiding place.

She heard Byron almost flop through the bathroom door mid way along the other side of the landing, almost opposite her, just as if he had collapsed from having his puppet strings cut. Natalie had locked the far left hand bedroom door in which she had deprived him of sleep with his continuous exposure to the floodlights, so that he couldn't get back in and see the inside of the room.

His mind would be in a whirl of panic, as hers had been and Natalie knew it. He would be desperate to find a secret hidey whole that would be unknown to her, where he could hopefully curl up and sleep in safety. She imagined she could see his face peeking from behind a bath as he lay in as small a size as his body could become, his breathing so shallow that he would think to himself that he was about to suffocate, the air hardly getting into his lungs, creating a feeling of claustrophobia despite the space around him. She remembered those thoughts, those feelings.

Father Byron would be scared in a way he had never been scared, like she had been, scared every night, too frightened to go to sleep although she pretended to be, hoping that he would leave her alone that night. She hadn't wanted to run or hide but she didn't want him pawing his sweaty, fat old body over her, feeling his weight push down on her. She just wished by some miracle that God would leave his false disciple and come to her on those nights and answer her prayers and that when she ran away from him, down a corridor and into a room, she would find her mother, waiting to save her, ready to wrap her warm, loving arms around her and that her nightly hell would finally be over.

With every frightened step along those corridors, she wished that God would grant her wish and wondered why God didn't take care of children in the way Father Byron and the other priests preached during the safety of day. She would lie fixed, almost corpse like, listening to the breathing of the other children, to see if she could tell if each one of them had fallen asleep or they were waiting like her, listening for the sound of his footsteps.

Natalie would try to look at her friends from underneath virtually closed eyelids while trying to stay perfectly still. Her eyes would strain to move as she kept her head fixed on her pillow, to see from where she was lying if any of the other children had their eyes open, looking for The Bogeyman coming to the side of their bed. Now she was The Bogeyman but there would only be this one last night for revenge.

Her walk continued slowly along the opposite side of the landing, deliberately and menacingly emphasising the sound of her feet against the carpet with each short step to drag out her approach, each step or stomp in time with the beat of the music. Her eyes were transfixed towards the bathroom door he had tumbled in through. Byron would be trying to visualise her in the same way she learnt to; listening to the sound of her steps, his eyes shut with concentration, trying to establish her location. His ears would be straining to listen for each sound coming from her feet as she had listened to the sound of his shoes. As the smallest of sounds reached his ears, he would shut his eyes even tighter, to analyse if her footsteps were getting louder and closer to him or if the sound of them was getting quieter, in the same way she had listened to him walking along the corridors or circling the children's beds.

The landing carpet and the music, made Natalie use her feet differently to how he used to use his. Byron had placed each step slowly, heel first, moving his weight though the length of his foot, enjoying the sound and threat his shoes made with the floor. His walk past each bed slowly, hesitant and deliberate, knowing his movement was being listened to by every awake child. That had excited him and now Natalie was using the same tension by stomping and scuffing along the carpet, transposing her memory of the rubber soles of his shoes as they squeaked with each step to each of her own short, artificial paces.

Natalie felt she was walking within the confines of those tiled dormitories, listening to the faintest of resonance coming off the walls, like the last remnant of an echo coming back down a valley. Her mind saw the gloomy light and shadows cast and created by each of the strangely out of character, matching Art Deco dancing lady, table mounted night lights at either end of the dormitory. They had seemed to let his body form, disappear like a black ghost moving along the length of the room and each footstep had told her where he was walking. Natalie could hear each part of the tread of his shoes pressing against the floor and every time his heel lifted with each step, peeling the length of his foot from the floor, it would make mouse like, little squeaks as the rubber pulled and finally lost contact with the tile.

When the sounds stopped, the silence told Natalie where he was standing. She could sense him and her anticipation had made her flesh crawl. She felt dirty and she didn't know why. She knew then if she was going to be his victim again that night or if she could try to go to sleep and be left alone. On the nights when his footsteps stopped by her bed, the silence of his motionless, hovering body was louder than thunder.

Natalie's temples had pulsed with her concentration in listening for the slightest sound of his clothes moving against his body. Her ears heard the sound of the silence around her like the noise from listening to the hollowness and the sea from a large conch shell. She could hear his chest rise and fall. After so many months of his visits, she could tell what clothing he was wearing by the sound they made when he moved. The quietest nights were when he wore a black woollen jumper which muffled the sound of his shirt straining against his body underneath but every night when it was her turn to play this unwanted, darkened game of hide and seek, she could smell his sweat and breath as he leant forward over her, her eyes locked shut, willing for him not to be there. Those same smells were floating around her now, emanating like an invisible fog from the room he thought he was hiding in.

She knew he would be shaking, conscious of trying to stop his fear from freezing his brain from thinking clearly as she had tried to stop herself from shaking. It was only when she got a bit older, through practice and her will, that she managed to gain control of the fright that used to shake through her involuntarily. That was when his visits to her started to lessen but even then, he would start his perversion in the same way by singing an almost silent whisper of another Elvis song, his mouth millimetres away from her ear, the deluge of halitosis enveloping her head.

"A very old friend came by today." He wouldn't sing any more not to her, not to any other child but would whisper, in a hissed, strangled voice, just loud enough for the ear next to his lips to hear, "are you lonesome tonight, will you kiss me tonight." He would change the words to suit his perversion and drain out the innocence and love within the meaning of those lyrics. The children thought The Bogeyman had been told by Father Byron about the things they had done that day to warrant his visit and that HE was Father Byron's friend.

Natalie stopped walking and stood silent, still staring at the doorway he had disappeared through. Every memory of every night showed in her face. Her eyes were wide open, filled with fury, her thoughts, her focus on him swamped by disgust. Her anger, her pursuit, her anticipation forced her head to shake, its vibrations rippling down through her body, her skeleton and skin taught with the effort of trying to hold her rage back from breaking through like the mushroom of energy from an exploding atom bomb and her losing control of her calculated superiority.

Her mind relived and manipulated her memories. She stood, motionless apart from her contained quivering re enacting his ritual. He used to wait for one minute, counting the seconds in his head as he closed his eyes, listening to the sounds of their bare feet slapping on the tiles as they ran away to hide. Natalie always wanted to cry out for help but there was no one who could help her, the only person who could help her was the person she was running from.

Natalie looked at her hands as she crouched down to put the glass bottle onto the floor. Her fingers slipped and wound almost unconsciously around themselves at the recollection of wiping his saliva off her ear as she ran away, its stickiness transferring to the palm of her hand and fingers. She would try to rub it off her hands into her night dress. Her eyes now remained fixed on the wall, staring through it, picturing him on the other side as if it was glass. When she hid, she had been frightened to breathe because her breathing made a noise and he might hear it and that would help him to find her quicker. The sooner he found her the more time he would have with her.

Even over the music, Natalie could hear him and he was trying to do the same not to give his hiding place away. She would have lay still in her hiding place, trying to make sure every part of her would be hidden if he walked by, looking for her. Younger children only covered their eyes thinking that made them invisible. He would pretend he hadn't seen them to keep his game going for longer, to give them false hope that he couldn't find them. She had tried to stop herself from crying, frightened again that the sound would be heard in that torrid game. He loved it but then he would because there was nothing she could do to stop him, nothing anyone could do to stop him because no one else as far as Natalie was aware, knew about it, just her and him. There was only one thing good about the night. He never picked on two children in one night.

There was no rush in her mind to end her game. Her hearing acted like sonar, painting a picture not just of his movements but his emotions from the sounds he was making as he moved from the bathroom into the adjoining bedroom and the noises that came uncontrollably out of his body.

Even as a child, she felt she had worked out that he was a failure as a man. Her disgust and derision for him had not wained over the years. His only success was his age and his size by comparison to children. She had realised that Father Byron, Father Elvis and The Bogeyman were the same person, despite the mask and his amateurish attempt to change the sound of his voice. Natalie knew despite her own fear in those dormitory days that he bristled with excitement at his own nightly superiority, his own alter ego, lost within the theatricality of his character. Natalie remembered the feeling of those goose bumps rising along her arms and across the back of her neck as the fear took hold of her body, chilling her as if ice had run down her spine and those goose bumps rose now as she glared psychotically at the wall.

The decor of her matching bedrooms had succeeded in confusing him, his still blurred vision no help to his tired brain which again struggled to place his position in the house. The newly oiled hinges on all of the doors were no help to him either, as their smoothness of opening had robbed them of an individual character or location and now worked against him.

She remembered the doors in the care home, how she would pray that they didn't squeak when she opened or closed them to give her location away. He used them to increase the terror of his pursuit but deliberately moving the doors slowly and exaggerating the hinges threat of his approach. Now, she could still smell him, hear him, her senses superior to his, given his immediate lack of vision. His footsteps scuffed against the carpet, his tiredness making his legs heavy, the tiny cuts stinging as his trousers rubbed against his open skin. Each sound transmitted and conveyed his exhaustion.

Natalie stood back up slowly; her athletic, powerful legs raising her torso like purposeful hydraulic ramps. There was no effort, just focused intent. She relished the control she now felt from the knowledge and her experiences of being hunted. The lack of light gave the appearance of her materialising from the floor, having come from another dimension; hell. The sound of his anguish at being lost in another bedroom, somewhere in her house caused her to start laughing again, first with a giggle which soon changed as the humour of her dominance and his demise became completely infused with pent up revenge. Her giggle changed to a sound more like a witch's cackle as her thoughts and feelings became more evil and it slammed back through the doors and walls to Father Byron.

Her laughter stopped him from moving in anyway, making him listen, his body static not to create any noise that would drown out any sound coming from Natalie. Byron listened as Natalie's laughter grew louder, until it drowned out Elvis' singing. Natalie folded her arms around her body, holding herself as she laughed louder and louder until it was difficult for Byron to believe he was listening to a woman laughing. She sounded out of control, swept away with hysteria. Natalie grabbed the top of the banister, instantly stopping her laughter, her eyes again glaring at the wall to the bedroom. Her silence made Byron look around, his mind convinced she would somehow be standing next to him. His sigh, a welcome feeling of relief to know he was still alone in the bedroom.

The light in the room went out.

"I know what you are thinking," she thought to herself, as she quietly walked back upstairs after slipping silently down stairs to turn the electric back off.

"Maybe I won't hear you, or I will have taken a wrong turn. I'll be somewhere else and nowhere near you. That's what you are wishing but I'm here and I know where you are."

She could visualise him feeling around the bedroom, his mind racing and falling over itself as he questioned and considered each nook and cranny as a possible hiding place. The stress of making a decision, to make the right decision in those split second moments knowing she was close, would make him cry, even at his age. He would try to muffle his sobbing, not to give his position away to her and this would make him panic more. He would second question his hiding place.

"Was it safe? Would she find him here? Were parts of his body sticking out? Was there enough light to give his hiding position away?"

Natalie deliberately stamped her feet harder than before as she resumed her walk along her side of the landing, enjoying the feeling of the carpet compacting under her feet. The end of the bannister turned to guide her across the width of the house to his side of the floor. Her stamping had the desired affect. The sound of his fearful, agitated fumbling of the door handle in order to get out of that room and into the next, clattered and rasped above the sound of Presley's voice which was now starting to sing Are You Lonesome Tonight?

Byron swept the perspiration off his forehead in an effort to cool himself again. Natalie was right, not that he knew her thoughts. As he went into the bathroom, he had been trying to breathe as quietly as possible but the effort of trying to get away and keeping his breaths shallow as well, while still trying to cope with the pain in his eyes was putting pressure on his heart and chest. The knife like feeling that cut across his torso, made him think that he was having a heart attack. His arms gripped around his upper body as far as he could reach, willing his heart to last through this ordeal. His words came out angrily through thin, tight lips. "I am not going to die here, not for this bitch."

His viciousness towards Natalie disappeared like a passing thought as he careered mindlessly on into the bedroom. He paused and bent over with his arms outstretched, the bed giving him support, stopping him from collapsing down onto his knees, his will telling him to stay standing, telling his legs to be strong. The quivering of his knees, the flaccidity of his thighs, their lack of power, put the feeling into his throat that his heart was trying to rise up his trachea and out through his mouth. His head was dizzy, making him feel the room was moving. He started to feel faint, that his mind was about to turn off. There were so many sensations and emotions happening all at the same time, his brain felt like it was being crushed inside his skull and the only way to escape, was to shut down.

This bedroom offered no consolation, no respite. Its shaded similarity shrouded its location in the house. Byron was none the wiser within his panic to getting his bearings.

He held his chest, his lungs felt tight as if they had shrivelled together like cling film that had shrunk around a dish being reheated in a microwave. Father Byron tried to take slow, silent deep breaths not to give himself away to Natalie's hearing. A sharp, stitch pain caught him on both sides of his body as his lungs peeled themselves open as the air started to inflate them. The perspiration continued to run down his face, the effort of trying to control the sound and speed of his breathing competing against his bodily need to gasp in great mouthfuls of oxygen to stabilise and stop his natural reaction to pant from his exertions.

His body felt like it was superheating as a result of the friction between his need for air and his efforts to control his breathing, forcing the blood to his temples and forehead, causing a constricted pulsing from the strain for oxygen. The veins in his head had swollen and in the dry of this bedroom, his mind displayed the vision of him grasping his way to the surface of the swimming pool, when a friend had pulled him a long way under when they were kids and the panic and suffocating confinement he had felt as he fought his way to the surface. He could still see the glare of the light above the surface of the water, its brightness, his safety and air. His lungs were all but empty as he broke the surface and he always remembered the relief that swept through his body on taking that first, life saving gasp, the dispersion of strain from his chest which followed, the disappearance from his head of the pulsing, pounding stress that felt like his brain wanted to escape from his skull. That experience had put him off swimming for the rest of his life and now the sensation and memory were back.

Byron pursed his lips and sucked in as much air as quietly as he could. The airflow dried his lips. He ran his tongue over them and sucked again. The dagger like pains cut across his chest again as his lungs expanded. His eyes squinted and grimaced as a reaction. He let out an unexpected whinge and caught himself almost child like, putting his right hand across his mouth to stop the sound escaping and being heard.

Natalie heard his pained squawk. She knew all to well. Even with him out of sight she could see him. His eyes darting, trying to look in all directions at once, looking at where he was hiding and where she may come from, trying to work out if he was hidden enough.

She thought again about those clinical, characterless corridors, their uniformity, their stealth to their anonymity. Byron would not be thinking clearly. Throughout her pursuit, his panic would be urging him to hide and run at the same time, this conflict overwhelming, flustering his thoughts so that they tumbled and jumbled into and over themselves. Natalie continued to meander around the landing, scuffing her feet again to give away her approach, each sound from her feet she knew, would make him question if she was getting closer or moving further away. His hearing would be directed totally to her footsteps. It would be trying to work out if each step were louder or quieter than the last as the sound of each step reached his ears; indicating which way she was walking but his concentration would be hampered as his brain went back over the sounds of her last footsteps at it tried to work out if his ears had been accurate. Was she getting closer? Was her last footstep really louder than the one before?

She could sense his effort and conflict and she felt the excitement running up and down her body, it made her feel momentarily that she needed a wee. Her own voice gave out a mixture of eeks, squeaks and giggles as her own emotions squeezed passed her control.

Her giggles developed into a second round of deeper, fuller laugh which dismissed the rest of her self control. Her left hand rested on top of the bannister and the wood within it creaked as the vibration from her laughing radiated down her arm.

Father Byron held his breath and listened, trying again to place Natalie on the landing. His hearing straining to reach beyond the door of the bedroom.

Natalie held her breath to control her laughter as the CD went quiet in between tracks, so that when she tinkled the glass she was holding, the shrill "ting" would travel to where he stood. Byron was still leaning on the bed when the threatening, high pitched noise reach him. His fingers gripped the duvet.

Byron's eyes widened fearfully when he heard Natalie's voice. It was filled with hate. He could hear it in every word. It chilled him in a way that his efforts to cool himself by wiping the sweat off his face had failed.

"I'm going to watch your eyeballs melt when I drop this acid into them. I'm going to smell your blood as it boils. I'm going to watch the smoke come out of your eyes as the acid burns through to the back of your head." There was no hint of weakness in her voice.

His eyes darted around the room just as Natalie had experienced. Byron's desperation flooded back like the water swelling through a breached dam. He went to take a breath, realising he had been holding it as he had been listening for Natalie.

The first breath was unexpectedly shallow, despite his efforts, the air entering his mouth and nose making him gag as it reached the top of his throat as it passed by his uvular. He tried again to get his lungs full of oxygen but he couldn't breathe in any deeper the second time. Father Byron felt anxious but for a different reason. His breathing had become ineffective. He gasped but still the air refused to be drawn into his lungs and his gasps became frantic, quick, shallow breaths empty of affect. He breathed and breathed again, his chest fluttering rather than expanding. His mind fought to make his chest expand, to pull in every gram of air it could; it didn't. It did not respond to his thoughts. His body felt weightless, heady. The feel of being submerged, fighting to get to the surface, swept through him again.

His memories panicked his thoughts adding to his anxious-ness. He gasped frantically at the warm air surrounding him within the bedroom, its stillness resisting his attempts to draw it into his body. The bed puffed slightly as he pushed himself upright, his head leading his body in a swerving, er-ratic almost snake like movement, swaying and twisting in the absence of a snake charmer as he urgently tried to get life into his lungs. Father Byron realised he was hyper ven-tilating, in the same way he remembered children on occa-sions after his pursuit along those corridors. The smell of his own bad breath took him by surprise as it filled his nostrils when he cupped his hands over his mouth and nose to breathe in carbon monoxide from his own exhalation in an effort to stabilise his breathing. There was no immediate change. His panting continued, rapid ineffective meaningless respiration. Byron writhed around the bedroom, his hands still over his face, bumbling into the side of the bed and bouncing away and backing into the chest of draws, the sharp edge digging into his back.

His muffled whinge of pain reached Natalie, like a top note of harmonics above the sound of the lower tones of thuds she heard his body making as he bumped around the bedroom.

"Come out, come out wherever you are.......come and play with me." Natalie's voice taunted him with recollections but hers were overlaid with evil sarcasm.

Father Byron's face had turned bright red from the lack of air and his excursions. He rubbed his eyes praying, in another at-tempt to gain clearer vision. His hands moved from cupping his face to holding his head. Both temples pulsed, straining under his skin, pushing against the soft, fleshy part of both his thumbs. The edge of the door dug sharply into his right collar bone, jarring it with a deadening thud as it kicked into clav-icle. His left hand went automatically from his left temple to rub the new area of his body, now hurting from another assailant.

Natalie sang with an aggressive, schizophrenic menace, punctuating every syllable unnaturally as she started walking towards the bedroom door again.

"It's...now....or ne...ver, come...hold....me... tight. Kiss... me... my... dar....ling, be... mine to....night. To...morr....ow...will.... be.... too... late. It's...now.... or... ne....ver, my...love...won't wait."

Father Byron knew this was where he had to come out of hiding. His lips quivered uncontrollably. He felt again the need to wee, his bladder contracting, his fear now escalating as his memories of his past control, frightening him. He feared what Natalie was promising to do, what was to come based on what had happened years ago.

"I'm here, I'm sorry, I'm sorry, I'm here. Please Natalie I'm sorry, I'm sorry, please, please."

His whole being sounded diluted, so vulnerable, scared, defeated. He caught his sub conscious thinking how child like he sounded as he stumbled back into the adjoining bathroom and out through the door onto the landing, his urgency now causing his entire body to shake with fear. His eyes squinted and strained to find Natalie on the landing as he blundered in a swirl of disorientation and turmoil; partly with the desperate thought of trying to overcome her with his size and partly with the feeling that nothing he could do would save him from what she was going to do. Father Byron slumped to his knees and felt he was going to collapse inward on himself, the remaining strength from his muscles and skeleton disappearing as his emotions swept aside any last remaining physical strength, leaving him a shaking mass of bewildered, beaten, squirming excuse for his previous deceitful, bully like persona. He held out his hands as if to plead, to pray to Natalie for some mercy.

Natalie stood motionless, like a carved ethereal demon, staring down on Byron, as she watched him regress to an isolated, frightened child, pleading to her for forgiveness, for mercy, for her to show him some compassion. She knew he had collapsed inside, tired from the pursuit and his efforts in trying to hide, from his attempts to double guess where she was in relation to where he was and his safety. Natalie looked at him as his outstretched arms started to slump as the feeling of helplessness and despair crushed his final feelings of trying to get away or of getting any sympathy or humanity from her. Natalie's eyes blazed her despise, knowing he was still unable to focus on her.

She tinkled the glass again. Her voice oozed evil "And now for the acid and those lovely eyes of yours."

28) HELPER

The cold edge of the steel handcuffs clamping around his wrists made him shiver from their unexpected chill. The ratcheting of their closing came and left his ears before his mind caught up the the fact that his weakened, still out-stretched aching arms had been restrained yet again.

Father Byron remained kneeling with his lower legs lying underneath him along the floor, his body bent forward over his thighs, his stomach acting like a large exercise ball stopping him from slouching fully forward.

"You seem to have everything under control." Jane said casually to Natalie.

Byron's face looked around, confused at the new voice joining in with his purgatory. His expression was cast with the bemused look of a Victorian doll, his eyes glazed and lifeless, staring blankly at the ceiling, the sound of Jane's voice surrounding him rather than he being able to distinguish the direction it was coming from.

Jane yanked viciously on the chain that she had looped around the connection between the two cuffs making them jerk and dig viciously into the skin around his wrists, the sensation reaching through his flesh and bruising the bones inside.

His voice whimpered. "Oh God no! Please.....not more. Who.....who are you?"

Jane's voice was calm, almost comforting but there was the same hint of threat "Someone you've met. Do you remember?.....my voice?.....you will........I remember you....you're someone I've never forgotten."

Jane made his mind jump as he tried to work out if he had heard her voice before. His memory careered through years of unchronicled encounters, searching for an audible match. In fleeting seconds he had tried to sift through a lifetime of voices.

Jane watched his blood shot eyes darting around in their sockets as they reacted with his brain in its attempts at recollection.

"Oh I see, you're trying to remember aren't you!" Jane's tone didn't change. It continued to unnerve him. Byron felt the hairs on the back of his neck prickle. Jane watched his body shiver involuntarily.

Father Byron's concentration on Jane's voice was stifled as the chloroform cloth clamped over his face. He tried to grab at Natalie's hands as they folded around his face from behind but she forced her right knee between his shoulder blades and pulled hard against his face. Jane watched his reaction and coolly tugged on the chain, pulling his hands sharply away from Natalie's hands. The force pulled his arms forwards, jarring them in his shoulder sockets. He whelped with the sharp, knife like burning sensation that cut through his tendons in his shoulder joint. His head pulled backwards as his body was pulled forward by his arms and Natalie's hands stayed held onto his face. His neck cricked from the opposing forces the two women were exerting on him.

"Aaacchhhh". His reaction was muffled behind the cloth. Father Byron tried to struggle to free his mouth and nose, to take in air instead of the mind numbing chemical soaked into the cloth.

Natalie held onto his face, forcing the fabric almost into his mouth and nostrils with the effort she was exerting. Byron started jerking as the suffocating affect from the lack of oxygen made his lungs snatch, forcing him to breathe in the coma inducing vapour. The swimming pool swamped his thoughts, the chloroform mimicking the sensation of being under water and him fighting his way to the surface. He opened his eyes, willing to see the light above the surface. His final gasped, frantic breath took him into total darkness. As he slumped into unconsciousness, he heard the tingling of a glass bottle being struck.

29) MOMENT

Byron's mind woke up. His eyes followed. They opened. There was no difference to them being shut. Everything was still black. He looked to find the smallest traces of light, to give him some indication of where he was and what was around him. There was nothing. As he became more alert and focused, he tried to move his arms. His wrists felt bruised as he sensed the restraints pulling against his skin. His legs twitched at the knee but nothing else. He concentrated hard, trying to clear his head. The smell of chloroform was still there, inside his nose. His stomach churned as he thought and remembered what had just happened. He tried to move his right leg and felt the strap dig into the ankle just above his right foot. He knew he was tied down. His body relaxed and he subsided into unconsciousness again.

30) DEFINITION

He heard Natalie's voice. It started in the distance to his hearing, like a muffled rumble of thunder, the hint of its growing strength and power playing with his ear drums, bringing him back to consciousness as it grew in volume. Her words started forming as she repeated them over and over, taunting him to open his eyes.

"Come on Elvis, come on Elvis, come on Elvis." She started to sing. "It's now or never......it's now or never......it's now or never.....it's now or never."

Natalie started to impersonate Elvis' voice and moves as she sang, much to Jane's amusement.

"It's now or never, it's now or never, come hold me tight. Kill me my darling, that's my delight."

The two women laughed at Natalie's connotations, like cauldron stirring witches as they circled Byron.

Father Byron slowly and covertly opened his eyes, fearful at what he might find around him. His senses scanned his body for sensations. He could breathe freely but he felt his head was restrained as he surreptitiously tried to turn it to one side. His fingers flexed but all movement was stopped at his wrists. His concentration moved down his legs. He felt his thigh muscles contract with his intention to lift them but there was nothing apart from the sense of his lower back pushing against something solid.

He closed his eyes as if to hide while he started to work out where and how he was. The firmness against the small of his back was unforgiving. It felt like wood. He flexed his legs again and he heard two different creaking sounds, almost in harmony, as his legs looked for space. Byron relaxed, now trying to work out these sounds. The one definitely sounded like wood. He flexed again and the same two sounds repeated themselves. The one sound coincided with his back pressing downwards as his legs attempted to move. His mind concluded he was lying on wood. The other sound? Byron pulled on his arms. Was that the same as the second sound he heard with his legs. He tried to move his legs again, his hearing focused on dissecting this second sound. He pulled on his forearms, there was no flexibility but the sound was the same. He felt the edges of his restraints cutting into his wrists as they groaned. His tried to lift his knees away and the matching sound repeated itself, this time with the lower bindings making their edges known to his flesh.

His eyes strained to confirm these sensations but their direction was restricted. He couldn't move his head. Most of the view he could see when looking down was the shape of his own cheeks. He was tied down with leather restraints, he was sure of it. Byron felt his heart and anticipation sink. The feeling of nausea swept over him as he accepted his situation.

Natalie stared down at his face, watching his eyeballs move his closed eyelids, giving away his consciousness. She bent down and deliberately forced some saliva through her lips as her voice gritted out a murderously infused final "it's now or never." She watched it drip and track around his left ear, her recollections of the stickiness on her own ears regurgitating and infusing themselves with the flow of her own spit now on his head. Her body quivered as the memorised revulsion transmitted through her nerves despite being in total control now.

Byron's eyes moved to his left as if trying to look at his ear, as the warm wet sensation he could feel, almost enveloped it.

The saliva tickled slightly as it found its way into his ear canal, oozing past his unkept ear hair.

His lips felt like they were being crushed, shocking him to open his eyes and to look straight in front of him. They parted as Jane pressed the clubbing end of her old police truncheon against his teeth, making him feel that they were going break out of his gums at their roots. Byron opened his mouth instinctively and Jane pushed the ebony weapon into his mouth.

"Uuugggghh". His tongue uncontrollably touched the truncheon and breathing instantly became difficult. His head started to jerk as he tried to pull it away, to lessen the suffocating, gagging affect it created. Byron's reactions were flooded with those same feelings of being under water and the air he needed to live was in another world above the surface. His eyes stared forward, open as wide as his eyelids would allow. Jane laughed as she locked down, watching his expression change from sedation, where all his muscles had slumped and relaxed, to one of rigid fear with every facial muscle straining in their effort to accommodate her truncheon and to breathe. She could see his jaw and top lip flex. His teeth bit against the ebony. It was unforgiving. They couldn't detect the slightest hint of leeway. It felt like he was biting on solid rock. His tongue had become independent as it darted around his mouth, playing against and around the polished wood shaft. His face had turned crimson as the trauma of long ago was recreated for a second time, that struggle of getting to light and oxygen. The sound of his nose sucking in air was strong, long and deep, like the noise of a vacuum cleaner hoovering in another room. He could hear his own breathing as if it was somewhere else and someone else's. His fists clenched as he attempted to regulate his breathing.

Jane followed the beads of perspiration oozing out of his face. His head glistened with the sheen that reminded her of pig"s head steaming on a silver salver, braised with the juices that should make a good gravy. Byron's aroma wafted into her nostrils more with the stench of stale sweat and rotten meat than a rich red wine jus, which her mind conjured up after the image of a banqueting hog had formed in her imagination. She leant back slightly and eased the truncheon away from the back of his throat, until just the end remained inside his lips and teeth. His gagging subsided as the tip moved away from his uvula. Jane watched the rigidity of his body ebb through his limbs and torso as the relief from the sensation of claustrophobia lessened. His breathing turned into short, sharp, deep breaths, eager to get as much air into his body as he could. He felt hot. The urge to wipe his face to cool himself swept across him but he couldn't. His restraints induced another wave of agitation as they held his hands down against his sides. As he tried to fill his lungs, he willed the air to cool him, hoping the speed of his inhalation would draw it over his features, like a damp cloud rising and spreading over the surface of a mountain. His head pulled against whatever was holding it firm. Jane watched his eyes shoot in different directions, not holding any direction for more than a second. She enjoyed his visual display of panic. His mind re lived the sensation of almost drowning and his body started to jerk and shake, the buckles of the belts they had used made the faintest of metallic clinks, virtually lost within the sounds of his groans and the straining of the leather.

Natalie's hearing picked up the sound of the buckles and she put her hands systematically on each restraint to reassure herself that they were secure, as she circled the single size old Victorian iron bed frame he was on.

The ageing greening discolouration of the iron caught her attention now that she found herself looking at it within the bright lights of the second floor attic room they had dragged him into. His dead body weight had been a struggle but their adrenalin had aided them like a third person as they moved him.

Jane pushed back down on the truncheon, leaning her body weight onto the end she was holding so that it eventually nestled against her sternum.

The veins in his arms and legs pumped blue as they swelled up under his skin. The truncheon felt like it was boring its way through the back of his throat as Jane's weight pressed down thorough it. His eyes fought against the pain the top of his spine was feeling as the vertebrae in his neck almost popped from the pressure. His whole body shook as the gagging feeling of the truncheon was surpassed by the feeling that it would snap the bones that connected his head to his spine. Jane became enveloped in the tears she watched erupt from his still reddened eyes as they started rolling down his face. The satisfaction from seeing his cheek puff was suddenly tempered with the imagined recollections of the children he took advantage of, struggling in the same way. She looked down on his snorting, wide eyed face and her disgust and anger ignited like the combination of magnesium and water she remembered from her school science lessons.

Jane wanted to gauge his eyes out with her thumbs. She thought back over the number of visits she had made as a police officer to the orphanage. The face of Father Byron, his white, holy dog collar standing in front of her; his smug, pious, devout face irritating her intelligence as he empathised with her about the "fantasised stories these naughty little devils dream up."

There weren't hundreds of visits but for Jane there had been a few more than the odd one or two over the years, just a few too many for her to think there was some horrid truth hidden behind his plausible placations. She hadn't liked him on their first meeting but as the accompanying female police officer, her older male officer, obviously uninterested in investigating children's tales, had lead the discussions.

Jane had watched Father Byron in silence as her male colleague approached his questioning at the orphanage, more interested at that first interview with reminiscing about the local football team. Father Byron had hardly glanced a look at the twenty or so old, blond haired police woman, who stood silent to one side.

Maybe because Jane was a woman but Byron seemed to her, to dismiss her presence. She looked at his eyes as he talked to the indifferent male office. Every dip in his eye contact, the furtive glance away from the male officer as they talked and he asked weak, inept questions, very quickly convinced Jane he was hiding something.

The young ten year old boy who had somehow, walked into the town police station and asked if he could go to sleep in a cell, just so he could get a nights sleep, was brought out to where they were talking in the garden of the orphanage.

The magnolia tree had formed a lasting image in Jane's mind, its white orchid like blossom, illuminated from the sun shining on the garden and from behind the tree. The flowers almost seemed to glow with a yellow halo and she remembered looking between him and the tree, she captured by its beauty and his ugly superciliousness.

The large oval of grass in the middle of the squared U shaped building that surrounded it on three sides, had a serenity of innocence emanating from it. Jane remembered it now as if she were still standing in it, listening to Father Byron's monotone, voice infused with religious sincerity. She'd watched the boys playing football look over at Simon Goldman, the curly blond boy that had asked in the police station if it was ok for The Bogeyman to put his hand into his pyjamas because he could never get to sleep.

Some forty odd years later, Jane looked down on his aged, puffed out face and she could still see where the youthful taught features of that slim, young Catholic Priest had been. They were close to the same age and she remembered wondering to herself during that first meeting, why a young man would lock himself away from the open world, behind the restrictions a Catholic Minister faced by taking those vows of chastity and poverty and whatever else those vows covered. Jane shook her head slightly to herself while she looked scathingly at Byron, as the realisation that had dawned on her innocence all those year ago jumped to mind. He hadn't locked himself away. He had locked himself into the world where he wanted to be.

His rotund belly now added a new dimension to his legacy. Jane had been back to follow up on other "children's complaints" but each time she went to the home, whether alone or with another officer, the child would be confused or unsure as to what had happened or what they had said, or had they dreamt it. Jane had followed each case privately but in her time on the force, had not come across Natalie at the home. It was a few years before retirement and the visits of Natalie and her mother to the house next door to hers, where they had met.

Jane looked at Natalie checking the adapted trouser belts now binding him to the frame of this old bed. They had used leather belts as they could pull them tighter around his wrists and legs and they would be far quieter than if they had used handcuffs, which would have clanked and jarred against the metal of the bed. Natalie became aware of Jane's gaze and smiled back, looking directly into Jane's eyes as she did.

Jane's expression changed from one of motherly support to questioning surprise. Since coming back into the house and man handling Byron's body with Natalie into this second floor attic room, she had not noticed any change in her until now. Natalie was not just feeling the buckles, she was bending over and looking at them as she checked their tension.

Jane hesitated, her mouth about to form the words but her brain questioning the plausibility of what she was thinking.

"Natalie.........can you......can you... see those belts? Can you see me?.....I mean clearly.........can you see my face?"

Natalie stopped her inspection and looked straight back at her, her smile unchanging until the truth of Jane's question hit home.

.............."My God, oh my God. I can almost see your face clearly. Jane! I can almost see your face."

Her hands left the buckles and cupped around her own mouth as if trying to guard and control what was coming out between her lips. Her hands and arms suddenly looked bewildered as to where they should be and how they should behave. They left her face after a second or so and stopped almost as quickly, as they shot out towards Jane, retracting as quickly, confused as to what they should do. Her fingers splayed open with shock and excitement and then turned into lose clenched fists as her nerves and muscles reacted to her eyes looking at Jane, looking at the walls around her, the wooden floor boards......Father Byron. Her fingers opened wide again and grabbed at the top of her own head, her hair interweaving instantly with them.

Jane watched Natalie's head quiver, the shaking transmitting down through her shoulders and along her arms. Her pyjama top shook like a curtain catching the wind through an open window where it hung and draped off the ends of her breasts.

"Natalie, darling.....Natalie." Jane's voice absorbed and reflected Natalie's excitement. She forgot all about Byron. She had become totally focused on Natalie.

Natalie clasped her hands back over her mouth, her eyes wide with anxiety, frightened that her eyes would suddenly go black.

"Jane I can almost see you without any blurriness. I can see your blond hair. I can see you are smiling from the shape of your lips and face. In can almost see all of your face in every detail."

Jane moved quickly towards Natalie, her arms outstretched to hug her and to hold in her excitement. She needed to contain the rising shock. As a police officer she had seen people who had witnessed an accident or been involved in one so she knew what she needed to do to try and calm Natalie, only the uniform had stopped her from giving victims a hug and the shock had often taken hold.

Her arms folded around Natalie, the heat of her body emanating through her night clothes, warming Jane's body. Jane squeezed her, her voice had an urgency in it despite Jane keeping her voice deliberately low and soft.

"Ok, ok, my darling.......look at me......look at me. Can you really see me? Natalie look at my eyes......tell me what colour are they?"

Jane wiped the tears that had started to run down Natalie's cheeks with her two thumbs as she held her face in her hands, their noses almost touching.

"They are blue. Jane they're blue. I can see they're blue. Oh God, thank you thank you."

Jane wanted to get her away and sit her down. "Come on, I need a cup of tea. He'll still be here when we get back." Jane kept one hand and arm touching and around Natalie's body as best she could while she bent down and pulled out an old cotton blouse from a bag of old clothes. She screwed the fabric up with her free right hand and rammed as much as she could into his mouth.

Byron cheeks puffed out as he breathed in deeply through his nose, a reaction to the surprise of having his mouth suddenly filled again, robbing him of a second air track. He felt his claustrophobia rise as they left the room, Jane flipping the remaining fabric of the blouse which she could not get in his mouth, over his face and eyes.

"Slowly!" Jane whispered as they walked down the wooden stairs.

Father Byron listened to their heavy footsteps as they walked down the stairs. That was all he could do.

31) EQUILIBRIUM

Jane guided Natalie to the kitchen stools, not that she needed that sort of help. She had watched her looking around her house as they walked down the stairs from the attic to the kitchen. Natalie's face beamed with approval as she looked at her own home for the first time, where everything had distinction.

Jane smiled and hugged her repeatedly as she casually tried to reduce Natalie's gushing excitement, her voice frenzied with elation at her eyesight seeing her furnishings, the decoration, just seeing.

"Oh my gosh, that's lovely, look at the carpet, I love the way it feels on my feet, between my toes, the bannister, the wood always feels cool. Look that's a nice painting, where did you get that Jane. I haven't seen the sea for years we must go but that looks great doesn't it? You could almost think you could put your hands in the water. Look at the shine on the hall floor. I can't believe it. I can't believe it. I can see this and this and this, that I can see Jane I can see I can really see I can't believe it, I can't believe it."

"Sit down Natalie, oh my God I can't believe it either, it's incredible."

Natalie and Jane eventually enjoyed that cup of tea. Making it had almost been a disaster with each of them falling over and bumping into each other, as they tried to do it for one another.

Their senses, reactions and emotions were on edge. Both women felt like streaking cheetahs hurtling across the savannah after an gazelle. Their arms, legs and bodies rippled energy, sending caustic excitement to their brains. They mutually and individually enveloped the kitchen with their movement in making the tea, darting cat like between the fridge, tap, cupboards, cups as Father Byron's capture, restraint and Natalie's miracle dominated this moment.

They said nothing strangely once the tea had been poured, until at least half a cup of the large tea mugs Jane had chosen had been drunk. Both their minds took those couple of minutes to think of what was happening. They exchanged glances as if to read each other's thoughts.

As the half cup level approached, each of them sipping in unison, the tea and their static posture started to easy off the tension inside them.

Their eyes met and they both sensed their own and each other's slowing metabolisms as the tea relaxed them. They both leaned onto their elbows, the granite cooling their skins through their clothing.

Jane watched as Natalie looked around at her kitchen, her eyes fluctuated with varying degrees of openness as she started to appreciate its appearance for the first time. Her left hand glided across the granite as she watched the black speckled stone appear as a stark contrast from behind her hand.

Jane smiled as Natalie moved the cup away from her lips. "I like the look of this work surface. I've always liked how it feels....really hard and cool but it looks alive. I love the way it sparkles and the colours jump out at you when you stare at them."

"I thought you would like it overall." Jane continued to smile as she thought back to when she helped Natalie choose a new kitchen, one which was tactile for Natalie's sense of touch, the real wooden doors with heavily routed design, warmer to the touch than the work surfaces; the long protruding handles which allowed Natalie a larger target to aim for when she wanted to grip onto them to open up the cupboard doors.

Jane felt the pleasure of her own satisfaction as she watched Natalie enjoy the appearance of her kitchen for the first time. She had been very involved with the kitchen designer, to get things well laid out so that it would be easy for Natalie to use.

They both finished the last drop of tea at the same time and cupped the mugs in their hands as they looked at each other in silence.

After about two minutes Jane said. "Do you think we should ring the others now?"

32) VICTIMS

Within fifty minutes, seven cars had parked on Natalie's crescent shaped drive and the eleven grown up children who had lived at the children's care home with, before or after Natalie, which Jane had managed to keep track of, all now congregated in Natalie's kitchen.

The atmosphere had fluctuated in intensity since the first childhood victim, Michael arrived within ten minutes of Jane's phone call, parking his dark blue 911 Porche as close to the exit of the drive, without protruding onto the pavement.

Michael was two years older than Natalie and had been in the care home for two years before Natalie arrived. He had been a very pretty little boy, bright blue eyes, smiley squared face and long straight blond hair. Father Byron had nick named him Thor when he pursued him around those same corridors.

He had been very lucky to be fostered by Ben and Kate Thomas for four years, two very outgoing people who had seen how introverted and shy he appeared when they first saw him and had decided there and then he was a little boy they could really help.

Michael had become a dentist and although he had never fully regained that childhood happiness, the horror of those nightly visits had been tamed, controlled and channelled into a very focused and intense young man, who for the most part was able to cope and deal with people from behind the security of a surgical mask. Outside of the surgery, he was still a bit of a loner with a few close friends he had made from dental college, Natalie and James.

His usual reserved disposition was bubbling over with infused, agitated aggression as he walked into Natalie's home, giving Jane a hug on the way in, when she opened the front door.

"Where have you got that God riddled slug?" His eyes looked victorious, wide with anticipation, his pupils almost looked luminous as the excitement pumped through his body.

Once in the kitchen with Natalie, it was seconds before he realised she could see him.

"Oh my God Natalie, you can see me can't you. Oh God........they said this might happen......I can't believe it........oh my God.....I'm so please for you. God!.....it's fantastic." Michael's hug transmitted every essence of his humanity to his long time friend and her regaining her sight.

He held her face firmly and lovingly in his hands as he planted a long, deep kiss on her forehead. Michael hugged her again and they were still stood in their embrace when Evelyn walked into the kitchen.

"Jane told me it was alright to come in. I'm Evelyn." She held out her hand but both Natalie and Michael altered how they were standing and sucked her into their hug.

"I'm Michael, do you remember me Evelyn? This is Natalie, I think ....I think you had left by the time Natalie came to the home."

Evelyn pulled her very round, reddened face away from the small group hug and looked at both of them. "I'd know you anywhere Michael. It's been such a long time. I never thought we would ever meet again, let alone we would ever get together like this. Has Jane told you anything?"

"Only that we've got Elvis......that's all she said along with Natalie's address.....that was enough!"

Evelyn turned and smiled at Natalie." I'm Evelyn please to meet you Natalie." She cupped the back of Natalie's neck and uninhibitedly pushed her own forehead against Natalie's as a sign of instant understanding and bonding, their pasts similar, an acknowledgement to their childhood history.

"Please to meet you Evelyn," responded Natalie as she put her right hand onto Evelyn's left shoulder. Natalie took in her reddened complexion, her black close cut, neck length hair; her eyes still sad twenty years later behind round black rimmed glasses, a sign to Natalie that her past had not left her. Her clothes were a drab grey shift dress that hung devoid of style and shape from her shoulders and lower than her knees, covering her undulating and disregarded body underneath.

"When can I gauge that perverts eyes out?" Evelyn's question stopped the animation of their hug as they both looked in reaction to the venom that came with her question.

"I don't think it's going to be as quick as that. There are quite a few of us and I'm sure lovely, everyone of us will want to do the same, if not worse. We've all waited a long time so we have to share everything out so we can all enjoy every bit of it."

Natalie patted Evelyn's shoulder as she broke the circle, smiling at them both while she walked towards the hall door and to Jane, who was now greeting Melony and Francis, both women who had been children at the home for almost the identical length of time as Natalie.

They had managed to keep in touch over the years, all three of them living within fifteen miles of each other after leaving the home and growing into adults.

Neither Melony or Francis first noticed any change in Natalie as they walked towards her from Melony's red Fiesta, which they parked side on to Michael's Porche. They held their arms outstretched towards Natalie and Jane and beaconed with their fingers for them to come and greet them. Jane put her hand on Natalie's right shoulder as she walked towards the on coming women. They still had not appreciated any change about Natalie as they hugged in a circle in front of the lounge bay windows.

All four of them still remained in a touching, holding, cuddling mix of bodies as they walked down the hallway into the kitchen. Their group split and rejoined, enlarged by Evelyn and Michael who they swept into the circle with their outstretched arms and greetings. Only Evelyn was the unknown face but within a few minutes, everyone's name was known or remembered.

The introductions and the reunions swelled and ebbed with excitement and vigour as the number of grown up victims came into Natalie's kitchen. Throughout the general tea and coffee making and the conversations of "how are you....where have you been?.....what have you been doing?....it's been such along time since I've seen you"; there was an underlying tension and electricity of anticipation at the immanency of seeing their mutually despised tormentor.

When Jane and Natalie finally came into the kitchen after the last person had arrived, they stood looking at the reunited children. They leant against the larder style fridge, smiling at the expectant group.

Their eyes looked slowly around at each person, both their minds individually thinking the same thoughts in unison, taking in how they looked now and comparing their memories of how they looked as children.

Francis had always been a pretty little, petite girl, long blond wavy hair, blue eyes, big smiley cheeks and she still looked the same twenty years on, only taller but still only five foot one. Francis had not had to endure Father Byron very often as his attention had been more focused on Natalie.

Melony, the friend she had come with was an Amazon by comparison, again long blond hair, not quite as wavy but with a swirl and life in it. She had always been tall as a child, nearly as tall as Byron had been despite their age difference but now at six foot one, no longer gangly and someone who had come to terms with her abuse and her size; was now very comfortable at being the person she had become. Melony had taken up netball and hockey as a young woman and still went to the gym three times a weak, transforming herself into an powerful, athletic woman with a very focused determination. She was never going to be used again, by anyone.

Evelyn stood out against her as they looked around, her grey dress made to look even more drab and shapeless as she stood next to Melony, her shapely figure in blue jeans and a red, long sleeved light weight jumper. It was obvious to them both, that Evelyn was still traumatised.

Harry and Nigel and been shy little boys, five years younger than Natalie and lived in the home at the same time as each other and Natalie. That shyness and insecurity had stayed with them for the rest of their lives and they recognised it in each other and it had perversely formed the basis of their friendship. They were there for each other.

Harry had become an accounting clerk for the council and just blended into the background of wherever he was. At five foot eight, he was not an ugly man by far but had never regained any confidence in himself to even make the best of how he looked. His black curly hair would benefit from being washed more than once a week as would his face and beard from only shaving twice a week, which resulted in him always looking scruffy and in need of sandblasting.

Nigel had become a painter and decorator, an occupation which meant he could work on his own, undisturbed or bothered by other people apart from when he first went to give a quote. He wore his light brown hair very close shaven so that he did not have to fuss with it but it emphasised the roundness of his face, making his head seem rounder and larger on his narrow shoulders than it really was. Although he had grown to only five foot nine, his slight, underdeveloped build made him look taller to the point of being lanky.

Unusual Natalie and Jane thought, they were both wearing virtually identical clothing, black jeans, blue shirts and brown shoes. Only Jane knew, given her long time contact with them both that they were not gay, nor did they live together but their dressing similarity happened quite often.

Michael stood midway between James on one side and Mary on his left, all of them leaning against the long work surface that faced the opposite side of the kitchen where the kitchen sink was located with the kettle to its right.

James had been brought into the care home a year after Michael, who had tried to look after him as he was six years younger and had only been four when he first arrived. James had been the youngest of Father Byron's victims and much as he could, Michael's big brotherly concern had tried to shield James from his attention and had tried to console and rejuvenate him when he had received it.

Although younger than the rest, James didn't look particularly young. For a twenty five year old man, he looked more like thirty to thirty five, still slim and lean as he had been as a child but his face showed the pain he had endured. He was still studying to become a surgeon as he had been influenced by Michael's choice in becoming a dentist but once he started to think about "a medical career", felt that working on and knowing about the whole of the human body would be more interesting and rewarding in the long run. His mental disturbance had told him that knowing how the body worked, what went where, what connected to what, what this bit working with that bit would do, would in some way give him the control he needed over himself.

Michael had tactfully tried to say to his prodigy that he had to also take in the mental connections as well as the physical bodily connections but James had not appreciated Michael subtlety and Michael had not wanted to hammer the point home. He did not want to put James down or back anymore than Byron had already done in this gentle boy's life.

Natalie's eyes hovered over his face, studying the lines around his eyes and his forehead not covered by his dark brown hair which was brushed forward, his own thoughts to make himself as discreet as possible by covering his face. She felt sorry for his prematurely aged face, his early jowl cheeks rather than the tight, taught cheek bones that his age should boast. His dark brown eyes lacked any real life spark but conveyed a sadness and emptiness from within. James' clothes were as sad as his eyes, brown trousers and shoes, brown shirt and brown V necked sweater.

Mary and Steph were heavily engrossed in their personal catching up as both their eyes flicked around, looking at the others in the kitchen. They had gone to the home within days of each other, both seven years old and black haired. Father Byron had mistakenly thought they were sisters, their similarity was such; same height at the time, four foot but now both five nine, same fair skin colouring, brown eyes. They had cut their long childhood hair to shoulder length. Mary was wearing a green woollen, long sleeved, high neck dress. It wasn't flattering to her figure but neither did it detract as did Evelyn's. It was a dress that allowed a person to be presentable and unnoticed.

Steph's black tight cotton jeans and black sweater were a bit more figure hugging but very understated for a mid to late twenty year old single woman who could have worn something which made people take notice of her.

Natalie watched their expressions change as they made reference to Father Byron in their one to one discussion. She could see the disgust that emanated from their eyes and faces as she heard them say that they couldn't wait to be standing above him, watching him helpless and unable to get away in the same way as he had made them feel when he pressed down his weight on their arms and chest. Steph's voice suddenly stood out from the ensemble as everyone unexpectedly stopped talking at the same time. "I still feel claustrophobic when ever I think of that fat bastard pushing down on me, that I can't move. I feel like that now when I'm talking to you, like I can't get my breath."

Natalie watched as Steph's face coloured up red from her recollection and the still very real lasting affect of those memories, as her voice and breathing changed to a higher pitched, constrained almost gasping, strangled sound as she finished her sentence to Mary. She suddenly looked positively flustered as she tried to calm her reaction. Mary hugged her, knowing exactly what she was going through and her embrace had an immediate soothing affect on her. Michael also walked over to her and put his arm around Steph's shoulders.

There was a thunderous silence after Steph finished speaking, everyone instantly transported back to those corridors and dormitories, their own memories rekindled. The looks between themselves conveyed more sympathy and empathy than anger as each of them felt for Steph as well as their awareness of their own traumas.

Jackie was the first to speak and break the silence. "I don't know how you did what you have done Natalie but I am sure we are all really grateful to you and Jane to be fair, for getting us here. I never thought I would ever get the chance to get my own back on that shit. What can we do to him? Have you got any plans or ideas or do we take it in turns to cut him into little bits? I don't know about the rest of you but I want to cut his bloody cock off with kitchen scissors and stuff it down his throat and make him eat it."

Julie, Jackie's identical red haired twin, clenched her right fist in agreement. "Yeah, that fat perverted bastard. I want to cut every bloody finger off one by one so that he will never ever be able to hold his own dick again."

Their thoughts like everyone else went back to their past, fuelling their hatred for Byron. Before they had their hair cut, they took it in turns or out of turn if the one of them was so upset from Byron's attention, whether it be very recent, prolonged or perverse. It seemed to make very little difference to the twins whoever physically endured Father Byron. It was that strange bond referred to, how identical twins somehow experienced the feeling and emotions of their twin. Julia nor Jackie had to say anything about what they had endured on any occasion when Byron had picked them for his entertainment. They knew.

The two sisters had now drawn the complete attention of everyone to them, not that it had been their intention to do so. It had been like that when they were children in the home. The other children had been transfixed by the fact they looked identical. No one could tell them apart for nearly a year until Father Byron made Julie have her hair cut shorter so he could tell which one of the girls he was going to use. Now it was Jackie who wore her hair short so Julie could wear it longer, a natural rebellion to Father Byron's influence on her life.

Their hair aside, it was still virtually impossible to tell either of them apart. They were both five foot seven, dark green eyes, defined thick lips, the luscious sort that just made you want to kiss them; their figures were the same so they often swapped and shared clothes and despite their misuse, they were very casual, warm smiling, friendly and inviting young women.

Natalie had met them nine months after she first went to the home when they were removed from their father who had been widowed and had lost himself in a whiskey bottle, with social services eventually taking them away from him and placing them in care.

When Natalie first lost her eyesight, they were close enough as friends to help Natalie learn how to compensate by feeling their faces to see if she could tell which one was which. Despite looking identical, Natalie eventually started to be able to feel the very slight difference in how their faces used to feel in her hands. Julie's eye brow line or more so the feeling of her skull beneath her eyebrows was just slightly more pronounced and it took easily six months of daily playing and feeling for Natalie to find this difference. It helped her intensely as she developed her tactile skills and she had been grateful to them for that.

It had been a strange combination of a game come therapy, for it benefited the three girls in different ways. For Jackie and Julie hearing Natalie saying she couldn't tell the difference between them, it seemed to strengthen the sisters bonds and determination to get through Father Byron's interferences. They would tell Natalie that she couldn't cheat when touching them by measuring the length of their hair but she had to name them just by feeling their faces.

For Natalie it had been an amazing gift to have two friends equally happy to let her explore their faces, their bone structure, so that it let her develop her tactile senses quicker than if they had not been there with her.

The three girls had formed an intense bond and they too, during the comings of everyone and Natalie's coming into and then out off the kitchen while different people arrived; had still not clicked onto the fact that she could see. Natalie had developed such a natural way about her, especially when she was within familiar environments, that it had become hard to tell she was not looking at what she was doing and going.

Even when Natalie walked away from the fridge she was leaning on, to go and give Julie a hug, did anyone even think she was doing it with eyesight rather than by sound and familiarity of her own kitchen. It was only when she held Julie's face in her hands, caressed the line of her eyebrows and then turned to Jackie who was standing to Julie's left and did the same, that her precision in placing her right thumb tip directly onto Jackie's left eyebrow, did the accuracy of her movement start to make people think she had done it with eyesight.

Julie followed Natalie's hand movement to her sisters face and turned her eyes back to stare straight into Natalie's eyes. The puzzlement on Julie's face started to diminish and transform into an expression filled with excitement and expectation as the possibility, the realisation that Natalie may be able to see started to dawn within her thinking.

Hesitantly, Julie started to ask, "Natalie?......can, can you see? Can you see me, my face? Did you, can you see Jackie's face?"

She watched as Natalie started to smile and became aware of everyone else in the kitchen slowly herding around the three of them, all looking intensely at Natalie, looking at her eyes almost as if to see through them, to see what she was seeing.

Natalie glanced around, smiling at everyone as she did, her smile, her eye contact conveying in those momentary glances that she could see. "Yes I can, my beautiful friend, I can see you. You are beautiful. You look the same as you did when I saw you last Julie... and you," Natalie turned towards Jackie and put her right thumb on her eyebrow again, "you are just as beautiful as well Jackie," as her thumb rubbed Jackie's eyebrow in her familiar way.

The three women became enveloped within their own hug, swamped almost instantly by everyone else in the kitchen, all immediately and simultaneously asking and saying the same things.

"When did this happen, Natalie are you alright? Can you see clearly? Natalie this is fantastic. They said this might happen years ago didn't they! How long have you been able to see for? Does everything around you look clear, can you see me? Does Jane know?"

The barrage of questions did not stop Natalie from smiling, nor from trying to answer all the questions she heard within the euphoria.

"It's only just happened and it started when I was taunting Elvis and following him around the house. I have to be honest, I wondered myself at first because it was just differences in light and then there seemed to be more shadows, then more colour and I could see the edges of shapes against other things, then I could see different things separate from other things. I could see Jane, her face got clearer." As Natalie tried to answer the deluge of questions, the tears started to form in her eyes and then run down her cheeks as the happiness and the reality of her eyesight coming back became stronger. The more she tried to answer and explain things, the more her emotions began to break down as the reality of her explanation became real.

"I could see Elvis down the far end of the landing as he tried to get away from me, I watched him duck into different rooms as he tried to hide from me but I could see and hear where he was going and what he was trying to do."

Natalie started to shake as she became emotional, her vision becoming blurred from her tears, her mind taking in and succumbing to the immediate here and now and how it had actually arrived, with long unseen friends and victims, all now surrounding her, eager to be told how she had captured Byron, what she had done and how she could see.

There was not enough space on her body for everyone to get an arm around Natalie or even a hand on her shoulders or arms but within that orgy of arms, legs, bodies, heads; emerged a feeling so strong of love and compassion for each other, that it became difficult for any of the other eleven damaged adults not to start crying along with Natalie.

After a few minutes of watching what was effectively the culmination of years of detective work, victim support, counselling and keeping in contact, Jane walked over to the swell of eye wiping, eye drying, hugging, kissing, squeezing grown ups who were sharing the emotions of past feelings wrapped and laced now with the anticipation of exacting uncontrolled revenge on their despised, unholy, sanctimonious demon.

Jane spoke softly, just so that her words would break gently into the hearing of the group without stopping the feelings that were evident amongst all of Byron's victims.

"Are you all alright? Are you ready to meet this cowardly bastard again?"

She stood, unhurried waiting for any response, knowing that one would filter through and back out to her. Jane looked on, smiling, understanding the moment she was watching.

Eventually, Julie turned her head to look away from the huddle and looked outwardly at Jane.

"Shall we see if that bastard is still breathing. I hope he is....." Julie's smile was not complimented by smiling eyes but a hard, stern gaze. It was obvious to Jane that Julie's mind was "in the zone."

The eleven splintered away from each other although there

was still plenty of contact and they looked as one towards Jane.

"You had better follow me then. We've got someone who we think is now dying to see you all !" Jane laughed naturally and enthusiastically at her own humour, a cross over from the sarcastic comebacks and police authoritarian attitude she leant while on the force.

Everyone followed Jane who lead the way from the kitchen, along the hall and then up the stairs. Natalie held her arms out and followed on behind everyone, like a Shepard herding sheep along a country lane.

Jane stopped at the first stair, pointed to her feet, put a thumbs up to Natalie who returned the gesture and then started to stomp slowly and purposely on each wooden stair, with each slow step. The others instantly picked up on what they should do by stomping slow and hard on each stair. By the time five of them were on the stairs, Julie and Jackie third on as a pair, side by side, Michael and Nigel before them, their combined stomping started to sound like the rumbling and vibrations of a small earth tremor.

33) SOUNDS

Father Byron had nodded on and off to sleep with exhaustion for the nearly two hours or so since Jane and Natalie left to go down stairs and have their cup of tea, before they started phoning his previous victims.

His drifting off into sleep was hindered by his own thoughts initially, about his bindings, his injuries and the constant pains that were circulating around his body, one replacing the other as his mind tried to categorise their level of intensity and which one was hurting the most.

He was just about to lose consciousness when he heard the voice of Michael as he came in through the front door, not that he knew it was Michael but he recognised the faint, gentle tones of Jane's voice talking to "someone" who had come into the house.

His ears strained to listen down the two flights of stairs to what was being said but he couldn't, not with this first new voice, it was too quiet and too far away. Michael coming into the house however did prompt him to wake up and to concentrate on what was happening on the ground floor.

Byron took deep breaths to try and clear his head and bring his level of concentration out of dozing and sleep orientation. It was an effort as he really wanted to just sleep so that he could recover his strength, what little there was and so that he could think straight. As he listened to Michael's voice, he knew that if more people arrived, he would be truly in the weakest of situations and would have lost any chance of regaining control or even being able to reason with just Natalie and Jane.

His brain however had not even thought that the voice he was trying to listen to, belonged to another of his victims, only that it was someone, another person coming into the house which would add to his difficulty in trying to get away. Despite his intentions, he slipped into sleep.

By the time Eveline arrived, which was only about seven minutes after Michael, Father Byron woke up and became as alert as his tiredness would allow. Eveline's voice was more shrill and carried more easily up to the attic. Byron did not associate it with anyone he had ever known and why would he. Eveline's voice, the last time he had heard it was that of a young teenager and Eveline's voice had changed since she was fourteen.

He could still not distinguish what this "next" person coming into the house was saying and his mind still had not even contemplated it would be a grown up childhood victim. He had started wondering why there were people coming to Natalie's home but his was too tired to think logically and to think things through. All he really wanted to do was sleep.

When Melony and Francis arrived and the sound of both their voices floated up to the attic, his wondering had started to turn a little towards concern. It was the combination of their voices, that interaction, the rhythm between them that prompted the vaguest of memories. Byron's brain wrestled with the thought that there was some sort of familiarity but he could not place that recollection.

Byron felt more and more agitated, as he listened to chattering voices walking down Natalie's hallway. Even though he counted the number of people who had arrived, the only voices he remotely recognised was Natalie's or Jane's. When everyone had arrived, all he could hear was the general mumble of sound coming up from the kitchen.

That mumbling, rumbling sound from eleven people all talking at once reached his ears with as much confusion and indistinction as it had within the kitchen. The silence that followed it although only about twenty seconds, seemed to last for more like twenty minutes and Byron's brain was racing, trying to work out a reason for so many people being here. Surely Natalie would be taking a chance of him being discovered by one of them if they used an upstairs bathroom and he was able to make some sort of noise to attract attention. Wasn't she taking a risk he thought. He tried to strain against his restraints, to loosen or break them but they were too tight and too strong and his second attempt virtually drained him of any final strength and his body resigned itself again to its bondage.

All he could do was listen.

The silence started to break very quietly, like that initial tiny glimpse of light at sunrise, with the first hint of sound coming from Jane's laughter, followed by the shuffling sounds of movement once the twelve started to walk down the hall after Jane.

The silence changed to a rumble and then the clear distinction of hard stamping feet on the wooden staircase which became rhythmic and uniform as every person joining the stairs, stamped in time, two abreast, like soldiers commencing to march in lines on a parade ground.

Father Byron opened his eyes as the volume of this increasing sound started to threaten an approach. He began trying to think why so many people were coming up the stairs, the sense of it for Natalie if one of these visitors came across him, strapped to a bed. How would she explain it?

The volume of their footsteps lessened as the first of the troupe arrived on the carpeted landing. They watched Jane emphasise her raised footsteps as she continued to stamp down on the carpet and as more followed and walked along the landing, the combined volume of their footsteps became a more muffled, muted sound.

Byron knew that they must now all be on the landing but still had not cottoned on to the concept they were coming to see him, not until he heard the harsh, hollow echo of the wooden stairs leading up to the attic room where he was prisoner.

His eyes widened at he listened to the growing volume of feet clomping on the bare wooden stairs to the attic rooms as it eventually dawned on him that he was what they were coming to see. Byron pulled frantically against his restraints to try and break them or at least create some slack within their tension so that he could hopefully start to twist and wriggle something free. He knew categorically now that if he didn't get free with all these other people becoming involved, he never would get free. The bindings around his wrists started to draw blood as he squirmed and twisted whatever ever part of his body he could to free himself in someway.

Jane's restraints had been well secured and despite the panic that had set in on hearing these loud approaching footsteps, no pumping adrenaline thrashings or pullings could loosen the tension that Jane had secured, to ensure Byron wouldn't get away.

The perspiration doused Byron's face within seconds of his first efforts to pull himself free and now, prostrate on his back along the bed like an exhausted runner, he could feel the trickle from the beads of sweat running back down across his cheeks and neck to the back of his head.

The long, despairing sigh that left his body accompanied a sad wishful pray to God, even though deep down, he had long given up on God helping him out. He tried one last time to break his restraints, his face screwed up to blood red, his temples pulsing, the veins in his neck bulging as his will to escape transposed itself into the every sinew and muscle in his body. His will was not enough.

The door creaked open, pushed slowly and deliberately by Jane. The light from the landing slipped through the opening gap and sliced a beam across Father Byron's head and body, illuminating a narrow band of his black clothing.

Byron tried to force his eyes to look above and passed his forehead and towards the opening door. There was just the fleeting glimpses of silhouettes.

34) REUNIONS

Father Byron's neck was as taught as a long bow string, as he tried to see who was standing at the doorway into the attic room. It still had not occurred to him despite the fact that he had already thought that they had come to see him, that they would be his grown up victims.

Jane came into the room first, the light from the landing almost acting like a spotlight as it illuminated Byron's shackled body to the old bed. Jane's tone of voice sent a chill along his back. He knew instantly that the level of danger he was in had just escalated beyond his previous perceptions. Her voice was filled with malice and sarcasm.

"Heeeellloo Elvis......it is Elvis isn't it? Uh huh..... It's nice to find you .....caught in a trap.......you remember that don't you.....how you used to love to sing that to "your little fans" when they couldn't run away any further.....when you had run them into a corner and they couldn't get away.....you remember that don't you!" Jane's voice rose to make the parody of the famous announcements that used to accompany an Elvis Presley concert.

"Well.....for one night only.... Elvis is still in the building and I've brought some of your biggest fans.........well they're big now........ to see you for ....one....last....time. Lets put our hands together for Elvis."

Jane's words made his spine go stiff at hearing his own "pursuit" words from his past stalkings and as the twelve walked slowly in through the door and filed around either side of the bed, they clapped a slow, solid hand clap which reverberated around the bareness of the room.

Byron's head turned from side to side, his eyes still blurred, darting from trying to look at the face of one person to the next, following them as they walked around the bed. He knew now that they used to be some of the children he had abused, why else would these people be here now. His brain was bursting for answers as to who they were. Even with the light coming in from the landing, there were still shadows moving and distorting the clarity he needed, to see anyone of them with any distinction. Reactively, he pulled again against his restraints as he turned and twisted to look at each of them as they clapped themselves into a position around the bed. Byron felt himself shaking, his fear and nerves now uncontrolled impulses running throughout his body. Every part of him quivered, causing the bed to emphasise his shaking as it rattled with its own metallic vibrations.

Byron's voice cracked and broke as he tried to speak. "Who are you? What are you doing? You can't get away with this."

Jane's voice responded. It was slow and threatening and her sarcasm remained.

"Ooooohhhhhh.............I think we will.........just think what we have done already and that was just the two of us, well.... actually, let me stop myself there......that was mainly just Natalie, a single blind woman, capturing a fat .... useless pig, or do you think that's unfair. You couldn't even compete with a blind woman, you are so useless, so pathetic as a human, that's why you used to pick on children, because they were the only people you could beat. Now, there are a few more of us and do you know what Elvis, no one knows you are here, not unless you told someone you were going to break into a blind woman's house and terrorise her.........and I don't think that is after dinner chat at a Catholic Priests retirement home, do you? So you are on your own, with just us to keep you company, to relive some ....old..... times."

Byron felt his bladder and groin becoming hot and uncomfortable as his body wanted to wet itself from the fear he was experiencing. He managed to suck in his stomach and held off the reaction to pee himself.

Jane motioned to the others to stop the slow hand clap, her voice full of sarcastic irony.

"We thought, well Natalie and myself thought, that you would like a reunion with some of your favourites so when we, well me actually this time, got in touch with everyone....they thought it would be a good idea as well. How ....about.... that.....they still remembered you and wanted to see you again."

Her voice rose again as she injected another layer of dramatic emphasis. "Oohhh, there is ....so .....much ......love." Jane started laughing.

Byron continued to force his head forward in an effort to try and see who was standing around the bed. "Oh God!" He thought, "I still can't see any of their faces properly. Who are they?"

Jane watched Byron's efforts and his squinting eyes and she knew he still couldn't see any of their faces. She was happy with that.

"Let's play a quick game! " she looked around at everyone who stood silently looking down at Byron. Evelyn had tears in her eyes and her face virtually showed the reenactment of her emotions as she fled from Byron all those years ago.

Michael's eyes glared with anger and hate, as did Harry's and Nigel's. Natalie followed Jane's eyes around the rest, all staring at Father Byron. With the exception of Melony, all the other women were wiping away a tear or two as they looked up and down his trussed up body. James held his hands around his head as if to stop it falling off his own shoulders, the horror of his own memories resurrected by looking at Byron's emasculated fat body.

Jane's voice brought everyone's attention back to her. "Let's see if Elvis here can remember one of you just from the sound of your voice. Thing is, I don't think he can see very well, can you Elvis?" Jane moved towards him giving him condescending little slaps across this left cheek as she spoke. She put her arm onto Michael's shoulder. "You go first darling on this occasion. What would you like to say to the old hound dog here."

Michael lent over so that his head was next to Byron's who tried to move his face away but was unable to do so to any degree. He grunted in his vain attempt to distance himself from the intimidation of Michael's presence.

It was all that Michael could do, to stop himself from punching Byron's face. Michael shook with anger as he whispered with a rasping voice into Byron's ear. "You look like an angel, walk like and angel, talk like and angel but I got wise, you're the devil in disguise."

Byron gripped at the bed, shocked by the recoil of his mind to twenty years ago and an Elvis song that he could only remember using specifically when perusing Michael. He had picked it because Michael was a named angel and that pretty little boy had been responsible in Byron's eyes, for tempting him with his childhood beauty, something Byron couldn't resist. It was soon after his abuse began that he nicknamed Michael, Thor because of his long blond hair and facial features. He still however kept that same song for Michael and he knew the instant he heard it, who was standing right by him. Byron could see he had grown into quite a large man.

Michael looked scathingly at Byron, waiting for his reaction.

Byron felt like he was spinning downwards through a hole, his mind and thoughts an avalanche of concerns and fears all tumbling over each other and he knew he was sweating again profusely, the panic inside was pumping his fluids out through every pore.

He blinked to look at Michael's face next to his as he tried to keep the perspiration out of his eyes. He shook his head as he felt the beads running down into his sockets towards his eyes. Michael stepped back as he felt some of the spray coming off Byron's face.

Father Byron voice was very tentative as he hoped he could appeal to some sort of compassion within Michael.

"Michael, my goodness, my little Michael. What a strapping man you've turned into. I was.....I was right to call you Thor."

Michaels voice had no compassion, no sympathy, nothing but disgust and distain."Thor! You think that it is... what....... some sort of consolation.....some childhood nick name is or was supposed to make me feel better about things. Trust me Elvis, we are all going to be back here to see you a bit later and then, ...then you fat disgusting bastard, every bit of everyone's life that you have ruined, will come back to you a hundred times worse than you ever did to us. You know what..........we are going to enjoy it, every second of it."

Michael slapped the side of Byron's face a couple of times just like Jane had done earlier, only harder.

Natalie took the opportunity to take people back out of the room. "Come on everyone. Let's leave him here for a little while. We need to decide who is going to do what. We just wanted to show he is here waiting....aren't you Elvis ?"

Byron listened to their footsteps and the new found aggression in their voices as they all walked back down into the kitchen. He lay there again, visualising his hearing following them down the two flights of stairs. Their voices were louder this time and the level of excitement had escalated.

Byron stared blindly at the ceiling. His mind for the moment had died, his thoughts had stopped.

35) COORDINATION

The eleven guests in Natalie's kitchen were reacting with each other and within themselves as if they had all been wired up to the electricity supply. There was an erratic, frantic eagerness to do something and everything to Byron, now that they had seen him strapped helpless to the bed.

Natalie and Jane stood silent with each other by the fridge as they waited for the fury of everyone's emotions to die down. Jackie and Julie were crying profusely and hugging each other. Natalie could still pick out their whispered support to each other above all the sobbing and angry, condemning voices that joined into one wall of sound. "We can get him back for what he did to us. I know, I know. I want to kill him for what he did to you, to us both."

Steph, Mary, Francis all had tears in their eyes but were more occupied with comforting Evelyn who was shaking from the jumbled emotions that were strafing through her body. One second she looked bewildered, the next triumphant at the thought that Byron was helpless and she could at last get her revenge for the times she had been helpless. Within moments, her expression changed, conveying her frightened, unsure inner self as she buried her head into the Mary's chest, her hands squeezing affection into Steph and Francis' arms, their bodies and contact giving Evelyn compassionate support.

Nigel and Harry also joined the huddle, putting their arms around the cuddling girls.

Michael, James and Melony stood together, leaning against the sink unit, their faces a mix of concern when they looked towards the huddle; anger and eagerness when they looked between themselves.

A natural lull occurred as Jane anticipated, allowing her to start the communal conversation.

"Well! ....Is everyone ok? ....Are we all alright?" Her smile drew their attention as equally as her question. "Now that you have all seen him, what do you want to do?"

Jane and Natalie looked around at each person individually, their gaze fixed to the pupils of their eyes, waiting for a response. There was a thoughtful silence as each of the eleven looked around at each other.

Melony stepped forward as she started to answer Jane. "We've all waited a long time, not that anyone I would guess ever thought we would ever have a chance to get him for what he's done, to get our own backs, so this is more than I, more I would think than any of us imagined. I'm quite happy in sharing out his ...let's say punishment and if someone can't do it for any reason, I'll happily do it for them."

There was a general murmur of agreement.

"Ok," said Natalie with a naughty, evil tone in her voice, "has anyone got an idea of what they would like to do to him, apart from kill him, that's out because it's too easy and.......too far, we can't do that. All we would say," Natalie motioned towards Jane, "is that whatever you do, it is either instantly and exceptionally painful and,.......or it stays with him for the rest of his life and hurts and reminds him everyday of us and what he did. It also needs to be subtle......so no cutting his head off."

There was a ripple of laughter while the eleven moved as if with one controlling brain, to form a non symmetrical, arms around each other circle, herded by the shape of the kitchen units, into becoming a squeezed out and bent oblong. The empathy they all felt for one another made them feel solid.

Slowly and surely, one by one, they started to quietly say what they wanted, what they intended to do to Father Byron.

As one spoke and then another, the next became more excited as their combined confidence grew on hearing what each wanted to do to Byron, how what they said and the way they said it, was what each of them felt and wanted as individuals.

Jane and Natalie listened until the point of the eleven's agitation had risen to where there was a barrage of conflicting, supporting, shouting, screaming, crying voices fuelled by erupting, uncontained, uninhibited, long buried emotions and memories; filling the kitchen with a single mindset on exacting the most horrific forms of revenge on the animal that had torn the innocence out of their child's body.

Jane lifted her arms and started to gently flap her hands to calm everyone down. "Ssssshhhh.....ok...ssshhh........ssshh-hh....ok, alright. We're so glad that you are all so in agreement. Some of you will have to share the things you want to do as you want to do the same things, so look...........take these......... dry your eyes, perhaps give your face a wash, while Natalie and myself go and get the things you need." Jane handed out two boxes of tissues so they could start composing themselves.

James held out his hand to touch Jane on the right arm. "Thanks Jane." His eyes were filled with tears and gratitude.

"It's ok James, give us about ten minutes and we'll be ready for everyone."

Jane and Natalie left the kitchen and walked out to Natalie's garden shed, returning after about five minutes with a whole mixture of implements which they put down on the long work surface opposite the sink units.

"I won't be long." Jane said as a general announcement to everyone and she walked out the kitchen towards the front door and back to her own house, returning ten minutes later with a cardboard box about the size of two combined shoe boxes, with more gadgets and implements.

While Jane was out, Natalie got some more gadgets from her kitchen draws.

Father Byron's feeling of panic rose again as he listened to the growing commotion from within the kitchen. Evelyn's almost hysterical shrieking sounded far louder than any other individual and was the only single, distinct sound he could hear. The vision of Evelyn squashing herself into a blackened corner along one of the little used corridors leading to the boiler room, forcing herself to try and morph into becoming a part of the old stone pillar as she tried to hide from him, came into his mind; her identity established by this perverse memory. It used to excite him but now on hearing it rise through two flights of stairs and it maintain its harshness, Byron felt himself shudder as if he had been surrounded by an icy breeze.

As Byron shivered, his nerves twitching with fright, the reality of who these people were, repeated itself to him, prompted by his recognition of Evelyn's wailing. His thoughts started talking to him, he lay there shaking his head to himself as he listened to his mind thinking.

"All these people, these were ALL children in the home. Oh God." His repeated epiphany hit home. "Oh God...... Oh God, oh God......they're going to kill me. No .....no they won't do that....oh no....noooo". His thoughts trailed off before they put into words what his subconscious had already formulated as he started listening again to the deliberate, heavy stamping footsteps coming up the first flight of stairs to the first floor landing.

This time, the stomping footsteps were accompanied by singing. "Return to sender ...do do do do do do, return to sender do do do do do do, return to sender do do do do do do return to sender do do do do do do."

36) PARADES

Byron's eyes were screwed tight, his face bloodshot and swollen, as he made one last effort to try and loosen or break his restraints. Whatever residual strength he may have had, was being drawn out of him the closer they approached Natalie's make shift torture chamber, as his despair sank lower.

Jane stood at the doorway and let the singing come to the end of the verse and then motioned with her finger to her lip for everyone to stop. She walked into the room, watching Elvis as he strained on the bed.

Her voice continued with the same sarcastic edge as earlier. "Still here! We're all so glad. It would not be as much fun without you, would it everyone?"

She motioned towards the group still more or less standing in two lines along the landing.
"No!" They all shouted in a high spirited, school like to a teacher response.

Byron tried to look at Jane as she slowly circled the bed, he now making the last feeble efforts to pull on his bindings.

"Now Elvis, we all know you but do you know all of your fans?" Jane struck an Elvis stage pose which made those who could see her from the landing laugh out aloud, "so let me bring on stage each one of these long lost fans from way back and let's see if you can remember them. I'm sure it will be better for you if you do, it will make them feel......well ......" Jane looked at Jackie and Julie who were the first two standing side by side in the doorway like they were waiting to walk on stage. Harry and Nigel were looking over their shoulders into the room and

Jane hesitated as she tried to think of the next word to say, conscious she had already used the word "remember" in her introduction and was looking for something else to say......it didn't come so she continued with the announcement for them to enter the room......"well.....remembered."

Jane shrugged her shoulders with a screwed face to show she was aware of her repeat and made a visual joke out of it. Jackie, Julie, Harry and Nigel laughed again as they were the only four who could really see Jane, the others could only catch glimpses of her through the gaps. She continued with her mock Elvis impersonation.

"Here are the first two young ladies and I'll give you a clue, they are very close. The first long haired lovely is sporting a natty little pair of garden pruning shears, they look new and therefore very sharp, what will she do with those I wonder; the other.......oooh....I'll let you guess but it's for the garden and think you might be drinking this.......not that you should, judging by the skull and cross bones on the label but hey......you can give it a go."

Julie walked in followed by Jackie and both took up standing either side of the bed by his head. Julie bent over him, looking him straight in the face, her own about two feet away and let her long red hair fall close to or just on his face. Jackie did the same from the other side. The smell and fleeting touches of Julie's hair seemed unreal for a second or so, taking Byron's mind out of the room. Julie could see the tension in his body relax and noticed him taking a deeper, slower breath as he smelt her hair by his nose.

Byron could hear the footsteps of the others walking into the room, a clattering, clicking, hollow conglomeration of different shoes and heels on the hollow sounding floor boards covered unknown to him, by heavy polythene.

Harry and Nigel stayed side by side and moved to the right

side of the room, to the left of the top of Byron's head which was closest to the doorway, followed by James and Evelyn who stood to their right.

Jane and Natalie had already walked in and stood to the right of Byron, against the wall, to give everyone a chance of a closer look.

Melony, Francis, Mary, Steph and Michael clustered in a group to the right of Byron's head, all with a clear view of his whole body and Jackie and Julie now either side of him.

Julie's voice growled with hatred. "Open your eyes Elvis, look closely, do you know me, do you know us?"

His eyes flickered into opening as he sniffed another breath, taking in the smell of Julie's red hair. She glared at him, her right hand squeezing and releasing the garden pruning shears. Even his smelling of her hair angered her and it was enough of an excuse.

"I said open your eyes and look at us. I didn't say smell anything did I!"

Byron's eyes jerked towards Julie. He opened his lids wider to try and see her face with some sort of clarity but his eyes were still affected by the sprays and lights and there was a blur around her features. He turned to look at Jackie. Her red hair made him look back at Julie's long hair hanging over the one side of his face and he realised the colour matched.

"AAAAHHH......." His hands tried to reach instinctively for his nose as a burning, knife life sensation cut into his right nostril, just where the soft outer edge joined his face. The bindings where still as tight as when Jane first made them despite his efforts and they cut again into his skin, his hands responded to the pain as he tried to get to his nose to form a cup or some other sort of contact relief. His face puffed up, his lips blowing with pain in between his screams. They all watched intently, some a bit surprised at the amount of reactive reaction the careful, quick little snip Julie had made through his skin had created. None of them had ever done anything like Julie had just done to Byron and they handled it in different measures.

Byron's voice screeched and quivered as he tried to speak. "Dear God, aaaahh, wha.....what on earth." The sensation continued and seemed to linger at the height of its intensity as he couldn't get to rub any soothing contact against it. His head thrashed around in an effort to alleviate the intensity. The little trickle of blood stuck to his skin and even tickled the side of his fulcrum, an almost welcome relief from the other feelings he was experiencing, as it tracked down from the cut, past his mouth and down his neck, running just under his right ear. His tongue pocked out of the right side of his lips just reaching the blood on his face, its taste confirming the snipping of his nose.

Julie looked down at him, her smile exaggerated by wet, drawling lips, her mouth unexpectedly salivating by the excitement and adrenaline of using the garden pruners to snip through about five millimetres of the skin at the base of his nostril. She looked across at her sister. "Oh yes .....that felt good Jackie. Do you want a go, on the other side."

"No" shouted Byron, "please no." Julie looked down and spoke to him like telling off a child who was trying to get attention.

"Now, ...we're weren't talking to you, were we. I ..was ..talking... to my sister......oops, have I given him a another clue? Do you know our names ....dear ....Father Byron."

Jackie looked across at Julie as she spoke, enjoying her involvement, herself eager to get physically involved. "Pass me those cutters a second, I might need them if Elvis here doesn't get our names right. Well then Elvis do you remember us?"

They both stared down at him, defying him to guess their

names.

Byron's voice could not hide his fear as he stared back at their hair, still the only thing he could see with any certainty, the colour. His head, his eyes moved from side to side as he started to mouth their names, still fearing he would get them wrong. "You're Julie and Jesse, you're sisters, you both use to have long hair."

As he said their names, his voice still exposed his fear, even when it changed to sound like he was pleased with himself for getting it right.

Julie adopted Jane's exaggerated, comedic announcement tone, "Ooh, so close, do you want to have another go and then tell me which one of us is which."

Byron felt the cold steel of the pruning shears lay across the left side of his top lip. He could sense the tips of the blades were on either side of his left nostril, the one blade just inside his nose.

Jackie forced the blades down onto face, the shape of their curves hard, flattening against his skin to stop his head from turning, as he tried to move his nose and face away from the cutting edges, which he knew had the skin of his left nostril between them. Her voice had no humorous tone just plain threatening instruction.

"No no, don't try to move away or I might just slip. We're giving you a chance here Elvis, you are half right. Get my name right now and perhaps I won't cut through your face......yet. So... what... is ....my ....name?"

Byron's head shook which delighted the sisters as they enjoyed how his terrified mind had lost control of his body. Jackie pressed down even harder on the shears, his skin around his lips changing colour from the pressure. Byron could feel the one blade slipping slightly deeper into the inside of his nose, touching the hairs inside.

His thoughts were frantic, his lips silently mouthed, other girls names beginning with J. He was certain the missing name ended in an E sound like Jesse. He listed them to himself,

"Jenny, Jackie, Janey, Jesse, Jackie ?........Jilly ...no ....it's Jackie not Jesse...you idiot....if you'd said that first time they might not have snipped you.'

There was so much urgency in his voice. "Jackie....it's Jackie not Jesse. I'm sorry it's Jesse, NO I mean Jackie, Jackie, please it's Jackie."

Jackie also changed her tone of voice to one of condescending patronage. "Well well, you have remembered....just. I'll give you a break for now as you've been a clever little Elvis but," she changed her voice again to sound like The Terminator's famous line, "I'll be back."

She flicked the shears off his face as she spoke, ensuring that the end of the blade just inside his nose, dug against it as she moved it away. "Oops, careless me!"

Byron sucked in through his mouth, reacting as the blade caught the inside of the end of his nose.

Jane announced the entry of Harry and Nigel. "And here are two young men, eager to be remembered to you and yes, they have brought you gifts as well. You....are....so.....lucky."

Jane swept her right arm in front of her, directing the two men to Byron. Jackie and Julie moved down to the bottom of the bed. "I haven't used the weed killer yet!" Jackie said as they made way for Harry and Nigel.

"Plenty of time for that, don't worry." Said Harry as he stood on the right side of Byron exchanging smiles with Jackie and Julie.

"Oh please, please in the name of God, please don't do this with everyone, please ....I'm sorry, I'm so sorry to all of you, please don't do this anymore."

Harry punched him in the face, an instant, uncontrolled re-action, the bed rattling as Byron's head pushed back against the springs. He followed it, less than a second later with an identical second straight punch to his right cheek bone, Byron's sound from the first blow was stopped mid exhalation by the impact of Harry's follow up punch, changing his voice into a low painful moan.

"Uh........aaarr."

Harry mocked him initially but as he started to speak to Father Byron, the affect Byron had on his life started to spill out and he became more angry and upset the more he spoke.

"Oh please stop, I'm sorry, I'm soooooo sorry. You're sorry because you've been caught you bastard. You didn't stop with me did you. You know, everyday you come into my mind be-cause I can't keep you out. I am in work, doing a shitty, boring job, numbers and bloody accounts for the council just so I can have a house to go home to on my own, just a cat and that's because its adopted me and that's the only thing that shares my life outside of the office, apart from meeting Nigel occa-sionally. No one wants to really know me, because I can't be with people because of you. People think I'm odd. How do I know? My boss has told me that I don't mix very well, that I'm stand offish, other people find me difficult to talk to. If there's an office do, I'm the one left on my own in the corner and everyone else is in a group, all laughing and joking and then there's me. And you know what, I don't know what to do, how to change, whatever I do, it doesn't work, I'm still Hilarious Harry as I've found out they call me, not because I'm funny and make them laugh but because they think I'm funny and they are laughing at me.

Do you know how that feels, going into work every day, expecting everyone at some time to be looking at me, Hilarious Harry and having a joke about me, laughing at me and that's because of you."

Harry was really worked up by now, his emotion at revealing his realisation of how people regarded him, dragging out his loneliness and self consciousness, his resentment towards Byron spitting out through his lips.

Harry grabbed hold of Byron's right hand with his left hand and splayed his fingers out so that he could take hold of each one individually with his right hand. Harry bent back Byron's little finger until it was as far back as it would move and he held it there. The pain from it being stretched made Byron arch his back along the bed, a token, instinctive reaction to try and ease the tension on his finger. It didn't. Byron stared up at Harry, trying to focus as his eyes started to water again.

"Do you remember how you used to take my hand. I thought the first time you were being nice to me. It was my first day at the home, the first day! I still remember all of that now, how you held my hand and you walked me around the garden, telling me you wanted me to be happy there, then doing a stupid Elvis song. I didn't know who Elvis was, I was six and I thought when you were telling me about "your friend", The Bogeyman, you were telling me so I wouldn't be frightened. I wasn't. It was the bloody opposite. When The Bogeyman turned up in the night, my very first night in the dormitory, I hadn't really even spoken to anyone much as you had kept me with you most of the day, everyone who was awake just watched The Bogeyman leading me out by my hand and he...YOU, your hold was really tight. I remember I couldn't move my fingers and they went numb as you pulled me along after you out of the room and I thought he was going to take me somewhere nice."

Harry's eyes slowly started to glaze over with tears as he

spoke. He held his breath and concentrated.

"Aaahh." Byron's voice shrieked as Harry tore back the little finger he had been holding so that it virtually met the back of his Byron's own hand, only being stopped from making direct contact by Harry's thumb which had acted as a fulcrum to break it from its knuckle joint.

Byron's cheeks puffed again, his head banging against the bare spring beds as he tried to cope with another inflicted agony.

"That seemed easy Harry, have another go." Natalie's voice was soft and encouraging to Harry, menacing to Byron who now on hearing Natalie, was whipping his head around still very much reacting to his first broken finger and also to try and look at where she was standing.

Byron's attention returned to his right hand as he felt harsh, pulsing, shooting pains up his right arm from his hand being manipulated again by Harry, so that he could get a grip on the next smallest finger. Harry looked away from Natalie and back down at Byron. He loved seeing the agony routed into every crease and fold of his face. Byron's back arched again as Harry started to bend his second finger back to just before breaking point. Byron tried to move his hand in an attempt to resist another finger being broken. The nerves along his arm and through his right hand were causing it to shake uncontrollably. Harry looked at the first broken finger dangling and jiggering on the end of his hand. He kept the tension on Byron's second finger and twisted and rotated the broken finger with his left hand. Byron screamed again. Harry let go with his left hand and broke his second finger in the same way as the first.

Byron's body jerked and banged on the bed as it went into a reactive spasm. His voice filled the room with a mixture of agony and whimpering screams.

Harry was shaking as he stood over him, his heart pumping as much as it had when he'd been trying to get away from The Bogeyman years ago. Byron was moaning and attempting to get back some regularity in his breathing. His mouth snatched at the air around him like it was in clumps and his teeth were wanting to take a bite.

Natalie's voice passed through Byron's hearing on its way to Harry. "See, was that even easier the second time? Now he's got three left on that hand."

Byron's voice gagged from the saliva that was nestling towards the back of his throat and another wave of terrorised agitation swept through him. "No Harry in Gods name, no more."

"Harry !....do you remember me? Do you remember my name?....do you? ..do you? or were you reminded by Jane and Natalie? DO YOU REMEMBER ME ?"

Byron's voice was tired, slow. "Harry I know you, yes I know you......from what you said about your first day."

"What about me, do you remember me?.....look closely." Nigel put his face right up to Byron's. The smell of his halitosis made Nigel recoil and take a deep breath. "Uugcchhh...you stank then and you stink now."

Nigel put his face back even closer to Byron. He continued to hold his breath as he spoke, to avoid taking in any more rotten mouth odour. "Look really close at my face. You have one chance with no clues to tell me my name."

Byron blinked his eyes hard and fast in his pain filled head, his right hand and all the nerves in his arm laying siege to any other cranial operation; his whole being still shaking along the length of the bed.

Nigel wasn't interested in Byron's bodily activity, he was worked up and impatient, screaming as he clamped his hand around Byron's throat above his dog collar. "What's my name? ....now !"

Byron's eyes just about stayed open as he struggled to stare at Nigel. "Your name is Nigel Harris. You used to love playing football. You even took your football to bed with you."

Within that second of recollection, Nigel and the other boys on hearing Byron, who had been there at the same time, remembered the sound of Nigel's football which he used to push out of the bed when The Bogeyman came and took him; the echoing, couple of taps as it bounced on the polished wood dormitory floor and then the sound of it rolling and bumping against another child's bed leg or wall. They all remembered that mix of sounds as they lay stone like within the petrified silence of the room and what it meant. They were safe that night as Nigel had been picked and he always threw his ball away for "safe keeping" and so that all the others knew, he was the one that night.

They all listened to the sound of The Bogeyman's shoes squeaking on the floor as he pulled or pushed Nigel back to his bed, the sound of the springs as his body slumped on the mattress and then Byron walking around between the beds looking for the football, which he put back onto Nigel's bed. No one else ever retrieved the ball, especially when Byron was picking Nigel, in case they drew attention to themselves and Byron changed his mind.

Byron even through his own frightened, nervous jerking, could feel Nigel's fingers and thumb shaking as they encompassed his throat. His mind jumped to an unthinkable conclusion. "Could Nigel be as weak now as he was as a child. He could never stand up for himself with the other kids, even girls, always relied on Michael or Harry. If he is still weak, perhaps I can appeal to him, use him to help me."

Byron's neck and head jerked forward violently as Nigel

ripped away his dog collar with his left hand.

"How could you still be wearing this, after all these years........" There was a long pause. Nigel's left hand was still shaking as he held the screwed, torn white symbol of divinity. He looked at it and back at Byron, crushing the collar even more.

"I'll give you the collar you deserve, the collar of the devil, something that you will never be able to take off or can hide from."

Byron tried to lift his head, to look up at Nigel but it was pushed back to the bed springs as violently as it had been pulled forward seconds earlier. Nigel looked at Jane and Natalie as he squeezed the final shape out of Byron's collar. "I really think now is the right time.......I feel ready!"

Both Jane and Natalie nodded, smiling, their eyes simultaneously flicked towards Byron.

Nigel's expression tore through Byron, his eyes psychotic, his face twisted as he asserted his confidence and domination, his nose again within an inch of Byron's, to where he could see Nigel's eyes penetrating into him. Any glimpse of weakness Byron may have sensed had disappeared when his collar was torn off and was now being confirmed by the look in Nigel's eyes. Byron flinched at the clicking sound of the kitchen blow lamp in Nigel's right hand and the flash of the flame from the nozzle as it flared in front of his face. As Nigel pressed the ignition button over and over again, the clicking became more threatening, eager, it conveyed an impatience to light....come on....come on.

Byron knew instantly, there was little to no chance in making Nigel any sort of alley, even a timid and frightened one. He swallowed to try and clear his mouth. His voice filled with tired, exasperated anxiousness "Nigel! What are you doing? Lets not be stupid now...come on......please.....everything up to now can be forgotten........I..........I can heal, all this can be forgotten. Natalie.......Jane......Michael..........come on Nigel, all this can stop."

Jane's blow lamp lit with a tiny roar, the flame intensely hot next to Byron's face, blue with heat more used to caramelising a creme brûlée.

Byron mentally tried to force his body through the bed springs to move away from the flame. They made the slightest of noise as his weak, restrained efforts naturally failed to transport the reality of his body through the coils away from Nigel.

Nigel turned the blow lamp to face Byron, its flame convecting to a point of intense heat close to Byron's left cheek.

Byron"s voice went up in pitch, screaming in panic, "Oh please god...Nigel no, ...all of you please....please, don't do this."

Nigel lifted the nozzle so that the heat projected above Byron's head as burning his cheek was not his intention. He put his mouth next to Byron's left ear so even the warmth of his breath felt threatening as his guttural whisper wafted around its curves and down the canal to his ear drum.

"How do you feel Elvis at the thought you can't get away, that whatever you do, you are mine? Remember those three words ...you are mine....those three words whispered in my ear. Well Elvis ......now.....YOU .....ARE ....MINE."

Byron's voice filled the room with a brain stopping agony filled cry, unplugging the adrenaline that had not fully started flowing through the veins of some of the others looking on. His screaming raised their delight on hearing Nigel's revenge take physical form, their spines tingling with elation as Nigel fanned the flame around Byron's neck where his dog collar usually rested.

They watched Byron jerk and tear against his restraints. The smell of burning skin filled their nostrils with a stench unknown to people, unused to a concentration camp's crematorium. Evelyn's life long weakness became confused at sensations that came at her from different directions, her ears dammed by Byron's voice, excluding every other sound around her from being heard, her nose filled with the vapours of his bubbling skin, smelling like burnt pork, turning her stomach to where she could feel the earlier cup of tea rising up through her trachea, the vision of his pain, exciting her as much as his smell repulsed her. These contradictions pounded in her skull, her ability to think, closing down by the domination of her senses.

Evelyn's consciousness started to cloud into a mist of dizziness and she began to sway, mirroring the increasing number of tiny smoke plumes rising from Byron's throat. James put his left arm around her to give her support. The participation, the atmosphere, infused through him with ghoulish devilment. His words started slow and quiet, as if not to startle her but then became more urgent.

"Deep.. breaths... Ev, you don't want to miss this. Smell the life coming out of him. Take him in and burn him inside you. Burn every bit of his memory to get rid of him from inside you for good. Watch the devil burn in our hell now. Enjoy this. I am."

James squeezed her left arm within his hug, shaking Evelyn gently as he did. He smiled and watched her eyes widen and refocus, feeling the strength come back into her body as she stood up straight.

Byron writhed, screaming like a dismembered demon from the bowels of hell, his ebbing strength and will redirected to his threatened vocal cords, the flame millimetres away from burning through his skin into the void of his throat and destroying them. They all watched from where they stood within the room, his torture burrowing its way into their decency, warping their morals with enthralling, uninhibited revenge, their minds releasing tormented memories fuelling their desire for retribution.

Nigel turned the blow lamp off and crossed his arms across his body in a comic mimic of a James Bond pose, making sure he kept the hot nozzle away from his left shoulder. He blew it, to add to the comedy and looked at Byron's neck which was oozing a mixture of blood, curling chard, blackened skin which resembled a burnt Indian nan bread smeared with tandoori sauce. There was a mixture of giggles, sniggers and out right laughter from everyone as they watched.

He stared down at Byron waiting for his reactions to stop until he lay still and barely conscious on the bed. A deafening silence eased its way through the group as they slowly stopped laughing, until everyone stood still, waiting for Nigel.

His voice was scathing, controlled. "That's the collar you will always wear and the one you deserve, so when you have the audacity to put this on, the real you is always there. You talk about God, well there's no God in you." Nigel threw the mangled collar into Byron's face. He moved slowly to one side to join Jackie and Julie at the foot of the bed, looking at the carefully burnt collar around the front and sides of Byron's throat which he had fanned like a car paint sprayer, to ensure the flame did not burn right through the several layers of skin. His retreat was an unspoken invitation for the next avenger to confront Father Byron.

Jane was the first to move, careful not to spill the jug of water she had brought up from the kitchen and poured it over Byron's throat. His cry from its chill was far less volatile. It was half hearted as it momentarily dragged him out of collapse.

Natalie walked around from the back of Jane, a smile on her

face looking around at everyone and spoke in a repetitive, bored tone of voice. "Salt and vinegar with that love!" She shook a large spray of ground salt from a long tubular salt re-fill container over his wounds which brought instant response as the granules dissolved within the mix of water and seeping blood.

"Ahh...ahh .aghh." His voice still didn't hit the same decibel level as when his neck was cooking.

"Come on Elvis, you've got to have salt and vinegar with your chips and you are getting your chips here." Natalie laughed and she threw apologetic glances at everyone. "I know, I know.....that was desperate wasn't it. I'm sure the jokes will get better through the day."

Byron's head seemed almost detached as it screamed a louder, garbled, teeth clenched grimace, which emanated more through his nose, as Natalie shook long dashes of malt vinegar all around his throat. His head went silent and his body took over, rattling the bed coils, reacting from his neck down, as his torso and legs visibly strained to cope with the alkaline dows-ing. His face had turned blood red again, the veins in his neck at breaking point and extremely visible within the scorched banding.

"Eeeehh, eeh....., feffff, feffff, eeeeehhhhh." He cried out and panted, the inside of his nose burning in a different way from the vinegar vapour that infiltrated into his sinuses. Byron sneezed three times.

"There there." Said Natalie sarcastically. "It's a shame we haven't got any curry sauce to go with it, a nice hot curry sauce. Battered Pasteur and chips with a curry sauce. That would be a new one on the menu for the Catholic Church." She laughter again at her own impromptu imagination. "Yes sorry again, that's even worse." She held her right hand up and around to everyone, still holding the vinegar bottle as she motioned her mock apology, her left wrist held out for a mock slapping but her smile continued at she listened to their laughter.

Jane put her left hand onto Natalie's shoulder.

"Do you know what, this is so much fun, isn't it Elvis?" She slapped him a few times on the right side of his face again, "I think we might be getting just a tinny whinny bit impatient so let's get everyone in, shall we Elvis? Come on everyone. Come closer one by one and I tell you what, let's make it even easier for him, everyone take a really close look at him so he can see you and hear you as well and we'll give him twenty seconds to see if he can remember each of your names. If you all take a bamboo skewer from Michael, if he doesn't guess your name, then stab it into him where ever you like but I'll pull his sleeves up a bit so you've got both his arms to play with."

Father Byron voice just about left his lips, the effort of speaking was even more draining. Despite his pleas for some sort of mercy and humanity, its tone did not convey any belief that it would happen.

"Ple......please, can we stop this. For the love of God again, please can you stop. I was wrong. Ple....please can all this stop?"

Jane sighed, her sarcastic tone unrelenting. "Yeeeessss, I suppose we could. You are looking tired. Perhaps you need a bit of a rest ....but there again. Now let's see if you can see clearly. Look at me, here, look."

She slapped his face again as she positioned her face in front of his, grabbing his chin and looked for the response in his eyes. "I'll give you a helping hand shall I? it's only fair."

Jane poured the rest of the jug of water onto his eyes as she held his head still with her left hand gripping into his hair on top of his head, pulling it back down towards the bed.

Byron instinctively tried to resist but his head just twitched uselessly from the combination of Jane's grip and his lack of strength. She wiped away the excess water from his eye recesses and off his cheeks, the trickles turning red as they mixed with the blood staining his skin from earlier.

"James have you got your surgical stapler?" Byron's eyes widened on hearing Jane's question. She could see the terror her words had created within his pupils which fixed on her face and followed her every twitch, trying to read what was coming. Jane's ongoing sarcastic tone continued but even that gave way to a dip towards venomous aggression, following years of frustrated policing in collaring Father Byron for his crimes and the pent up hatred his, pious sanctity had created within her.

"Oh, sorry, I haven't told you. I...well James probably, he's got more experience than me, is going to staple your eye lids open so you can see everyone else clearly, well again I suppose, as clearly as you can. After all, you only have twenty seconds to tell the rest of them their names, to show them that after all the years they had to suffer, ...your early... attention, you remember each and everyone of them, that they mean something to you and that you haven't forgotten them as if they were worthless, that you didn't just use them because they were just defenceless, small, trusting, innocent children......you know the sort of thing I mean, that they were special, that everyone is equal in the sight of God and that they were as important as you, as important as you thought you were."

James had walked to her side while he listened to Jane's voice lose some of her usual control and become incensed with the indignant anger within her. He flinched in surprise as she grabbed the surgical stapler out of his right hand.

In a swirl of movement, Jane turned back on Byron, rolling

270

his left eyelid up from over his eyeball. He felt the cold steel edge push up from the underside of his eyelid as Jane used it to help her left thumb lift the lid towards his forehead. The staple that went through it, pinning it to the top of his eye socket sent slicing shards of pain ricocheting around his head, streaking past his temples, hitting the nerves at the top of his neck making him feel like his head was going to fall off from where it is connected to his spine. As he cried out, his vocal chords collapsed, his voice disappeared into a hiss. His face contorted against the impalement, the lid straining against the staple as his nerves told his eyes to shut, to contain and control the pain. It felt totally unnatural to Byron, to feel his right eye closed and his left eye open? They both gushed tears, soaking his face with snake like salty streams running all over his cheeks and towards the back of his head and neck, just as the water from Jane's jug had done before.

Jane seemed to be vibrating along the whole of her body as the indignation surged through her. She forced her left thumb onto his right eyelid, dragging it up like the first. He could feel her aggression through the pressure she exerted, pushing initially down against his eyeball, in spite of the sensations screaming around the inside of his skull. His eyes had become independent, darting uncontrollably to look at every part of Jane's face, the room space either side of her, the shapes of the others standing to the side where they were just within his peripheral vision. The hard edge of the stapler found the underside of the lid. His eyes widened with petrification at the imminent expectation of what was about to happen again, helping Jane more than with his first eye. Her expression was totally insular, oblivious within her own world in those moments of anything or anyone other than the two of them. The staple found a solid securing point in the bone just under his eyebrow and another wave of scorching nerve impulses shot around his skull. His face repeated the involuntary gurning rearrangement of his features. Jane's eyes were wide, they emitted delight. Byron's throat emitted nothing, his agony couldn't get passed his vocal chords but got caught somewhere between his brain and the pit of his stomach, his back arched where it could, stopping the connection, trapping any audible response. Jane watched his mouth move and relished its muteness.

She felt James put his left hand on her right shoulder, the touch brought her back.

"What! No song Elvis?" Her voice had the hint of a quiver as she regained all her self control. "Sorry! What? ....I didn't hear you."

James squeezed her shoulder as he said, "well ! I know where to come if I need a surgical assistant. You did that ....rather well, uh....rather quick in fact."

Jane looked at James. The humour had returned to her voice. "Yeah....sorry, you were supposed to do that but do you know what,.... that felt good.....do you use anaesthetic? Personally, I think it's overrated. What do you think Elvis?"

Byron's eyes looked almost dead as they looked blankly upwards, tears still oozing out at their sides, the flow now only running down the sides of his face and onto his ears. They barely moved when Jane spoke to him. She could hear his breathing, again short, sharp, quick breaths. His head twitched every seven to eight seconds. Jane knew he was in shock and she needed to bring him back. She slapped his face a couple of times again, with quick little flicks.

"I think we are ready everyone for Elvis here to start playing the name game. And now, without further a do, live before Elvis, here are your long lost fans."

37) TERRORISATION

Jane held her arm out to beckon Melony, Mary, Steph, Francis and Evelyn to form a line on the right hand side of the bed. Each of them held the sharp wooden skewer they had taken from Michael; some playing with the tip with their thumb, feeling its sharpness, some rolling it between their fingers.

As each one of them approached having naturally ordered themselves into a single file, Byron's stapled, open eyes drew their gaze into his, everyone in some way waiting to contribute to his torture and to test his recollection of them. A few, still subdued by their own memories, their personalities trapped, lent towards him either pensively, frightened to some extent that he would still even now, be able to control them; others, their aggression brimming through them burning their complexions red.

Melony put her face within inches of Byron's halitosis and winced as the stink from his mouth captured her nostrils. Within that instant, the dormant overpowering, swamping presence of his adult body leaning over her when she was ten started to make her quiver, those frightened thoughts grabbing her mind from two decades ago. Steph put her right hand on her shoulder and felt her shaking through her body. She squeezed Melony's shoulder.

"Stab the bastard in the leg. Make him squeal. You're in control now. What's her name Elvis and now I'm here, what's my name ......do you remember.....quick, what are our names?" Steph's impatience was agitated, the aggression exuding from her, overwhelming and obliterating Melony's timidness.

Byron's eyes moved to look at Melony, her eyes although still fixed on his enforced expression, transmitted her own apprehension. Steph stabbed Byron in the top of his right thigh just to the right of his groin. He shrieked as his skin burnt like lightning had struck him through a thunder clap, his back arching against his restraints as his body kicked in reaction. Small droplets of blood formed around the staples in his eyelids as they strained to close, elongating the holes through them. Byron started to hyper ventilate, puffing and straining as the droplets slowly broke their globular form and trickled into his eyes. He shook his head as best he could, in an effort to get the blood from around his pupils but it had already mixed and diluted into his tears. Red watery smears washed over his lower eyelids and down onto his cheeks.

"What,.....are......our.....names?" Steph impaled each question into Byron's thigh with the wooden skewer, increasing Melony's confidence to interrogate Byron.

"Ahh, ahh . Ahhh. A................ " Byron screamed as the skewer gauged repeatedly into his leg, his last scream disappearing into a silent agonising breath.

Steph grabbed his chin with her left hand, forcing it down to his right making his face look towards her. Byron's objections pleaded in between each of Steph's words. She could feel the resistance from the muscles in his neck pushing his chin against her hand.

"What"
"No"
"Are"
"No"
"Our"
"No"
"Names?"

Steph's voice was assertive. "Look at us... Our names you fat bastard." She pushed his chin upwards, directing his eyes towards Melony.

He tried to shake the murky blood from his eyes so he could see their faces more clearly, forcing Steph to release the pressure off his chin. Byron stared manically upwards at their faces, flicking from one to the other, the strain of trying to remember their names showing itself in the tension of his forehead and cheeks.

Byron's body stiffened as if over come with rigor mortis as he girded himself to name Melony and Steph. His mind was a jumble of names from the past. His brain dredged through years of abused children, their young faces his lasting images. His eyes now were very little help while looking at these two women and ageing his memories of those children so that matched up to now adult faces threatening down on him.

Melony's inhibitions were leaving her as quickly as the adrenaline now surged around her body. She spoke up. "I'm beginning to really enjoy this. Last time ! ....what...are ... our ......names?" Her fist had now clamped tight around the skewer as she hammered its point even deeper into his right thigh muscle with every word.

"EEEEEEEEEEEEEE." Byron let out a long, pained, plaintive crying of despair, his thoughts of trying to remember their names again hijacked by the burning wooden point penetrating his nerves as it stabbed into his right leg.

The two women looked at each other and then back expectantly at Byron, waiting for his answer. They watched the tension seep out of his body as the initial pain subsided from his lower limbs.

His voice had lost all strength and volume. It sounded like he had run a marathon, gasping in between words. "You.....you are

Melony.........you're Melony."

He tried to direct his head and eyes towards Melony, to convince her that he knew her, even though unexpectedly through all their fury, his memory grabbed her name and face and managed to match her up to the woman stabbing him.

"And me ?" Steph snarled at him.

"Oh God, I'm sorry, I can't ....I can't see your face clearly enough to recognise you and.... and it's been so long.......you've changed so much."

"Ok, let me give you a clue. Do you remember the name of the girl who carried a little blue parrot everywhere with her? Do you remember taking that parrot and telling her she can only have it back if she's a good girl for The Bogeyman......Do you? Do you remember Beaky?"

The bird's name opened his memory. "Stephanie !"

"Yes, Stephanie. What a shame you can't remember me. I remember every night you bastard." Steph, incensed now and pumped full of hate stabbed her skewer into his groin and turned to walk away."

Byron's scream this time erupted from the back of his throat and was deafening, as the first numbing impact from her fist slamming into his testicles was followed by a searing, sharp, burning, excruciating rapier like sensation, shutting his senses down to everything other than the undiscovered agony that now engulfed his whole body. Steph looked casually over her shoulder as she put her arm around Melony, to walk away from Byron in order that others could move closer to test his memory. The end of the wooden skewer flicked erratically like a gale blown palm tree, its base buried deep into his scrotum. Byron's face could not distort enough to shut out the excruciation from his private parts.

She noticed the fresh blood as it started to form matching red shrouds around his wrists which strained against his restraints. His second scream was as loud as his first, almost seamlessly a continuation without noticeably taking in any air to re inflate his empty lungs. Byron's head was ruby, ready to explode. His right eyelid had shut over his eye, the staple pulled out of his bone around the socket now protruding through both sides of the skin. The holes through his eyelids were shredded into elongated slices through the thin flesh as his bodily reaction to this virgin pain forced his eyelids to try and close, only the right lid succeeding. His left eyelid looked twisted as the staple pulled out slightly on one side from its bedding. Fresh blood leaked profusely out from the torn holes in his eyelids, running instantly as four tiny, rapidly flowing red tributaries filling up the two lakes within his eyes, obscuring any hint of distinction between the whites of his eyeballs and his pupils.

Jane stepped forward almost awkwardly just for her first two paces, herself caught off guard slightly by Melony's totally unexpected change in character. She held her arm out, sliding it around her shoulder and steered both woman towards the foot of the bed.

"Well done Melony." She said in a congratulatory manner. "Good on you darling but I think we will keep that area to last......you know.... save the best till last." She smiled as she nuzzled her head against Steph and Melony.

Byron was still screaming, the impaled skewer sending wave after wave of unbearable pulsing pain along every nerve. Every sinew and muscle through each arm, leg, his body, his face, pushed to breaking point. Jane noticed Mary, Francis and Evelyn had their hands over their ears, all three despite their pent up hatred for Byron, momentarily shocked by the yin and yang of Steph and Melony's face off.

"Come forward ladies. We'll just let Elvis here gather his senses, just to give him a fair chance." Jane held her arm out to coax them into their presentation position in front of his face.

Jane walked around to the lower half of the bed. Byron was still screaming, his own involuntary shaking inadvertently creating his own purgatory as the skewer moved around inside his scrotum. "I'll have this back for now. We will need this for later."

Byron screamed equally as loud as Jane yanked the skewer out from his groin. His body convulsed and shook uncontrollably, his left eyelid again tearing at the staple, increasing the tiny spray of blood into and just beyond his eye and onto the top of his cheek. The blood from his wrists had run down to his fingers. His fists were sticky but he was beyond noticing. Jane glanced down at his trousers and saw the slight discolouration in the black cotton from the blood draining from his groin. Suddenly there was silence. She looked up at Byron's face and then to Natalie. Byron had passed out, his brain unable to cope or function with the level of torture his nervous system was transmitting.

Jane sighed, her breath and expression conveying her frustration to Natalie.

"Well,.......that's a bit of a party pooper isn't it. Mary did I see you pick up the second kitchen blow lamp?"

"Yes I did Jane. Do you want it?"

"No." She said nonchalantly. "Light it and give the back of his right hand a little suntan to wake him up. We can't have him sleeping here with all of us waiting for him."

Mary fumbled with the lamp, not having used anything like it before until she got it to ignite.

"Well done lovely. Now toast his hand."

Mary shyly held the blue roaring flame about four inches from the back of Byron's right hand. The wet blood started to bubble instantly.

"Make sure you move the flame back and fore, otherwise you will set his hand on fire.....you might even burn through and we don't want that when he is asleep."

Mary followed Jane's instructions, moving the flame forward and back across his hand. They all watched as she started to look like a body shop paint sprayer admiring the coating she was giving a car. The layer of blood that coated his hand acted initially like tin foil, protecting his hand from direct contact with the tip of the flame.

Byron's hand retracted into a fist and his body shuddered back to life, his wrists again tearing more skin away as they pull against the restraints.

"AAAAAHHHHHHH.......his eyes opened, shocked into consciousness, his heart pleading Jesus!. mother of god......aaahhh for pity sake no more please no more."

Jane looked around at everyone, smiled and announced, "Elvis has just entered the building. That was very eloquent Elvis I must say considering but it was Mary who was the mother of God, not Jesus and I would have thought a man of the cloth would know that."

Her tone remained sarcastic and scathing and it brought a ripple of laughter from everyone as she continued with her compere style. "Ok ladies, present your beautiful, grown up faces and let's see if Elvis can win some brownie points and possibly even some human compassion." She made the sound of a game show buzzer when a contestant gives the wrong answer. "Uuh uuh NO .....so come on Elvis, can you name these faces.....get all three and win a sip of water.........I know the prizes aren't very good but it's all down to cut backs and the small budget we've got to work with."

Mary turned the blow lamp off and remained standing in the same position letting Francis and Evelyn join her on her left hand side. They looked down in unison, putting their faces closer to Byron.

"Uuhhh......Jane, I think we need some water to wash his eyes out. We can't see them so I assume he can't see us. They're full of blood."

Jane looked at Francis and then at Byron, "oh yes so they are. I'll go and get some water. Hang on in there Elvis. I'll Return to Sender in a minute." Jane flicked her outstretched fingers to beckon a false cheer at the awfulness of her humour.

The blood swelled and diluted as Jane returned quickly from the bathroom below and poured the glass of water into one eye and then the other, ramming scrunched up toilet paper into the recesses of his eyes to wipe away the residue.

"Now Elvis, can you see the Three Degrees in front of you?"

Elvis's voice was weak. "Jane, please can I have some water...... please.?"

"Ooohhhh so polite ....No, not until you have named all three and only if you name all three."

She pushed his head back into their direction. "Cast your mind back Elvis. Name them."

Elvis' right eye blinked, his left eyelid still just about stapled open, each lid showing renewed signs of blood bleeding out of the wounds. He moved his head to help his eyes move from one face to the next, his right eye blinking repeatedly to alleviate the sensation of blood still trickling and mixing into his tears.

Byron deliberately tried to sound unduly pleased and happy

at seeing Mary, putting effort into his voice. "You are Mary. I would know you anywhere. You've not changed a bit. You are still the same."

Byron was right. Mary was instantly recognisable to everyone. She looked exactly the same only bigger.

"Well done! One down, two to go." Natalie's voice came from the other side of the bed. Her voice was mockingly encouraging. "Come on Elvis. Get that sip of water."

Mary unconsciously stood back allowing Evelyn and Francis to remain, hovering above Elvis's face. Evelyn spoke first. She had a distinct Scottish accent and had not lost it since being an eleven year old brought into the home away from abusive parents, only to then meet Elvis. Her move down from Scotland to Oxfordshire was prompted by the location of her mother's sister who unfortunately fell seriously ill after she had been taken away from her drunken, drug taking parents. The long term physiological damage was still with her. Evelyn lived alone, unable to commit to anyone, to fully trust any man. She unknowingly overcompensated by being louder within company. She wasn't confrontational but conveyed an appearance of being confident, eager to pass opinion and contribute to a conversation, giving her the persona that she would not be someone to be walked over.

She venomously stabbed the skewer without any hint of warning straight through the scapha area of his right ear, blood instantly emerging from the back and front of his ear. Byron screamed again, his voice showing signs of fatigue, both from his eroded strength and the excess amount of screaming it had already had to voice from the pains he had been put through.

Evelyn mercilessly pumped the skewer up and down through the hole as if she were rodding a drain, watching his head shudder with its movement through the cartilage of his ear. As the hole enlarged the blood flowed more quickly having no time to congeal. She squeaked with delight as she dropped her head to look at the skewer coming out from the back of his ear, just to make sure that it had gone all the way through. Evelyn swapped her left hand onto the skewer and yanked his head to turn towards her, his whimpering increased instantly to a squeal which delighted Evelyn as she clamped her right hand over his mouth, squeezing the skin under both cheeks together, forcing his lips to twist and open.

"My name runt." She pulled repeatedly on the skewer, dragging his ear out from the side of his head as she held his face firmly with her right hand.

Byron's wailing and simpering sounded a mixture of a dog pining to be let in and someone gagging about to be sick. His brain reeled from the reception of so many different sensations of pain. Evelyn's eyes were transfixed to his. She could see how weak he appeared. "Don't you pass out runt, not before you tell me my name. You wouldn't let me sleep would you, not even when I was crying myself to sleep."

"It's Evelyn." His voice was defeated. She watched his right eye flutter a few times as he drifted off into unconsciousness.

Natalie's voice adopted the same comedic announcers tone Jane had been using. "Well what a cheek. To fall asleep again in your own party. This is just not good enough and he was so close to having a sip of water. Now we will have to throw it over him to wake him up. Don't worry Francis your turn isn't far away."

Michael spoke up. "I think we need to give him a little longer to recover, otherwise we are not going to have the fun we want as he will keep passing out. Let's let him come around in his own time or say in about an half an hour if he hasn't woken up. Let's have a drink or something."

They all filed out the door, the sound of the thick, heavy duty polythene squeaking and rustling under their feet. There was quite a lot of blood under the bed having built up from the various drips coming from his body. Evelyn excited pointed to the blood pool below his head. "Ohh....I did most of that. Do you think he still has a lot of blood left?"

Francis said, "I'm sure there is still enough to go around. It's my turn next."

38) TEA

Everyone was talking at once as they all virtually fell over each other in a pumped up frenzy of activity, all eager to talk about their revenge on Byron so far and all wanting to contribute to making the tea, coffee or a beer.

The half hour passed in a blur and their attention was soon back on their return to the attic room. There was a feeling of delight as they stomped from the kitchen and all the way along the wooden floors to his cell.

Byron had come to some five minutes earlier. He lay still for the first minute or so trying to assess how he was, what hurt, what would move, what part of him was still bleeding. His thoughts moved on to how long he had to get away, how long he had before they came back to continue their retribution. He tried moving his hands but the pain from his wrists and the restraints instantly stopped any attempt to test their strength. His thoughts were stolen by the deliberate and emphasised regimented sound of their shoes as they marched upwards towards him, the sound from the wooden floors which helped Natalie around her home changing, as first some then others mounted the stairs from the hall, then the diminishment of volume as they reached the carpeted landing and its thunderous increase as they started up the creaking hollow stairs to the attic floor.

39) UNRECOGNISABLE

Everyone without saying a word, stopped as one in their orderly line and looked towards Francis, letting her go into the the room first and walk up to the bed. They all then followed and formed a circle just like General Custer's last stand around the bed to watch. The echo's from their footsteps died away and they all remained totally silent as they looked at Francis.

Francis stared at him motionless, her breathing controlled and normal. She held her right index finger to her lips to tell Byron to remain silent. He obeyed. When she eventually spoke a minute or so later, her voice was calm, gentle but chilling.

"I want you to look at me now and when I ask you my name...........when I ask you and not before, you have the one chance to tell me."

Byron blinked his right eye. His face winced from the strain of his left eyelid which still remained loosely stapled open. He tried to keep his blinking to a minimum but the bright lights in the room didn't help. They encouraged his eyes to water.

Now close up and studying her victim, Francis could see the affect the lighting was having.

"I think I can do something for that....your tears....the light." She looked around at everyone watching. The polythene rustled again as some people adjusted their stances to her glances.

"Tell me Elvis, do you like cats now, now that you have got

older?"

He moved his head slightly to respond. Francis leaned down to his face to listen, her voice remained gentle, inquisitive.

"Tell me Elvis ......do you........do you like cats.......now? You didn't all those years ago when I was with you. That may help you with my name but I would really like you to take a close look at me now ....you have one chance, so no guessing, just take a long look at my face and get it right.......for your sake."

Francis pulled her blond hair back away from where it fell against her face. Her blue eyes remained with a fixed intensity staring Elvis down. "Think of that sip of water, it may not be much but I'm sure it will taste wonderful. When was the last time you had anything to drink?....just think of that water. Now, one name and one name only. Have you had enough time to look at my face, perhaps put the sound of my voice to it although that would have changed in some way I know over the years as I've got older."

Her look directly at Elvis became even more intimidating. He stared blankly back as his mind feverishly trawled back through his memories of hundreds of children's faces. Francis did not come to mind. He started to try and give himself more time by umming and ahhing to show his mind was thinking but after thirty seconds it conveyed to Francis that he didn't remember.

"Times up.......one name......my name......what's your answer?" Francis could see the agitation in his body and head twitches, the anxiousness in his garish expression which came out in his voice.

"Uuhhh.....it's...........Alexandra. She had, you had, have .....blue eyes and black hair." He tried to convince her he had the right name.

"Alexandra! Not even close. I even gave you a clue when I

asked you if you like cats. I had a cat, well a kitten when they brought me to the home and you took it off my as soon as I arrived. You didn't ask its name, just said pets were not allowed cos if one child had one they would all want a pet of some sort, so no pets. You didn't even say sorry to me. You just took it away. When I started crying you told me to grow up. I was nine.

Now I have a little present for you. It's from my cats, something they left in the garden which when I knew you were here, I've saved specially for you."

Francis lifted up a plastic supermarket bag which flopped to one side with the weight of what was in it, filling one corner. She held the bag up to his nose, the stench hit him turning his stomach. Byron recoiled as much as he could.

"Uugghh...what on earth?"

Francis' voice was just so matter of fact, no threat, no anger, just a simple explanation and statement of facts as she looked around at everyone in the room while she spoke to Byron. "Cats.....well cat shit mixed with a little weed killer; apparently if you get this into your eyes, it can seriously affect your eyesight......you know make you go blind or that sort of thing. So we think we are going to do exactly what you did to Natalie only her condition was more psychosomatic ....I think that's right isn't ....you know something brought on physically because of mental trauma. Now we can't guarantee to do the same just from playing with your mind, that's sick enough already but Natalie's wasn't, none of ours were, you've done that to all of us in one way and that's not right. We've waited a long time. To be honest, I think most of us are surprised you are even here but thankfully," her voice changed to gush sarcasm, "our dear beloved Elvis, you are, so we are going to have to do it from a physical approach and see if that works. If it doesn't well there are a few medical people here who have the stomach and ability just to slice your eyes open; not quite as subtle we know but just as affective. Just think the rest of your life unable to see, not knowing when one of us might be standing behind your chair or your bed in that lovely Catholic Ministers retirement home.....just waiting.......just watching you."

Byron strained to move his head again as a natural reaction to hearing the immanency of what Francis had just said and the runaway thoughts that now stampeded through his brain.

His mind spoke to him as if he were speaking to another person. "Oh God, this is not going to end is it? Whatever they do next..... it's not going to be over ....it's .....it's just the start."

His hearing focused on the sound of the plastic supermarket bag rustling as Francis put it down on the floor. From where she stood, she made a show of putting on yellow rubber washing up gloves.

"You better have this." Jane handed her a clothes peg.

Her voice continued with an air of ridicule. "Now because we all love you, without this peg, there's a good chance you may be sick and choke from the smell of this stuff, so we are going to be nice and considerate and shove this on you nose. Oh and by the way, you didn't win that sip of water," she made the sound of a game show buzzer......"uuhh....ugh; only two names....bad luck."

Byron instinctively tried to pull his head away from the approaching peg, letting out a mouthy gasp as it clamped over his nostrils. Francis turned her attention to the bag of cat excrement. It smelt repulsive. Byron could almost taste the smell of the mixture as Francis laid a thick layer into each eye socket. His body and head quivered frantically as he tried to control his panic and the sensation of the slimy mix resting against his eyes. His voice sounded like he was full up with a cold as his crushed nasal passages changed the sound of his vocal chords.

"I'm so sorry....I'm so sorry, to all of you. I couldn't help it. I loved you all. Please stop this please, please."

There were glances between everyone, some now, the more timid ones, despite everything, looking a little awkward and sheepish at listening to his pleas; others, their faces evilly gleeful at seeing this pedophile at their total mercy.

Harry lent forward to take a closer look and recoiled at the smell.

"Holy cow, that really.....really stinks. How long do you think it should take before his eyes get really infected from that stuff?"

"About two hours is my guess from stuff I've read. The mix will work its way in, apparently it will start affecting the optic nerves, get behind his eyeball and then hopefully we won't have to cut his eyes out. That will be a bonus won't it Elvis?"

Francis patted him on the right shoulder as she watched him go stiff on hearing her last words. She smiled at everyone. Henry spoke a second time. "Should we wait here to see what happens?"

Everyone looked quizzically at each other. Jane spoke. "I think waiting here for two hours with that stench is not going to be very pleasant. I think we'll leave Elvis here to enjoy it. Come on, let's go back to the kitchen, we've got plenty of time."

40) REMINISCING

Back in the kitchen, the tea and coffee were left to one side by most people and the gin, vodka, wine and beers started to pour. There was a electricity between everyone with the euphoria of their captured hypocrite.

As the alcohol flowed, there were lots of hugs and cuddles as long parted friends told each other of occasions they remembered about their childhood together in the home. The unity with everyone became stronger as the drinks refilled. A few people were tearful as they remembered happy occasions and memories and their empathy with each other increased the longer they stayed in the kitchen.

The two hours disappeared quickly and their return to torment Elvis was announced by Jane who had been keeping an eye on the time.

Time for Father Byron had dragged on for an eternity. The smell of the mixture they had laid across his eyes still permeated through the taste buds on his tongue making him wretch as if he was tasting the smell. The feeling of the slimy mixture touching his eyeballs had made him feel claustrophobic inducing gasping, panicky breaths. He felt like he had been buried alive. The pressure pushing down on his eyes, the feeling of the slime running underneath his lower eyelids and squeezing below his one moveable top eyelid felt unpleasant, unnatural, adding to the panic that pumped through his body. Each minute of his isolation made him feel more mortal, that his life was on a thin string waiting to be cut and then it would end. Byron visualised Hercules, the Disney film he had watched with some of the children from years ago and saw

Hercules swimming after Meg in the sea of souls with the scissors about to cut his lifeline. He had laid there seeing his life ending the same way over and over again as he couldn't see a way out from the revenge that had impaled him on a bed.

The sound of the raucous, happy capturers stomping up the wooden stairs again, back up to the attic room brought him out of his mixture of semi sleep, unconsciousness and to another degree of fright. He knew from the sounds of their voices that they were different to how they had left him. There was a feeling of abandonment and that made him feel even more uneasy. They sounded intoxicated and that added to his concern. He strained at the wrists, hoping his bindings would break by some miracle. They didn't. There would be no reasoning with them now. He knew instinctively that his situation had worsened even more. Harry kicked the partly opened door so that it bounced back off the wall, the effect of its bang and subsequent shaking had the desired affect on Byron.

41) DAN

Harry held his nose as the stench hit his nostrils. "Jesus Christ, it's worst than when we left. Francis you need to get your cat crap off his face. You.....you seem to be ok with that."

Francis seemed unperturbed at almost being given an instruction from Harry. She emphasised the snap of the yellow rubber gloves, turning Byron's head as much as he could move it. In a flash of her hands, Francis scooped away the pungent mix laying in the recesses of his eyes and flicked it off her gloves, back into the plastic bag.

Natalie moved forward out of the huddle and poured a jug of warm water over both his eyes to wash away any residue. Byron's head and body stiffened and twitched as the remnants of Francis' mixture splashed onto the thick polythene covering the bare floorboards.

Byron blinked his right eye frantically, half expecting to be blind, half wanting to get rid of the last drops of water and excreta. Everyone looked expectantly to see in some illogical way, if he had gone blind. Byron continued to blink, his left eye still straining against the staple. Michael bent over Byron face and stared at his pupils to see if they looked different and if Byron reacted.

Byron stopped moving and stared back, a vague, directionless stare. Michael moved his head from one side to the other. Byron's eyes did not follow but remained fixed, almost zombie like, lifeless.

"Is he blind?" Mary asked. Michael looked back towards her. I don't know. His eyes are just..... staring. Can you see me Elvis."

Michael's voice raised in volume. "Elvis ....can you see me?"

Byron's eyes and unstapled eyelid flicked and blinked again as if in a spasm. His voice was remote almost as if he was talking to himself. "Kind of!"

Mary became agitated. "Is he blind or not Michael?"

"I can't tell Mary, I just can't tell. Would it be obvious, would it be instant?" He looked around for answers.

Jane walked up to Michael and put her hand on his shoulder. "No it won't be instant, not unless we are incredibly lucky. It will infect his eyes, they should be infected now, so it's just a matter of waiting." She turned to Byron, "it's just a matter of waiting Elvis, like the children used to wait for you but now we want to do other things. She put her hand down around his testicles and squeezed.

Byron let out a shriek which curtailed quickly into a deep groan as Jane's surprise attention brought sharp, pulsing throbbing burning to his genitals. His thoughts spoke rhetorically within his own mind. He was conscious of his body shaking. "I wondered how long it would take before this would come."

His own expectation of what they might do next made him shake involuntarily causing the bed to rattle ominously which delighted everyone. Their cackling laughter drew the very last grain of self control out of him. Byron exploded into a twitching, straining mass of aged unmaintained muscle and sinuses struggling against his restraints with every last oxygenated breath he could gasp in, to put strength into his trust up limbs and body. His voice screamed, its volume to Byron in a direct connection to the power he was exerting in trying to break free. His pleading almost became a babble of language, virtually indecipherable as his total panic robbed his brain of logical, coordinated and constructed sentences.

Everyone laughed hysterically as they saw his final implosion into a jabbering, quaking blob of God forsaken priest.

Byron's face was blood red with his efforts, the sweat still pumping out of his forehead, neck and cheeks and swilling around his head, his hair matting from the perspiration that oozed out of his scalp. He screamed where his voice allowed, breaking erratically as he begged his captures for mercy.

"No God....Jesus Christ..name mercy. I.... forgive, can't forgive myself....... please forgive me.....no more... more... I can't ......more , god no please no more....tell me.....me....what I can do ....I can't do anything.....it's too late......I can't I can't..... please help me......stop this now please.... PLEASE....nothing good.....children no.... I know that's me ......stop... forgive me, you forgive .....I deserved this but now no.....stop....STOP... let's ...can we please? Yes ? "

His delirium, his struggle, his ineloquent panic delighted everyone.

Eveline leaned in and grabbed his throat, her fingers unconsciously slipping around the back of his trachea so that his wind pipe became clamped. She could feel the ridges of the cartilages which made up the inside of his neck.

Byron gagged instantly at the fear she would squeeze her fingers and thumb together, crushing the framework of his neck. He shook again, wetting himself in the process.

"You disgusting little turd!" Eveline's voice growled out her revulsion, the veins in her neck and forehead pumped to breaking point, her control on the edge of slipping over and beyond regaining any sort of footing.

"I didn't think I would be able to do this but I can, trust me you snivelling, pathetic runt, I am going to.... I'm going to burn your balls off with a blow lamp so you know how I felt. You will never be able to piss again. By the time we've dumped you .....wherever, you will beg the hospital if you get to one, to make you a eunuch because there will be nothing left to work with between your scabby legs."

Jane's voice was calm. Her years of policing had taught her self control so that she had a calculated, manipulative manner to control people she was confronting. "Don't squeeze any more lovely. We don't want to kill him." She glanced down at Byron, his face as crimson as Eveline's, both people balancing on the boundaries; Eveline with self control, Byron with the abyss.

Jane deliberately added a bedevilled rider to make sure Byron didn't think there was the remotest chance of any leniency. "Well not yet. There's a long way to go and lots of people want to do what you have just said."

Eveline turned to look at Jane, the tension in her hands easing off as Jane rubbed her right shoulder. Her straining veins subsided, her face and complexion regaining normality as her grip around his throat slackened.

Jane could see the vodkas Eveline had in the kitchen, had given her the courage to break lose from societies conventions and her training and to go beyond her normal character. She smiled at Jane as she slammed the heel part of the palm of her right hand down along the bridge of Byron's nose, breaking it open across his face, the cartilage inside fragmenting to puncture the skin and split it virtually along its whole length.

Byron screamed a gurgling, cold like blocked nose scream as the blood spurted across his face and ran down his cheeks and down his neck, following the same blood tracks from his eyelids.

Jane leant back, looking admiringly at Eveline, her right hand still on Eveline's right shoulder, her voice influenced by her wry smile as she asked her question. "So you took those martial arts lessons I suggested?"

"Oh yes darling. I got myself to second Dan because no man, no one was ever going to do what he did to me ever again." She smiled another smile at Jane, this one conveyed thanks for the encouragement Jane had given her on one occasion she had visited the home and while looking around in a casual way so as not to spook Byron, came across Eveline hiding under a massive chrysanthemum bush, its blue flowers in full bloom.

Jane had heard a little voice talking to itself, one asking, one responding and had crawled under the canopy of the bush as best she could and found Eveline. With a little coaxing and some roll play with a one armed Cindy doll, Jane was for the first time given something positive against Byron. Eveline was only nine and Jane cuddled her under the bush and whispered, "I will try to help you and what I am about to say will I think, be difficult to understand but you are a big girl Eveline."

Within these glances which passed between the two women, both remembered that July afternoon from twenty odd years ago and the strangeness of a woman police officer trying to explain to a hiding child that as soon as she can, she should take up martial arts, Kung Fu so that she could fight nasty men.

For some unknown but lucky reason, Eveline remembered this conversation two years later when she was fostered out to a family with two six year old twin boys and to parents who had lost a daughter of eleven, three years earlier when she ran across the road in front of a car to get to mum who was looking in shops along the waterfront in Bodrum.

The parents who Jane had never met, after their two years of grief and disbelief at loosing their daughter, had watched a program about fostering and decided to give a least one child, particularly a girl as first choice, a chance at getting a normal life.

Eveline had been lucky and the twins and her foster parents all clicked together very quickly so that after fourteen months, they adopted her. The twins were boisterous and one day when they were watching Pokemon, Eveline asked if she could do martial arts and her new parents were encouraging people who gave her the opportunity.

Now it showed. The power with which she broke Byron's nose was evident to Jane and she appreciated the technique having done martial arts herself in her forties, while still on the force.

Byron lay shuddering from the impact, his head bolstered by the bed frame below, not allowing any concession to Eveline's aggression.

The two women now hand in hand as Jane eased Eveline away from striking distance of Byron, heard a round of applause and cheers from the others as Byron quivered along the length of the bed.

"Nice one Bruce!" Michael shouted from the background. Everyone laughed, their spirits heighten by the spirits they had been drinking.

42) DEBAGGING

"Hit him again Eveline, smash his throat in so we can watch him suffocate to death. I remember his hand over my mouth so I couldn't scream. Kill him slowly so we can watch it." Michael's voice was aggressive but not towards Eveline.

"There will be plenty of time for that but killing is too quick and too good and there's plenty of other things to do." Jane looked back at Byron, "assuming Elvis you are able to stay alive, stay alive....ah, ah ah staying alive, staying alive." She slipped into the Bee Gees song from Saturday Night Fever and laughed. Everyone started to do the dance actions as if rehearsed.

Byron had slipped again into semi consciousness, his body exhausted from hours of degradation and torment. His will to live had all but gone. His belief in God and that he would in some way, in any way conceivable, come to his aid, obliterated. His mind sparked with semblances of thought, nothing coherent or formed, just a multitude of reactions triggering wishes from the depths of his brain that he wanted to live somehow.

He felt the belt around his waist being pulled and it slipping through the belt hooks of his trousers around the small of his back.

His ears heard the roar of a blow lamp ignite simultaneously as the chill of a wide knife blade was laid across his Adam's apple and drawn slowly across the surface of his skin.

Jane voice was stern. "Don't either of you do anything yet. We need him to be fully conscious otherwise it's wasted."

He felt his trousers and underpants being pulled down around his ankles as his remaining awareness left him and passing out gave him momentary and unwarranted oblivion.

43) INSATIABLE

Byron was dragged back to consciousness by the raucous laughter and cackling of everyone in the room. His mind meandered from dark silence to first a distant hint of sound and it fooled him into thinking he was lying out in the sun on a sun bed. He felt hot and with his trousers down, he felt free, like he was wearing a pair of light weight swimming shorts. The laughter increased in volume as he came out from his delusion back to the reality of where he was. He partly opened his eyes, hoping his thoughts were real and he would find himself elsewhere other than tied to a bed.

"Elvis is back in the room!" Harry announced as Byron eyes fluttered. His voice obliterated the last bit of Byron's delusion.

He felt something cold and wet pour over his penis. The odour from the liquid was familiar but within the first ten seconds of the dowsing, he struggled to place it. The liquid ran past his scrotum and to his buttocks. He briefly enjoyed the tickling sensation as it tracked around his sensitive areas.

"Mentholated Spirit ! Oh God they're going to set fire to me." Instinctively he pulled and strained against those unyielding restraints, only rattling the bed as again his efforts failed to do anything else.

"You just do not learn do you." Harry said, as he deliberately tapped a box of matches lightly against the mis sharpened remnants of Byron's nose, so that he could see what he was holding; adding to Byron's spiralling terror.

"Oh God...." Byron was cut off by Harry continuing to talk over him deliberately to heighten the impending torture.

"Well," Harry said looking around at everyone now crowded around the bed, "you're not like we remember you....is he everyone?.......you are so much.......smaller now."

There were a few belly laughs and a few guarded, controlled stifles from Mary and Eveline, still inwardly scared that even now, in some way, if they were seen by Byron to be enjoying his predicament, he would still be able to control them.

"Please...please......every" .....Harry clamped his hand over Byron's mouth, cutting off his sentence. His retort was scathing, full of loathing and sarcasm......"what Father Byron? Please don't do this? Is that why you didn't stop when you heard me, Natalie, Nigel, Steph, Julie, everyone, beg you to "please don't do this, ...to leave us alone", that you just carried on. Do you honestly think that after .....let's just say twenty years to keep it simple, that you think one of us, any of us are going to stop because you have asked.......no...PLEADED us to stop.......I think the term you "holy" men would use, "hell will freeze over" before anyone of us will ever give a thought to letting you go.

What you did to us was unholy, inhuman. You were, ...are, a disgrace to the collar you wear and the hypocrisy from you and all the other Fathers who did nothing, knowing what you were doing to us. You deserve God's revenge, if there is a God. No, you deserve Satan's revenge because there was certainly no God in you, or them when we were in that God forsaken home, so don't expect God's mercy here. Am I right everyone ? Do I speak to Elvis here on everyone's behalf?"

There was a general, subdued agreement "hum" from some still concerned at Elvis's possible superiority and resounding YES's from those significantly more confident of their impending revenge. Those more certain put their arms around the likes of Mary and Eveline to give them reassurance, that their time had come and now this scourge of a man was going to get his reward.

Harry continued as the closest face leaning over, to put his features directly in Byron's vision. "So you see Elvis." He broke into a very off key rendition, "it's now or never, come hold me tight."

Melony spoke up. "oh no not that one, please Harry. It haunts me. He used to singing it walking through the corridors looking ....for me.....for us. I turn the radio off even now if it comes on."

Her face looked worried as if Byron could rise up and take immediate retaliation.

Harry went back through the mix of people standing in between him and Melony, passed Michael, James and Jackie to give her a big hug. They were in the home at exactly the same time, give or take a few days and that had given them a special bond even within this group of people as a whole.

He put his arm around her and said softly. "He is never going to be hurting anyone of us again after tonight.'

He squeezed her shoulders reassuringly while he asked. "So what should we do now my fellow sodomites .....now that we have this little.....frail....gnarled prick in front of us. Should we set fire to it now that it's saturated in meths or should we cut it off?"

"Both" Francis shouted with unexpected and unrestrained zeal.

"There you have it." His voice extended Elvis's clerical title. "Faaaather Byyyyron...one person has spoken but I would guess for all of us in fact.....can we wait to do this?".......... He looked around. "Can't wait for the little man here to light up like a little squirming glow worm."

He turned to ask who had the kitchen blow lamp but before he could, he heard the "poullll" of a flame igniting.

Jane came over to Harry and whispered in his ear. "Span this out. Remember we don't actually want to kill him. This is only the first part of it. We want him to suffer for years and years and years, so when Francis lights his shrivelled little dick in a second or so, I will be throwing a bucket of water over him to put it out. Then we can use the garden shears and whatever else comes to hand."

Harry looked at Jane and nodded affectionately, his forehead touching hers as he spoke.

Jane glanced down at Byron. "Well I tried to talk them out of it Elvis, but Marie's the name of his latest flame."

Francis approached the bed. Jane gave the little kitchen creme brûlée blow lamp carefully to her. Mary and Eveline walked through the group and stood beside her, either side and clicked the two other culinary blow lamps, all three looking at each other with now almost satanic expressions of revenge for roasting Byron, any hint of human hesitation now devoid from their ethics.

"After three girls, I'll count you in," said Francis, "just so he knows what's about to happen in the same way as we all did, when this fat prick pinned us down and he was on top of us."

Francis looked straight into Byron's eyes, glaring, her confidence brimming, hate exuding from her pupils. "Now Elvis, sing us a song which you think sums you up..........." She waited, the three blow lamps roaring blue and intense.

Byron's mouth twitched as if to start singing whatever song he thought would help him. No sound came out.

Francis looked at Eveline and Mary. "Well girls. No answer so far from the king himself. What do you think?"

Mary spoke up, her body twitching with unnatural evil, unnatural excitement as she looked first at Francis and then back down at Elvis. "I think" she sang......"you're the devil in disguise." She smiled delightedly as if she had answered the winning question in a pop quiz. Francis changed the song. "Try this one Mary...and Marie's the name of his latest flame."

"I totally agree." Said Eveline. "Well girls shall we toast this little sausage?"

Mary and Francis looked at Eveline and then around to the rest of his abused victims who had now all started spontaneously clapping in time to them singing "and Marie's the name of his latest flame........and Marie's the name of his latest flame."

All three of them looked back down at Elvis. Byron had found reserve strength at the impending incineration and was writhing on the bed, pulling frantically against his restraints, the skin on his wrists and ankles gauging chunks of flesh as the leather or plastic belts cut even deeper into already open wounds, drawing ribbons of blood.

Byron had become oblivious to the bindings and the slicing affect on his skin as he wrenched every last remaining muscle throughout his body to break their hold on his arms and ankles. His only focus and his primeval motivation was to save the unsedated burning off of his genitalia.

All three women without planning, held the three blow lamp flames so that they crossed like swords of the musketeers over his shackled body and looked down on Byron with a unison expression of revulsion and despise.

Byron was frantic. "Christ no! In God's name no." Byron screamed as he turned, twisted and fought to get his rotund body away from the flames.

"We all said something similar didn't we but did you?" Francis's voice was unforgiving. She looked at Eveline and Mary and they then guided their flames down to Byron's penis with her eyes. All three flames touched the bottom end of its shaft where it joined his scrotum.

The meths irrupted in a purple blue flame on his skin igniting his greying soaked pubic hair. In less then a second the flame had tracked around past his ball sack to the underside of his buttocks where the meths had flowed less than a minute earlier.

Byron's scream was louder than anyone had ever heard anyone scream and in that instant a few, including Mary and Francis despite their musketeers approach, wondered if anyone would have heard Byron from outside the house.

"AAAAAAAAAAAAAHHHHHHHHHHHHHH,   AAAAAAAAAHHHHHHHHHHH."

The blood pumped out from the open skin around the belts which had become mini guillotines, as he convulsed uncontrollably while the purple flames danced over his skin.

"Sploosh" the impact of the water from the bucket Jane was holding, hit him between the legs as if he had been kicked.

His screams continued at the same volume as the shock of his testicles being hit with a projected wall of water took the wind out of his lower stomach. His hands still instinctively jerked and strained towards holding himself, tearing away even more skin as they tore against the bindings.

"AAAAAAAAHHHHH, AAAAAAAHHHHHH, AAAAAAAHHHHHH." The volume of his pain infused a collective euphoria within his victims. Even those who had looked on with a little bit of squeamishness at the anticipation, had lost their reserve after the mentholated spirits ignited.

Byron's face was blood red. Harry looked on and wondered if

he might have a heart attack and spoil everything they had talked about over recent months with Jane.

They all turned to see where the water had come from, all surprised at the flames abrupt extinction.

Jane was holding the empty red bucket, which was still extended at the end of her throwing motion over Byron." Everyone wants a go at this fat, perve's dick, so if it gets burnt off on the first go, no one else gets a chance, so we all have to enjoy this and the little bit we get to do, so everyone can join in the fun. The day is still young. Let's give him a minute......poor boy and then some others can......" She paused, glancing around......."enjoy their turn." Jane continued with evil humour. "I think that's going to smart a little bit, I really do, I really think that's going to smart!"

She enjoyed the laughter back.

Byron face was covered with blood again, the pressure from his screaming forcing fresh flows from his broken nose. He shook from the contrast of cold water dousing the heat from the meths, the shock of its impact into his groin making him gasp for breath.

Natalie came around from the back of everyone, with a blue mop and matching bucket, acting like an old woman fussing over wiping her kitchen floor and started to soak up the water which was trapped from draining through the gaps in the floor boards by the heavy polythene sheeting laid across the whole floor under Byron. As she bent down to reach under the bed, the mop mixed the blood with the water into swirls of red.

"Someone's been careless with his blood, letting it drip everywhere. You need to be careful with this dear. If you lose too much you could die." Natalie patted his chest with her left hand as she mocked and taunted him.

Everyone laughed loudly as she continued to comically emphasise her mopping actions.

They watched expectantly for three minutes or so, as Byron slowly returned to a level of controlled breathing.

Jane stood over Byron, looking around at everyone as she took a pair of yellow rubber gloves out of her jeans right hand back pocket and made an equally comic display in putting them on, like a mad Frankenstein frantic around the monster he had just brought to life.

She took hold of his penis and moved it from side to side, examining the degree of burn damage.

"Well Elvis....you look a bit worse for wear but," her voice changed to mimic a sports commentator, "the good news everyone, he's hardly been torched, I mean touched, so there is everything to play for!"

Byron's mind had mulched into spaghetti. One strand of a thought would start to form and disappear into the mix. Another would start and end up in the same mix, inter twined and lost in the tangle. As Jane handled him, he instinctively tried to look down to see how much damage had been done.

Despite the way in which Jane announced his seemingly good fortune after the flames, his head slumped back in despair, knowing there was more to come.

Jackie shuffled to look more intently at what Jane was doing and stared down at what was left of his singed pubic hair, blackened and matted flat against his body from the water Jane had thrown over him

"Not a pretty sight is it lovely?" Jane said to Jackie. "Never was Jane." She paused........
"The times I had that in my face and he would stick it in my mouth." There was the glaze of tears over her eyes.

"Aaaahhh" Jackie punched him straight in the testicles, her

second punch following in an instant, the third as quickly.

Byron's body strained again as his nerves and brain responded to the onslaught from her right fist.

Michael shouted out. "That's the way girl. Punch it into his throat so he can see what it tastes like."

Jackie punched him three time again, his body shaking and jumping as her punches struck hard into his scrotum.

Jane left go of his penis and it retracted from the stretched organ it had been while she had been holding it up as she carried out her inspection and Jackie had carried out her own personal reprisal when she had timely become involved while Jane unplanned, had held it up for her, exposing his testicles.

She turned around, the same commentators voice.

"Ooh, I think he felt that one. Mohamed Ali would have been proud of those punches. What do you think champ?"

Jane turned to Jackie and grabbed his penis again, this time like a microphone. Jackie caught on, bending down to speak into it.

"Well Jane, it's been a hard fight and it's been a long time coming but I think I got the better of him in this one. What do you all think?" She turned, her arms wide open, beckoning for approval.

"Yeaaaahhh" came back from everyone like a tidal wave, sweeping Jackie back into the enjoyment of her roll play.

She continued to ham it up, the five vodkas in the kitchen and the adrenaline, a perfect combination for the loss of any inhibitions she may have had.

"I don't know if the fight is all over yet. Personally I think there is a little way to go but he's looking tired. I think anyone of us could take him in the final round."

Jane took hold of Jackie's right hand and held it high, as if she had just won a boxing match.

"Let's hear it for champion Jackie, the best ball breaker in town."

Everyone again shouted out a resounding "yeeaaahh," with clapping, cheering and a few with in keeping comedic back slaps on Jackie.

"Go for it champ" shouted Michael, "punch his balls through the top of his head."

Jackie again looked around at everyone and then specifically at Jane, almost seeking final approval.

"There's your target Hun. Do you want me to hold this little............... little chipolata sausage out of the way, so you can get the final knock out punch?"

Jane pulled on his penis, stretching it taught like a fleshy elastic band, lifting Byron's scrotum so that his testicles were on show again.

Byron vomited whatever little he had left in his stomach on the impact of Jackie's final punch, his exhausted body barely able to cope with any more abuse. The contents of his stomach regurgitated and then slowly oozing out of the side of his mouth, somehow stifled his cry of pain into a gagging, squeak; his head turned to his right to let the trickling vomit leave his mouth, falling through the gaps in the springs to join the watery mixture of blood on the polythene.

"Ladies and gentlemen ....the winner by a definite knockout." She again held Jackie's hand high.

Everyone looked at Father Byron who had passed out.

There was a happy murmur around the room as they laughed and waited for Byron to come too. After about five minutes he started to stir. He jerked awake. Michael kept up the torment.

"Right, we need to start cutting this bastards balls off. Who's for the scalpels?" Byron was instantly aware, his voice vibrating with the effort to speak.

"NNNOOOOOOOOOO. For the love of God no, please please please don't do this please."

Byron found another reserve of strength, forcing him to strain and sit up as much as he could, the bindings still strong and in control, his head and neck straining to lift away from the bed as he tried to look down the length of his body and to plead with Jane who was still hovering over his groin.

Jane's voice was authoritative, calm, conveying no leeway to Byron or to everyone else.
"For the love ...of God ? You keep saying this as if this is going to make a difference. God has no place here and he certainly didn't have any place with you when all these were just kids. So I afraid this little monster is going to have to go."

Byron's anticipation was again uncontrolled, raw panic. There were tears streaming from his eyes. His breathing had degenerated into a mixture of sobbing, gagging, gasping gulps, just bodily impulses divorced from his brain. His head thrashed around, looking at everyone moving around the bed, his mind totally focused on the impending castration.

The belts continued to draw fresh blood from his wrists and ankles but he was still obvious to it. He watched Jane purposely parade around the bottom of the bed, crossing from one side to another, her right marigold protected hand still stretching his private parts to the extreme of their elasticity, like walking around a human maypole.

Michael walked around the bed and down to stand next to Jane. He opened James' small black canvas pouch he had brought up from the kitchen for James and let it slowly unfold in front of Byron. James watched and smiled. There was a glint of the surgical steel handles of four scalpels, their blades sheathed within the segregated canvas compartments.

Byron's voice disappeared into a conglomeration of hisses, grunts and terrified indistinguishable worlds as he writhed and jerked.

Michael's voice was as controlled as Jane's.......calm, deliberate, threatening.

"I think he's getting excited. We are going to give you a face lift but ......it's not on your face."

Each movement of his ex victims, became like lions stalking a wounded deer. They could feel and see his panic streaming around every sinew and vein in his body as they walked around the bed. They were in unison. As if choreographed, they all transformed their movements to slow, menacing shapes, leaning in over his face as they circled the bed, some flicking their arms out as they past further down his body to draw his attention away from whoever was looking down into his eyes, the distraction causing him greater agitation and they knew it; they loved it.

Byron was demented, his mind was in total melt down. His past digressions from decency with the now adult faces of the children he had abused, brought wave after wave of horror as he watched them circle him. He could recall virtually very lurid, disgusting defamation he had inflicted on everyone of them and now he was regretting for the first time because of their superiority, his past actions. Twenty odd years ago the concept of today, what he was enduring now, had not even entered his thoughts. Those nights of stalking any one of these children down the darkened corridors had been an excitement, a game he couldn't loose, with no consequences. He was too clever, too superior. Now those consequences were punching into every conception of life he had ever had, every nerve, every muscle was experiencing retribution and his anonymity had been destroyed.

His voice was still hoarse and strained, his words just about distinguishable, his speech had again lost consciousness coherency. Everything he was trying to say, was a desperate   man rambling through panic, his brain not fully connecting to his tongue. "Jesus Christ, ...God please, you don't, you don't ....what?, can you help........., you can't ....no don't .....don't....can you?   Stop this ....yes...no stop it all .....have you lost your, ...my minds ?" There was just no continuous train of thought that he could string together, it was just delirium.

Michael stopped circling the bed and stood next to Jane still pulling Byron's penis as taught and as long as it would stretch. She was grateful she had chosen the marigold rubber gloves. As she stood there, the thought of actually holding his flesh repulsed her.

She had never liked that aspect of men, having seen what she had seen from a very young age of nineteen, by becoming a police woman.

Her years on the force had brought her into contact with, to her, the unfathomable degradation of how men treated women: the calls to domestic violence in people's homes, where a woman would be lying on the floor, curled in a corner, blood covering her face and a Neanderthal macho man striding around the living room spraying out his territory like a feral cat. The only thing that was missing was a wooden club, the sort Jane always associated with Fred Flintstone.

She had watched and listened to these men as they tried to justify their incredulous aggression against the women they professed to love while the women backed down.

Going to the care home and listening to a five year old, ten year old child, trying to explain to her, something so unnatural, so alien in their innocent lives, had torn her heart out. She had become obsessed with wanting to bring the perpetrators to justice. Unfortunately Father Byron had always managed to talk his way out of things and just through his presence with the kids, had conveyed enough intimidation to influence them into changing what they had said so that it became a contradiction or too confused for Jane to either officially report or arrest him. There had been no help from the other Fathers in confirming anything like some of the children who had been brave enough to say anything; had said to her and their covering up and closing ranks had galled her. Jane felt they were almost as guilty as she had suspected Father Byron of being and it disgusted her that they had remained mute, their silence condoning what he was doing.

The Chief Constable at the time had demanded that she obtain solid evidence before he authorised any action against a Catholic Priest and that it would not happen based on hear say or the ramblings or the confusions of a child.

Nigel leant forward over Byron's face and stayed looking down on him. Byron's eyes were still full of tears, his breathing still sharp, shallow breaths. He tried to stare back, for a moment his focus totally on Nigel who angrily glared into his eyes.

Byron glanced down towards his groin where Jane was still pulling tight on his shrunken penis, the foreskin stretched to its extreme, like a straining snail trying to get its head over the finish line in a race.

Nigel brought up from his left hand side a little stuffed rabbit, about eight inches tall which had faded from the bright yellow of his childhood to lemon white. The backs of the rabbits very long ears had kept a lot more of their original colour where the sun and light had not had such an ageing affect.

Nigel held the rabbit directly in front of Byron's damaged nose. He took a deep breath as he gently shook the toy, making his six inch ears dance from side to side.

"Do you remember Mr Ears?" He waited for Byron to answer. He didn't. Byron shook his head slightly bemused as he tried to clear the water from in his eyes, so that he could see more clearly.

Nigel asked again, more aggressively as he glanced again down to Jane and Michael.

"Do you remember Mr. Ears?"

"Uhh !....." Nigel didn't wait for the rest of Byron's response. He carried on as if he were playing with a six year old child.

"Mr. Ears remembers you, don't you Mr. Ears ?" He turned Mr. Ears to look back at himself, nodding the rabbits head, his ears giggling.

Byron looked hard at the rabbit, his puzzled expression fixed on the rabbits nose which Nigel was twitching by manipulating Mr. Ears' head.

Nigel continued to talk as if talking to a child, turning Mr. Ears head back to looking at Byron, the rabbit clearly telling him off through his animation. "Mr. Ears is not going to be very happy with you if you don't remember him. He remembers when you took him off me and put him in a cupboard. He was so lonely and he thought he would never see me again. HE remembers YOU putting me in that same cupboard with Mr. Ears as well because I didn't want to do any of those nasty, horrible things you made me do. Mr. Ears remembers you making him show me what to do because you made Mr. Ears do those things to me first and he didn't like that either."

Nigel turned Mr. Ears to look back at himself and brought the rabbit close to his head so it could talk into his left ear.

"That's right Mr. Ears. I know you didn't think you would ever see this nasty man again but now that he's here, what would you like to do to him for all those naughty, naughty things he did to you?"

Mr. Ears whispered into Nigel's ear and then went back to looking directly into Byron's face. The rabbit was motionless, just staring and waiting.

Everyone around had stopped moving and had become engrossed instantly, listening silently apart from a few giggles, to Mr. Ears; some remembering Nigel as he had been with them, a quiet, shy boy but a caring little boy.

Nigel turned Mr. Ears head so that he looked at everyone standing around Byron. Mr. Ears looked back at Byron, his head moving slowly from side to side, his long ears swinging. Mr. Ears looked down at Jane and Michael and then at Father Byron's penis. He turned his head to look back at Nigel and then turned back, putting his nose right up to Byron's eyes.

Byron stared back, blinking occasionally as he wondered at what Mr. Ears was doing.

"AAAAAAAAAAAAHHHHHHHHHHHHHHHHHHHHHHHH-HHH, AAAAAAAAAHHHHHHHHHHH, AAAAAAAAA-AAAHHHHHHHHHHHHHHHHH."

Byron's voice was shatteringly loud. His whole body jerked and shook, every sinew straining, the veins in his face, neck and all along his arms instantly and un expectantly bursting to prominence as his brain reacted to the slamming nerve endings within his foreskin as Nigel snipped off the end with the wire cutters he had discretely held in his right hand.

Nigel said nothing. Mr. Ears looked expectantly around at everyone. Everyone was cheering, back slapping and cuddling each other. Mr. Ears nodded his face frantically in front of

Byron who was shuddering and convulsing with the excruciating pain shooting from the end of his penis, or at least where it used to be, through his nervous system and cudgelling his brain with sensations he had never felt before.

Every inch of his body was pulling against where he had been restrained, the belts gauging mercilessly into his open woulds, cutting deeper to his bones.

Byron was unaware of any pain from the restraints as he thrashed around, his hands and arms instinctively moving inwardly to try and clutch his penis, to alleviate the agony he was experiencing. Wave after wave of nauseating revenge pounded his head. His mouth frothed, blood seeping from lips bitten unintentionally as Byron's body struggled to cope.

He could do nothing. He was helpless just as these children had been helpless years before.

Mr. Ears looked back at Byron, putting his nose right up against his face as the restrained Byron writhed uncontrollably.

Nigel moved the wire cutters upwards along Byron's body and dropped the foreskin onto his chest.

Mr. Ears twitched with excitement and leant down to Byron's chest, where the bloodied foreskin lay. He looked back down to Byron's groin area and twitched as he watched the blood pump out of the severed skin which had contracted back around the shaft of his penis, the purple tinged main body of his abusive genitals deluged crimson. Mr. Ears twisted to watch it running down to his testicles in a free flowing torrent of red.

Father Byron's mind could no longer function through this purgatory. His screams and cries continued to delight his childhood victims as his body reacted to his unanaesthetised circumcision.

Mr. Ears looked up at Jane and Michael and then at everyone around them. He turned his head to one side, conveying he was thinking what to do next. Byron was still beyond gaining control and continued to scream.

The rabbit looked down at the penis flesh on Byron's chest laced with his own blood and with Nigel's help, picked it up with the end of his little front paws. He looked around again for approval to resounding cheers and squawks from all of his fellow colluders.

"Feed it to the bastard. Make him eat his own prick, like we had to do." Melony's anger brimmed with venom, her memories now controlled over years of self reconciliation.

Mr. Ears looked at Melony and then back at the foreskin and then into Byron's eyes. Nigel started singing, "Return to Sender, return to sender!" as Mr. Ears carefully held the un bloodied end of the foreskin with his paws, his head jiggling furiously, conveying hysterical laughter.

Byron's face was still grimacing from the pain of his circumcision, his face contorted and sweating, his breathing almost extinct as he fought to cope with the waves of pain throbbing and burning from his groin, the veins around his temples swollen to bursting from the lack of fresh oxygen as his natural functions were almost shut down by excruciation.

Mr. Ears hovered with the bloodied skin above Byron's mouth, waiting for Byron to realise he was there. Seventy to eighty seconds passed as everyone waited for Byron to rejoin them. His face wet with bloodied tears, swathes of red across his cheeks, running into multiple streams down onto either side of his neck.

The rabbit turned his head again and looked around at everyone, nodding as he did so.

Everyone started singing, "return to sender". Mr. Ears looked back at Byron watching his breathing reestablish itself. Byron's lips relaxed, parting as they did so.

Mr. Ears stuffed Byron's own body part deep into his mouth, clamping his jaw shut with his paws, shaking Byron's head to encourage him to chew his own flesh.

"Uuummm, uummm, uuhhhh, uuhhhh." Nigel sounded. Byron wasn't allow to speak. His jaws were forced together so that he couldn't do anything other than chew his own body. He gagged as he swallowed the inch or so of his blood coated genital.

Melony was the closest to Nigel as he bore down on Elvis from behind Mr. Ears. He was still grimacing "return to sender" through gritted teeth.

Melony was excited. "Cut another part of his cock off now. Make him eat it bit by bit." She grabbed the cutters out of Nigel's hand, smiling satanically as she did. She was elated.

"Crack"

"Eeeeeeee" Natalie dropped a bag of ice that she had slipped away to get and dropped it on Byron's bleeding penis, the jagged edges and cold creating a new un welcomed and contradictory burning sensation.

"That should help take the pain away and bring things back to size!" She pressed down on the bag, forcing the freezing affect to burn and the jaggedness of the ice protrude painfully against his skin.

Melony looked at Natalie with surprise and a slight hint of anger at being stopped from snipping off another half inch.

Natalie put her left arm around Melony and gave her a hug. She said reassuringly, "there's still plenty of time, ...plenty of time. Remember......let's share it out." She turned to look at Byron. "HEY ...... Elvis how are you feeling. Are you ready for an encore?"

Her question passed Byron by. His mind had melted into a gunge of pulp. He was no longer thinking, just feeling and reacting, just about existing.

Mr. Ears looked back at Nigel and then to Byron, not that he noticed and waved bye bye with his right paw. Nigel and Mr. Ears moved back into the group to resounding cheers.

Natalie slapped Byron hard on his chest with the palm of her right hand to bring his attention back.

"Right Elvis, let's keep this concert rolling."

Michael lifted up the open, dangling pouch with the four scalpels and held it where Byron could see its contents.

"I'll only need one, well unless one goes blunt."

Natalie started to sing, "I saw him lying with a scalpel" changing the words to one of Elvis' songs and then started laughing, her laughter gaining momentum as the funnier it became to her. She held onto the side of the bed as it developed into a belly laugh, infecting the others around her, turning them into a curved wall of cuddling, huddling friends, all laughing with her.

She continued laughing, talking to herself out aloud. "Oh God, I'm sorry.....come on Nat, get a grip girl.....oh dear, I kill myself, no I mean you, I'll kill you."

She slammed the palm of her hand down hard again on his chest creating a hollow, dull thud. The response from Byron was weak. "Uhh."

By comparison to Nigel's attack, this was easy.

"Now Michael, what do you want to do with his balls?" Jane

lifted the bag of ice off his groin. Byron's penis had shrunk back almost up into his body. Jane looked at it and then at Michael. "You haven't got much to work with there Michael. Shall I get you a magnifying glass?"

"Na, it's ok, as a dentist Hun, I'm used to working on abscesses and lumps which....well let's say are about what.........I know, the size of a small cat's balls. In fact, I think a cat's ball would be bigger than Elvis here."

Elvis shrieked as he saw Michael swish the blade in front of his face for the first time like a buccaneer. His voice was weak and shaky, almost too exhausted to protest as the blade glinted.

"Is there anyone who would like to assist doctor? I have a spare pair of marigolds if they want them." Jane looked around at everyone. For a moment no one responded apart from the giggles that were still filtering around the group.

"What colour are the marigolds. Will they match my eyes?" Francis asked, laughing as she moved forward.

"Not unless your eyes are pink." Jane handed the gloves to Francis, who then followed Jane's earlier lead and hammed it up putting them on.

Francis' four gin and tonics from earlier in the kitchen were well into her blood stream and she had lost her usual inhibitions.

She grabbed Byron's penis as if she were seizing the last cooked sausage on a plate, when you come in after a drink and you are starving. Byron cried out as her fingers crushed the severed end of his private part. She yanked it taught, his scrotum and testicles appearing to come out from inside his body.

Her tone started humorously but transformed into one full of anger as she remembered those same words which used to echo slowly after her in the empty, hollow corridors and rooms she fled into, to get way from The Bogeyman. "Still a bit cold dear from the ice? We had better coax them out so Doctor Michael can do his stuff. Come out, come out wherever you are. I know you are in there. You can't hide from The Bogeyman. Father Byron tells me you've been a little naughty, so I've had to come here, to show you what to do."

Byron's efforts to recoil and struggle wilted and appeared half hearted, even to his vanquishers around him. His eyes were pouring with tears, fuelled by the pain from his partly mutilated private part solidly in Francis' hand and the traumatised terror his whole being was engulfed in.

He was now reduced to a sobbing shell, unable to think anything through. His mind could only cope with the primal instinct to survive and it told his mouth to save himself. Byron could not hear his own voice, as it repeated over and over again the same thing. "Have some mercy, please, please, please, please, have some mercy, have some mercy, please, please, please."

Francis tore on his penis, her anger still boiling. "I remember saying that. Do you remember, do you?" She screamed it again. "DO YOU?"

Byron's bottom almost raised off the bed as Francis exerted a monumental lift using his private as a handle. His mouth grimaced, his teeth grinding together, his scream emerging through puffed cheeks, his forehead visibly enlarging as his blood pressure burst into his skull, almost crushing his brain as it swelled from his excruciation.

Francis held him there, his weight irrelevant. She was focused as she looked at Michael. "Now castrate this fat bastard. Can you see his balls, cut them off and stuff them done his throat to follow the end of his dick."

Byron's scream again surprised nearly everyone around him,

preempting the blade cutting into his scrotum. Unlike Nigel who caught him by surprise, the terror of his anticipation, escalated the impending incision a thousand fold. His attempt to break free reached a monumentous height as he tried unconsciously to build on his already elevated level and go beyond the braking strain of his bindings. His mind had turned off to any pain they were creating as they cut unforgivingly through already open flesh wounds, down to where they were scraping against his bones. Fresh blood geysered from the slices in his skin, his wrist and ankles burning as the bindings cut relentlessly through more tissue but this was irrelevant, his brain could only see the scalpel and his imagination had jumped to its conclusion before it was about to become reality.

Everyone looked around at each other as some held their hands over their ears, as his screaming went beyond expectation.

Steph went frantic. "Holy cow, shut him up someone, they will hear him outside. I didn't think anyone could be that loud. Put something in his mouth, cover his head. Do something, someone is bound to hear outside." She started to look around for anything to put over his head, to stuff in his mouth. She couldn't and then realised she was wearing a blue and yellow scarf. She grappled with the knot, tightening it in her panic to get it off from around her neck, her frustration within seconds encouraging a flow of tears.

Natalie put her arms around her. "Darling, the room has been sort of sound proofed. There is, well, let's call it padding on every wall and where the window is. Superman would have a job hearing him. Natalie squeezed her reassuringly. Steph's panic subsided.

"Really? Are you sure?

Natalie watched her come back to calm, her arms still hugged around her.

"Yes. Absolutely. Now let's enjoy him screaming just like most of us did. Carry on Michael, you can do us proud."

Michael turned to James. "Do you want to do this? After all, theses are yours." He flashed the staple towards his friend.

"No no, it's fine, you carry on and enjoy yourself. Show me how it's done."

There was a collective laugh from everyone.

Michael flashed the scalpel in front of Byron's eyes for a second time. This time everyone, after hearing Natalie's reassurance to Steph, joined in with Byron's screaming, transforming their screams and shrieks into cheers, almost drowning out Byron's purgatory as he convulsed and shook to the scolding sensation the surgical steel created as Michael carefully sliced around his testicles.

"You have to be fair, that is loud, I mean really loud." Harry quipped with a purposeful amount of volume within his voice, to be heard within the gaps of Byron's screaming. The few who were still cheering, responded to Harry. They went silent to listen to their friend. Harry continued. "Day ooh, day-yyyy oh, like tooooo loud man, toooo loud." He mimicked the Harry Belafonte record of the sixties.

Michael looked up. "Nice one Harry," and went back to his castration. "You are doing really well there Francis. Pull him a little tighter. It doesn't help me it's just more painful for Elvis."

Elvis screams started to slow, his body started to slump back onto the bed and then he collapsed into a state of relapse. He was unconscious. His brain had shut down, unable to cope with the intolerable pain, its sub conscious safety mechanism trying unknowingly to save this satanic paedophile.

Michael looked around at everyone who had become silent

while watching The Bogeyman having his dreaded weapon dissected, fall "asleep", in the middle of it all.

Jackie spoke up after a twenty second stunned silence. "That's wasn't supposed to happen was it?"

"Uhh.......I don't think so." Said Julie, " I mean we don't want him unconscious do we?"

Michael paused from cutting open Byron's scrotum. He sounded frustrated. "Well.....what do you want me to do. Do I carry on while he is out of it or what?"

Jane's voice was firm and matter of fact. "It would have been nice if we could have cut these off while he had been awake but you can't have everything. Michael can you finish on his balls and then split his dick down the length of his urethra so that every time he pisses it virtually kills him."

"Not a problem. It's a pleasure." Michael was about to insert the point of the scalpel when Jackie put her hand on his. "No, making him feel everything is the only way, don't do this when he can't feel anything. We felt everything so he must as well. He didn't show us any........" she paused to think of the right word to use.........."any mercy....I .....we, we all had to endure everything he did to us and live with it for years, so he has to as well. How can we wake the bastard up? Do we have smelling salts? Do we throw water over him? Have we have a cattle prod or something?"

Her questions stopped and she paused again, her eyes darting around everyone, her thinking process written all over her face. "A cattle prod would do it, wouldn't it? I mean it will, jolt him awake won't it. He can't get away with this, bloody passing out stuff. I didn't, did any of you? I just remember.." there was a very long, thoughtful, poignant recollection back to when she was nine, the tears welling up in her eyes. Her voice changed from the determined certainty of the adult she now was, standing in front of her friends, back to the vulnerability and innocence of twenty years ago, when she was The Bogeyman's target for that night, for that two weeks of consecutive nightly pursuit.

"I just remember everything, every night, every detail, his weight on me, squashing me, his smell and we all do, so no, he has to feel everything and feel what we have done to him today for the rest of his life. Killing him is too quick. So how do we wake this bastard up?"

Everyone looked around at each other for some kind of response. James put his arm around Jackie. "Well......it just so happens," he started to talk as if to wind an audience up, "that I anticipated this and I have a pungent little bottle in my scalpel pouch. They will wake the dead. Here, you do the honours."

He handed the small purple labelled bottle to Jackie, who was now smiling gleefully.

"You clever man." She took the bottle and pressed it up under Byron's nostrils. Its smell was so strong within fifteen to twenty seconds some others were starting to wipe their eyes. Byron remained still. His brain had gone into deep shutdown to avoid the agonising traumas his body, his nerves had been sending it. It had reached a point when it was frightened to exist.

They watched expectantly and he remained motionless. Then............his damaged nose, crusted with drying blood twitched. Jackie glanced around excitedly again as his head moved to his right, just the smallest of movements. He returned static. Another fifteen or so seconds past and his nostrils flared as the vapours continued to attack his sense of smell, dominating and excluding anything else that his nose might detect.

His head jerked, a still unconscious reaction to the salts strength.

"Come on Elvis, come back to us. That's a good boy, come on, come on." Jackie talked as if she was talking to her dog. "Good boy Elvis, come on, we're waiting, come on."

His head continued to move from side to side slowly at first, its reaction as the smell and the salts waking affect made their presence known, accelerating its movement until it was trashing around, straining to escape the burning the vapours started to inflict within his sinuses. Jackie could not keep up with Byron as his head jumped for relief so she held the bottle centrally and everyone started laughing when she gave up trying to follow it.

Byron's eyes opened and instantly began to water. He was still not back in the room. Jackie went to remove the bottle but Michael stopped her. "A bit longer, he's not fully awake yet."

His eyes darted erratically. They had no focus and then a scream as the latent pains around his body reconnected with his consciousness. "Aaahhhh, aaahhhh."

Jane announced. "Elvis is back in the building and we are all back in business. Hip hip.. Hooray." Everyone joined in.

Jane put her right hand back onto his chest. "How are you feeling Elvis, ready for another prong?"

His voice was weak, just above a whisper. It conveyed defeat. "Please, ...please, I ....will give you anything I can for.......for you to stop this. I'm sorry..... for everything I did, to ......all of you. I will give you ....anything, please !"

Mary spoke from behind. "Can you give us childhood back."

"What?"   "Can you give us our childhood back?

"Uuhh.........no." His answer was cautious.

"Then you can't give us anything." Mary swept forward, past Jackie and straight down to his groin area. As she moved in front of Michael, she smiled as she used her body to encourage him to give her a bit more space.

"This is taking too long." Her voice was determined and impatient. Almost robotically, devoid of any human emotion, she grabbed his flaccid penis, as if she were holding an overlooked, limp withered carrot she had taken out of the salad draw of a fridge, straightened it as she held it in her left hand, lifted the small battery operated drill she had chosen in the kitchen, looked at it for a second, as if wondering how to use it and then without any further hesitation, drilled down through his urethra, the small black drill bit designed for wood drilling, gauging out tiny bits of flesh, her hand, his penis and scrotum engulfed by another deluge of blood.

Incredibly, the plastic belt on his left wrist snapped as the force of his reaction to grab himself passed beyond anything he had consciously been able to generate before. His wrist, was covered in dried and wet blood, the fresh blood dripping off his fingers as he tried to clutch himself to ease the pain. With one hand free, his body was able to turn a bit more off the bed allowing his convulsing to be wilder as he shook and writhed within his greater level of freedom.

Everyone jumped or shuffled back, all surprised and startled as they watched him thrash around, his left hand virtually crushing the previously mutilated end of his private part and now the unimaginable pain from having the soft inner core drilled out without anaesthetic. His mind unbelievably recalled when he had a catheter inserted a few years back and how uncomfortable that had been even while sedated and it tried to measure the difference in pain as if when quantified, he would be able to cope.

He screamed without stopping, his body movements uncontrollably violent while trying to subdue the unfathomable sensation burning from within his bored out penis. The bed rattled like it was in an earthquake. The conglomeration of all the noise, swelled to an incredulous crescendo and remained undiminished, its intensity and volume unreal. Even some of his torturers, all unused to anything they were doing now, despite their years of pent up aggression and loathing towards him, felt unnerved. Byron's body shuddered and jerked as if he was being continuously electrocuted.

Whatever bodily fluid he had within him became transformed into a regurgitated gungy foam of vomit and bile oozing out between teeth bitten lips, blood seeping out from their swollen surfaces. He could not speak. Byron had fallen into the depths of hell as he had portrayed so many times. "Your will be in eternal torment," whatever "eternal torment" was, though he had never envisaged the torment would be as painful as he was humanly experiencing over a significantly shorter period. Whatever Lucifer had planned for the souls of those that arrived in Hades, he could have taken lessons from this group of novices. They, after years of self doubt, insecurity and the longing for revenge and come to a point where they had lost their humanity without realising it. Had they, it wouldn't have mattered.

They looked at Byron and each other, their glances intense and erratic with excitement and tension which conveyed the elation they were all feeling at watching him bleed and convulse, his screaming transcending from being noise, to fill them with energy and satisfaction. Byron's mind had lost control. His reactions were primitive and basic. Every nerve was burning, an inferno of pain, his mouth wide and taught as his screams exploded out of his lungs and then seconds later, his agony still escaping through clamped teeth, his cries still swamped with torture but the sound of his torment changing as his mouth involuntarily switched from open to closed.

They giggled and laughed, some awkwardly as they partici-
pated in his destruction.

Byron's struggle started to slacken after about two minutes,
his eyes gushing tears, his withered strength evaporating until
he shut down for a third time as he passed out.

Byron woke up, not knowing he had been unconscious for fifteen or so minutes, his forehead on the bed springs. He felt
different, everything about him was different angles, different
pressures on his body. He tried to focus his eyes. As they adjusted, he could see the spring coils and through the gaps, the
polythene covering the floor boards underneath. He blinked,
things looked unusually blurred. His head somehow had more
freedom but as his muddle cleared, he realised he was facing in
completely the opposite direction from previously.

He shook himself as best he could to gain composure, like a
dog that had just come out of the sea and in doing so, felt fresh
bindings holding him into a different position than before he
had passed out. He rocked his head, trying to get clarity. The
sniggers of his capturers filtered in as they watched him working out what was happening while his consciousness visibly
returned. The steel from the bed frame pressed unforgivingly
into his knee caps. He became aware that his legs from the
knees down, splayed away from each other.

As his mind sent signals around his body looking for answers,
the answers coming back started to stoke up his fears again.
The memory of what he had already endured spun around in a
whirl of half finished thoughts and the pain each had created
became real again. The intensity from his penis suddenly hit
him as did the freezing, burning feeling that surrounded it,
caused by the economy family pack of frozen peas which Jane
had stuffed down between his legs after they all manhandled
him off his back and turned him, arranging him like a cat
about to pounce; placing his legs, bent at knees, to support his

weight along with his elbows and wrists laid along the frame in front of his body, all of which were belt tied again to the bed. The overhang from his stomach jammed the peas in place. Byron tried to move on his knees, to ease the pressure from the solid bed frame but the ties around the back of them and at his ankles stopped any movement he tried to make. His bottom was sticking up in the air, the bag of peas, shrinking his scrotum, eliminating what would normally have been a hanging pair of testicles for any man in this position, like a cow need milking. It was still, not a pretty sight but it had everyone in raucous laughter as he struggled when he got back to full realisation.

Despite now regaining full consciousness, inwardly he slumped but his body's position remained unchanged. Nothing had been said but he knew what the next depravity was to come.

As he listened to their laughter he jolted with the shock from the chill of the KY jelly or what other lubricant jelly they had picked, as Eveline slapped a dollop onto his anus.

James crouched down in front of his face and looked directly into Byron's eyes. "Well well, who would have thought twenty two years later I would be here." Byron lifted his head, as heavy as it felt and looked back at James, waiting motionless, for the next comment.

He had already come to the conclusion, once he was fully aware, that his strapped up, bottom up position would be for his annul sodomising.

His voice was even weaker than when he was lying on his back. There were still tears in his eyes from the discomfort of his contrived position. His voice declined to a level of despair as he talked. "James, please James. Help me, you, they...you, don't have to do anymore to me. You've beaten me. I'm done. Kill me if you want to. I really can't take anymore. I am so, so sorry for what I did to you, all of you."

James was patronising, putting his right hand on Byron's left shoulder as he talked back to him. "Well the thing is Elvis, we have all heard this over and over and over again, over these last few, memorable hours but as Jackie said, we had to endure everything so you must as well. Killing you is too easy, too quick, although I admit there are a few, no names, no pack drill, that would do that without hesitation I think but over the last few hours, despite I admit, months and months of planning, once Jane had found out about the new retirement home for priests and that you were in it: we have more or less planned tonight as we all wanted to meet up with you again and thanks to Natalie.....let's hear it for Natalie!" James broke off from conversation with Byron to promote Natalie with an air punch for her achievements, "Natalie you were, are...... beyond anything or anyone I have ever met and I love you Hun. You have been so brave especially as you couldn't see to do what you did to get him for all of us. You are brilliant and to be fair Jane........Jane, you never gave up on us and now you've got him..............we've got him and it's thanks to both of you."

He looked back relentlessly into Byron's eyes. There was no hint of mercy. "So you see Elvis, uh hah, we are going to give you the same experience as all of us endured in one way or another."

This confirmed Byron's new fears and he tried to slouch his body to his right side, to protect his back passage. The mixture of the belts, his age, his weight and shape didn't allow for much movement so all he felt was strain and pain on his joints and within his tired, weak muscles.

"So! " James continued. "What would be the equivalent size of a pigs, sorry preachers dick to let's say, an eleven year old?" Have anyone of us got something we can use.

Mary shouted out, "a cucumber."

"Good suggestion." James replied, he paused and then used the thumb and fore finger of each hand by touching their finger-tips together, to try and make a comparison to the sizes he had just asked for.

"Don't think that's big enough. Something a little bigger. Let's stretch the imagination."

There was a pause as people thought. Byron glanced around, his face clearly showing he was dreading the next suggestion.

By now the affect of the earlier alcohol and the few top ups when Byron was unconscious had everyone virtually in game mode. Only Natalie and Jane had controlled their drinking as all this, was taking place in Natalie's house.

"A fire extinguisher!" Nigel shouted.

"He's not an elephant. James shouted back, laughing as he re-plied. He look back purposefully at Byron. "Think a fire extin-guisher is a good comparison?"

Byron's eyes widen at the thought he might actually be ser-ious. He went after a few moments to answer. James put his hand across Byron's mouth. "We'll find something suitable."

Byron shook his head as much as he could in protest while James still clamped his hand over his bloodied, swollen lips.

"We'll find something that you will appreciate. Now anymore suggestions?"

There were various shout outs. "A wine bottle, a fist" Jackie stopped herself, "perhaps not a fist....uuhhhh...,,,, sorry .....didn't think that one through!" Everyone including Jane and Natalie were now hysterical.

Nigel shouted out, "A chair leg." "What?" James said surprised. "A chair leg?. no....do you mean a Chippendale one of those curved ones. That would find his G spot."

The laughter continued. Mary leant forward and looked Byron straight into his face. "I've got Thor, a twelve inch long dildo. It's about five inches around." She looked around at everyone listening and enjoying her turn to torment. "Is that big enough do you all think?"

"Five inches around makes it about two inches in diameter. No that's not thick enough for this arse hole."

Julie had a brain wave as she started to try and explain what she was thinking, despite the hilarity of the moment. "How about a flexible toilet brush! Are there flexible toilet brushes, you know what I mean, ones which bend around the U bend.?"

The laughter dwindled as people began to think about her suggestion.

She continued as everyone looked at her. Even Byron strained his eyes to look upwards at her as she stood to his left hand side, trying to explain.

"Think about it. The brush will be bristly and if it's flexible will go up inside him. When it's in his butt, we can roger that in and out and the bristles will ....what?.........." she hesitated as she thought, "they will rub against his insides." She stopped talking but her thinking continued, which she then shared. "No......they won't just rub against his insides ....They will cut his insides.....won't they? .... Do they do flexible toilet brushes?" She looked around again with everyone now looking at each other.

"Well" said Michael pensively, "that's a really good thought. What about a stiff brush, the sort you use in wine making when you need to clean the demijohn. I used those when I was in university and did brewing and wine making, ...it was cheaper."

There was a moments silence as everyone looked at everyone in the hope that someone had one of these brushes. Even Byron who had now subsided into an almost semi relaxed state listened and wondered to the conversation.

Suddenly it hit his brain. "Those brushes aren't soft, the bristles are .....are hard...oh god that's ....that's going to tear me up inside." The panic reappeared on his face and he thought in some bizarre way, he was part of this conversation and that his concern would be registered and accepted by everyone else. It wasn't. Their almost collective thought was, "what a good idea!"

Some of the older ones recalled in that instant the feeling of Byron on top of them.

Mary stood up from her continued face to face with Byron. "Have we got one of these things. I mean if we have, let's get on with it." There was another short silence with Byron looking as best he could up at everyone, with expectancy.

Jane had waited patiently listening to the humour was thin al of their suggestions and then spoke up as if she had had a brain wave. "Hang on a minute I've got one of those. Give me five minutes and I'll be back."

Jane started walking to the bedroom door, taking off the yellow marigolds as she did, smiling to herself for anticipating the culmination at their thinking as to how and with what to violate Byron. She thought to herself, "here's one I prepared earlier!"

Nigel spoke just before she left through the doorway. "Jane... great if you have but don't rush. I don't know about everyone else but I need a top up and a loo, so let's have a fifteen minute or so break. What does everyone else think?"

There was a general murmur of agreement and everyone shuffled out of the room back down to the kitchen, leaving Father Byron strapped firmly to the bed frame. In the silence he became aware, now that his thoughts and his body were his own, of how much everything hurt. The old iron frame was unforgiving, pressing against his knees and elbows. His lower back started to send signs that it needed to be stretched out of the bent position he was in. The bag of peas had lost the frozen intensity and as he moved with the overall restriction within his bindings, his mind dismayed about this instant, this here and now.

In the kitchen, more drinks flowed after toilet stops for virtually everyone.

In the attic room, silence. Byron had lapsed into being barely awake, yet within his reduced awareness, he thought about what was coming. Years ago in the care home, he and some of the other Fathers had done home brewing. It was cheap and it gave them access to more alcohol than they were expected to have, as priests.

"This brush" that had been referred to was a familiar item in the brewing process as it got right down inside the demijohn and the bristles were firm enough to scrap off the film and scum left inside the fermentation jar.

Despite the light being on, things didn't look particularly clear. He blinked his eyes repeatedly to get more clarity. He started thinking about the cat excrement from hours ago. The panic mounted within his contemplations. Was he going to go blind as they planned because of the infection? His mind jumped. "The cleaning brush! How stiff was it?" He tried to remember how it flexed or didn't, when he used it twenty to thirty years ago, to clean out the one gallon glass jars. He became aware again of the KY jelly on his anus, its chill, waining but the slimy affect still there, between his buttocks. He made a half hearted attempt to pull on his bindings but nothing gave way. The only thing noticeable was that he felt the cheeks of his bottom pushing together as he tried to exert some strength to break free. The large dollop of jelly squished between his buttocks.

He tried to move his left hand to unstrap his right and then realised that someone must have re strapped it too the bed so he was once again, completely bound to its frame.

Again, the now familiar stomping up the wooden stairs, bellowed their return. He tried to work out how long they had been down in the kitchen and by working that out, how many extra drinks they may have had. Byron stopped himself when he realised the stupidity of his thoughts in trying to work this out. He could feel his previously subdued heart rate rising as their approach grew louder.

They were all laughing from the extra shots of alcohol when they walked back in on Byron.

They had talked about their approach, how they would treat him on this last confrontation. The gin, vodka etc were having their affect. None of them said anything to him, they were just silent apart from giggles and sniggers as they walked into the room. They again, formed a circle around him.

Byron's neck strained as he tried to look upwards at every-one standing around him. The light was bright in the room and worked against his eyes, restricting his focus, especially from the angle he was looking up at them. They remained si-lent, each of them controlling their laughter in different ways. There was a collective feeling emanating from them that this was to be the last act of revenge.

Their presence hovered over him, their silence becoming more intimidating than their laughter. He felt his bottom pro-truding in the air and he tried to make it discreet by lowering it but his bindings argued against his intentions, reminding him of his wounds. His eyes caught a glimpse of something which on a quick glance, looked like a bicycle pump being passed around his grown up predators.

He started to think about asking for mercy again but then slumped as much as he could, giving up on the idea. In the quiet, was a brief moment of unnatural peace.

It didn't last long.

He felt the extremely uncomfortable and unnatural sensation of something touching the outer edges of his rectum. He tried to move away from it but he couldn't break the contact it had made with his skin. Byron willed himself to move further down the bed but again his bindings stopped him dead.

The pressure of the thoroughly smothered demijohn cleaning brush, started to force open his anus. It was slow at first and he could feel the mass of KY jelly ooze around the inside of his buttocks as the tip of the brush ingress into the large dollop they had plopped onto his back passage earlier. He started to grip the sides of the bed in anticipation and struggled to look behind him, the fear of not being able to see what was happening as great as being able to see what his torturers were doing.

Mary knelt down in front of his face. "Yes I've seen that face before. I've seen it on your face Michael, that night you tried to help me."

Michael looked at her from the other end of Byron. He was eight years older than Mary and had been fifteen and a long time unselected resident at the home when Mary first arrived at seven. People wanted younger children than he had been when he first went there at twelve years old. He had been a gangly kid and tall for his age but not much physical strength, despite Byron's nick name of Thor for him.

He heard Byron with Mary one night very soon after she came to the Catholic orphanage and had gone out into the corridor and followed them. She was younger and reminded him of his sister who had been the same age when Louise and his parents were killed in a car crash, on their way to pick him up from his friends house as he had stayed there longer than he should have. He never forgave himself for that and the aftermath of guilt had made him very insular and sullen as he beat himself inwardly every day for what had happened.

This had been a major factor on why he had been left on the shelf. People didn't want problem baggage.

The Bogeyman had turned on him when he had grabbed hold of him, to pull him away from Mary, who was crying because the room he had taken her into was totally dark and she was still scared of the dark even now.

Byron abused Michael with just one table lamp turned on so Mary could see what he was doing. "This is your fault Mary, all your fault for crying. Get down on your hands and knees and tell me what he looks like and remember it because you did this to him."

Mary sobbed as she told him "Michael's face is all screwed up and its wet."

That had excited Byron more.

Mary looked back at Byron. "His face is beginning to screw up and his eyes are wet." She said with a big grin across her face.

Michael pushed hard and slow on the stem of the brush, the top part of the gunged up bristles pushing into Byron's back passage. The KY squidged and squelched as the brush head penetrated his colon.

"Now his face really looks like yours did." Mary said with glee-ful, childish tone. She could remember exactly how Michael had looked that night and the masked face of The Bogeyman that Father Byron, Elvis had warned would come if they had been naughty. Mary could never remember what she had done that day that could have ever been seen as naughty. She remembered playing on the swings, colouring in a Disney Princess picture of Cinderella in her ball gown and singing along with Elvis with some other children, on the grass under a big tree in the garden. She hadn't been naughty.

She remembers crying out aloud, "stop you're hurting him," but The Bogeyman was unforgiving.

Michael started to push and pull the brush backwards and forwards, the jelly almost regurgitating from his back passage. Byron's face grimaced and contorted as the amount of pain increased with every thrust, the bristles starting to protrude through the lubricant as it dissipated, nicking the soft tissue of his anal track.

Michael thrusted and retracted harder and faster, enjoying watching Byron visibly ripple as the discomfort transformed itself into pain. The bristles closest to the handle of the bush started to turn pink and with every retraction, the shade grew darker, becoming red, transposing the clear jelly matted within the bristles, with first a coating and then the infestation of the lubricant with Byron's blood as they shredded the soft inner tissue of his back passage.

Byron writhed and pulled against his bindings, squealing in agony as this unknown, hideous sensation tore him open from the inside. It felt like nothing he had ever experienced before and it confused his mind as he could not see his injuries. This divorce from connecting a cut or bruise visible on any outer part of his body and the feeling his nerves were sending smashing into his cranium, violated all logic. His head throbbed from the pressure of blood flooding into it as his neurones tried to cope with this oscillating agony, while the bristles snatched and clawed at his bowel wall.

"Michael, Michael, Michael." As if one body, everyone started to chant in rhythm to Michael's thrusting, getting louder with each stroke, speeding up to increase the violence against

Byron. Their encouragement was virtually drowned out as Byron's yelps and whines transposed into raped, guttural screams of sodomy.

The brush had turned totally red, the bristles flicking splatterings of blood on Byron's buttocks and folded up legs as they exited his rectum.

Michael finished with a flurry, totally out of time with the frantic and now, unsynchronised chanting of his name to exact revenge. Byron continued to jolt and jump as Michael threw the bloodied brush into the half emptied bucket of water Jane had used to wake him up. The water swirled red.

Those that couldn't see clearly from where they were standing, shuffled around to look victoriously at Byron backside and the blood oozing from his anus and running down the inside of his quivering thighs.

Mary looked around at everyone and then back firmly at Michael. "And that's what you call a good rogering I think Michael! How about you?"

Michael was rubbing the top of his right arm, his shoulder muscle aching from the exertion.

He went and gave Mary a hug, others closest to the pair joining in.

Byron's head was covered in perspiration, his hair flat to his head from the water poured over him earlier and his new sweat. His face had contorted into a grimaced, twisted mass of expression and muscles, his features almost unrecognisable as he struggled to cope with the latest abomination his body had endured. He wretched repeatedly, his gagging inducing a similar reaction in a few around him, until he expelled a small amount of bile and then virtually passed out, his mind shutting down again, to block out every feeling and sensation.

There was silence as some swallowed or coughed to control their own throats and regain composure. Byron still remained their focus of attention as they all stared at this fallen, evil hypocrite.

Slowly their attention started to spread, catching the eye of each other as they looked around, each feeling a surge of mutual approval and satisfaction at everything each one had done and contributed to their combined revenge on Byron. Their faces expressed their uniform transformation as smiles started to spread, the realisation to all of them, that they had done as much as they could without actually killing him.

The smiles became sniggers, to giggles to a few uncontrolled short sharp almost self conscious outbursts and then into a wave of combined raucous, body folding laughs and shrieks of elation as his punishment became their realisation.

Byron remained unconscious to the bedlam of the hysterical laughter surrounding him. As if dancing the conga, everyone walked around his tethered body looking at him from all angles, their laughter beginning to ebb after they had walked around the bed for the third time.

As if in homage to Jane and Natalie, everyone in turn broke away from the line and hugged them individually, either kissing their thanks on their cheeks or the simple "thank you" whispered lovingly, affectionately, gratefully Into one of their ears, with a heart felt hug.

When the procession had finished, they all stood looking at Jane and Natalie.

"Well!" Said Natalie jokingly. "He can't stay here. I've lived with him too long now. Once is enough, so let's get rid of him. How about a final drink before we dump him back by the home."

There was a final nod and gurgles of approval from everyone as they walked down the stairs back to the kitchen for a last top up.

Jane watched them leave the room and then stood still, just staring at Byron's motionless, bleeding, mutilated body. She stood there for at least two minutes, soaking in the final view of this sanctified paedophile.

"Got you, you bastard."

Jane turned, closing the door behind her as she walked down to join the others.

44) DISPOSAL

The atmosphere in the kitchen was boisterous, the final drink turning into three or four.

Jane took hold of Michael and Nigel's arms as they
laughed and chatted, Nigel occasionally throughout their conversation, mimicking Michael's "rogering" action, provoking more laughter between them.

"I need to hose off all the blood and tidy him up a bit, just a bit before we dump him close to the home. Can you two help me?"

Jane unbuckled the belts. Byron's body didn't move he was still unconscious and he stayed that way as the four of them including Harry, manhandled him down the stairs, down through the kitchen and out into the back garden, where they stripped him off totally, before Jane hosed him down. Even then, his body was so far in shut down that she had almost finished sponging and washing off the blood and stains before he started to come to.

He shuddered violently awake as his senses regained awareness, turning onto his front instinctively to hide himself, the patio slabs hard and cold as the water pooled on them temporarily.

"I wouldn't worry about that Elvis. That's way too late? Jane's voice was unemotional, a statement of fact.

She threw him an old, holed towel. Dry yourself off and listen. Her voice remained the same but the threat it carried was clear.

The three men, Natalie and Jane watched as his pained, slow movements to dry himself off was clearly a monumental effort. He remained kneeling. Byron face winced and twisted as each movement became more and more uncomfortable, each twinge increasing in pain and adding to the next. His hands involuntarily darted to his groin and bottom as his movements reminded him of the injuries and attacks those parts of his body had suffered.

Jane walked around him, inspecting him for blood, there was none.

"Elvis!" Her voice was raised to grab his attention. "Elvis.........Byron..............Thhhheeee Bogeyman ....whatever your pathetic little mind thinks you are or were.....listen."

Her voice returned to its normal level but the threat still obvious within her words.

"What has happened to you will happen to every other priest in that God forsaken home you live in, if you breathe a word of this to anyone, like every child here you threatened with worse to come if they told "your little secret," worse will come to you and every other Father that knew you and probably knew what you were doing. It's up to you. You "keep this little secret" or everyone around you will suffer and then we will be back for you.........especially you. Do you understand?"

She gave him a gentle final kick between his legs which made him gag as he tried to breathe. Jane didn't need to kick him any harder. The last hours and mutilations had weakened and sensitised his body. Harry and Michael pulled Byron back up onto his knees as his strength to hold himself up had disappeared.

They lifted him onto his feet, the weight of his body increasing the pain in his groin and back passage as it pushed down onto his hips and through his legs.

Jane continued. "Yes you can feel it can't you. We can be back. Now help him dress boys so we can get rid of this perve."

Harry and Nigel did what they were asked, happily enjoying his grimaces and whines as each movement proved to be more and more agonising, while Michael helped more to support his weight.

Everyone clapped him as they supported his slouched body through the kitchen and down the hallway out to Jane's white Honda Jazz.

It was 2.30 am now so there was little risk of being seen by the neighbours as they pushed him into the left rear passenger seat.

"Remember!" Michael said as he stood by the door waiting to close it, "it's our little secret."

Byron said nothing only his head moved with the slightest of nods. The three men got into the car and Jane got behind the wheel and drove out through the gates slowly and back to the rear lane, close to the priests retirement home. The journey took about four minutes and it was silent, only Byron made squeaks and squawks as the bumps found his injuries. All four smiled to themselves at first with continuous looks to each other as the journey progressed.

Jane pulled the car into the lane to which, the rear garden of the home had a high, locked wooden gate. She looked in the mirror. Her voice was harsh. "Chuck him out. He can crawl back to the front door."

Michael got out of the front passenger and opened the back door. He grabbed Byron by the scruff of his neck. Nigel pushed him from the side, between them Byron scraped against the door sill and collapsed onto the floor by the side of the rear wheel.

Harry had walked around to where he was lying and gave him a final kick to his chest. Byron rolled over, holding his groin and at the same time trying to find enough hands to reach around to his back passage. Pain returned from every direction.

Harry's voice slurred from the alcohol. "Remember, it's our secret."

Byron lay on his back, holding himself, the darkness folding around him as the rear lights faded out of sight at the far end of the lane.

45) SANCTUARY ?

"Father Byron, Father Byron, are you alright ? Can you hear me?" Byron thought he felt his right arm being shaken gently. His eyes remained closed as his brain started to function.

"Father." The voice filtered through his ear drums and sounded familiar. "Father." There was a softness to it.

"Is he waking up?" A different woman's voice, agitated and quick, came from the other side of the bed with a broad Scottish accent. "Father! Father! The shake on his left arm was frantic. "Father, dear God, Father wake up! Are you alright?"

The shaking awoke pains and nerves which brought Byron slowly around. His holed eye lids twitched, the staples having been removed while he had been unconscious but they still felt like they were scrapping across his eyeballs as he blinked against the light seeping into his irises.

His head turned slowly towards the Hebridean accent, his eyes squinting to try and focus on Iona's voice. He tried to lift his right hand. The agitated voice continued.

"Dear Mother of God, Father, what happened to you. Have you been hit by a car? Your hands, your ankles! Your.....your....your ....face Where have you been? You've been gone for days. What's, what's, what's?"

The first woman's voice remained calm and slow but through his waking haze, he still heard a strange menace within it. "Iona, shhhhhhhh. What ever it is, Father Byron will tell us......if he thinks he should...... or can."

His brain waded through its memories to identify this voice, the familiarity unnerving him as he couldn't put a name to it. His eyes opened fully and he blinked rapidly against the light. He turned his head to face Iona and went to speak.

"Uhh...."

The other voice stopped Byron from continuing. "Shhhhhh, save your strength. You are going to need it." The hidden intimidation still laced her words.

Byron turned his head and squinted to try and see who was talking to him but nothing he looked at was clear, there was just differences in light.

Iona took hold of his left hand. "Jane is right, save your strength. You can tell us when you're feeling better."

His thoughts froze and his fingers stiffened around Iona's. "Jane...who's Jane? Which Jane?"

He tried to look around himself at where the voices were coming from and who was standing by his bed. Nothing was clear. He started to panic. "Who's Jane ?"

Jane put her hand firmly onto his right arm to settle him. Byron stopped moving and looked towards her.

Iona carried on trying to reassure him. "You've not met Jane before, she's only been here for a couple of months, part time and mostly in the kitchen, oh....and sorting out the news papers and books for you all and laundry, so you probably have not have seen her around, she's been back stage so to speak."

Byron pulled his arm away from Jane as he made the connection and recoiled into the soft bed mattress as much as it would let him. He felt déjà vue as he rubbed his eyes again to try and see her face clearly but her silhouette remained blurred. His mind played tricks. It thought he was back, tied to the metal bed frame and his hands unconsciously felt around the side of the mattress. His eyes followed his fingers to re-assure himself that what he was feeling wasn't the same bed he had been strapped to. Now Byron looked agitated and his body shook involuntarily. Iona continued to press him to tell her what had happened, her voice rising in pitch as she became more impatient.

"Father you must remember what has happened to you, where you have been, how have you got so many injuries?"

Jane put her hand back onto his upper arm and squeezed her finger nails discreetly around the inside of his bicep. Her voice was subdued but direct. He still detected her threat, both in her voice and fingers. "Come on Father, you need to rest. It looks like you have been through the mill.......somewhere. Now we've met, I just want you to know, I will be happy to help Iona keep an eye on you, make sure you are safe. We wouldn't want anything else to happen to you."

Jane turned to Iona, her face innocent and deceiving. "Would you still like me to work those extra hours we talked about a few weeks ago, to help you out ? I think Father Byron here may be glad of the attention. Oh...and you know that doctor I told you about, well, he's a surgeon actually but he is happy to come here for an hour or so each week and ...well I suppose, give a little bit of medical advice if any of the Fathers have any sort of issue. Don't get me wrong Iona, I know he's a surgeon but he's very knowledgeable. His name is James, James Don-aldson. Do you think he would be helpful Iona?"

Byron looked towards the shape he took for Iona, his face showing apprehension on hearing the name "James."

Jane gave his arm a second undetected squeeze with her nails. "From what Iona tells me Father, James used to be in the care home you used to be in when he was a child. I'm sure you would like to meet him again and see how he's turned out. Is it right that some of the other retired Fathers here used to be in the same orphanage as you?"

Iona was surprised and hesitant. "Well.....yes, uh of course he would be, wouldn't you Father Byron," she said on his behalf, looking at Byron then Jane. "Yes, you're right, there's also Fathers Patrick, Lewis and John. They all cared in the same orphanage at the same time as Father Byron here. You'll see Jane, they are all great friends. I'll introduce you to them soon.

Jane responded casually as she looked demurely at Iona. "Yes......that will be nice, getting to know a few more of The Fathers."

Byron held out his right arm, his hand pointing to the bedside draw unit, his fingers gripping at thin air.

An Irish accent filled the room, stopping everyone by surprise as Father Patrick dressed in black trousers and red tea shirt blundered through into the bedroom, followed by a middle aged policeman, helmet in hand. "Byron! Good grief what's happened to you where have you been? Father Lewis said you crawled back into the house in the middle of the night. Where in heavens name have you been since Thursday night? That's the last time anyone saw you."

Everyone turned to look at Father Patrick. He stared at Byron for a few moments expecting him to give some sort of an answer and then glanced at Iona and then Jane. The policeman looked on silently, waiting for the opportune moment, having assessed the situation he had walked into.

Father Patrick interrupted himself on seeing Jane. "Oh, uh, who are you.......you....you look familiar. Have we met before? I'm Father Patrick. Do you know what happened to Father Byron?" He held his hand out to shake Jane's hand.

Jane didn't answer but looked back at Byron as if to. Byron

still had his hand outstretched. He looked back at Jane furtively. Jane turned back to Father Patrick and shook his hand and asked quizzically. "Do I look familiar? Come to think of it, I think you look familiar as well.....Father Patrick did you say? Did you work in the same orphanage as Father Byron here?"

"Yes I did for twenty years."

Jane glanced at the policeman and smiled widely. "Hi Paul, nice to see you again. How are you getting on?"

He went to respond, a surprised and curious look on his face as he looked at Jane for his first concentrated moment..... "Jane! good God Jane." His voice lightened as he smiled, his recognition of his senior mentor from his early days. Iona's voice turned their attention back to Byron. "What do you want Father, something from your draw?

Byron made some sort of noise which was indecipherable to Iona but she took it as a yes.

She opened the top draw of the old oak cabinet, the draw scagging on the runners as she pulled on it. After a few pushes in and pulls out, she managed to open the draw to look inside. There was an A5 size brown envelope at the back of the draw. Iona took it out and went to hold it towards Byron but the contents tumbled out onto the floor as she spoke.

"Is this what you wanted?....oh God, sorry Father."

Iona looked down on the pile of white, oblong pieces of card, or so she thought. She bent down. "What on earth are all these....just pieces of card? What have you got these for?"

Iona turned them over like a pack of playing cards. Her eyes widened as she thumbed through.

"Why have you got pictures of children? She paused bemused. " Are these...... the children you looked after?"

Jane smile, beckoning to Paul to follow her out of the room and then looked back at Father Patrick.

46) TAXI TO !

Natalie walked slowly into the taxi rank office, her right hand leaving the door handle and stretching out in front of her, guiding her to the desk covered with two flat computer screens and connected keypads, papers, log books, two full ash trays and a half drunk two litre bottle of full fat coke. Her nose twitched at the stench from the cigarette smoke that had infiltrated everything within the fourteen foot square office that had been made from an old store room at the side of a small convenience store which had long closed as a result of the competition from the supermarket which had been built opposite.

"Can I help you love?" The controller's blue collared shirt was covered in fag ash as the cigarette in his mouth moved around within his lips as he spoke.

"Yes I hope you can. I used one of your taxis last Friday, it was a Mondeo I think and it had a big dent on the back of the right hand side. The driver was Indian or Pakistani from his voice. I left my umbrella in the back, well I think so, I haven't seen it since. Has it been handed in or is he here?"

"Pick up at number six Stanley Close, 5.30 Mrs Morgan, John have you got that?"

Natalie waited while she listened to John confirming he had received the information the controller had also sent from his computer.

"Still can't break the habit of telling them the addresses despite all these gadgets." Natalie smiled. He continued. Yes that's Raj, well they're all Raj to me but he's the only Indian we've got.

He's over there." He pointed to some cars parked to one side, by the side of the road where a few drivers were chatting and waiting for pick ups or passing customers from the supermarket.

"Where?" Said Natalie. "Sorry, I don't see too well. She touched her dark glasses."

"Oh sorry luv, I didn't realise." The controller got up and walked around his desk and took Natalie gently by the arm, leading her carefully out of the office door.

"Raj......Raj." He shouted louder on the second calling. "Help this lady out. She left her umbrella she thinks in the back of your car last Friday. Have a look for her."

Raj waived to acknowledge and opened the rear right door and started looking under the seats and around the car. "Some chance of finding that." He thought to himself.

"Is he free to take me home now by the way?"

"Sure luv." He shouted over to Raj. "Come here and walk her to your cab, she needs a hand. I've got to go back in luv. Raj will sort you out."................Natalie waited.

Previous Publications - Adult

New Pews for Sunday

Future Publications

The Third Incarnation

It's all in the Bag

Possession is Nine Tenths of the Law

My Grandfather Child

New Pews Eucharist

Damocles Scalpel

Children's

Captain Flash, The Cuddely Horse and his Magic Dreams.

Stories Include.

Admiral Roarandsnarl and the Pirate Penguins.

Captain Flash and the Frothing Whirlpool.

Grampy's Stories

Ned and Alf, The Giants, The Golden Eagle and The Indian Minor

Facebook : Stephen E. Scott

The Next Release : The Third Incarnation

If you believe in the immortal soul, reincarnation, heaven, hell, the afterlife; the afterlife of one life, is the pre life of the next.

The Third Incarnation takes you through the lives of Rebecca's soul as she tries to live her next life with her new parents and twin sister but this incarnation for her, is like no other.

The First Release : New Pews for Sunday

The new pews delivered to John Rowlands church would be welcomed into their church life. What wouldn't be welcome, was the evil that accompanied them as their presence in the church incredulously drew the worst out of the congregation, changing believers, manipulating their imaginations with the reality of their history.

The Second Release : It's all in The Bag

I see this hopefully as a "self help", short 11 month autobiography, when initially after diagnosis, I thought I was going to die. Aside from my wife, daughter, family and friends; the most important thing I wanted to do, was to publish the books I had been writing but hadn't yet published.

Hopefully, it will help someone and those they care about, avoid going through what I went through because, it's not just the person diagnosed that "goes through it" but everyone who cares about the person who's been told "we're sorry to tell you, you have cancer."

Your life is too important, read this, don't lose it, live it.

Printed in Poland
by Amazon Fulfillment
Poland Sp. z o.o., Wrocław

54818250R00211